Isaac Bickerstaff

The Maid of the Mill

A Comic Opera

Isaac Bickerstaff

The Maid of the Mill
A Comic Opera

ISBN/EAN: 9783743392571

Manufactured in Europe, USA, Canada, Australia, Japa

Cover: Foto ©Andreas Hilbeck / pixelio.de

Manufactured and distributed by brebook publishing software (www.brebook.com)

Isaac Bickerstaff

The Maid of the Mill

BELL's

RITISH THEATRE.

VOLUME the TWENTY-FIRST.

Bell's
BRITISH THEATRE;
OPERAS.

LONDON

Printed for John Bell near Exeter Exchange in the
Strand. May 1st. 1777.

BRITISH THEATRE,

Confisting of the moft efteemed

ENGLISH PLAYS.

VOLUME the TWENTY-FIRST.

Being the Second Volume of OPERAS.

CONTAINING

MAID of the MILL, by Mr. BICKERSTAFF.

LOVE in a VILLAGE by Mr. BICKERSTAFF.

JOVIAL CREW, from ~~BEAUMONT and FLETCHER~~.

ACCOMPLISHED MAID, from the Italian of GOLDONI.

LIONEL and CLARISSA, by Mr. BICKERSTAFF.

LONDON:

Printed for JOHN BELL, *Britifh Library, Strand.*

MDCCLXXXI.

T O

His Royal Highnefs

W I L L I A M,

DUKE OF GLOUCESTER.

May it pleafe your Royal Highnefs,

WHEN I prefumed to folicit the honour of laying the fubfequent trifle at your Royal Highnefs's
feet, it was not without a thorough confcioufnefs of the
little value of the offering I was going to make; but I
confidered, mean as it was, it would ferve as a teftimony
of my devotion; and to a Prince happy in love of the
arts, nothing could be unacceptable, which bore the re-
moteft analogy to them.

How far the Comic Opera, under proper regulations,
has a right to be acknowledged for a junior offspring of
the Drama, and as fuch become candidate for a fhare
of public encouragement, I fhall not pretend to determine; but if it can be rendered an agreeable amufe-
ment, the Englifh Theatre has never fcrupled to adopt
what was capable of pleafing there; and though as a
work of genius, it is by no means to be fet in competi-
tion.

tion with good Tragedies and Comedies, it may, I apprehend, be permitted as an occafional relief to them, without bringing either our tafte or underftanding into queftion.

I need not inform your Royal Highnefs, that in France, where the ftage has been cultivated with more care, and fuccefs, than in any other country, this fpecies of entertainment is received with very great applaufe; nor is it thought an injury to Corneille, and Moliere, that the pieces of Anfeaume and Favart, meet with fuccefs.

It is true, among the French, Comic Operas have very often the advantage of being extremely well written; of which, On ne S'avife jamais de tout, Le Roy, et le Fermier, and fome others, are an inftance; nor would the beft compofition of the greateft mafter, make a very contemptible poem pafs on an audience: I wifh I could affert with truth, that in this refpect we fall nothing behind our neighbours, and that what I here prefent to your Royal Highnefs, might lay claim to fome degree of merit, even in the writing: but though I cannot do this, permit me to fay, I have attempted to render it a little interefting, and not wholly undiverting, as far as the mufic, my principal care, would give me leave.

But I humbly beg your Royal Highnefs's pardon; in applying to the connoiffeur, I forget that I am at the fame time addreffing a Great Prince: indeed, there is a fubject on which I could dwell with the trueft pleafure; but I am too well inftructed in your Royal Highnefs's character, to dare to offend you with a language which forms and cuftoms too often impofe upon princes,

a ne-a neceſſity of hearing; I mean their own praiſe; to thoſe who are moſt deſerving, ever leaſt welcome.

I therefore, ſubſcribe myſelf,

　With the profoundeſt reſpect,

　　May it pleaſe your Royal Highneſs,

　　　Your Royal Highneſs's,

　　　　Moſt obedient,

　　　　　Moſt devoted, and

　　　　　　Moſt humble ſervant,

　　　　　　　　THE AUTHOR;

Dramatis Personæ.

M E N.

Lord Aimworth	Mr. *Mattocks.*
Sir Harry Sycamore	Mr. *Wilson.*
Mervin	Mr. *Robson.*
Fairfield	Mr. *Hull.*
Giles	Mr. *Reinhold.*
Ralph	Mr. *Quick.*

W O M E N.

Lady Sycamore	Mrs. *Pitt.*
Theodosia	Mrs. *Morton.*
Patty	Miss *Satchell.*
Fanny	Miss *Catley.*

THE
MAID OF THE MILL.

*** *The lines diſtinguiſhed by inverted comas, ' thus,' are omitted in the Repreſentation.*

ACT I. SCENE I.

A rural proſpect, with a mill at work. Several people em-
ployed about it ; on one ſide a houſe, PATTY reading in
the window ; on the other a barn, where FANNY ſits
mending a net ; GILES appears at a diſtance in the mill ;
FAIRFIELD and RALPH taking ſacks from a cart.

CHORUS.

FREE from ſorrow, free from ſtrife,
  O how bleſt the miller's life !
Chearful working through the day,
Still he laughs and ſings away.
    Nought can vex him,
    Nought perplex him,
While there's griſt to make him gay.

DUET.

Let the great enjoy the bleſſings
  By indulgent fortune ſent :
What can wealth, can grandeur offer
  More than plenty and content.

Fairf. Well done, well done; 'tis a ſure ſign work
goes on merrily when folks ſing at it. Stop the mill
there ; and doſt hear, ſon Ralph, hoiſt yon ſacks of

B

ſlour

flour upon this cart, lad, and drive it up to lord Aim-worth's ; coming from London laft night with ftrange company, no doubt there are calls enough for it by this time.

Ralph. Ay feyther, whether or not, there's no doubt but you'll find enow for a body to do.

Fairf. Whot doft mutter ? Is't not a ftrange plague that thou can'ft never go about any thing with a good will ; murrain take it, what's come o'er the boy ? So then thou wilt not fet a hand to what I have defired thee !

Ralph. Why don't you fpeak to fufter Pat to do fome-thing then ? I thought when fhe came home to us after my old lady's death, fhe was to have been of fome ufe in the houfe ; but inftead of that, fhe fits there all day, reading outlandifh books, dreffed like a fine madumafel, and the never a word you fays to fhe.

Fairf. Sirrah, don't fpeak fo difrefpectfully of thy fifter ; thou wilt never have the tyth of her deferts.

Ralph. Why I'll read and write with her for what fhe dares ; and as for playing on the hapficols, I thinks her rich good mother might have learn'd her fomething more properer, feeing fhe did not remember to leave her a le-gacy at laft.

Fairf. That's none of thy bufinefs, firrah.

Ralph. A farmer's wife painting pictures, and playing on the hapficols ; why I'll be hang'd now, for all as old as fhe is, if fhe knows any more about milking a cow, than I do of fewing a petticoat.

Fairf. Ralph, thou haft been drinking this morning.

Ralph. Well, if fo be as I have, it's nothing out of your pocket, nor mines neither.

Fairf. Who has been giving thee liquor, firrah ?

Ralph. Why it was wind—a gentleman guve me.

Fairf. A gentleman !

Ralph. Yes, a gentleman that's come piping hot from London ; he is below at the Cat and Bagpipes ; I cod he rides a choice bit of a nag ; I dare to fay fhe'd fetch as good as forty pound at ever a fair in all England.

Fairf. A fig's end for what fhe'd fetch ; mind thy bu-finefs, or by the lord Harry ———

Ralph.

Ralph. Why I won't do another hand's turn to-day
now, so that's flat.

Fairf. Thou wilt not——

Ralph. Why no I won't ; so what argufies your putting yourself in a paſſion, feyther ! I've promiſed to go
back to the gentleman ; and I don't know but what he's
a lord too, and mayhap he may do more for me than
you thinks of.

Fairf. Well, ſon Ralph, run thy gait ; but remember
I tell thee, thou wilt repent this untowardneſs.

Ralph. Why, how ſhall I repent it ? Mayhap you'll
turn me out of your ſervice; a match ; with all hearts
—I cod I don't care three braſs pins.

A I R.

If that's all you want, who the plague will be ſorry,
'Twere better by half to dig ſtones in a quarry ;
  For my ſhare I'm weary of what is got by't :
S'fleſh ! here's ſuch a racket, ſuch ſcolding and coiling,
You're never content, but when folks are a toiling,
  And drudging like horſes from morning 'till night.

You think I'm afraid, but the diff'rence to ſhew you ;
Firſt, yonder's your ſhovel ; your ſacks too I throw you ;
  Henceforward take care of your matters who will ;
They're welcome to ſlave for your wages who need 'em,
Tol lol derol lol, I have purchas'd my freedom,
  And never hereafter ſhall work at the mill.

S C E N E II.

F A I R F I E L D, P A T T Y.

Fairf. Dear heart, dear heart ! I proteſt this ungra-
cious boy puts me quite beſide myſelf. Patty, my dear,
come down into the yard a little, and keep me company
—and you, thieves, vagabonds, gypſies, out here, 'tis
you debauch my ſon.

B 2

A I R.

A I R.

Patty.   *In love to pine and languish,*
     Yet know your passion vain ;
     To harbour heart felt anguish,
     Yet fear to tell your pain.

     What pow'rs unrelenting,
     Severer ills inventing,
     Can sharpen pangs like these ;
     Where days and nights, tormenting,
     Yield not a moment's ease !

Fairf. Well, Patty, Master Goodman, my lord's steward, has been with me juft now, and I find we are like to have great doings ; his lordfhip has brought down Sir Harry Sycamore and his family, and there is more company expected in a few days.

Patty. I know Sir Harry very well ; he is by marriage a diftant relation of my lord's

Fairf. Pray what fort of a young body is the daughter there ? I think fhe ufed to be with you at the caftle, three or four fummers ago, when my young lord was out upon his travels,

Patty. Oh ! very often ; fhe was a great favourite of my lady's : pray father is fhe come down ?

Fairf. Why you know the report laft night, about my lord's going to be married ; by what I can learn fhe is, and there is likely to be a nearer relationfhip between the families, ere long. It feems, his lordfhip was not over willing for the match, but the friends on both fides in London preffed it fo hard : then there's a fwinging fortune : mafter Goodman tells me a matter of twenty or thirty thoufand pounds,

Patty. If it was a million, father, it would not be more than my lord Aimworth deferves ; I fuppofe the wedding will be celebrated here at the manfion-houfe.

Fairf. So it is thought, as foon as things can be properly prepared————And now, Patty, if I could but fee thee a little merry—Come, blefs thee, pluck up thy fpirits—To be fure thou haft fuftained, in the death of

thy

thy lady, a heavy lofs; fhe was a parent to thee; nay, and better, inafmuch as fhe took thee when thou wert but a babe, and gave thee an education which thy natural parents could not afford to do.

Patty. Ah! dear father, don't mention what, perhaps, has been my greateft misfortune.

Fairf. Nay then, Patty, what's become of all thy fenfe, that people talk fo much about?——But I have fomething to fay to thee which I would have thee confider ferioufly. ——I believe I need not tell thee, my child, that a young maiden, after fhe is marriageable, efpecially if fhe has any thing about her to draw people's notice, is liable to ill tongues, and a many crofs accidents; fo that the fooner fhe's out of harm's way the better.

Patty. Undoubtedly, father, there are people enough who watch every opportunity to gratify their own malice; but when a young woman's conduct is unblameable——

Fairf. Why, Patty, there may be fomething in that; but you know flander will leave fpots, where malice finds none: I fay, then, a young woman's beft fafeguard is a good hufband. Now there is our neighbour, Farmer Giles; he is a fober, honeft, induftrious young fellow, and one of the wealthieft in thefe parts; he is greatly taken with thee; and it is not the firft time I have told thee I fhould be glad to have him for a fon-in-law.

Patty. And I have told you as often, father, I would fubmit myfelf entirely to your direction; whatever you think proper for me, is fo.

Fairf. Why that's fpoken like a dutiful, fenfible girl; get thee in, then, and leave me to manage it———— Perhaps our neighbour Giles is not a gentleman; but what are the greateft part of our country gentlemen good for?

Patty. Very true, father. The fentiments, indeed, have frequently little correfpondence with the condition; and it is according to them alone we ought to regulate our efteem.

B 3   ·   A I R.

A I R.

What are outward forms, and shews,
To an honest heart compar'd?
Oft the rustic, wanting those,
Has the nobler portion shar'd.

Oft we see the homely flower,
Bearing at the hedge's side,
Virtues of more sov'reign pow'r,
Than the garden's gayest pride.

S C E N E III.

FAIRFIELD, GILES.

Giles. Well, master Fairfield, you and Miss Pat have had a long discourse together; did you tell her that I was come down?

Fairf. No, in truth, friend Giles; but I mentioned our affair at a distance; and I think there is no fear.

Giles. That's right—and when shall us—You do know I have told you my mind often and often.

Fairf. Farmer, give us thy hand; nobody doubts thy good will to me and my girl; and you may take my word, I would rather give her to thee than another; for I am main certain thou wilt make her a good husband.

Giles. Thanks to your kind opinion, master Fairfield; if such be my hap, I hope there will be no cause of complaint.

Fairf. And I promise thee my daughter will make thee a choice wife. But thou know'st, friend Giles, that I, and all belongs to me, have great obligations to lord Aimworth's family; Patty, in particular, would be one of the most ungrateful wretches this day breathing if she was to do the smallest thing contrary to their consent and approbation.

Giles. Nay, nay, 'tis well enough known to all the country, she was the old lady's darling.

Fairf.

Fairf. Well, mafter Giles, I'll affure thee fhe is not one whit lefs obliged to my lord himfelf. When his mother was taken off fo fuddenly, and his affairs called him up to London, if Patty would have remained at the caftle, fhe might have had the command of all ; or if fhe would have gone any where elfe, he would have paid for her fixing, let the coft be what it would.

Giles. Why, for that matter, folks did not fpare to fay, that my lord had a fort of a fneaking kindnefs for her himfelf : and I remember, at one time, it was rife all about the neighbourhood, that fhe was actually to be our lady.

Fairf. Pho, pho ! a pack of woman's tales.

Giles. Nay, to be fure they'll fay any thing.

Fairf. My lord's a man of a better way of thinking, friend Giles——But this is neither here nor there to our bufinefs——Have you been at the caftle yet ?

Giles. Who I ! Blefs your heart I did not hear a fyllable of his lordfhip's being come down, 'till your lad told me.

Fairf. No ! why then go up to my lord, let him know you have a mind to make a match with my daughter ; hear what he has to fay to it ; and afterwards we will try if we can't fettle matters.

Giles. Go up to my lord ! I cod if that be all, I'll do it with the biggeft pleafure in life.—But where's Mifs Pat ? Might one not ax her how fhe do ?

Fairf. Never fpare it ; fhe's within there.

Giles. I fees her—odd rabbit it, this hatch is locked now————Mifs Pat——Mifs Patty—She makes believe not to hear me

Fairf. Well, well, never mind ; thoul't come and eat a morfel of dinner with us.

Giles. Nay, but juft to have a bit of a joke with her at prefent——Mifs Pat, I fay——won't you open the door ?

A I R.

A I R.

Hark ! 'tis I your own true lover,
  After walking three long miles,
One kind look at leaft difcover,
  Come and fpeak a word to Giles.
  You alone my heart I fix on :
  Ah, you little cunning vixen !
I can fee your roguifh fmiles.
Addflids ! my mind is fo poffeft,
Till we're fped, I fhan't have reft ;
  Only fay the thing's a bargain,
    Here an you like it,
    Ready to ftrike it,
  There's at once an end of arguing :
I'm her's, fhe's mine ;
Thus we feal, and thus we fign.

S C E N E   IV.

FAIRFIELD, PATTY.

Fairf. Patty, child, why would'ft not thou open the door for our neighbour Giles ?

Patty. Really, father, I did not know what was the matter.

Fairf. Well, another time ; he'll be here again prefently. He's gone up to the caftle, Patty ; thou know'ft it would not be right for us to do any thing without giving his lordfhip intelligence, fo I have fent the farmer to let him know that he is willing, and we are willing ; and, with his lordfhip's approbation—

Patty. Oh dear father—what are you going to fay?

Fairf. Nay child, I would not have ftirr'd a ftep for fifty pounds, without advertifing his lordfhip beforehand.

Patty. But furely, furely, you have not done this rafh, this precipitate thing.

Fairf How rafh, how is it rafh, Patty? I don't underftand thee.

Patty. Oh, you have diftrefs'd me beyond imagination —but why would you not give me notice, fpeak to me firft?

Fairf.

Fairf. Why han't I spoken to thee an hundred times? No, Patty, 'tis thou that would'ſt diſtreſs me, and thou'lt break my heart.

Patty. Dear father!

Fairf. All I deſire is to ſee thee well ſettled; and now that I am likely to do ſo, thou art not contented; I am ſure the farmer is as ſightly a clever lad as any in the country; and is he not as good as we?

Patty. 'Tis very true, father; I am to blame; pray forgive me.

Fairf. Forgive thee! Lord help thee, my child, I am not angry with thee; but quiet thyſelf, Patty, and thou'lt ſee all this will turn out for the beſt.

SCENE V.

PATTY.

What will become of me?—my lord will certainly imagine this is done with my conſent——Well, is he not himſelf going to be married to a lady, ſuitable to him in rank, ſuitable to him in fortune, as this farmer is to me; and under what pretence can I refuſe the huſ-band my father has found for me! Shall I ſay that I have dared to raiſe my inclinations above my condition, and preſumed to love, where my duty taught me only gra-titude and reſpect? Alas! who could live in the houſe with lord Aimworth, ſee him, converſe with him, and not love him! I have this conſolation, however, my folly is yet undiſcover'd to any; elſe, how ſhould I be ridiculed and deſpiſed; nay, would not my lord himſelf deſpiſe me, eſpecially, if he knew that I have more than once conſtrued his natural affability and politeneſs into ſentiments as unworthy of him, as mine are bold and ex-travagant. Unexampled vanity! did I poſſeſs any thing capable of attracting ſuch a notice, to what purpoſe could a man of his diſtinction caſt his eyes on a girl, poor, meanly born, and indebted for every thing to the ill-placed bounty of his family?

A I R.

A I R.

Ah! why should fate, pursuing
A wretched thing like me,
Heap ruin thus on ruin,
And add to misery?
The griefs I languish'd under,
In secret let me share;
But this new stroke of thunder,
Is more than I can bear.

SCENE VI.

Changes to a Chamber in Lord AIMWORTH's *House.*

SIR HARRY SYCAMORE, THEODOSIA.

Sir Har. Well, but Theodosia, child, you are quite unreasonable.

Theo. Pardon me, papa, it is not I am unreasonable: when I gave way to my inclinations for Mr. Mervin, he did not seem less agreeable to you and my mama, than he was acceptable to me. It is therefore you have been unreasonable, in first encouraging his addresses, and afterwards forbidding him your house; in order to bring me down here, to force me on a gentleman——

Sir Har. Force you, Doffy, what do you mean? By the la, I would not force you on the Czar of Muscovy.

Theo. And yet, papa, what else can I call it? for tho' lord Aimworth is extremely attentive and obliging, I assure you he is by no means one of the most ardent of lovers.

Sir Har. Ardent, ah! there it is; you girls never think there is any love, without kissing and hugging; but you shou'd consider child, my lord Aimworth is a polite man, and has been abroad in France and Italy, where these things are not the fashion; I remember when I was on my travels, among the madames and signoras, we never saluted more than the tip of the ear.

Theo. Really, papa, you have a very strange opinion of my delicacy; I had no such stuff in my thoughts.

Sir Har. Well come, my poor Doffy, I see you are chagrin'd, but you know it is not my fault; on the con-

trary,

trary, I aſſure you, I had always a great regard for young Mervin, and ſhould have been very glad————

Theo. How then, papa, could you join in forcing me to write him that ſtrange letter. never to ſee me more; or how indeed could I comply with your commands? what muſt he think of me?

Sir Har. Ay, but hold Doſſy, your mama convinced me that he was not ſo proper a ſon-in-law for us as Lord Aimworth.

Theo. Convinced you! Ah, my dear papa, you were not convinced.

Sir Har. What don't I know when I am convinced?

Theo. Why no, papa; becauſe your good-nature and eaſineſs of temper is ſuch, that you pay more reſpect to the judgment of mama, and leſs to your own, than you ought to do.

Sir Har. Well, but Doſſy, don't you ſee how your mama loves me; if my finger does but ach, ſhe's like a betwitched woman; and if I was to die, I don't believe ſhe would outlive the burying of me: nay ſhe has told me as much herſelf.

Theo. Her fondneſs indeed is very extraordinary.

Sir Har. Beſides, could you give up the proſpect of being a counteſs, and miſtreſs of this fine place?

Theo. Yes, truly could I.

A I R.

With the man that I love, was I deſtin'd to dwell,
On a mountain, a moor, in a cot, in a cell,
Retreats the moſt barren, moſt deſert, would be
More pleaſing than courts or a palace to me.

Let the vain and the venal, in wedlock aſpire
To what folly eſteems, and the vulgar admire;
I yield them the bliſs, where their wiſhes are placed,
Inſenſible creatures! 'tis all they can taſte.

S C E N E VII.

SIR HARRY, THEODOSIA, LADY SYCAMORE.

La. Syc. Sir Harry, where are you?

Sir Har. Here my lamb.

La. Syc.

La. Syc. I am juſt come from looking over his lordſhip's family trinkets.——Well, Miſs Sycamore, you
are a happy creature, to have diamonds, equipage, title,
all the bleſſings of life poured thus upon you at once.

Theo. Bleſſings, madam! Do you think then I am
ſuch a wretch as to place my felicity in the poſſeſſion of
any ſuch trumpery?

La. Syc. Upon my word, Miſs, you have a very dif-
dainful manner of expreſſing yourſelf; I believe there
are very few young women of faſhion, who would think
any ſacrifice they cou'd make, too much for them.——Did
you ever hear the like of her, Sir Harry?

Sir Har. Why, my dear, I have juſt been talking to
her in the ſame ſtrain, but whatever ſhe has got in her
head————

La. Syc. Oh, it is Mr. Mervin, her gentleman of
Bucklerſbury.——Fye Miſs, marry a cit! Where is your
pride, your vanity; have you nothing of the perſon of
diſtinction about you?

Sir Har. Well, but my lady, you know I am a piece
of a cit myſelf, as I may ſay, for my great-grandfather
was a dry-ſalter.

Theo. And yet, madam, you condeſcended to marry
my papa.

La. Syc. Well, if I did miſs, I had but five thouſand
pounds to my portion, and Sir Harry knows I was paſt
eight and thirty, before I would liſten to him.

Sir Har. Nay, Doſſy, that's true, your mama own'd
eight and thirty, before we were married : but by the
la, my dear, you were a lovely angel ; and by candle-
light nobody would have taken you for above five and
twenty.

La. Syc. Sir Harry, you remember the laſt time I was
at my lord duke's.

Sir Har. Yes, my love, it was the very day your little
bitch Minxey pupt

La. Syc. And pray what did the whole family ſay ;
my lord John, and my lord Thomas, and my lady Du-
cheſs in particular ? Couſin, ſays her Grace to me——
for ſhe always called me couſin.

Theo. Well, but madam, to cut this matter ſhort at
once, my father has a great regard for Mr. Mervin, and
would conſent to our union with all his heart.

La. Syc. Do you fay fo, Sir Harry?

Sir Har. Who I love!

La. Syc. 'Then all my care and prudence are come to nothing.

Sir Har. Well, but ftay my lady—Doſſy, you are always making miſchief.

Theo. Ah! my dear ſweet————

La. Syc. Do miſs, that's right, coax————

Theo. No, madam, I am not capable of any ſuch meannefs.

La. Syc. 'Tis very civil of you to contradiĉt me however.

Sir Har. Eh! what's that—hands off Doſſy, don't come near me.

A I R.

Why how now miſs pert,
Do you think to divert
My anger by fawning and ſtroking,
Would you make me a fool?
Your play-thing, your tool,
Was ever young minx ſo provoking?
Get out of my fight,
'Twould be ſerving you right,
To lay a ſound doſe of the laſh on;
Contradiĉt your mama,
I've a mind by the la!
But I won't put myſelf in a paſſion.

S C E N E VIII.

SIR HARRY, LADY SYCAMORE, LORD AIMWORTH, GILES.

L. Aim. Come farmer, you may come in, there are none here but friends.—— Sir Harry, your ſervant.

Sir Har. My lord, I kiſs your lordſhip's hands—I hope he did not overhear us ſquabbling——" I have " been chattering here with my wife and daughter, my " lord————We have been examining your lordſhip's " piĉtures.

L. Aim. " I flatter myſelf, then her ladyſhip found

C

" ſome-

" fomething to entertain her; there are a few of them
" counted tolerable."———Well now, mafter Giles,
what is it you have got to fay to me? If I can do you
any fervice, this company will give you leave to fpeak.

Giles. I thank your lordfhip, I has not got a great
deal to fay; I do come to your lordfhip about a little
bufinefs, if you'll pleafe to give me the hearing.

L. Aim. Certainly, only let me know what it is.

Giles. Why an pleafe you my lord, being left alone,
as I may fay, feyther dead, and all the bufinefs upon
my own hands, I do think of fettling and taking a wife,
and am come to ax your honour's confent.

L. Aim. My confent farmer! if that be neceffary,
you have it with all my heart—I hope you have taken
care to make a prudent choice.

Giles. Why I do hope fo, my lord.

L. Aim. Well, and who is the happy fair one? Does
fhe live in my houfe?

Giles. No, my lord, fhe does not live in your houfe,
but fhe's a parfon of your acquaintance.

L. Aim. Of my acquaintance!

Giles. No offence, I hope, your honour.

L. Aim. None in the leaft: but how is fhe an acquaintance of mine?

Giles. Your lordfhip, do know Miller Fairfield?

L. Aim. Well———

Giles. And Patty Fairfield, his daughter, my lord?

L. Aim. Ay, is it her you think of marrying?

Giles. Why if fo be as your lordfhip has no objection;
to be fure we will do nothing without your confent and
approbation.

L. Aim. Upon my word, farmer, you have made an
excellent choice—It is a god-daughter of my mother's,
madam, who was bred up under her care, and I proteft I do not know a more amiable young woman.———
But are you fure, farmer, that Patty herfelf is inclinable
to this match?

Giles. O yes, my lord, I am fartain of that.

L. Aim Perhaps then fhe defired you to come and
afk my confent?

Giles. Why as far as this here, my lord; to be fure,
the miller did not care to publifh the banns, without
making

making your lordſhip acquainted—But I hope your honour's not angry with I.

L. Aim. Angry farmer! why ſhould you think ſo?— what intereſt have I in it to be angry?

Sir Har. And ſo, honeſt farmer, you are going to be married to little Patty Fairfield? She's an old acquaintance of mine; how long have you and ſhe been ſweethearts?

Giles. Not a long while, an pleaſe your worſhip,

Sir Har. Well, her father's a good warm fellow; I' ſuppoſe you take care that ſhe brings ſomething to make the pot boil?

La. Syc.. What does that concern you, Sir Harry? how often muſt I tell you of meddling in other people's affairs?

Sir Har. My lord, a penny for your thoughts.

L. Aim. I beg your pardon, Sir Harry; upon my word, I did not think where I was.

Giles. Well then, your honour, I'll make bold to be taking my leave; I may ſay you gave conſent for Miſs Patty and I to go on.

L. Aim. Undoubtedly, farmer, if ſhe approves of it ᷄ but are you not afraid that her education has rendered her a little unſuitable for a wife for you?

La. Syc. Oh my lord, if the girl's handy——

Sir Har. Oh, ay— when a girl's handy——

Giles. Handy! Why, ſaving reſpect, there's nothing comes amiſs to her; ſhe's cute at every varſal kind of thing.

A I R.

Odd's my life, ſearch England over,
   An you match her in her ſtation,
   I'll be bound to fly the nation:
And be ſure as well I love her.

Do but feel my heart a beating,
   Still her pretty name repealing,
   Here's the work 'tis always at.
Pitty, patty, pat, pit, pat.

C 2

When.

When she makes the music tinkle,
  What on yearth can sweeter be?
Then her little eyes so twinkle,
  'Tis a feast to hear and see.

SCENE IX.

LORD AIMWORTH, SIR HARRY, LADY SYCAMORE.

Sir Har. By dad this is a good merry fellow, is not he in love, with his pitty patty——And so my lord you have given your confent that he shall marry your mother's old houfekeeper.   Ah, well, I can fee——

L. Aim. Nobody doubts, Sir Harry, that you are very clear-fighted.

Sir Har. Yes, yes, let me. alone, I know what's what: I was a young fellow once myfelf; and I fhould have been glad of a tenant, to take a pretty girl off my hands now and then, as well as another.

L. Aim. I proteft my dear friend, I don't underftand you.

La. Syc. Nor nobody elfe—Sir Harry you are going at fome beaftlinefs now.

Sir Har. Who I, my lady? Not I, as I hope to live and breathe; 'tis nothing to us you know, what my lord does before he's married; when I was a batchelor, I was a devil among the wenches, myfelf; and yet I vow to George, my lord, fince I knew my lady Sycamore, and we fhall be man and wife eighteen years, if we live till next Candlemas-day, I never had to do——

La. Syc. Sir Harry, come out of the room, I defire.

Sir Har. Why, what's the matter, my lady, I did not fay any harm?

La. Syc. I fee what you are driving at, you want to make me faint.

Sir Har. I want to make you faint, my lady!

La. Syc. Yes you do—and if you don't come out this inftant I fhall fall down in the chamber——I beg, my lord, you won't fpeak to him.——Will you come out, Sir Harry.

Sir Har. Nay, but my lady!

La. Syc. No, I will have you out.

SCENE

SCENE X.

LORD AIMWORTH.

This worthy baronet, and his lady, are certainly a very whimfical couple; however, their daughter is perfectly amiable in every refpect: and yet I am forry I have brought her down here; for can I in honour marry her, while my affections are engaged to another? To what does the pride of condition and the cenfure of the world force me! Muft I then renounce the only perfon that can make me happy; becaufe, becaufe what? becaufe fhe's a miller's daughter? Vain pride, and unjuft cenfure! has fhe not all the graces that education can give her fex; improved by a genius feldom found among the higheft? Has fhe not modefty, fweetnefs of temper, and beauty of perfon, capable of adorning a rank the moft exalted? But it is too late to think of thefe things now; my hand is promifed, my honour engaged: and if it was not fo, fhe has engaged herfelf; the farmer is a perfon to her mind, and I have authorized their union by my approbation.

A I R.

The mad-man thus, at times, we fee,
  With feeming reafon bleft;
His looks, his words, his thoughts are free,
  And fpeak a mind at reft.

But fhort the calms of eafe and fenfe,
  And ah! uncertain too;
While that idea lives from whence
  At firft his frenzy grew.

SCENE XI.

Changes to the profpect of the mill.

Enter RALPH, *with* MERVIN, *in a riding drefs, followed by* FANNY.

Fanny. Ah, pray your honour, try if you have not fomething to fpare for poor Fanny the gipfey.

C 3

Ralph.

Ralph. I tell you, Fan, the gentleman has no change about him; why the plague will you be fo trcublefome?

Fanny. Lord what is it to you, if his honour has a mind to give me a trifle? Do pray, gentleman, put your hand in your pocket.

Mer. I am almoft diftracted! Ungrateful Theodofia, to change fo fuddenly, and write me fuch a letter! However, I am refolved to have my difmiffion face to face; this letter may be forced from her by her mother, who I know was never cordially my friend: I could not get a fight of her in London, but here they will be lefs on their guard; and fee her I will, by one means or other.

Fanny. Then your honour will not extend your cha-rity?

A I R.

I am young, and I am friendlefs,
  And poor, alas! withal;
Sure my forrows will be endlefs;
  In vain for help I call.
Have fome pity in your nature,
To relieve a wretched creature,
  Though the gift be ne'er fo fmall.

May you, poffeffing every bleffing,
  Still inherit Sir, all you merit Sir,
And never know what it is to want;
Sweet Heaven, your worfhip all happinefs grant.

S C E N E XII.

RALPH, MERVIN.

Ralph. Now I'll go and take that money from her and I have good mind to lick her, fo I have.

Mer. Pho, pr'ythee ftay where you are.

Ralph. Nay, but I hate to fee a toad fo devilifh greedy.

Mer. Well come, fhe has not got a great deal, and I have thought how fhe may do me a favour in her turn.

Ralph. Ay, but you may put that out of your head, for I can tell you fhe won't.

Mer.

Mer. How fo?

Ralph. How fo, why fhe's as cunning as the Devil.

Mer. Oh fhe is—I fancy I underftand you. Well, in that cafe, friend Ralph——Your name's Ralph, I think?

Ralph. Yes, fir, at your fervice, for want of a better.

Mer. I fay then, friend Ralph, in that cafe, we will remit the favour you think of, till the lady is in a more complying humour, and try if fhe cannot ferve me at prefent in fome other capacity——There are a good many gipfies hereabout, are there not?

Ralph. Softly—I have a whole gang of them here in our barn; I have kept them about the place thefe three months, and all on account of fhe.

Mer. Really.

Ralph. Yea,——but for your life don't fay a word of it to any Chriftian——I am in love with her.

Mer. Indeed!

Ralph. Feyther is as mad with me about it, as Old Scratch; and I gets the plague and all of anger; but I don't mind that.

Mer. Well, friend Ralph, if you are in love, no doubt you have fome influence over your miftrefs; don't you think you could prevail upon her, and her companions, to fupply me with one of their habits, and let me go up with them to-day to my lord Aimworth's.

Ralph. Why do you want to go a mumming? We never do that here but in the Chriftmas holidays.

Mer. No matter: manage this for me, and manage it with fecrefy; and I promife you fhall not go unrewarded.

Ralph. Oh! as for that fir, I don't look for any thing, I can eafily get you a bundle of their rags; but I don't know whether you'll prevail on them to go up to my lord's, becaufe they're afraid of a big dog that's in the yard: but I'll tell you what I can do; I can go up before you and have the dog faftened, for I know his kennel

Mer. That will do very well——By means of this difguife I fhall probably get a fight of her; and I leave the reft to love and fortune.

A I R.

A I R.

Why quits the merchant, bleft with eafe,
The pleafures of his native feat,
To tempt the dangers of the feas,
And crimes more perilous than thefe;
  Midft freezing cold, or fcorching heat.

He knows the hardfhips, knows the pain,
The length of way, but thinks it fmall;
The fweets of what he hopes to gain,
  Undaunted, make him combat all.

SCENE XIII.

PATTY, RALPH, GILES, FANNY.

Giles. So his lordfhip was as willing as the flowers in May————and as I was coming along, who fhou'd I meet but your father————and he bid me run in all hafte and tell you———— for we were fure you would be deadly glad.

Patty. I know not what bufinefs you had to go to my lord's at all, farmer.

Giles. Nay, I only did as I was defired————Mafter Fairfield bid me tell you moreover, as how he wou'd have you go up to my lord out of hand, and thank him.

Ralph. So fhe ought; and take off thofe cloaths, and put on what's more becoming her ftation; you know my father fpoke to you of that this morning too.

Patty. Brother, I fhall obey my father.

  Lye ftill my heart; oh! fatal ftroke,
    That kills at once my hopes and me.

Giles.   *Mifs Pat!*
Patty.   ————*What?*
Giles.   ———————— *Nay, I only fpoke:*
Ralph.   *Take courage, mon, fhe does but joke.*
    Come, Sufter, fomewhat kinder be.

Fanny.   *This is a thing the moft oddeft,*
    Some folks are fo plaguily modeft;

Ral. Fan. { *Were we in the case,*
To be in their place,
We'd carry it off with a different face.

Giles. *Thus I take her by the lilly hand,*
So soft and white.

Ralph. —————————— *Why now that's right ;*
And kiss her too, mon, never stand.

Pat. Giles. { *What words can explain*
My pleasure—my pain ?
It presses, it rises,
My heart it surprises,
I can't keep it down, tho' I'd never so fain.

Fanny. *So here the play ends,*
The lovers are friends ;

Ralph. *Hush !*

Fanny. ———— *Tush !*

Giles. ———— ———— *Nah !*

Patty. ————————————— *Psha !*

All. *What torment's exceeding, what joys are above,*
The pains and the pleasures that wait upon love.

The End of the First Act.

ACT II.   SCENE I.

*A marble portico, ornamented with statues, which opens
from Lord* Aimworth's *house ; two chairs near the front.*

Enter Lord AIMWORTH *reading.*

IN how contemptible a light would the situation I am
now in shew me to most of the fine men of the present age ? In love with a country girl ; rivalled by a
poor fellow, one of my meanest tenants, and uneasy at
it ! If I had a mind to her, I know they would tell me,
I ought to have taken care to make myself easy long ago,
when I had her in my power.   But I have the testimony
of

of my own heart in my favour ; and I think, was it to do again, I fhould act as I have done. Let's fee, what we have here ? perhaps a book may compofe my thoughts; [*reads and throws the book away*] it's to no pur-pofe, I can't read, I can't think, I can't do any thing.

A I R.

Ah ! how vainly mortals treafure
Hopes of happinefs and pleafure,
  Hard and doubtful to obtain ;
By what ftandards falfe we meafure :
    Still purfuing
    Ways to ruin,
Seeking blifs, and finding pain.

S C E N E II.

Lord AIMWORTH, PATTY.

Patty. Now comes the trial : no, my fentence is al-ready pronounc'd, and I will meet my fate with pru-dence and refolution.

L. Aim. Who's there ?

Patty. My lord !

L. Aim. Patty Fairfield !

Patty. I humbly beg pardon, my lord, for preffing fo abruptly into your prefence ; but I was told I might walk this way ; and I am come by my father's com-mands to thank your lordfhip for all your favours.

L. Aim. Favours, Patty ? what favours ? I have done you none : but why this metamorphofis ? I proteft, if you had not fpoke, I fhould not have known you ; I never faw you wear fuch cloaths as thefe in my mother's life-time.

Patty. No, my lord, it was her ladyfhip's pleafure I fhould wear better, and therefore I obeyed ; but it is now my duty to drefs in a manner more fuitable to my ftation, and future profpects in life.

L. Aim. I am afraid, Patty, you are too humble—— come fit down—nay, I will have it fo.—What is it I have been told to-day, Patty ? It feems you are going to be married.

Patty. Yes, my lord.

L. Aim.

L. Aim. Well, and don't you think you could have made a better choice than farmer Giles ? I fhould imagine your perfon, your accomplifhments, might have intitled you to look higher.

Patty, Your lordfhip is pleafed to over-rate my little merit : the education I received in your family, does not intitle me to forget my origin ; and the farmer is my equal.

L. Aim. In what refpeft ? The degrees of rank and fortune, my dear Patty, are arbitrary diftinctions, unworthy the regard of thofe who confider juftly ; the true ftandard of equality is feated in the mind : thofe who think nobly are noble.

Patty. The farmer, my lord, is a very honeft man.

L. Aim. So he may : I don't fuppofe he would break into a houfe, or commit a robbery on the highway : what do you tell me of his honefty for ?

Patty. I did not mean to offend your lordfhip. ᐧ

L. Aim. Offend ! I am not offended, Patty ; not at all offended——But is there any great merit in a man's being honeft ?

Patty. I don't fay there is, my lord.

L. Aim. The farmer is an ill-bred, illiterate booby ; and what happinefs can you propofe to yourfelf in fuch a fociety?——Then, as to his perfon, I am fure—But perhaps, Patty, you like him ; and if fo, I am doing a wrong thing.

Patty. Upon my word, my lord——

L. Aim. Nay, I fee you do : he has had the good fortune to pleafe you ; and in that cafe, you are certainly in the right to follow your inclinations.—I muft tell you one thing Patty, however—I hope you won't think it unfriendly of me——But I am determined farmer Giles fhall not ftay a moment on my eftate, after next quarter-day.

Patty. I hope, my lord, he has not incurred your difpleafure——

L. Aim That's of no fignification.—Could I find as many good qualities in him as you do, perhaps——. But 'tis enough, he's a fellow I don't like ; and as you have a regard for him, I would have you advife him to provide himfelf.

Patty.

Patty. My lord, I am very unfortunate.

L. Aim. She loves him, 'tis plain————Come, Patty, don't cry; I would not willingly do any thing to make you uneasy.—Have you feen Mifs Sycamore yet?—I. fuppofe you know fhe and I are going to be married.

Patty. So I hear, my lord.————Heaven make you both happy!

L. Aim. Thank you, Patty; I hope we fhall be happy.

Patty. Upon my knees, upon my knees I pray it: may every earthly blifs attend you! may your days prove an uninterrupted courfe of delightful tranquility; and your mutual friendfhip, confidence and love, end but with your lives!

L. Aim. Rife, Patty, rife; fay no more—I fuppofe you'll wait upon Mifs Sycamore before you go away—at prefent I have a little bufinefs————As I faid Patty, don't afflict yourfelf: I have been fomewhat hafty with regard to the farmer; but fince I fee how deeply you are interefted in his affairs, I may poffibly alter my defigns with regard to him————You know—You know, Patty, your marriage with him is no concern of mine—I only fpeak ————

A I R.

My paffion in vain I attempt to diffemble;
   Th' endeavour to hide it, but makes it appear:
Enraptur'd I gaze; when I touch her I tremble,
   And fpeak to and hear her, with falt'ring and fear.

By how many cruel ideas tormented!
   My blood's in a ferment: it freezes, it burns:
This moment I wifh, what the next is repented;
   While love, rage, and jealoufy, rack me by turns.

S C E N E   III.

P A T T Y,   G I L E S.

Giles. Mifs Pat—Odd rabit it, I thought his honour was here; and I wifh I may die if my heart did not jump into my mouth—Come, come down in all hafte, there's fuch rig below as you never knew in your born days.   *Patty.*

" *Patty.* Rig!

" *Giles.* Ay, and fun "—There's as good as forty of the tenants, men and maidens, have got upon the lawn before the caftle, with pipers and garlands·; juft for all the world as tho'f it was May-day ; and the quality's looking at them out of the windows.—'Tis as true as any thing ; on account of my lord's coming home with his new lady——" Look here, I have brought a ftring of " flowers along with me."

Patty. Well, and what then ?

Giles. Why I vas thinking, if fo be as you would come down, as we might take a dance together : little Sal, farmer Harrow's daughter, of the Green, would fain have had me for a partner ; but I faid as how I'd go for one I liked better, one that I'd make a partner for life.

Patty. Did you fay fo ?

Giles. Yes, and fhe was ftruck all· of a heap——fhe had not a word to throw to a dog—for Sal and I kept company once for a little bit

Patty. Farmer, I am going to fay fomething to you, and I defire you will liften to it attentively. It feems you think of our being married together.

Giles. Think, why I think of nothing elfe ; it's all over the place mun, as how you are to be my fpoufe ; and you would not believe what game folks make of me.

Patty. Shall I talk to you like a friend, farmer—— You and I were never defigned for one another ; and I am morally certain we fhould not be happy.

Giles. Oh ! as for that matter, I never has no words with nobody.

Patty. Shall I fpeak plainer to you then—I don't like you.

Giles. No !

Patty. On the contrary, you are difagreeable to me—

Giles. Am I !

Patty. Yes, of all things : I deal with you fincerely.

Giles. Why, I thought, Mifs Pat, the affair between you and I was all fix'd and fettled.

Patty. Well, let this undeceive you—Be affured we fhall never be man and wife. No offer fhall perfuade, no command force me.—You know my mind, make your advantage of it.

A I R.

Was I sure a life to lead,
Wretched as the vilest slave,
Every hardship would I brave;
Rudest toil, severest need;
Ere yield my hand so coolly,
To the man who never truly,
Could my heart in keeping have.

Wealth with others success will insure you,
Where your wit and your person may please;
Take to them your love, I conjure you,
And in mercy set me at ease.

S C E N E IV.

G I L E S.

Here's a turn ; I don't know what to make of it : she's gone mad, that's for sartin ; wit and learning have crack'd her brain——Poor soul, poor soul——It is often the case of those who have too much of them.—Lord, Lord, how sorry I be—But hold, she says I baint to her mind—mayn't all this be the effect of modish coyness, to do like the gentlewomen, because she was bred among them ? And I have heard say, they will be upon their vixen tricks, till they go into the very church with a man.—Icod there's nothing more likelier ; for it is the cry of one and all, that she's the moral of a lady in every thing : and our farmer's daughters, for the matter of that, tho'f they have nothing to boast of but a scrap of red ribbon about their hats, will have as many turnings and windings as a hare, before one can lay a fast hold of them,—There can no harm come of speaking with master Fairfield, however.—Odd rabbit it, how plaguy tart she was—I am half vext with myself now that I let her go off so.

A I R.

A I R.

When a maid, in way of marriage,
  Firſt is courted by a man,
  Let 'un do the beſt he can,
She's ſo ſhame-fac'd in her carriage,
  'Tis with plain the ſuit's began.

Tho'f mayhap ſhe likes him mainly,
  Still ſhe ſhams it coy and cold ;
Fearing to confeſs it plainly,
  Leſt the folks ſhould think her bold.

But the parſon comes in ſight,
  Gives the word to bill and coo ;
'Tis a different ſtory quite,
  And ſhe quickly buckles too.

S C E N E V.

Changes to a view of Lord AIMWORTH's *houſe, and im-*
provements ; a ſeat under a tree, and part of the garden
wall, with a Chineſe pavillion over it ; ſeveral country
people appear, dancing, others looking on, among whom
are, MERVIN, *diſguiſed,* RALPH, FANNY, *and a num-*
ber of gipſies. After the dancers go off, THEODOSIA
and PATTY *enter through a gate ſuppoſed to have a con-*
nection with the principal building.

Theo. Well then, my dear Patty, you will run away
from us : but why in ſuch a hurry, I have a thouſand
things to ſay to you ?

Patty. I ſhall do myſelf the honour to pay my duty to
you ſome other time, madam ; at preſent I really find
myſelf a little indiſpoſed.

Theo. Nay, I would by no means lay you under any
reſtraint. But methinks the entertainment we have juſt
been taking part of, ſhould have put you into better
ſpirits : I am not in an over-merry mood myſelf, yet, I
ſwear, I could not look on the diverſion of thoſe honeſt
folks, without feeling a certain *gaiete de cœur.*

Patty. Why, indeed, madam, it had one circumſtance
attending it, which is often wanting to more polite
amuſements ; that of ſeeming to give undiſſembled ſatisfaction to thoſe who were engaged in it.

D 2

Theo.

Theo. Oh, infinite, infinite! to fee the chearful, healthy looking creatures, toil with fuch a good will! To me there were more genuine charms in their aukward ftumping and jumping about, their rude meafures, and homefpun finery, than in all the drefs, fplendor, and ftudied graces, of a birth-night ball-room.

Patty. 'Tis a very uncommon declaration to be made by a fine lady, madam : but certainly, however the artful delicacies of high life may dazzle and furprize, nature has particular attractions, even in a cottage, her moft unadorned ftate, which feldom fails to affect us, tho' we can fcarce give a reafon for it.

Theo. But you know, Patty, I was always, a diftracted admirer of the country ; no damfel in romance was ever fonder of groves and purling ftreams : had I been born in the days of Arcadia, with my prefent propenfity, inftead of being a fine lady, as you call me, I fhould certainly have kept a flock of fheep.

Patty. Well, madam, you have the fages, poets and philofophers, of all ages, to countenance your way of thinking.

Theo. And you, my little philofophical friend, don't you think me in the right too?

Patty. Yes indeed, madam, perfectly.

A I R.

Truft me, would you tafte true pleafure,
Without mixture, without meafure,
No where fhall you find the treafure
*   Sure as in the fylvan fcene :*

Bleft, who, no falfe glare requiring,
Nature's rural fweets admiring,
Can, from groffer joys retiring,
*   Seek the fimple and ferene.*

S C E N E VI.

THEODOSIA, MERVIN, FANNY.

Mer. Yonder fhe is feated ; and, to my wifh, moft fortunately alone. Accoft her as I defired.

Theo. Heigh !

Fanny.

Fanny. Heaven bless you, my sweet lady——bless your honour's beautiful visage, and send you a good husband, and a great many of them.

Theo. A very comfortable wish upon my word : who are you, child ?

Fanny. A poor gipsey, an' please you, that goes about begging from charitable gentlemen and ladies—If you have ere a coal or bit of whiting in your pocket, I'll write you the first letter of your sweetheart's name ; how many husbands you will have ; and how many children, my lady : or, if you'll let me look at your line of life, I'll tell you whether it will be long or short, happy or miserable.

Theo. Oh ! as for that, I know it already—you cannot tell me any good fortune, and therefore I'll hear none. Go about your business.

Mer. Stay, madam, stay, [*Pretending to lift a paper from the ground*] you have dropt something—Fan, call the young gentlewoman back.

Fanny. Lady, you have lost——

Theo. Pho, pho, I have lost nothing.

Mer. Yes, that paper, lady ; you dropt it as you got up from the chair.—Fan, give it to her honour.

Theo. A letter with my address !—[*Takes the paper and reads*] " Dear Theodosia ! Though the sight of me was " so disagreeable to you, that you charged me never to " approach you more, I hope my hand-writing can have " nothing to frighten or disgust you. I am not far off ; " and the person who delivers you this, can give you " intelligence,"——Come hither, child : do you know any thing of the gentleman that wrote this ?

Fanny. My lady——

Theo. Make haste, run this moment, bring me to him, bring him to me ; say I wait with impatience ; tell him I will go, fly any where ——

Mer. My life, my charmer !

Theo. Oh, Heavens !——Mr. Mervin !

          SCENE

SCENE VII.

Theodosia, Mervin, Sir Harry, Lady Sycamore, Fanny, Gipsies.

La. Syc. Sir Harry, don't walk fo faft, we are not
running for a wager.

Sir Har. Hough, hough, hough.

La. Syc. Hey day, you have got a cough; I fhall have
you laid upon my hands prefently.

Sir Har. No, no, my lady, it's only the old affair.

La. Syc. Come here, and let me tie this handkerchief
about your neck; you have put yourfelf into a muck-
fweat already. [*Ties a handkerchief about his neck.*] Have
you taken your Bardana this morning? I warrant you
know now, though you have been complaining of
twitches two or three times; and you know the gouty
feafon is coming on. Why will you be fo neglectful of
your health, Sir Harry? I proteft I am forced to watch
you like an infant.

Sir Har. My lovey takes care of me, and I am obliged
to her.

La. Syc. Well, but you ought to mind me then, fince
you are fatisfied I never fpeak but for your good.—I
thought, Mifs Sycamore, you were to have followed
your papa and me into the garden——How far did you
go with that wench?

Theo. They are gipfies, madam, they fay. Indeed I
don't know what they are.

La. Syc. I wifh, mifs, you would learn to give a rational anfwer.————

Sir Har. Eh! what's that? gipfies! Have we gipfies
here! Vagrants, that pretend to a knowledge of future
events; diviners, fortune-tellers?

Fanny. Yes, your worfhip, we'll tell your fortune, or
her ladyfhip's, for a crum of bread, or a little broken
victuals: what you throw to your dogs, an pleafe you.

Sir Har. Broken victuals, huffey! How do you think
we fhould have broken victuals?——If we are at home,
indeed, perhaps you might get fome fuch thing from the
cook: but here we are only on a vifit to a friend's houfe,
and have nothing to do with the kitchen at all.

La.

La Syc. And do you think, Sir Harry, it is neceſſary to give the creature an account.

Sir Har. No, love, no; but what can you ſay to obſtinate people?——Get you gone, bold face——I once knew a merchant's wife in the city, my lady, who had her fortune told by ſome of thoſe gipſies. They ſaid ſhe ſhould die at ſuch a time; and I warrant, as ſure as the day came, the poor gentlewoman actually died with the conceit.————Come, Doſly, your mama and I are going to take a walk ———My lady, will you have hold of my arm?

La Syc. No, Sir Harry, I chooſe to go by myſelf.

Mer. Now, love, aſſiſt me——[*Turning to the gipſies.*] Follow, and take all your cues from me———Nay, but good lady and gentleman, you won't go without remembering the poor gipſies.

Sir Har. Hey! here is all the gang after us.

Gip. Pray, your noble honour.

La. Syc. Come back into the garden; we ſhall be covered with vermin.

Gip. Out of the bowels of your commiſeration.

La. Syc. They preſs upon us more and more; yet that girl has no mind to leave them: I ſhall ſwoon away.

Sir Har. Don't be frighten'd, my lady; let me advance.

A I R.

You vile pack of vagabonds, what do ye mean?
I'll maul you, raſcallions,
Ye tatter-demallions——
If one of them comes within reach of my cane.

Such curſed aſſurance;
'Tis paſt all endurance.
Nay, nay, pray come away.
They're lyars and thieves,
And he that believes
Their fooliſh predictions,
Will find them but fictions,
A bubble that always deceives.

SCENE

SCENE VIII.

MERVIN, THEODOSIA, FANNY, GIPSIES.

Fanny. Oh! mercy, dear—The gentleman is so bold, 'tis well if he does not bring us into trouble. Who knows but this may be a justice of peace! and see, he's following them into the garden!

1st Gip. Well, 'tis all your seeking, Fan.

Fanny. We shall have warrants to take us up, I'll be hang'd else. We had better run away, the servants will come out with sticks to lick us.

Mer. Cursed ill fortune—[*Here Mervin returns with gipsies.*]—She's gone, and, perhaps, I shall not have another opportunity—And you, ye blundering block-head, I won't give you a halfpenny —— Why did you not clap too the garden door, when I called to you, before the young lady got in? The key was on the out-side, which would have given me some time for an explanation.

2d Gip. An please your honour I was dubus.

Mer. Dubus! plague choak ye———However, it is some satisfaction that I have been able to let her see me, and know where I am [*Turning to the gipsies, who go off.*] ——Go, get you gone, all of you, about your business.

Theo. Disappeared, fled! [*Theodosia appears in the pavilion*]—Oh, how unlucky this is!—Could he not have patience to wait a moment?

Mer. I know not what to resolve on.

Theo. Hem!

Mer. I'll go back to the garden-door.

Theo. Mr. Mervin!

Mer. What do I see!——'Tis she, 'tis she herself!—Oh, Theodosia!——Shall I climb the wall and come up to you?

Theo. No; speak softly: Sir Harry and my Lady sit below at the end of the walk—How much am I obliged to you for taking this trouble.

Mer. When their happiness is at stake, what is it men will not attempt?—Say but you love me.

Theo. What proof would you have me give you?—I know but of one: if you please I am willing to go off with you.

Mer.

Mer. Are you !—Would to Heaven I had brought a carriage !

Theo. How did you come ?—Have you not horses ?

Mer. No; there's another misfortune.——To avoid suspicion, there being but one little public-house in the village, I dispatched my servant with them, about an hour ago, to wait for me at a town twelve miles distant, whither I pretended to go; but alighting a mile off, I equipt myself, and came back as you see : neither can we, nearer than this town, get a post-chaise.

Theo. You say you have made a confidant of the miller's son :—return to your place of rendezvous : —————— my father has been asked this moment, by Lord Aimworth, who is in the garden, to take a walk with him down to the mill : they will go before dinner; and it shall be hard if I cannot contrive to be one of the company.

Mer. And what then——————

Theo. Why, in the mean time, you may devise some method to carry me from hence : and I'll take care you shall have an opportunity of communicating it to me.

Mer. Well, but dear Theodosia——————

A I R.

Theo. *Hist, hist! I hear my mother call——————*
  Pr'ythee be gone;
  We'll meet anon :
  Catch this, and this——————
  Blow me a kiss,
In pledge promis'd truth, that's all.
Farewell!——————and yet a moment stay ;
Something beside I had to say :——————
  Well, 'tis forgot ;
  No matter what——————
  Love grant us grace ;
  The mill's the place :
She calls again, I must away.

SCENE IX.

MERVIN, FANNY.

Fan. Pleafe your honour, you were fo kind as to fay you would remember my fellow-travellers for their trouble : and they think I have gotten the money.

Mer. Oh, here ; give them this—[*Gives her money.*] And for you, my dear little pilot, you have brought me fo cleverly through my bufinefs, that I muft——

Fan. Oh, Lord !—your honour—[*Mervin kiffes her*] Pray don't——kifs me again.

Mer. Again, and again.————There's a thought come into my head.—Theodofia will certainly have no objection to putting on the drefs of a fifter of mine.—So, and fo only, we may efcape to-night.—This girl, for a little money, will provide us with neceffaries.————

Fan. Dear gracious! I warrant you, now, I am affured as my petticoat: why would you royfter and touzle one fo?——If Ralph was to fee you, he'd be as jealous as the vengeance.

Mer. Hang Ralph ! Never mind him.—There's a guinea for thee.

Fan. What, a golden guinea ?————

Mer. Yes ; and if thou art a good girl, and do as I defire thee, thou fhalt have twenty.

Fan. Ay, but not all gold.

Mer. As good as that is.

Fan. Shall I though, if I does as you bids me ?

Mer. You fhall.

Fan. Precious heart ! He's a fweet gentleman !—Icod I have a great mind————

Mer. What art thou thinking about ?

Fan. Thinking, your honour ?—Ha, ha, ha !

Mer. Indeed, fo merry.

Fan. I don't know what I am thinking about, not I—— Ha, ha, ha !—Twenty guineas !

Mer. I tell thee thou fhalt have them.

Fan. Ha, ha, ha, ha, ha !

Mer. By Heaven I am ferious.

Fan. Ha, ha, ha !—Why then I'll do whatever your honour pleafes.

Mer.

Mer. Stay here a little, to fee that all keeps quiet: you'll find me prefently at the mill, where we'll talk farther.

A I R.

Yes, 'tis decreed, thou maid divine!
I muft, I will poffefs thee :
Oh, what delight within my arms to prefs thee !
To kifs, and call thee mine !
Let me this only blifs enjoy ;
That ne'er can wafte, that ne'er can cloy :
All other pleafures I refign.

Why fhould we dally ;
Stand fhilli fhally :
Let fortune fmile or frown.?
Love will attend us ;
Love will befriend us ;
And all our wifhes crown.

SCENE X.

FANNY, RALPH.

Fan. What a dear kind foul, he is—Here comes Ralph—I can tell him, unlefs he makes me his lawful wife, as he has often faid he would, the devil a word more fhall he fpeak to me.

Ralph. So, Fan, where's the gentleman ?

Fan. How fhould I know where he is ; what do you afk me for.?

Ralph. There's no harm in putting a civil queftion, be there.? Why you look as crofs and ill-natured————

Fan. Well, mayhap I do—and mayhap I have where-withal for it.

Ralph. Why, has the gentleman offered any thing un-civil ? Ecod, I'd try a bout as foon as look at him.

Fan. He offer—no—he's a gentleman every inch of him : but you are fenfible, Ralph, you have been pro-mifing me, a great while, this, and that, and t'other ; and, when all comes to all, I don't fee but you are like the reft of them.

Ralph.

Ralph. Why, what is it I have promifed?

Fan. To marry me in the church, you have a hundred times.

Ralph. Well, and mayhap I will, if you'll have patience.

Fan. Patience, me no patience; you may do it now if you pleafe.

Ralph. Well, but fuppofe I don't pleafe? I tell you, Fan, you're a fool, and want to quarrel with your bread and butter; I have had anger enow from feyther already upon your account, and you want me to come by more. As I faid, if you have patience, mayhap things may fall out, and mayhap not.

Fan. With all my heart, then; and now I know your mind, you may go hang yourfelf.

Ralph Ay, ay.

Fan. Yes, you may—who cares for you?

Ralph. Well, and who cares for you, an you go to that?

Fan. A menial feller—Go mind your mill and your drudgery; I don't think you worthy to wipe my fhoes —feller.

Ralph. Nay, but Fan, keep a civil tongue in your head : odds flefh! I would fain know what fly bites all of a fudden now.

Fan. Marry come up, the beft gentlemen's fons in the country have made me proffers ; and if one is a mifs, be a mifs to a gentleman, I fav, that will give one fine cloaths, and take one to fee the fhow, and put money in one's pocket.

Ralph. Whu, whu—*(hits him a flap)* What's that for?

Fan. What do you whiftle for, then? Do you think I am a dog?

Ralph. Never from me, Fan, if I have not a mind to give you, with this fwitch in my hand here, as good a lacing————

Fan. Touch me, if you dare : touch me, and I'll fwear my life againft you.

Ralph. A murrain! with her damn'd little fift as hard as fhe could draw.

Fan. Well, it's good enough for you ; I'm not neceffitated to take up with the impudence of fuch a low-

lived

lived monkey as you are.—— A gentleman's my friend, and I can have twenty guineas in my hand, all as good as this is.

Ralph. Belike from this Londoner, eh ?

Fan. Yes, from him—fo you may take your promife of marriage ; I don't value it that—*(fpits)* and if you fpeak to me, I'll flap your chops again.

A I R.

Lord, fir, you feem mighty uneafy ;
　　But I the refufal can bear :
I warrant I fhall not run crazy,
　　Nor die in a fit of defpair.
If fo you fuppofe, you're miftaken ;
　　For, fir, for to let you to know,
I'm not fuch a maiden forfaken,
　　But I have two ftrings to my bow.

S C E N E XI.

R A L P H.

Indeed ! Now I'll be judg'd by any foul living in the world, if ever there was a viler piece of treachery than this here ; there is no fuch a thing as a true friend upon the face of the globe, and fo I have faid a hundred times ! A couple of bafe deceitful——after all my love and kindnefs fhewn　Well, I'll be revenged ; fee an i be'nt——Marfter Marvint, that's his name, an he do not fham it : he has come here and difguifed unfelf ; whereof 'tis contrary to law fo to do : befides, I do partly know why he did it ; and I'll fifh out the whole conjuration, and go up to the caftle and tell every fyllable ; a fhan't carry a wench from me, were he twenty times the mon he is, and twenty times to that again ; and moreover than fo, the firft time I meet un, I'll knock un down, tho'f 'twas before my lord himfelf ; and he may capias me for it afterwards an he wull.

E.A I R.

A I R.

As they count me such a ninny,
  So to let them rule the roast;
I'll bet any one a guinea
  They have scor'd without their host.
But if I don't shew them in lieu of it,
A trick that's fairly worth two of it,
Then let me pass for a fool and an ass.

To be sure yon sly cajoler
  Thought the work as good as done,
When he found the little stroller
  Was so easy to be won.
But if I don't shew him in lieu of it,
A trick that's fairly worth two of it,
Then let me pass for a fool or an ass.

S C E N E XII.

Changes to a room in the Mill; two Chairs, with a Table
and a Tankard of Beer.

F A I R F I E L D, G I L E S.

Fairf. In short, farmer, I don't know what to say to thee. I have spoken to her all I can ; but I think children were born to pull the grey hairs of their parents to the grave with sorrow.

Giles. Nay, master Fairfield, don't take on about it: belike Miss Pat has another love ; and if so, in Heaven's name be't : what's one man's meat, as the saying is, is another man's poison ; and, tho'f some might find me well enough to their fancy, set in case I don't suit her's, why there's no harm done.

Fairf. Well but, neighbour, I have put that to her ; and the story is, she has no inclination to marry any one ; all she desires, is, to stay at home and take care of me.

Giles. Master Fairfield——here's towards your good health.

Giles.

Fairf. Thank thee, friend Giles—and here's towards thine.——I promiſe thee, had things gone as we propoſed, thou ſhould'ſt have had one half of what I was worth, to the uttermoſt farthing.

Giles. Why to be ſure, Maſter Fairfield,. I' am not the leſs obligated to your good-will; but, as to that matter,. had I married, it ſhould not have been for the lucre of gain ; but if I do like a girl, do you ſee, I. do like her ; ay, and I'll take her, ſaving reſpect, if ſhe had. not a ſecond petticoat.

Fairf. Well ſaid——where love is, with a little induſtry, what have a young couple to be afraid of ? And,. by the Lord Harry, for all that's paſt, I cannot help thinking we ſhall bring our matters to bear yet—Young women, you know, friend Giles——

Giles. Why, that's what I have been thinking with. myſelf, Maſter Fairfield.

Fairf. Come, then, mend thy draught.—Duce take· me if I let it drop ſo—But, in any caſe, don't you go to make yourſelf uneaſy.

Giles. Uneaſy, Maſter Fairfield ; what good would· that do ?—For ſarten, ſeeing how things were, I ſhould have been very glad they had gone accordingly : but if they change, 'tis no fault of mine, you know.

A I R.

Zooks ! why ſhould I ſit down and grieve ?
   No caſe ſo hard, there mayn't be had
Some med'cine to relieve.

Here's what maſters all diſaſters :
   With a cup of nut-brown beer,
   Thus my drooping thoughts I cheer :
If one pretty damſel fail me,
   From another I may find
   Return more kind ;
What a murrain then ſhould ail me !
   All girls are not of a mind.

He's a child that whimpers for a toy ;
So here's to thee, honeſt boy.

E 2   S C E N E.

S C E N E XIII.

Fairfield, Lord Aimworth.

Fairf. O the goodnefs, his lordſhip's honour—you
are come into a litter'd place, my noble ſir—the arm-
chair—— will it pleaſe your honour to repoſe you on
this, till a better——

L. Aim. Thank you, miller, there's no occaſion for
either.————I only want to ſpeak a few words to you,
and have company waiting for me without.

Fairf. Without——won't their honours favour my
poor hovel ſo far——

L. Aim. No, miller, let them ſtay where they are.—I
find you are about marrying your daughter—I know the
great regard my mother had for her ; and am ſatisfied,
that nothing but her ſudden death could have prevented
her leaving her a handſome proviſion.

Fairf: Dear, my lord, your noble mother, you, and
all your family, have heaped favours on favours on my
poor child.

L. Aim. Whatever has been done for her ſhe has fully
merited————

Fairf. Why, to be ſure, my lord, ſhe is a very good
girl.

L. Aim. Poor old man—but thoſe are tears of ſatisfaction.—— Here, Maſter Fairfield, to bring matters
to a ſhort concluſion, here is a bill of a thouſand pounds.
—— Portion your daughter with what you think con-
venient of it.

Fairf. A thouſand pound, my lord ! Pray excuſe me ;
excuſe me, worthy ſir ; too much has been done already,
and we have no pretenſions————

L. Aim. I inſiſt upon your taking it.———Put it up,
and ſay no more.

Fairf. Well, my lord, if it muſt be ſo : but indeed,
indeed————

L Aim. In this I only fulfil what I am ſatisfied would
pleaſe my mother. As to myſelf, I ſhall take upon me
all the expences of Patty's wedding, and have already
given orders about it.

Fairf.

Fairf. Alas, fir, you are too good, too generous ; but I fear we fhall not be able to profit of your kind intentions, unlefs you will condefcend to fpeak a little to Patty.

L. Aim. How fpeak !

Fairf. Why, my lord, I thought we had pretty well ordered all things concerning this marriage ; but all on a fudden the girl has taken it into her head not to have the farmer, and declares fhe will never marry at all.——But I know, my lord, fhe'll pay great refpect to any thing you fay ; and if you'll but lay your commands on her to marry him, I'm fure fhe'll do it.

L. Aim. Who, I lay my commands on her ?

Fairf. Yes, pray, my lord, do ; I'll fend her in to you.

" *L. Aim.* Mafter Fairfield ! [*Fairfield goes out and* " *returns.*]—What can be the meaning of this ?---Re-" fufe to marry the farmer !---How, why ?---My heart " is thrown in an agitation ; while every ftep I take, " ferves but to lead me into new perplexities.

" *Fairf,* She's coming, my lord ; I faid you were " here ;" and I humbly beg you will tell her, you infift upon the match going forward ; tell her, you infift upon it, my lord, and fpeak a little angrily to her.

<h2 style="text-align:center">S C E N E XIV.</h2>

Lord AIMWORTH, PATTY.

L. Aim. I came hither, Patty, in confequence of our converfation this morning, to render your change of ftate as agreeable and happy as I could : but your father tells me, you have fallen out with the farmer ; has any thing happened, fince I faw you laft, to alter your good opinion of him ?

Patty. No, my lord, I am in the fame opinion with regard to the farmer now as I always was.

L. Aim. I thought, Patty, you loved him, you told me——

Patty. My lord !

L. Aim. Well, no matter—It feems I have been miftaken in that particular——Poffibly your affections are

E 3

engaged

engaged elfewhere: let me but know the man that can make you happy, and I fwear————

Patty. Indeed, my lord, you take too much-trouble upon my account.

L. Aim. Perhaps, Patty, you love fomebody fo much beneath you, you are afhamed to own it; but your efteem confers a value wherefoever it is placed. I was too harfh with you this morning: our inclinations are not in our own power; they mafter the wifeft of us.

Patty. Pray, pray my lord, talk not to me in this ftile: confider me as one deftined by birth and fortune to the meaneft condition and offices; who has unhappily been apt to imbibe fentiments contrary to them! Let me conquer a heart, where pride and vanity have ufurped an improper rule; and learn to know myfelf, of whom I have been too long ignorant.

L. Aim. Perhaps, Patty, you love fome one fo much above you, you are afraid to own it ———— If fo, be his rank what it will, he is to be envied: for the love of a woman of virtue, beauty, and fentiment, does honour to a monarch.————What means that downcaft look, thofe tears, thofe blufhes? Dare you not confide in me? —Do you think, Patty, you have a friend in the world would fympathize with you more fincerely than I?

Patty. What fhall I anfwer!—No, my lord, you have ever treated me with a kindnefs, a generofity of which none but minds like yours are capable: you have been my inftructor, my advifer, my protector: but, my lord, you have been too good: when our fuperiors forget the diftance between us, we are fometimes led to forget it too: had you been lefs condefcending, perhaps I had been happier.

L. Aim. And have I, Patty, have I made you un-happy: I, who would facrifice my own felicity, to cure your's?

Patty I beg, my lord, you will fuffer me to be gone: only believe me fenfible of all your favours, though un-worthy of the fmalleft.

L. Aim. How unworthy!—You merit every thing; my refpect, my efteem, my friendfhip, and my love!— Yes, I repeat, I avow it: your beauty, your modefty, your underftanding, has made a conqueft of my heart.

But

—But what a world do we live in! that, while I own this; while I own a paſſion for you, founded on the juſteſt, the nobleſt baſis, I muſt at the ſame time confeſs, the fear of that world, its taunts, its reproaches—

Patty. Ah, ſir, think better of the creature you have raiſed, than to ſuppoſe I ever entertained a hope tending to your diſhonour: would that be a return for the favours I have received? Would that be a grateful reverence for the memory of her—————Pity and pardon the diſturbance of a mind that fears to enquire too minutely into its own ſenſations.—————I am unfortunate. my lord, but not criminal.

L. Aim. Patty, we are both unfortunate: for my own part, I know not what to ſay to you, or what to propoſe to myſelf.

Pat. Then, my lord, 'tis mine to act as I ought: yet, while I am honoured with a place in your eſteem, imagine me not inſenſible of ſo high a diſtinction; or capable of lightly turning my thought towards another.

L Aim. How cruel is my ſituation!————I am here, Patty, to command you to marry the man who has given you ſo much uneaſineſs.

Pat. My lord, I am convinced it is for your credit and my ſafety, it ſhould be ſo: I hope I have not ſo ill profited by the leſſons of your noble mother, but I ſhall be able to do my duty, wherever I am called to it: this will be my firſt ſupport; time and reflection will complete the work.

A I R.

Ceaſe, oh ceaſe, to overwhelm me,
  With exceſs of bounty rare;
What am I? What have I? Tell me,
  To deſerve your meaneſt care?
'Gainſt our fate in vain's reſiſtance,
  Let me then no grief diſcloſe;
But reſign'd at humble diſtance,
  Offer vows for your repoſe.

SCENE

SCENE XV.

Lord AIMWORTH, PATTY, *Sir* HARRY SYCAMORE,
THEODOSIA, GILES.

Sir Har. No justice of peace, no bailiffs, no head-borough!

L. Aim. What's the matter, Sir Harry?

Sir Har. The matter, my lord—While I was examining the construction of the mill without, for I have some small notion of mechanics, Miss Sycamore had like to have been run away with by a gipsey man.

Theo. Dear papa, how can you talk so? Did not I tell you it was at my own desire the poor fellow went to shew me the canal.

Sir Har. Hold your tongue, miss. I don't know any business you had to let him come near you at all : we have stayed so long too ; your mama gave us but half an hour, and she'll be frightened out of her wits—she'll think some accident has happened to me.

L. Aim. I'll wait upon you when you please.

Sir Har. O! but my lord, here's a poor fellow ; it seems his mistress has conceived some disgust against him : pray has her father spoke to you to interpose your authority in his behalf?

Giles. If his lordship's honour would be so kind, I would acknowledge the favour as far as in me lay.

Sir Har. Let me speak—[*Takes Lord Aimworth aside*]. a word or two in your lordship's ear.

Theo. Well, I do like this gipsey scheme prodigiously, if we can but put it into execution as happily as we have contrived it—[*here Patty enters*] So, my dear Patty, you see I am come to return your visit very soon ; but this is only a call *en passant*—will you be at home after dinner?

Patty. Certainly, madam, whenever you condescend to honour me so far : but it is what I cannot expect.

Theo. O fye, why not———

Giles. Your servant, Miss Patty.

Patty. Farmer, your servant.

Sir Har. Here, you goodman delver, I have done your business ; my lord has spoke, and your fortune's

made

made : a thoufand pounds at prefent, and better things
to come ; his lordfhip fays he will be your friend.

Giles. I do hope, then, Mifs Pat, will make all up.

Sir Har. Mifs Pat, make up ; ftand out of the way,
I'll make it up.

> *The quarrels of lovers, adds me ! they're a jeft ;*
> *Come hither, ye blockhead, come hither :*
> *So now let us leave them together.*

L. Aim.   *Farewell, then !*

Patty.   ————————— *For ever !*

Giles.   ———————————— *I vow and proteft,*
> *'Twas kind of his honour,*
> *To gain thus upon her ;*
> *We're fo much beholden it can't be expreft.*

Theo.   *I feel fomething here,*
> *'Twixt hoping and fear :*
> *Hafte, hafte, friendly night,*
> *To fhelter our flight ——*

L. Aim. }
Patty, } *A thoufand diftractions are rending my breaft.*

Patty.   *Oh mercy,*

Giles.   ————*Oh dear !*

Sir Har. *Why mifs, will you mind when you're fpoke to, or not?*
> *Muft I ftand in waiting,*
> *While you're here a prating ?*

L. Aim. }
Theo. } *May ev'ry felicity fall to your lot.*

Giles.   *She curtfies !—Look there,*
> *What a fhape, what an air !—*

All.   *How happy ! how wretched ! how tir'd am I !*
> *Your lordfhip's obedient ; your fervant ; good bye.*

A C T

ACT III. SCENE I.

The Portico to LORD AIMWORTH'*s House.*

Enter LORD AIMWORTH, SIR HARRY, LADY SYCA-
MORE.

La. Syc. A Wretch! a vile, inconfiderate wretch! coming of fuch a race as mine; and having an
example like me before her!

L. Aim. I beg, madam, you will not difquiet yourfelf: you are told here, that a gentleman lately arrived
from London has been about the place to-day; that he
has difguifed himfelf like a gipfey, came hither, and had
fome converfation with your daughter; you are even
told, that there is a defign formed for their going off
together; but poffibly there may be fome miftake in all
this.

Sir Har. Ay, but, my lord, the lad tells us the gentleman's name: we have feen the gipfies; and we know
fhe has had a hankering———

La. Syc. Sir Harry, my dear, why will you put in
your word, when you hear others fpeaking—I proteft,
my lord, I'm in fuch confufion, I know not what to fay :
I can hardly fupport myfelf.———

L. Aim. This gentleman, it feems, is at a little inn
at the bottom of the hill.

Sir Har. I wifh it was poffible to have a file of muf-
queteers, my lord; I could head them myfelf, being in
the militia : and we would go and feize him directly.

L. Aim. Softly, my dear fir; let us proceed with a
little lefs violence in this matter, I befeech you. We
fhould firft fee the young lady———Where is Mifs Sycamore, madam ?

La. Syc. Really, my lord, I don't know; I faw her
go into the garden about a quarter of an hour ago, from
our chamber window.

Sir Har. Into the garden! perhaps fhe has got an
inkling of our being informed of this affair, and is gone
to throw herfelf into the pond. Defpair, my lord, makes
girls do terrible things. 'Twas but the Wednefday before

fore we left London, that I saw, taken out of Rosa-
mond's pond, in Saint James's Park, as likely a young
woman as ever you would desire to set your eyes on, in
a new callimancoe petticoat, and a pair of silver buckles
in her shoes.

L. Aim. I hope there is no danger of any such fatal
accident happening at present; but you will oblige me,
Sir Harry?

Sir Har. Surely, my lord——

L. Aim. Will you commit the whole direction of this
affair to my prudence?

Sir Har. My dear, you hear what his lordship says.

La. Syc. Indeed, my lord, I am so much asham'd, I
don't know what to answer; the fault of my daughter——

L. Aim. Don't mention it, madam; the fault has been
mine, who have been innocently the occasion of a young
lady's transgressing a point of duty and decorum, which,
otherwise, she would never have violated. But if you,
and Sir Harry, will walk in and repose yourselves, I hope
to settle every thing to the general satisfaction.

La. Syc. Come in, Sir Harry.   [*Exit.*

L. Aim. I am sure, my good friend, had I known that
I was doing a violence to Miss Sycamore's inclinations,
in the happiness I proposed to myself——

Sir Har. My lord, 'tis all a case——My grandfather,
by the mother's side, was a very sensible man---he was
elected knight of the shire in five successive parliaments;
and died high sheriff of his county---a man of fine parts,
fine talents, and one of the most curiosest docker of horses
in all England (but that he did only now and then for
his amusement)————And he used to say, my lord, that
the female sex were good for-nothing but to bring forth
children, and breed disturbance.

L. Aim. The ladies were very little obliged to your
ancestor, Sir Harry: but for my part, I have a more
favourable opinion————

Sir Har. You are in the wrong, my lord: with submission, you are really in the wrong.

A I R.

To speak my mind, of woman kind,
   In one word 'tis this ;
By nature they're defign'd,
   To fay and do amifs.

Be they maids, be they wives,
   Alike they plague our lives :
Wanton, headftrong, cunning, vain ;
Born to cheat, and give men pain.

Their ftudy day and night,
Is mifchief, their delight :
And if we fhould prevent,
At one door their intent ;
They quickly turn about,
And find another out.

SCENE II.

" *Lord* AIMWORTH," *Enter* FAIRFIELD, " RALPH."

" *Ralph.* Dear goodnefs, my lord, I doubts I have
" done fome wrong here ; I hope your honour will for-
" give me ; to be fartin, if I had known———
" *L. Aim.* You have done nothing but what's very
" right, my lad ; don't make yourfelf uneafy."—How
now, mafter Fairfield, what brings you here ?

Fairf. I am come, my lord, to thank you for your
bounty to me and my daughter this morning, and moft
humbly to intreat your lordfhip to receive it at our
hands again.

L. Aim. Ay—why, what's the matter ?

Fairf. I don't know, my lord ; it feems your generofity to my poor girl has been noifed about the neighbourhood ; and fome evil-minded people have put it into
the young man's head, that was to marry her, that you
would never have made her a prefent fo much above her
deferts and expectations, if it had not been upon fome
naughty account : now, my lord, I am a poor man, 'tis
true, and a mean one ; but I and my father, and my
father's

father's father, have lived tenants upon your lordſhip's eſtate, where we have always been known for honeſt men ; and it ſhall never be ſaid, that Fairfield, the miller, became rich in his old days by the wages of his child's ſhame.

L. Aim. What then, Maſter Fairfield, do you be-lieve ————

Fairf. No, my lord, no, Heaven forbid : but when I conſider the ſum, it is too much for us ; " it is indeed, " my lord," and enough to make bad folks talk : be-ſides, my poor girl is greatly alter'd ; ſhe us'd to be the life of every place ſhe came into ; but ſince her being at home, I have ſeen nothing from her but ſadneſs and watry eyes.

L. Aim. The farmer then refuſes to marry Patty, not-withſtanding their late reconciliation.

Fairf. Yes, my lord, he does indeed ; and has made a wicked noiſe, and uſed us in a very baſe manner : I did not think farmer Giles would have been ſo ready to believe ſuch a thing of us.

L. Aim. Well, Maſter Fairfield, I will not preſs on you a donation, the rejeſtion of which does you ſo much credit; you may take my word, however, that your fears upon this occaſion are entirely groundleſs : but this is not enough, as I have been the means of loſing your daughter one huſband, it is but juſt I ſhould get her ano-ther ; and, ſince the farmer is ſo ſcrupulous, there is a young man in the houſe here, whom I have ſome in-fluence over, and I dare ſay he will be leſs ſqueamiſh.

Fairf. To be ſure, my lord, you have, in all honeſt ways, a right to diſpoſe of me and mine, as you think proper.

L. Aim. Go then immediately, and bring Patty hither; I ſhall not be eaſy till I have given you entire ſatisfaction. But, ſtay and take a letter, which I am ſtepping into my ſtudy to write : I'll order a chaiſe to be got ready, that you may go back and forward with greater expedition.

F   A I R.

A I R.

Let me fly————hence tyrant fashion,
Teach to servile minds your law ;
Curb in them each gen'rous passion,
Ev'ry motion keep in awe.

Shall I, in thy trammels going,
Quit the idol of my heart :
While it beats, all fervent, glowing !
With my life I'll sooner part.

SCENE III.

Fanny *following* Ralph.

Fanny. Ralph, Ralph !

Ralph. What do you want with me, eh ?

Fanny. Lord, I never knowed such a man as you are, since I com'd into the world ; a body can't speak to you, but you falls strait ways into a passion : I followed you up from the house, only you run so, there was no such a thing as overtaking you, and I have been waiting there at the back door ever so long.

Ralph. Well, and now you may go and wait at the fore door, if you like it : but I forewarn you and your gang not to keep lurking about our mill any longer ; for if you do, I'll send the constable after you, and have you every mother's skin clapt into the county gaol : you are such a pack of thieves, one can't hang so much as a rag to dry for you : it was but the other day that a cou‐ e of them came into our kitchen to beg a handful of dirty flour to make them cakes, and before the wench could turn about, they had whipped off three brass can‐ dlesticks, and a pot-lid.

Fanny. Well, sure it was not I.

Ralph. Then you know that old rascal, that you call father ; the last time I catch'd him laying snares for the hares, I told him I'd inform the game-keeper, and I'll expose all————

Fanny. Ah, dear Ralph, don't be angry with me.

Ralph. Yes I will be angry with you—what do you come nigh me for ?—You shan't touch me—There's the

skirt

ſkirt of my coat, and if you do but lay a finger on it, my lord's bailiff is here in the court, and I'll call him and give you to him.

Fanny. If you'll forgive me, I'll go down on my knees.

Ralph. I tell you I won't.—No, no, follow your gentleman; or go live upon your old fare, crows and pole-cats, and ſheep that die of the rot ; pick the dead fowl off the dung-hills, and ſquench your thirſt at the next ditch, 'tis the fitteſt liquor to waſh down ſuch dainties— ſkulking about from barn to barn, and lying upon wet ſtraw, on commons, and in green lanes—go and be whipt from pariſh to pariſh, as you uſed to be.

Fanny. How can you talk ſo unkind ?

Ralph. And ſee whether you will get what will keep you as I did, by telling of fortunes, and coming with pillows under your apron, among the young farmers wives, to make believe you are a breeding, with " the Lord Almighty bleſs you, ſweet miſtreſs, you cannot tell how ſoon it may be your own caſe." You know I am acquainted with all your tricks—and how you turn up the white's of your eyes, pretending you were ſtruck blind by thunder and lightning.

Fanny. Pray don't be angry, Ralph.

Ralph. Yes but I will tho' ; ſpread your cobwebs to catch flies, I am an old waſp, and don't value them a button.

A I R.

When you meet a tender creature,
Neat in limb, and fair in feature.
Full of kindneſs and good nature,
*   Prove as kind again to ſhe ;*
Happy mortal ! to poſſeſs her,
In your boſom, warm, and preſs her,
Morning, noon, and night, careſs her,
*   And be fond, as fond can be.*

* But if one you meet that's frow-ard,*
Saucy, jilting, and untow-ard,
Should you act the whining coward,
*   'Tis to mend her ne'er the will :*

F 2

Nothing's

Nothing's tough enough to bind her ;
Then agog, when once you find her,
Let her go, and never mind her ;
Heart alive, you're fairly quit.

SCENE IV.

FANNY.

" I wish I had a draught of water. I don't know
" what's come over me ; I have no more strength than
" a babe ; a straw would fling me down."—He has a
heart as hard as any parish officer ; I don't doubt now
but he would stand by and see me whipt himself; and
we shall all be whipt, and all through my means ———
The devil run away with the gentleman, and his twenty
guineas too, for leading me astray : if I had known
Ralph would have taken it so, I would have hanged myself before I would have said a word—but I thought he
had no more gall than a pigeon.

A I R.

O! what a simpleton was I,
  To make my bed at such a rate !
Now lay thee down, vain fool, and cry,
  Thy true love seeks another mate.

  No tears, alack,
  Will call him back,
No tender words his heart allure ;
  I could bite
  My tongue, thro' spite———
Some plague bewitch'd me, that's for sure.

SCENE V.

Changes to a Room in the Miller's House.

Enter GILES, *followed by* PATTY *and* THEODOSIA.

" A I R.

" Giles   *Women's tongues are like mill-clappers,*
       " *And from thence they learn the knack,*
       " *Of for ever sounding clack.*"———
                                   Giles.

Giles. Why, what the plague's the matter with you
-What do you fcold at me for ? I am fure I did not fay
an uncivil word, as I do know of : I'll be judged by the
young lady if I did.

Patty. 'Tis very well, farmer ; all I defire is, that
you will leave the houfe : you fee my father is not at
home at prefent ; when he is, if you have any thing to
fay, you know where to come.

Giles. Enough faid, I don't want to ftay in the houfe,
not I ; and I don't much care if I had never come into
it.

Theo. For fhame, farmer, down on your knees and
beg Mifs Fairfield's pardon for the outrage you have
been guilty of.

Giles. Beg pardon, mifs, for what ?—Icod that's well
enough ; why I am my own mafter, be'nt I ?—If I have
no mind to marry, there's no harm in that, I hope : 'tis
only changing hands.——This morning fhe would not
have me ; and now I won't have fhe.

Patty. Have you !—Heav'ns and earth ! do you think
then 'tis the miffing of you that gives me concern ?—
No : I would prefer a ftate of beggary a thoufand times
beyond any thing I could enjoy with you : and be affured, if ever I was feemingly confenting to fuch a facrifice, nothing fhould have compelled me to it, but the
cruelty of my fituation.

Giles. O, as for that, I believes you ; but you fee
the gudgeon would not bite as I told you a bit agone
you know : we farmers never love to reap what we don't
fow.

Patty. You brutifh fellow, how dare you talk——

Giles. So, now fhe's in her tantrums again, and all for
no manner of yearthly thing.

Patty. But be affured my lord will punifh you feverely
for daring to make free with his name.

Giles. Who made free with it ; did I ever mention my
lord ? 'Tis a curfed lie.

Theo. Blefs me ! farmer !

Giles. Why it is, mifs——and I'll make her prove
her words——Then what does fhe mean by being punifhed ? I am not afraid of nobody, nor beholding to
nobody, that I know of ; while I pays my rent, my

F 3

money,

money, I believe, is as good as another's : egad, if it goes there, I think there be thofe deferve to be punifhed more than I.

Patty. Was ever unfortunate creature purfued as I am, by diftreffes and vexations!

Theo. My dear Patty—See, farmer, you have thrown her into tears—Pray be comforted.

A I R.

Patty. *Oh leave me, in pity ! The falfhood I fcorn ;*
For flander the bofom untainted defies :
But rudenefs and infult are not to be borne,
Tho' offer'd by wretches we've fenfe to defpife.

Of woman defencelefs, how cruel the fate !
Pafs ever fo cautious, fo blamelefs her way,
Nature, and envy, lurk always in wait,
And innocence falls to their fury a prey.

S C E N E VI.

MERVIN, THEODOSIA.

Theo. You are a pretty gentleman, are not you, to fuffer a lady to be at a rendezvous before you ?

Mer. Difficulties, my dear, and dangers——None of the company had two fuits of apparel ; fo I was obliged to purchafe a rag of one, and a tatter from another, at the expence of ten times the fum they would fetch at the paper-mill.

Theo. Well, where are they ?

Mer. Here, in this bundle———and tho' I fay it, a very decent habiliment, if you have art enough to ftick the parts together : I've been watching till the coaft was clear to bring them to you.

Theo. Let me fee——I'll flip into this clofet and equip myfelf——— All here is in fuch confufion, there will no notice be taken.

Mer. Do fo; I'll take care nobody fhall interrupt you in the progrefs of your metamorphofis *(fhe goes in)* —and if you are not tedious, we may walk off without being feen by any one.

Theo.

Theo. Ha! ha! ha!—— What a concourfe of atoms are here? tho', as I live, they are a great deal better than I expected.

Mer. Well, pray make hafte; and don't imagine yourfelf at your toilette now, where mode prefcribes two hours, for what reafon would fcarce allow three minutes.

Theo. Have patience; the outward garment is on already; and I'll affure you a very good ftuff, only a little the worfe for the mending.

Mer. Imagine it embroidery, and confider it is your wedding fuit.————Come, how far are you got?

Theo. Stay, you don't confider there's fome contrivance neceffary.——Here goes the apron, flounced and furbelow'd with a witnefs—Alas! alas! it has no ftrings! what fhall I do? Come, no matter, a couple of pins will ferve——And now the cap——oh, mercy! here's a hole in the crown of it large enough to thruft my head through.

Mer. That you'll hide with your ftraw-hat; or, if you fhould not——What, not ready yet?

Theo. Only one minute more—Yes, now the work's accomplifh'd.

A I R.

Who'll buy good luck, who'll buy, who'll buy
The gipfey's favours ?————Here am I!

Through the village, through the town,
What charming fav'ry fcraps we'll earn!
Clean ftraw fhall be our beds of down,
And our withdrawing-room a barn.

Young and old, and grave, and gay,
The mifer and the prodigal;
Cit, courtier, bumpkin, come away;
I warrant we'll content you all.

SCENE

SCENE VII.

MERVIN, THEODOSIA, FAIRFIELD, GILES.

Mer. Plague, here's somebody coming.

Fairf. As to the past, farmer, 'tis past; I bear no malice for any thing thou hast said.

Giles. Why, Master Fairfield, you do know I had a great regard for Miss Patty; but when I came to consider all in all, I finds as how it is not adviseable to change my condition yet awhile.

Fairf. Friend Giles, thou art in the right; marriage is a serious point, and can't be considered too warily.—Ha, who have we here!—Shall I never keep my house clear of these vermin?——Look to the goods there, and give me a horse-whip—by the lord Harry, I'll make an example—Come here, Lady Light-fingers, let me see what thou hast stolen.

Mer. Hold, miller, hold!

Fairf. O gracious goodness! sure I know this face—Miss——young Madam Sycamore————Mercy heart, here's a disguise!

Theo. Discover'd!

Mer. Miller, let me speak to you.

Theo. What ill fortune is this!

Giles. Ill fortune————Miss! I think there be nothing but crosses and misfortunes of one kind or other.

Fairf. Money to me, sir! not for the world; you want no friends but what you have already—Lack-a-day, lack-a-day—see how luckily I came in: I believe you are the gentleman to whom I am charged to give this. on the part of my Lord Aimworth——Bless, you, dear sir, go up to his honour, with my young lady—There is a chaise waiting at the door to carry you————I and my daughter will take another way.

SCENE VIII.

MERVIN, THEODOSIA, GILES.

Mer. Pr'ythee read this letter, " and tell me what
" you think of it."

Theo. Heavens, 'tis a letter from lord Aimworth !
—— We are betray'd.

Mer. By what means I know not.

Theo. I am so frighted and flurried, that I have
scarce strength enough to read it.

" SIR,
" It is with the greatest concern I find, that I have
" been unhappily the occasion of giving some uneasiness
" to you and Mifs Sycamore : be assur'd, had I been
" appriz'd of your prior pretensions, and the young
" lady's disposition in your favour, I should have been
" the last person to interrupt your felicity. I beg, sir,
" you will do me the favour to come up to my house,
" where I have already so far settled matters, as to be
" able to affure you, that every thing will go entirely
" to your satisfaction."

Mer. Well ! what do you think of it !——Shall we
go to the castle ?
" *Mer.* Well !——
" *Theo.* Well !——
" *Mer.* What do you think of it ?
" *Theo.* Nay, what do you think of it ?
" *Mer.* Egad, I can't very well tell——However, on
" the whole, I believe it would be wrong of us to pro-
" ceed any further in our design of running away, even
" if the thing was practicable.
" *Theo.* I am entirely of your opinion. I swear this
" Lord Aimworth is a charming man : I fancy 'tis
" lucky for you I had not been long enough acquainted
" with him to find out all his good qualities.—But how
" the deuce came he to hear——
" *Mer.* No matter ; after this, there can be nothing
" to apprehend.———What do you say, shall we go up
" to the Castle ?"

Theo.

Theo. By all means : and in this very trim ; to fhew what we were capable of doing, if my father and mo-ther had not come to reafon.————" But, perhaps,
" the difficulties being removed, may leffen your *pen-*
" *chant :* you men are fuch unaccountable mortals.—
" Do you love me well enough to marry me, without
" making a frolic of it ?
    " *Mer.* Do I love you !————
    " *Theo.* Ay, and to what degree ?
    " *Mer.* Why do you afk me ?————

" A I R.

" *Who upon the oozy beech,*
    " *Can count the num'rous fands that lie ;*
" *Or diftinctly reckon each*
    " *Tranfparent orb that ftuds the fky ?*

" *As their multitude betray,*
    " *And fruftrate all attempts to tell :*
" *So 'tis impoffible to fay*
    " *How much I love, I love fo well?"*

But hark you, Mervin, will you take after-my father, and be a very hufband now ?—Or don't you think I fhall take after my mother, and be a commanding wife !
    Mer. Oh, I'll truft you.
    Theo. But you may pay for your confidence. *(Exeunt.*

S C·E N E IX.

G I L E S.

So, there goes a couple ! Iccd, I believe Old Nick has got among the people in thefe parts. This is as queer a thing as ever I heard of. ——— Mafter Fairfield, and Mifs Patty, it feems, are gone to the caftle too ; where, by what I larns from Ralph in the mill, my lord has promifed to get her a hufband among the fervants. Now fet in cafe the wind fets in that corner, I have been thinking with myfelf who the plague it can be : there are no unmarried men in the family, that I do know of, excepting little Bob, the poftillion, and mafter Jonathan,
the

the butler; and he's a matter of fixty or feventy years old. I'll be fhot if it beant little Bob.————Icod, I'll take the way to the caftle, as well as the reft; for I'd fain fee how the nail do drive. It is well I had wit enough to difcern things, and a friend to advife with, or elfe fhe would have fallen to my lot.————But I have got a furfeit of going a courting, and burn me if I won't live a batchelor; for, when all comes to all, I fee nothing but ill blood and quarrels among folk when they are married.

A I R.

Then hey for a frolickfome life!
I'll ramble where pleafures are rife:
Strike up with the free-hearted laffes;
And never think more of a wife.
Plague on it, men are but affes,
To run after noife and ftrife.

Had we been together buckl'd;
'Twould have prov'd a fine affair:
Dogs would have bark'd at the cuckold;
And boys, pointing, cry'd————Look there.

S C E N E X.

Changes to a grand Apartment in LORD AIMWORTH's *Houfe, opening to a View of the Garden.*

Lord AIMWORTH, FAIRFIELD, PATTY, RALPH.

L. Aim. Thus, Mafter Fairfield, I hope I have fully fatisfied you with regard to the falfity of the imputation thrown upon your daughter and me————

Fairf. My lord, I am very well content; pray do not give yourfelf the trouble of faying any more.

Ralph. No, my lord, you need not fay any more.

Fairf. Hold your tongue, firrah.

L. Aim. I am forry, Patty, you have had this morti- fication.

Patty. I am forry, my lord, you have been troubled about it; but really it was againft my confent.

Fairf. Well, come children, we will not take up his honour's time any longer; let us be going towards home

Heav'n

—— Heav'n profper your lordfhip ; the pray'rs of me
and my family fhall always attend you.

L. Aim. Miller, come back —— Patty, ftay——

Fairf. Has your lordfhip any thing further to command us?

L. Aim. Why yes, Mafter Fairfield, I have a word or
two ftill to fay to you———In fhort, though you are
fatisfied in this affair, I am not ; and you feem to forget the promife I made you, that, fince I had been the
means of lofing your daughter one hufband, I would find
her another.

Fairf. Your honour is to do as you pleafe.

L. Aim. What fay you, Patty, will you accept of a
hufband of my chufing ?

Patty. My lord, I have no determination ; you are
the beft judge how I ought to act ; whatever you command, I fhall obey.

L. Aim. Then, Patty, there is but one perfon I can
offer you——and I wifh, for your fake, he was more
deferving———Take me————

Patty. Sir !

L. Aim. From this moment our interefts are one, as
our hearts ; and no earthly power fhall ever divide us.

Fairf. " O the gracious !" Patty—my lord—Did I
hear right !——You, fir, you marry a child of mine !

L. Aim. Yes, my honeft old man, in me you behold
the hufband defigned for your daughter ; and I am happy
that, by ftanding in the place of fortune, who has alone
been wanting to her, I fhall be able to fet her merit in a
light, where its luftre will be rendered confpicuous.

Fairf. But good, noble fir, pray confider ; don't go to
put upon a filly old man : my daughter is unworthy——
Patty, child, why don't you fpeak ?

Patty. What can I fay, father ! what anfwer to fuch
unlook'd-for, fuch unmerited, fuch unbounded generofity !

Ralph. Down on your knees, and fall a crying.

Patty. Yes, fir, as my father fays, confider —— your
noble friends, your relations—It muft not, cannot be—

" *L. Aim.* I muft, and fhall——Friends ! relations !
" from henceforth I have none, that will not acknow-
" ledge you : and I am fure, when they become ac-
" quainted with your perfections, thofe, whofe fuffrage
"

" I moſt eſteem, will rather admire the juſtice of my
" choice, than wonder at its ſingularity."

A I R.

L. Aim.	*My life, my joy, my bleſſing,*
	In thee, each grace poſſeſſing,
	All muſt my choice approve :
Patty.	*To you my all is owing ;*
	O ! take a heart o'erflowing,
	With gratitude and love.
L. Aim.	*Thus infolding,*
	Thus beholding,
Both.	*One to my ſoul ſo dear :*
	Can there be pleaſure greater !
	Can there be bliſs compleater !
	'Tis too much to bear.

S C E N E   XI.

Enter SIR HARRY, LADY SYCAMORE, THEODOSIA,
MERVIN.

Sir Har. Well, we have followed your lordſhip's coun-
ſel, and made the beſt of a bad market——So my lord,
pleaſe to know our ſon-in-law, that is to be.

L. Aim. You do me a great deal of honour—I wiſh
you joy, ſir, with all my heart.—And now, Sir Harry,
give me leave to introduce to you a new relation of
mine——This, ſir, is ſhortly to be my wife.

Sir Har. My lord !

La. Syc. Your lordſhip's wife !

L. Aim. Yes, madam.

La. Syc. And why ſo, my lord ?

L. Aim. Why, faith, ma'am, becauſe I can't live
happy without her——And I think ſhe has too many
amiable, too many eſtimable qualities to meet with a
worſe fate.

Sir Har. Well, but you are a peer of the realm ; you
will have all the ſleerers——

L. Aim. I know very well the ridicule that may be
thrown on a lord's marrying a miller's daughter ; and I
own, with bluſhes, it has for ſome time had too great

G   weight-

weight with me : but we fhould marry to pleafe ourfelves, not other people : and, on mature confideration,
I can fee no reproach juftly merited, by raifing a deferving woman to a ftation fhe is capable of adorning, let
her birth be what it will.

Sir Har. Why 'tis very true, my lord.　I once knew
a gentleman that married his cook-maid : he was a relation of my own—You remember fat Margery, my lady !
She was a very good fort of a woman, indeed fhe was,
and made the beft fuet dumplings I ever tafted.

La. Syc. Will you never learn, Sir Harry, to guard
your expreffions ?————Well, but give me leave, my
lord, to fay a word to you——There are other ill confequences attending fuch an alliance.

L. Aim. One of them I fuppofe is, that I, a peer,
fhould be obliged to call this good old miller father-in-
law.　But where's the fhame in that ? He is as good as
any lord, in being a man ; and if we dare fuppofe a
lord that is not an honeft man, he is, in my opinion,
the more refpeftable charafter.　Come, Mafter Fairfield,
give me your hand ; from henceforth you have done
with working ; we will pull down your mill, and build
you a houfe in the place of it ; and the money I intended
for the portion of your daughter, fhall now be laid out
in purchafing a commiffion for your fon.

. *Ralph.* What, my lord, will you make me a captain ?

L. Aim. Ay, a colonel, if you deferve it.

Ralph. Then I'll keep Fan.

SCENE XII.

LORD AIMWORTH, SIR HARRY, LADY SYCAMORE,
　　PATTY,　THEODOSIA,　MERVIN,　FAIRFIELD,
　.RALPH, GILES.

Giles. Ods bobs, where am I running—I beg pardon
for my audacity.

Ralph. Hip, farmer ; come back, mon, come back
—Sure my lord's going to marry fifter himfelf ; feyther's
to have a fine houfe, and I'm to be a captain.

L. Aim.

L. Aim. Ho, Mafter Giles, pray walk in ; here is a lady who, I dare fwear, will be glad to fee you, and give orders that you fhall always be made welcome.

Ralph. Yes, farmer, you'll always be welcome in the kitchen.

L. Aim. What, have you nothing to fay to your old acquaintance——Come, pray let the farmer falute you——Nay, a kifs—I infift upon it.

Sir Har. Ha, ha, ha—hem !

La. Syc. Sir Harry, I am ready to fink at the mon-ftroufnefs of your behaviour.

L. Aim. Fye, Mafter Giles, don't look fo fheepifh ; you and I were rivals, but not lefs friends at prefent. You have acted in this affair like an honeft Englifhman, who fcorned even the fhadow of difhonour, and thou fhalt fit rent-free for a twelvemonth.

Sir Har. Come, fhan't we all falute——With your leave, my lord, I'll——

La. Syc. Sir Harry !

A I R.

L. Aim.   *Yield who will to forms a martyr,*
　　　　　While unaw'd by idle fhame,
　　　Pride for happinefs I barter,
　　　　　Heedlefs of the millions blame.
　　　Thus with love my arms I quarter ;
　　　　　Women grac'd in nature's frame,
　　　Ev'ry privilege, by charter,
　　　　　Have a right from man to claim.

Theo.   *Eas'd of doubts and fears prefaging,*
　　　　What new joys within me rife !
　　　While mama, her frowns affuaging,
　　　　Dares no longer tyrannize.
　　　So long ftorms and tempefts raging,
　　　　When the bluft'ring fury dies,
　　　Ah ! how lovely, how engaging,
　　　　Profpects fair, and cloudlefs fkies !

Sir

Sir Har. *Dad but this is wond'rous pretty,*
    Singing each a roun-de-lay ;
And I'll mingle in the ditty,
    Tho' I scarce know what to say.
There's a daughter, brisk and witty ;
    Here's a wife, can wisely sway :
Trust me, masters, 'twere a pity,
    Not to let them have their way.

Patty. *My example is a rare one ;*
    But the cause may be divin'd :
Women want not merit———dare one
    Hope discerning men to find.
O ! may each accomplish'd fair one,
    Bright in person, sage in mind,
Viewing my good fortune, share one
    Full as splendid, and as kind.

Giles. *Laugh'd at, slighted, circumvented,*
    And expos'd for folks to see't,
'Tis as tho'f a man repented
    For his follies in a sheet.
But my wrongs go unresented,
    Since the fates have thought them meet :
This good company contented,
    All my wishes are complete.

END OF THE OPERA.

ADDITIONAL AIRS.

ACT I.

FAIRFIELD.

THE great folks are noble, and proud let 'em be,
  Of title, of honour, and wealth,
That I am a Briton is title to me,
  And I'm rich in a ftock of good health.
    Lads, ftop the mill;
    Be the hopper ftill;
    When low the fun,
    Our work is done;
Then we'll fit to our homely board with glee,
For fweet is the bread of induftry.

Though in fummer I copied the provident ant,
  For winter fome grains to provide;
Yet, what I could fpare to a friend when in want,
  I ne'er was the friend who denied.
    Lads, ftop the mill, &c.

ACT II.

GILES.

Gadzooks! there's fuch gig, and nice rig on the lawn,
Little Sal for a partner wou'd fain have me on;
    But when your's I fhall be,
    How 'twill mortify fhe,
    Then I'll bet twenty pound,
    That the whole village round,
Cannot fhew fuch a couple as Patty and me.

For you, the fweeteft flowers I chofe,
  See here the wreath I've wove;
Of this a chaplet I'll compofe,
  And crown you queen of love.

Tho' Jemmy fo fupple,
  And Jenny fo taper,
Caft off the firft couple,
  Becaufe they can caper;

Poll jigs it with Roger,
　　Blythe Betty with Cudden;
And Cudden's a codger
　　Won't tire of a sudden.

Tho' Tim of the valley,
　　So nimble when tipsey,
Foots up to fly Sally,
　　That arch little gypsy;

Tho' spruce Davy Dumble,
　　Is partner with Dolly,
And old Gaffer Grumble
　　Is link'd to young Polly;

Yet you and I'll dance for a crown or a guinea,
'Gainst Poll, Tim, Sal, Jem, Bet, Bill, Cudden, and Jenn

FANNY.

　　The fields were gay
　　And sweet the hay,
Our gang of gypsies seated,
　　Upon the grass,
　　Both lad and lass,
By you we all were treated.

　　Young chicken, geese,
　　With ducks and peafe,
And beans and bacon dainty;
　　With punch and beer,
　　The best of cheer,
You gave us then in plenty.
　　'Twas all to cheat poor silly Fan,
　　　　And pilfer that same jewel;
　　You're sworn to me, you perjur'd man,
　　　　Tho' now so false and cruel.

　　Whene'er we'd meet,
　　With kisses sweet,
And speeches soft you won me;
　　The hawthorn bush
　　Should make you blush,
'Twas there you first undone me.

What fignifies
Your fhams and lies,
Your jokes no more fhall jeer me ;
A licenfe bring,
And golden ring,
Or never more come near me.
For you have cheated filly Fan, &c.

FAIRFIELD.

Of afpect fair, and temper mild,
 My Patty tho' you fee ;
When yet a babe, a' fweeter child
 Ne'er bleft a parent's knee.

The infant flower, for tender care,
 Cou'd ev'ry joy impart ;
But now a bramble proves, to tear
 Her aged father's heart.

A C T III.

FAIRFIELD.

Ere round the huge oak, that o'erfhadows my mill,
 The fond ivy had dar'd to entwine ;
Ere the church was a ruin, that nods on the hill,
 Or a rook built her neft on the pine.

Cou'd I trace back the time, a much earlier date,
 Since my forefathers toil'd in yon field ;
For the farm I now hold on your Lordfhip's eftate,
 Is the fame that my grandfather till'd.

He dying, bequeath'd to his fon, a good name
 Which unfullied defcended to me ;
For my child I've preferv'd it, uncrimfon'd with fhame,
 And it ftill from a fpot fhall be free.

THEODOSIA.

A thoufand charms the lover fees
In her he loves, while bolts and keys

Keep two fond hearts afunder;
But foon each envious bar re nov'd,
His paffion cools, and why he lov'd,
Is now his caufe of wonder.

My heart is your's, you know my mind,
In vain to anfwer nay ;
But will you be for ever kind,
For ever and a day ?

Your faith, if proof to female wiles,
And beauty's fweet alluring fmiles,
You'll never play the rover;
Nor I of cold neglect accufe,
Or in the lordly hufband lofe
The fond the tender lover.
My heart is your's, &c.

VERSE *for* RALPH, *in the Vaudville, after* PATTY.

Captain Ralph, my Lord will dub me.
Soon I'll mount a huge cockade;
Mounfeer fhall powder, queue, and club me,
'Gad, I'll be a roaring blade.

If Fan fhall offer once to fnub me,
When in fcarlet all array'd;
Or my feather dare to drub me,
Frown your worft——but who's afraid ?

AIR   Page

ACT III.

Mrs **WRIGHTEN** in the Character of **MADGE**

Since Hodge proves ungrateful no farther I'll seek

MISS PRUDOM *in the Character of* ARBACES
in ARTAXERXES.

BELL'S EDITION.

LOVE IN A VILLAGE;

A COMIC OPERA.

AS IT IS PERFORMED AT THE

Theatre-Royal in Covent-Garden.

DISTINGUISHING ALSO THE

VARIATIONS OF THE THEATRE.

Regulated from the Prompt-Book,

By *PERMISSION of the MANAGERS,*

By Mr. W I L D, Prompter.

L O N D O N:

Printed for JOHN BELL, at the BRITISH LIBRARY in the *Strand.*

M DCC LXXXI.

T O

Mr. B E A R D.

S I R,

IT is with great pleafure I embrace this opportunity
to acknowledge the favours I have received from you.
Among others I would mention in particular, the warmth
with which you efpoufed this piece in its paffage to the
ftage; but I am afraid it would be thought a compliment to your good-nature, too much at the expence of
your judgment.

IF what I now venture to lay before the public is
confidered merely as a piece of dramatic writing, it will
certainly be found to have very little merit: in that
light no one can think more indifferently of it than I do
myfelf; but I believe I may venture to affert, on your
opinion, that fome of the fongs are tolerable; that the
mufic is more pleafing than has hitherto appeared in
compofitions of this kind; and the words better adapted,
confidering the nature of the airs, which are not common ballads, than could be expected, fuppofing any degree of poetry to be preferved in the verfification.

MORE than this few people expect in an Opera; and
if fome of the feverer critics fhould be inclined to blame
your indulgence to one of the firft attempts to a young

A 2

writer,

writer, I am perfuaded the public in general will applaud your endeavour to provide them with fomething new, in a fpecies of entertainment in which the performers at your theatre fo eminently excel.

You may perceive, Sir, that I yield a punctual obfervance to the injunctions you laid upon me, when I threatened you with this addrefs, and make it rather a preface than a dedication : and yet I muft confefs I can harldly reconcile thofe formalities which render it indelicate to pay praifes where all the world allows them to be due ; nor can I eafily conceive why a man fhould be fo ftudious to deferve what he does not defire : but fince you will not allow me to offer any panegyric to you, I muft haften to beftow one upon myfelf, and let the public know (which was my chief defign in this introduction), that I have the happinefs to be,

S I R,

Your moft obliged,

and moft obedient fervant,

The AUTHOR.

A Table of the Songs, with the Names of the feveral Compofers. *N. B.* Thofe marked thus* were compofed on purpofe for this Opera.

A New Overture by Mr. Abel.

A C T I.

1	Hope thou nurfe of young defire	Mr. Weldon
2	Whence can you inherit	Abos
3	My heart's my own, my will is free	Arne
4	When once love's fubtile poifon gains	Arne
5	*Oh had I been by Fate decreed	Howard
6	Gentle youth, ah tell me why	Arne
7	*Still in hopes to get the better	Arne
8	There was a jolly miller once	
9	Let gay ones and great	Baildon
10	The honeft heart whofe thoughts are free	Fefting
11	Well, well, fay no more	*Larry Gorgan*
12	Cupid, god of foft perfuafion	Gardini
13	How happy were my days till how	Arne
14	A medley	

A C T II.

15	We women like weak Indians trade	Paradies
16	Think my faireft, how delay	Arne
17	*Believe me, dear aunt	Arne
18	When I follow'd a lafs that was forward and fhy	
19	Let rakes and libertines refign'd	Handel
20	How bleft the maid whofe bofom	Gallupi
21	In vain I every art affay	Arne
22	Begone, I agree	Arne
23	Oh how fhall I in language weak	Cary
24	Young I am, and fore afraid	Gallupi
25	Oons neighbour ne'er blufh	Arne
26	My Dolly was the faireft thing	Handel
27	Was ever poor fellow	Agus
28	Ceafe, gay feducers, pride to take	Arne
29	Since Hodge proves ungrateful	Arne
30	In love fhould there meet a fond pair	Bernard
31	*Well come let us hear.	

A C T III.

32	The world is a well furnifh'd table	Arne
33	It is not wealth, it is not birth	Gardini
34	*The traveller benighted	Arne
35	If ever a fond inclination	Geminiani
36	Plague o' thefe wenches, &c.	*St. Patrick's Day*
37	*How much fuperior beauty awes	Howard
38	When we fee a lover languifh	Arne
39	All I wifh in her obtaining	Arne
40	If ever I'm catch'd in thofe regions	Boyce
41	*Go, naughty man, I can't abide you	Arne
42	Hence with cares	Boyce

DRAMATIS PERSONÆ.

M E N.

SIR WILLIAM MEADOWS,	MR. FEARON.
YOUNG MEADOWS,	MR. LEONI.
JUSTICE WOODCOCK,	MR. WILSON.
HAWTHORN,	MR. REINHOLD.
EUSTACE,	MR. ROBSON.
HODGE,	MR. DOYLE.

W O M E N.

ROSSETTA,	MRS. MARTYR.
LUCINDA,	MRS. MORTON.
MRS. DEBORAH WOODCOCK,	MRS. CATLEY.
MARGERY,	MRS. WILSON.

Country Men and Women, Servants, &c.

SCENE, A VILLAGE.

LOVE IN A VILLAGE.

₩ *The lines distinguished by inverted comas, 'thus,' are omitted in the representation.*

ACT I.   SCENE I.

A garden with statutes, fountains, and flower-pots. Several Arbours, appear in the side-scenes: ROSSETTA *and* LU-CINDA *are discovered at work, seated upon two garden-chairs.*

AIR I.

Rossetta.   *H*OPE! *thou nurse of young desire,*
     Fairy promiser of joy;
Painted vapour, glow-worm fire,
    Temp'rate sweet, that ne'er can cloy:

Lucinda. *Hope! thou earnest of delight,*
    Softest soother of the mind;
Balmy cordial, prospect bright,
    Surest friend the wretched find:

Both.   *Kind deceiver, flatter still,*
    Deal out pleasures unpossest;
With thy dreams my fancy fill,
    And in wishes make me blest.

Lucin. Heigho——*Rossetta?*
Ross. Well, child, what do you say?
Lucin. 'Tis a devilish thing to live in a village an hundred miles from the capital, with a preposterous gouty father, and a superannuated maiden aunt.—I am heartily sick of my situation.

B

Ross.

Roff. And with reafon—But 'tis in a great meafure your own fault : here is this Mr. Euftace, a man of cha-racter and family ; he likes you, you like him ; you know one another's minds, and yet you will not refolve to make yourfelf happy with him.

A I R II.

Whence can you inherit
So flavifh a fpirit ?
Confin'd thus and chain'd to a log!
Now fondl'd, now chid,
Permitted, forbid :
'Tis leading the life of a dog.

For fhame, you a lover !
More firmnefs difcover ;
Take courage, nor here longer mope ;
Refift and be free,
Run riot like me,
And to perfeƐ the piƐure, elope.

Lucin. And this is your advice ?
Roff. Pofitively.
Lucin: Here's my hand ; pofitively I'll follow it—I have already fent to my gentleman, who is now in the country, to let him know he may come hither this day ; we will make ufe of the opportunity to fettle all prelimi-naries—And then—But take notice, whenever we de-camp, you march off along with us.

Roff. Oh ! madam, your fervant ; I have no inclina-tion to be left behind, I affure you—But you fay you got acquainted with this fpark, while you were with your mother during her laft illnefs at Bath, fo that your father has never feen him ?

Lucin. Never in his life, my dear ; and I am confident he entertains not the leaft fufpicion of my having any fuch conneƐion : my aunt, indeed, has her doubts and furmifes ; but, befides that my father will not allow any one to be wifer than himfelf, it is an eftablifhed max-im between thefe affeƐionate relations, never to agree in any thing.

Roff.

Roff. Except being abfurd; you muft allow they fympathize perfectly in that——But now we are on the fubject, I defire to know what I am to do with this wicked
old juftice of peace, this libidinous father of yours?
He fol'ows me about the houfe like a tame goat.

Lucin. Nay, I'll affure you he has been a wag in his
time—you muft have a care of yourfelf.

Roff. Wretched me! to fall into fuch hands, who have
been juft forced to run away from my parents to avoid
an odious marriage——You fmile at that now; and I
know you think me whimfical, as you have often told
me; but you muft excufe my being a little over delicate
in this particular.

A I R .III.

My heart's my own, my will is free,
 And fo fhall be my voice;
No mortal man fhall wed with me,
 Till firft he's made my choice.

Let parents rule, cry nature's laws;
 And children ftill obey;
And is there then no faving claufe,
 Againft tyrannic fway?

Lucin. Well, but my dear mad girl——
Roff. Lucinda, don't talk to me—Was your father to
go to London, meet there by accident with an old fellow as wrong-headed as himfelf; and in a fit of abfurd
friendfhip agree to marry you to that old fellow's fon,
whom you had never feen, without confulting your inclinations, or allowing you a negative, in cafe he fhould
not prove agreeable——

Lucin. Why, I fhould think it a little hard, I confefs—
yet, when I fee you in the character of a chambermaid—

Roff. It is the only character, my dear, in which I
could hope to lie concealed; and I can tell you, I was
reduced to the laft extremity, when, in confequence of
our old boarding-fchool friendfhip, I applied to you to
receive me in this capacity: for we expected the parties
the very next week.

B 2

Lucin,

Lucin. But had not you a meſſage from your intended ſpouſe, to let you know he was as little inclined to ſuch ill-concerted nuptials as you were ?

Roſſ. More than ſo ; he wrote to adviſe me, by all means, to contrive ſome method of breaking them off, for he had rather return to his dear ſtudies at Oxford ; and after that, what hopes could I have of being happy with him ?

Lucin. Then you are not at all uneaſy at the ſtrange route you muſt have occaſioned at home ? I warrant, during this month you have been abſent—

Roſſ. Oh ! don't mention it, my dear ; I have had ſo many admirers ſince I commenced Abigail, that I am quite charmed with my ſituation—But hold, who ſtalks yonder into the yard, that the dogs are ſo glad to ſee ?

Lucin. Daddy Hawthorn, as I live ! He is come to pay my father a viſit ; and never more luckily, for he always forces him abroad. By the way, what will you do with yourſelf while I ſtep into the houſe to ſee after my truſty meſſenger, Hodge?

R ſ. No matter, I'll ſit down in that arbour and liſten to the ſinging of the birds : you know I am fond of melancholy amuſements.

Lucin. So it ſeems, indeed : ſure, Roſſetta, none of your admirers had power to touch your heart ; you are not in love, I hope ?

Roſſ. In love ! that's pleaſant : who do you ſuppoſe I ſhould be in love with, pray ?

Lucin. Why, let me ſee——What do you think of, Thomas, our gardener ? There he is, at the other end of the walk—He's a pretty young man, and the ſervants ſay he's always writing verſes on you.

Roſſ. Indeed, Lucinda, you are very ſilly.

Lucin. Indeed, Roſſetta, that bluſh makes you look very handſome.

Roſſ. Bluſh ! I am ſure I don't bluſh.

Lucin. Ha, ha, ha !

Roſſ. Pſhaw, Lucinda, how can you be ſo ridiculous ?

Lucin. Well, don't be angry, and I have done—But ſuppoſe you did like him, how could you help yourſelf ?

A I R

AIR IV.

When once Love's subtile poison gains
A passage to the female breast ;
Like lightning rushing through the veins,
Each wish, and every thought's possest.
To heal the pangs our minds endure,
Reason in vain its skill applies ;
Nought can afford the heart a cure,
But what is pleasing to the eyes.

SCENE II.

Enter YOUNG MEADOWS.

Y. Meadows. Let me see—on the fifteenth of June at half an hour past five in the morning *(taking out a pocket-book)* I left my father's house, unknown to any one, having made free with a coat and jacket of our gardener's which fitted me, by way of a disguise:—so says my pocket-book ; and chance directing me to this village, on the twentieth of the same month I procured a recommendation to the worshipful Justice Woodcock, to be the superintendant of his pumpkins and cabbages; because I would let my father see I chose to run any lengths rather than submit to what his obstinacy would have forced me, a marriage against my inclination, with a woman I never saw. *(Puts up the book and takes up a watering-pot)*. Here I have been three weeks, and in that time I am as much altered as if I changed my nature with my habit. 'Sdeath, to fall in love with a chambermaid! And yet, if I could forget that I am the son and heir of Sir William Meadows—But that's impossible.

AIR V.

O! had I been by Fate decreed
Some humble cottage swain ;
In fair Rossetta's sight to feed
My sheep upon the plain ;

What.

What bliſs had I been born to taſte,
Which now I ne'er muſt know?
Ye envious pow'rs! why have ye plac'd
My fair one's lot ſo low?

Ha! who was it I had a glimpſe of as I paſt by that arbour! Was it not ſhe ſat reading there! The trembling
of my heart tells me my eyes were not miſtaken—Here
ſhe comes.

SCENE III.

Young Meadows, Rossetta.

Roſſ. Lucinda was certainly in the right of it, and yet
I bluſh to own my weakneſs even to myſelf—Marry hang
the fellow, for not being a gentleman.

Y. Meadows. I am determined I won't ſpeak to her
(turning to a roſe-tree, and plucking the flowers.) Now or
never is the time to conquer myſelf: beſides I have ſome
reaſon to believe the girl has no averſion to me: and, as
I wiſh not to do her an injury, it would be cruel to fill
her head with notions of what can never happen *(hums
a tune.)* Pſhaw! rot theſe roſes, how they prick one's
fingers!

Roſſ. He takes no notice of me; but ſo much the better, I'll be as indifferent as he is. I am ſure the poor
lad likes me; and if I was to give him any encouragement, I ſuppoſe the next thing he talked of would be
buying a ring, and being aſked in church—Oh, dear
pride, I thank you for that thought.

Y. Meadows. Hah, going without a word! a look!
—I can't bear that—Mrs. Roſſetta, I am gathering a few
roſes here, if you pleaſe to take them in with you.

Roſſ. Thank you, Mr. Thomas, but all my lady's
flower-pots are full.

Y. Meadows. Will you accept of them for yourſelf,
then? *(catching hold of her.)* What's the matter? you
look as if you were angry with me.

Roſſ. Pray let go my hand.

Y. Meadows. Nay, pr'ythee, why is this? you ſhan't
go, I have ſomething to ſay to you.

Roſſ. Well, but I muſt go, I will go; I deſire, Mr.
Thomas—

A I R

AIR VI.

Gentle youth, ah, tell me why
Still you force me thus to fly ;
Cease, oh ! cease, to persevere.
Speak not what I must not hear ;
To my heart its ease restore ;
Go, and never see me more.

SCENE IV.

YOUNG MEADOWS.

This girl is a riddle—That she loves me, I think there
is no room to doubt ; she takes a thousand opportunities
to let me see it: and yet when I speak to her, she will
hardly give me an answer ; and if I attempt the smallest
familiarity, is gone in an instant—I feel my passion for
her grow every day more and more violent—Well, would
I marry her ? would I make a mistress of her if I could ?
Two things, called prudence and honour, forbid either.
What am I pursuing, then ? A shadow. Sure my evil
genius laid this snare in my way. However, there is
one comfort, it is in my power to fly from it ; if so,
why do I hesitate ? I am distracted, unable to determine any thing.

AIR VII.

Still in hopes to get the better
Of my stubborn flame I try ;
Swear this moment to forget her,
And the next my oath deny.
Now prepar'd with scorn to treat her,
Ev'ry charm in thought I brave ;
Boast my freedom, fly to meet to her,
And confess myself a slave.

SCENE

SCENE V.

A hall in Justice WOODCOK's *house. Enter* HAWTHORN *with a fowling-piece in his hands, and a net with birds at his girdle: and afterwards Justice* WOODCOCK.

AIR VIII.

There was a jolly miller once,
   Liv'd on the river Dee ;
He work'd and sung, from morn till night ;
   No lark more blythe than he.
And this the burthen of his song,
   For ever us'd to be,
I care for nobody, not I,
   If no one cares for me.

Houfe here, houfe! what all gadding, all abroad ; houfe I fay, hilli ho ho!

J. Woodcock. Here's a noife, here's a racket! William, Robert, Hodge! why does not fomebody anfwer? Odds my life, I believe the fellows have loft their hearing! *(Entering)* Oh mafter Hawthorn! I guefled it was fome fuch mad cap—Are you there?

Hawth. Am I here? Yes: and if you had been where I was three hours ago, you would find the good effects of it by this time : but you have got the lazy unwhole-fome London fafhion, of lying a bed in a morning, and there's gout for you—Why, Sir, I have not been in bed five minutes after fun-rife thefe thirty years, am generally up before it ; and I never took a dofe of phyfic but once in my life, and that was in compliment to a coufin of mine, an apothecary, that had juft fet up bufinefs.

J. Woodcock. Well but, mafter Hawthorn, let me tell you, you know nothing of the' matter ; for I fay fleep is neceflary for a man ; ay and I'll maintain it.

Hawth. What, when I maintain the contrary ?——— Look you, neighbour Woodcock, you are a rich man, a man of worfhip, a juftice of peace, and all that ; but learn to know the refpect that is due to the found from the infirm ; and allow me that fuperiority a good con-ftitution gives me over you—Health is the greateft of

all

all poffeffions; and 'tis a maxim with me, that an hale cobler is a better man a fick king.

J. Woodcock. Well, well, you are a fpórtfman.

Hawth. And fo would you too, if you would take my advice. A fportfman! why there is nothing like it: I would not exchange the fatisfaction I feel while I am beating the lawns and thickets about my little farm, for all the entertainments and pageantry in Chriftendom.

A I R IX.

Let gay ones and great
Make the moft of their fate;
From pleafure to pleafure they run:
Well, who cares a jot,
I envy them not,
While I have my dog and my gun.
For exercife, air,
To the fields I repair,
With fpirits unclouded and light:
The bliffes I find,
No ftings leave behind,
But health and diverfion unite.

S C E N E VI.

JUSTICE WOODCOCK, HAWTHORN, HODGE.

Hodge. Did your worfhip call, Sir?

J. Woodcock. Call, Sir; where have you and the reft of thefe rafcals been? but I fuppofe I need not afk— You muft know there is a ftatute, a fair for hiring fervants, held upon my green to-day; we have it ufually at this feafon of the year, and it never fails to put all the folks hereabout out of their fenfes.

Hodge. Lord, your honour, look out, and fee what a nice fhow they make yonder; they had got pipers, and fidlers, and were dancing as I came along, for dear life —I never faw fuch a mortal throng in our village in all my born days again.

Hawth. Why I like this now, this is as it fhould be.

　　　　　　　　　　J. Woodcock.

J. Woodcock. No, no, 'tis a very foolish piece of business; good for nothing but to promote idleness and the getting of bastards: but I shall take measures for preventing it another year, and I doubt whether I am not sufficiently authorized already; for by an act passed *Anno undecimo Caroli primi*, which impowers a justice of peace, who is lord of the manor——

Hawth. Come, come, never mind the act; let me tell you this is a very proper, a very useful meeting; I want a servant or two myself, I must go see what your market affords;—and you shall go, and the girls, my little Lucy and the other young rogue, and we'll make a day on't as well as the rest.

J. Woodcock. I wish, master Hawthorn, I could teach you to be a little more sedate: why wont you take pattern by me, and consider your dignity!—Odds heart, I don't wonder you are not a rich man; you laugh too much ever to be rich.

Hawth. Right, neighbour Woodcock! health, good-humour, and competence, is my motto: and if my executors have a mind, they are welcome to make it my epitaph.

A I R X.

The honest heart, whose thoughts are clear
   From fraud, disguise, and guile,
Need neither fortune's frowning fear,
   Nor court the harlot's smile.

The greatness that would make us grave
   Is but an empty thing;
What more than mirth would mortals have?
   The chearful man's a king.

S C E N E VII.

LUCINDA, HODGE.

Lucin. Hist, hist, Hodge!
Hodge. Who calls? here am I.
Lucin. Well, have you been?

Hodge.

Hodge. Been, ay I ha' been far enough, an that be all: you never knew any thing fall out fo crofsly in your born days.

Lucin. Why, what's the matter?

Hodge. Why you know, I dare not take a horfe out of his worfhip's ftables this morning, for fear it fhould be miffed, and breed queftions; and our old nag at home was fo cruelly beat i'th'hoofs, that, poor beaft, it had not a foot to fet to ground; fo I was fain to go to farmer Ploughfhare's, at the Grange, to borrow the loan of his bald filly: and would you think it! after walking all that way—de'el from me, if the crofs-grained toad did not deny me the favour.

Lucin. Unlucky!

Hodge. Well, then I went my ways to the King's-head in the village, but all their cattle were at plough: and I was as far to feek below at the turnpike: fo at laft, for want of a better, I was forced to take up with dame Quickfet's blind mare.

Lucin. Oh, then you have been?

Hodge. Yes, yes, I ha' been.

Lucin. Pfha! Why did not you fay fo at once?

Hodge. Aye, but I have had a main tirefome jaunt on't, for fhe is a forry jade at beft.

Lucin. Well, well, did you fee Mr. Euftace, and what did he fay to you?—Come, quick—have you e'er a letter?

Hodge. Yes, he gave me a letter, if I ha'na loft it.

Lucin. Loft it, man!

Hodge. Nay, nay, have a bit of patience: adwawns, you are always in fuch a hurry *(rummaging his pockets)* I put it fomewhere in this waiftcoat pocket. Oh here it is.

Luncin. So, give it me *(reads the letter to herfelf.)*

Hodge. Lord-a-mercy! how my arms achs with beating that plaguy beaft; I'll be hang'd if I won'na rather ha' thrafh'd half a day, than ha' ridden her.

Lucin. Well, Hodge, you have done your bufinefs very well.

Hodge. Well, have not I now?

Lucin. Yes—Mr. Euftace tells me in this letter, that he will be in the green lane, at the other end of the village, by twelve o'clock—You know where he came before.

Hodge.

Hodge. Ay, ay.

Lucin. Well, you muſt go there; and wait till he arrives, and watch your opportunity to introduce him acroſs the fields, into the little ſummer-houſe, on the left ſide of the garden.

Hodge. That's enough.

Lucin. But take particular care that nobody ſees you.

Hodge. I warrant you.

Lucin. Nor for your life drop a word of it to any mortal.

Hodge. Never fear me.

Lucin. And Hodge——

A I R XI.

Hodge.   *Well, well, ſay no more;*
        Sure you told me before;
     I ſee the full length of my teather;
        Do you think I'm a fool,
        That I need go to ſchool?
     I can ſpell you and put you together.

        A word to the wiſe,
        Will always ſuffice;
    Addſniggers go talk to your parrot;
        I'm not ſuch an elfe,
        Though I ſay it myſelf,
    But I know a ſheep's head from a carret.

S C E N E VIII.

LUCINDA.

How ſevere is my caſe! Here I am obliged to carry on a clandeſtine correſpondence with a man in all reſpects my equal, becauſe the oddity of my father's temper is ſuch, that I dare not tell him I have ever yet ſeen the perſon I ſhould like to marry—But perhaps he has quality in his eye, and hopes, one day or other, as I am his only child, to match me with a title—vain imagination!

A I R

AIR XII.

Cupid, God of soft persuasion,
  Take the helpless lover's part :
Seize, oh seize some kind occasion,
  To reward a faithful heart.

Justly those we tyrants call,
Who the body would enthral ;
Tyrants of more cruel kind,
Those who would enslave the mind.

  What is grandeur ? foe to rest ;
  Childish mummery at best ;
  Happy I in humble state ;
  Catch, ye fools, the glittering bait.

SCENE IX.

A field with a stile.   Enter HODGE, *followed with* MAR-
GERY ; *and in some time after, enter* YOUNG MEADOWS.

Hodge. What does the wench follow me for ? Odds
flesh, folk may well talk, to fee you dangling after me
every where, like a tantony pig : find fome other road,
can't you ; and don't keep wherreting me with your
nonfenfe.

Marg. Nay, pray you Hodge ftay, and let me fpeak
to you a bit.

Hodge. Well ; what fayn you ?

Marg. Dear heart, how can you be fo barbarous ?
and is this the way you ferve me after all ; and won't
you keep your word, Hodge ?

Hodge. Why no I won't, I tell you ; I have chang'd
my mind.

Marg. Nay but furely, furely—Confider Hodge, you
are obligated in confcience to make me an honeft woman.

Hodge. Obligated in confcience ! How am I obligated ?

Marg. Becaufe you are ; and none but the bafeft of
rogues would bring a poor girl to fhame, and afterwards
leave her to the wide world.

C

Hodge.

Hodge. Bring you to fhame! Don't make me fpeak, Madge, don't make me fpeak.

Madge. Yes do, fpeak your worft.

Hodge.   Why then, if you go to that, you were fain to leave your own village down in the Weft, for a baftard you had by the clerk of the parifh, and I'll bring the man fhall fay it to your face.

Marg. No, no, Hodge, 'tis no fuch thing, 'tis a bafe lie of farmer Ploughfhare's—But I know what makes you falfe-hearted to me, that you may keep company with young madam's waiting-woman, and I am fure fhe's no fit body for a poor man's wife.

Hodge. How fhould you know what fhe's fit for? She's fit for as much as you mayhap; don't find fault with your betters, Madge [*Seeing Young Meadows.*] Oh! mafter Thomas, I have a word or two to fay to you; pray did not you go down the village one day laft week with a bafket of fomething upon your fhoulder?

Y. Meadows. Well, and what then?

Hodge. Nay, not much, only the oftler at the Greenman was faying as how there was a paffenger at their houfe as fee'd you go by, and faid he know'd you; and axt a mort of queftions—So I thought I'd tell you.

Y. Meadows. The devil! afk queftions about me! I know nobody in this part of the country; there muft be fome miftake in it— Come hither, Hodge.

Marg. A nafty ungrateful fellow, to ufe me at this rate, after being to him as I have.—Well, well, I wifh all poor girls would take warning by my mifhap, and never have nothing to fay to none of them.

A I R   XIII.

How happy were my days, till now!
I ne'er did forrow feel,
I rofe with joy to milk my cow,
Or take my fpinning-wheel.

My heart was lighter than a fly,
Like any bird I fung,
Till he pretended love, and I
Believ'd his flatt'ring tongue.

Oh

Oh the fool, the silly fill—ing fool,
Who knows not what man may be;
I wish I was a maid again,
And in my own country.

SCENE X.

A green with the prospect of a village, and the representation of a statute or fair. Enter JUSTICE WOODCOCK, HAWTHORN, *Mrs.* DEBORAH WOODCOCK, LUCINDA, ROSSETTA, YOUNG MEADOWS, HODGE, *and several country people.*

Hodge. This way, your worship, this way. Why don't you stand aside there! Here's his worship acoming.

Countrymen. His worship!

J. Woodcock. Fye, fye, what a croud's this! Odd, I'll put some of them in the stocks. [*Striking a fellow*] Stand out of the way, sirrah.

Hawth. For shame, neighbour. Well, my lad, are you willing to serve the king?

Countryman. Why, can you list ma! Serve the king, master! no, no, I pay the king, that's enough for me. Ho, ho, ho!

Hawth. Well said, Sturdy-boots.

J. Woodcock. Nay, if you talk to them, they'll answer you.

Hawth. I would have them do so, I like they should. —Well, madam, is not this a fine sight? I did not know my neighbour's estate had been so well peopled.—Are all these his own tenants?

Mrs. Deb. More than are good of them, Mr. Hawthorn. I don't like to see such a parcel of young husseys fleering with the fellows.

Hawth. There's a lass [*beckning to a country girl.*] Come hither, my pretty maid. What brings you here [*Chucking her under the chin.*] Do you come to look for a service?

C. Girl. Yes, an't please you.

Hawth. Well, and what place are you for?

C. Girl. All work, an't please you.

C 2

J. Woodcock.

J. Woodcock. Ay, ay, I don't doubt it; any work you'll put her to.

Mrs. Deb. She looks like a brazen one—Go hussy.

Hawth. Here's another. [*Catching a girl that goes by.*] What health, what bloom!—This is Nature's work; no art, no daubing. Don't be ashamed, child; those cheeks of thine are enough to put a whole drawing-room out of countenance.

SCENE XI.

JUSTICE WOODCOCK, HAWTHORN, *Mrs.* DEBORAH WOODCOCK, LUCINDA, ROSSETTA, YOUNG MEADOWS, HODGE, *and men and women servants.*

Hodge. Now, your honour, now the sport will come. The gut-scrapers are here, and some among them are going to sing and dance. Why there's not the like of our statute, mun, in five counties; others are but fools to it.

Servant-man. Come, good people, make a ring, and stand out, fellow servants, as many of you as are willing, and able to bear a bob. We'll let my masters and mistresses see we can do something at least; if they won't hire us, it shan't be our fault. Strike up the Servants Medley.

AIR XIV.

HOUSE-MAID.

I pray ye, gentles, list to me,
I'm young, and strong, and clean you see;
I'll not turn tail to any she,
 For work that's in the country.
Of all your house the charge I take,
I wash, I scrub, I brew, I bake;
And more can do than here I'll speak,
 Depending on your bounty.

FOOTMAN.

*Behold a blade, who knows his trade
  In chamber, hall, and entry ;
And what tho' here I now appear,
  I've serv'd the best of gentry.
    A footman would you have,
    I can dress, and comb, and shave ;
For I a handy lad am ;
    On a message I can go,
    And slip a billet-doux,
With your humble servant, madam.*

COOK-MAID.

*Who wants a good cook, my hand they must cross ;
For plain wholesome dishes I'm ne'er at a loss ;
And what are your soups, your ragouts, and your sauce,
Compar'd to old English roast beef ?*

CARTER.

*If you want a young man, with a true honest heart,
Who knows how to manage a plough and a cart,
Here's one for your purpose, come take me and try ;
You'll say you ne'er met with a better nor I,
    Ge ho Dobbin, &c.*

CHORUS.

*My masters and mistresses, hither repair ;
What servants you want you'll find in our fair ;
Men and Maids fit for all sorts of stations there be ;
And, as for the wages we shan't disagree.*

END OF THE FIRST ACT.

ACT

ACT II SCENE I.

A Parlour in JUSTICE WOODCOCK'*s House.*

LUCINDA, EUSTACE.

Lucin. WELL, am not I a bold adventurer, to bring you into my father's houfe at noon-day? Though, to fay the truth, we are fafer here than in the garden; for there is not a human creature under the roof befides ourfelves.

Euft. Then why not put our fcheme into execution this moment? I have a poft-chaife ready.

Lucin. Fye: how can you talk fo lightly? I proteft I am afraid to have any thing to do with you; your paffion feems too much founded on appetite; and my aunt Deborah fays——

Euft. What! by all the rapture my heart now feels——

Lucin. Oh to be fure, promife and vow; it founds prettily, and never fails to impofe upon a fond female.

AIR XV.

We women like weak Indians trade,
Whofe judgment tinfel fhew decoys;
Dupes to our folly we are made,
While artful man the gain enjoys:
We give our treafure to be paid,
A paltry, poor return! in toys.

Euft. Well, I fee you've a mind to divert yourfelf with me; but I wifh I could prevail on you to be a little ferious.

Lucin. Serioufly then, what would you defire me to fay? I have promifed to run away with you; which is as great a conceffion as any reafonable lover can expect from his miftrefs.

Euſt. Yes; but, you dear provoking angel, you have not told me when you will run away with me.

Lucin. Why that, I confeſs, requires ſome conſideration.

Euſt. Yet remember, while you are deliberating, the ſeaſon, now ſo favourable to us, may elapſe, never to return.

A I R XVI.

Think, my faireſt, how delay
Danger every moment brings;
'Time flies ſwift, and will away;
Time that's ever on its wings;
Doubting and ſuſpence at beſt,
Lovers late repentance coſt;
Let us, eager to be bleſt,
Seize occaſion e'er 'tis loſt.

S C E N E II.

LUCINDA, EUSTACE, JUSTICE WOODCOCK, *Mrs.*
DEBORAH WOODCOCK.

J. Woodcock. Why here is nothing in the world in this houſe but catter-wäwling from morning till night; nothing but catter-wawling. Hoity toity; who have we here?

Lucin. My father and my aunt!

Euſt. The devil! What ſhall we do?

Lucin. Take no notice of them, only obſerve me. *(Speaks aloud to* Euſtace) Upon my word, Sir, I don't know what to ſay to it, unleſs the Juſtice was at home; he is juſt ſtepped into the village with ſome company! but, if you will ſit down a moment, I dare ſwear he will return *(pretends to ſee the Juſtice)*—Oh! Sir, here is my papa!

J. Woodcock. Here is your papa, huſſey! Who's this you have got with you? Hark you, ſirrah, who are you, ye dog? and what's your buſineſs here?

Euſt. Sir, this is a language I am not uſed to.

J. Woodcock. Don't anſwer me, you raſcal—I am a
juſtice

juftice of the peace; and if I hear a word out of your mouth, I'll fend you to jail, for all your lac'd hat.

Mrs Deb. Send him to jail, brother, that's right.

J. Woodcock. And how do you know it's right? How fhould you know any thing's right?—Sifter Deborah, you are never in the right.

Mrs. Deb. Brother, this is the man I have been telling you about fo long.

J. Woodcock. What man, goody Wifeacre!

Mrs. Deb. Why the man your daughter has an intrigue with; but I hope you will not believe it now, though you fee it with your own eyes—Come huffey, confefs, and don't let your father make a fool of himfelf any longer.

Lucin. Confefs what, aunt? This gentleman is a mufic-mafter: he goes about the country teaching ladies to play and fing; and has been recommended to inftruct me; I could not turn him out when he came to offer his fervice, and did not know what anfwer to give him till I faw my papa.

J. Woodcock. A mufic-mafter!

Euf. Yes, Sir, that's my profeffion.

Mrs. Deb. It's a lye, young man; it's a lye. Brother, he is no more a mufic-mafter, than I am a mufic-mafter.

J. Woodcock. What then you know better than the fellow himfelf, do you? and you will be wifer than all the world?

Mrs. Deb. Brother, he does not look like a mufic-mafter.

J. Woodcock. He does not look! ha! ha! ha! Was ever fuch a poor ftupe! Well, and what does he look like then? But I fuppofe you mean, he is not dreffed like a mufic-mafter, becaufe of his ruffles, and this bit of garnifhing about his coat—which feems to be copper too —Why, you filly wretch, thefe whipperfnappers fet up for gentlemen, now-a-days, and give themfelves as many airs as if they were people of quality.—Hark you friend, I fuppofe you don't come within the vagrant act? You have fome fettled habitation?—Where do you live?

Mrs Deb. It's an eafy matter for him to tell you a wrong place.

J. Woodcock. Sifter Deborah, don't provoke me.

Mrs. Deb.

Mrs. Deb. . I wish, brother, you would let me examine him a little.

J. Woodcock. You shan't say a word to him, you shan't say a word to him.

Mrs. Deb. She says he was recommended here, brother; ask him by whom ?

J. Woodcock. No, I won't now, because you desire it.

Lucin. If my papa did ask the question, aunt, it would be very easily resolved.

Mrs. Deb. Who bid you speak, Mrs. Nimble Chops? I suppose the man has a tongue in his head, to answer for himself.

J. Woodcock. Will nobody stop that prating old woman's mouth for me? Get out of the room.

Mrs. Deb. Well, so I can, brother; I dont want to stay; but remember, I tell you, you will make yourself ridiculous in this affair; for through your own obstinacy you will have your daughter run away with before your face.

J. Woodcock. My daughter! who will run away with my daughter ?

Mrs. Deb. That fellow will.

J. Woodcock. Go, go, you are a wicked censorious woman.

Lucin. Why, sure madam, you must think me very coming indeed.

J. Woodcock. Ay, she judges of others by herself; I remember when she was a girl, her mother dared not trust her the length of her apron-string ; she was clambering upon every fellow's back.

Mrs. Deb. I was not.

J. Woodcock. You were.

Lucin. Well, but why so violent ?

A I R   XVI.

Believe me, dear aunt,
If you rave thus, and rant,
You'll never a lover persuade ;
The men will all fly,
And leave you to die,
Oh, terrible chance ! an old maid.

How

How happy the lass,
Must she come to this pass,
Who ancient virginity 'scapes:
'Twere better on earth
Have five brats at a birth,
Then in hell be a leader of apes.

SCENE III.

JUSTICE WOODCOCK, LUCINDA. EUSTACE.

J. Woodcock. Well done, Lucy, send her about her business; a troublesome, foolish creature, does she think I want to be directed by her—Come hither my lad, you look tolerable honest.

Eust. I hope, sir, I shall never give you cause to alter your opinion.

J. Woodcock. No, no, I am not easily deceived, I am generally pretty right in my conjectures.—You must know, I had once a little notion of music myself, and learned upon the fiddle; I could play the Trumpet Minuet, and Buttered Peas, and two or three tunes. I remember when I was in London, about thirty years ago, there was a song, a great favourite at our club at Nando's coffee-house; Jack Pickle used to sing it for us: a droll fish; but 'tis an old thing, I dare swear you have heard of it often.

AIR XVIII.

When I follow'd a lass that was froward and shy,
Oh! I stuck to her stuff, till I made her comply;
Oh! I took her so lovingly round the waist,
And I smack'd her lips and held her fast:
    When hug'd and haul'd,
    She squeal'd and squall'd;
But though she vow'd all I did was in vain,
Yet I pleased her so well that she bore it again:
    Then hoity, toity,
    Whisking, frisking,
Green was her gown upon the grass;
Oh! such were the joys of our dancing days.

Eust.

Euſt. Very well, Sir, upon my word.

J. Woodcock. No, no, I forget all thoſe things now; but I could do a little at them once:—Well, ſtay and eat your dinner, and we'll talk about your teaching the girl—Lucy, take your maſter to your ſpinnet, and ſhew him what you can do—I muſt go and give ſome orders; *then hoity, toity,* &c.

SCENE IV.

LUCINDA, EUSTACE.

Lucin. My ſweet pretty papa, your moſt obedient, humble ſervant; hah, hah, hah! was ever ſo whimſical an accident! Well ſir, what do you think of this?

Euſt. Think of it! I am in a maze.

Lucin. O your aukwardneſs! I was frigthened out of my wits, leſt you ſhould not take the hint; and if I had not turned matters ſo cleverly, we ſhould have been utterly undone.

Euſt. 'Sdeath! why would you bring me into the houſe? we could expect nothing elſe: beſides, ſince they did ſurpriſe us, it would have been better to have diſcovered the truth.

Lucin. Yes, and never have ſeen one another after-wards. I know my father better than you do; he has taken it into his head, I have no inclimation for a huſ-band; and let me tell you, that is our beſt ſecurity; for if once he has ſaid a thing he will not be eaſily perſua-ded to the contrary.

Euſt. And pray what am I to do now?

Lucin. Why, as I think all danger is pretty well over, ſince he has invited you to dinner with him, ſtay; only be cautious of your behaviour; and, in the mean time, I will conſider what is next to be done.

Euſt. Had not I better go to your father?

Lucin. Do ſo, while I endeavour to recover myſelf a little out of the flurry this affair has put me in.

Euſt. Well, but what ſort of a parting is this, with-out ſo much as your ſervant, or good bye to you? No ceremony at all? Can you afford me no token to keep up my ſpirits till I ſee you again?

Lucia. Ah childiſh!

Euſt. My angel!

AIR

AIR XIX.

Euſt.   *Let rakes and libertines reſign'd*
           To ſenſual pleaſures, range!
           Here all the ſex's charms I find,
           And ne'er can cool or change.

Lucin.   *Let vain coquets, and prudes conceal,*
           What moſt their hearts deſire ;
           With pride my paſſion I reveal,
           Oh! may it ne'er expire.

Both.   *The ſun ſhall ceaſe to ſpread its light,*
           The ſtars their orbits leave ;
           And fair creation ſink in night,
           When I my dear deceive.

SCENE V.

A Garden.

Enter ROSSETTA, *muſing.*

Roſſ. If ever poor creature was in a pitiable condition, ſurely I am. The devil take this fellow, I cannot get him out of my head, and yet I would fain perſuade myſelf I don't care for him: well but ſurely I am not in love : let me examine my heart a little: I ſaw him kiſſing one of the maids the other day; I could have boxed his ears for it, and have done nothing but find fault and quarrel with the girl ever ſince. Why was I uneaſy at his toying with another woman ? what was it to me? —Then I dream of him almoſt every night—but that may proceed from his being generally uppermoſt in my thoughts all day: Oh ! worſe and worſe !—Well, he is certainly a pretty lad ; he has ſomething uncommon about him, conſidering his rank : —And now let me only put the caſe, if he was not a ſervant, would I, or would I not prefer him to all the men I ever ſaw ? Why, to be ſure, if he was not a ſervant—In ſhort, I'll aſk myſelf no more queſtions, for the further I examine, the leſs reaſon I ſhall have to be ſatisfied.

AIR

AIR XX.

How bless'd the maid, whose bosom
No head-strong passion knows;
Her days in joys she passes,
Her nights in calm repose.
Where e'er her fancy leads her,
No pain, no fear invades her;
But pleasure,
Without measure,
From ev'ry object flows.

SCENE VII.

Young Meadows, Rossetta.

Y. Meadows. Do you come into the garden, Mrs. Rossetta, to put my lillies and roses out of countenance; or to save me the trouble of watering my flowers, by reviving them? The sun seems to have hid himself a little, to give you an opportunity of supplying his place.

Ross. Where could he get that now? he never read it in the Academy of Compliments.

Y. Meadows. Come don't affect to treat me with contempt; I can suffer any thing better than that; in short, I love you; there is no more to be said: I am angry with myself for it, and strive all I can against it: but in spite of myself, I love you.

AIR XXI.

In vain I ev'ry art essay,
To pluck the venom'd shaft away
That wrankles in my heart;
Deep in the centre fix'd, and bound,
My efforts but enlarge the wound,
And fiercer make the smart.

Ross. Really, Mr. Thomas, this is very improper language; it is what I don't understand; I can't suffer it and in short, I don't like it.

Y. Meadows. Perhaps you don't like me.

Ross. Well, perhaps I don't.

D

Y. Meadows

Y. Meadows. Nay, but 'tis not fo ; come, confefs you ove me.

Rof. Confefs ! indeed I fhall confefs no fuch thing: befides, to what purpofe fhould I confefs it ?

Y. Meadows. Why, as you fay, I don't know to what purpofe ; only it would be a fatisfaction to me to hear you fay fo ; that's all.

Rof. Why, if I did love you, I can affure you, you wou'd never be the better for it—Women are apt enough to be weak ; we cannot always anfwer for our inclinations, but it is in our power not to give way to them; and, if I was fo filly ; I fay, if I was fo indifcreet, which I hope I am not, as to entertain an improper regard, when people's circumftances are quite unfuitable, and there are obftacles in the way that cannot be furmounted—

Y. Meadows. Oh ! to be fure, Mrs. Rofetta, to be fure : you are entirely in the right of it—I—know very well, you and I can never come together.

Rof. Well then, fince that is the cafe, as I affure you it is, I think we had better behave accordingly.

Y. Meadows. Suppofe we make a bargain, then, never to fpeak to one another any more ?

Rof. With all my heart.

Y. Meadows. Nor look at, nor, if poffible, think of, one another ?

Rof. I am very willing.

Y. Meadows. And, as long as we ftay in the houfe together, never to take any notice ?

Rof. It is the beft way.

Y. Meadows. Why, I believe it is—Well, Mrs. Rofietta—

A I R XXII.

Rof   *Be gone——I agree*
         From this moment we're free:
         Already the matter I've fworn:
Y. Mead. *Yet let me complain*
         Of the fates that ordain,
         A tryal fo hard to be borne.
Rof.   *When things are not fit,*
         We fhould calmly fubmit;

No cure in reluctance we find:
Y. Mead. *Then thus I obey,*
Tear your image away,
And banish you quite from my mind.

Roff. Well, now, I think, I am somewhat eafier: I am glad I have come to this explanation with him, becaufe it puts an end to things at once.

Y. Meadows. Hold, Mrs. Roffetta, pray ftay a moment—The airs this girl gives herfelf are intolerable: I find now the caufe of her behaviour; fhe defpifes the meannefs of my condition, thinking a gardner below the notice of a lady's waiting-woman: 'sdeath, I have a good mind to difcover myfelf to her.

Roff. Poor wretch! he does not know what to make of it. I believe he is heartily mortified, but I muft not pity him.

Y. Meadows. It fhall be fo; I will difcover myfelf to her, and leave the houfe directly—Mrs. Roffetta— *(ftarting back)*—Pox on it, yonder's the Juftice come into the garden!

Roff. O Lord! he will walk round this way; pray go about your bufinefs; I would not for the world he fhould fee us together.

Y. Meadows. The devil take him: he's gone acrofs the parterre, and can't hobble here this half hour: I muft and will have a little converfation with you.

Roff. Some other time.

Y. Meadows. This evening, in the green-houfe, at the lower end of the canal; I have fomething to communicate to you of importance. Will you meet me there?

Roff. Meet you!

Y. Meadows. Ay; I have a fecret to tell you; and I fwear, from that moment, there fhall be an end of every thing betwixt us.

Roff. Well, well, pray leave me now.

Y. Meadows. You'll come then?

Roff. I don't know, perhaps I may.

Y. Meadows. Nay, but promife.

Roff. What fignifies promifing; I may break my promife—but I tell you I will.

Y. Meadows. Enough—Yet before I leave you, let me defire you to believe I love you more than ever man

loved

loved woman ; and that, when I relinquish you, I give
up all that can make my life supportable.

A I R XXIII.

Oh! how shall I in language weak,
My ardent paffion tell;
Or form my falt'ring tongue to fpeak,
That cruel word, Farewell!
Farewell!—but know, tho' thus we part,
My thoughts can never ftray:
Go where I will, my conftant heart
Muft with my charmer ftay.

S C E N E IV.

Rossetta, Justice Woodcock.

Roff. What can this be that he wants to tell me: I
have a ftrange curiofity to hear it, methinks—well—

J. Wood.ock. Hem : hem: Roffetta!

Roff. So, I thought the devil would throw him in my
way; now for a courtfhip of a different kind; but I'll
give him a furfeit—Did you call me, Sir?

J. Woodcock. Ay, where are you running fo faft?

Roff. I was only going into the houfe, Sir.

J. Woodcock. Well, but come here : come here, I fay.
(Looking about) How do you do, Roffetta?

Roff. Thank you, Sir pretty well.

J. Woodcock. Why you look as frefh and bloomy to-
day—Adad, you little flut, I believe you are painted.

Roff. O! Sir, you are pleafed to comp liment.

J. Woodcock. Adad, I believe you a. e—let me try—

Roff. Lord, Sir!

J. Woodcock. What brings you into this garden fo
often, Roffetta? I hope you don't get eating green fruit
and trafh ; or have you a hankering after fome lover in
dowlas, who fpoils my trees by engraving true-lovers
knots on them, with your horn and buck-handled knives?
I fee your name written upon the ceiling of the fervants
hall, with the fmoak of a candle ; and I fufpect—

Roff. Not me, I hope, Sir—No, Sir; I am of another
guefs

guefs mind, I affure; you for, I have heard fay, men are
falfe and fickle—.

J. Woodcock. Ay, that's your flanting, idle young fellows ; fo they are ; and they are fo damn'd impudent;
I wonder a woman will have any thing to fay to them ;
befides, all that they want is fomething to brag of, and
tell again.

Roff. Why, I own, Sir, if ever I was to make a flip it
fhould be with an elderly gentleman—about feventy, or
feventy-five years of age.

J. Woodcock. No child, that's out of reafon ; tho' I
have known many a man turned of threefcore with a
hale conftitution.

Roff. Then, Sir, he fhould be troubled with the gout,
have a good ftrong, fubftantial, winter cough—and I
fhould not like him the worfe—if he had a fmall touch
of the rheumatifm.

J. Woodcock. Pho, Pho, Roffetta, this is jefting.

Roff. No, Sir, every body has a tafte, and I have
mine.

J. Woodoock. Well, but Roffetta; have you thought of
what I was faying to you ?

Roff. What was it, Sir ?

J. Woodcock. Ah ! you know, you know, well enough,
huffey.

Roff. Dear Sir; confider "my foul ; would you have
"me endanger my foul ?

J. Woodcock. "No, no—Repent.

Roff. "Befides, Sir confider," what has a poor fervant
to depend on but her character ? And, I have heard,
you gentlemen will talk one thing before, and another
after.

J. Woodcock. I tell you again, thefe are the idle, flafhy
young dogs : but when you have to do with a ftaid, fober
man—

Roff. And a magiftrate, Sir !

J. Woodcock. Right; it's quite a different thing——
Well, fhall we, Roffetta, fhall we ?

Roff. Really, Sir, I don't know what to fay to it.

AIR XXIV.

Young I am, and fore afraid:
Wou'd you hurt a harmlefs maid?

D 3

Lead

Lead an innocent astray ?
Tempt me not, kind Sir, I pray.
Men too often we believe :
And should you my faith deceive,
Ruin first and then forsake,
Sure my tender heart wou'd break.

J. Woodcock. Why, you silly girl, I won't do you any harm.

Roff. Won't you, Sir?

J. Woodcock. Not I.

Roff. But won't you indeed, Sir?

J. Woodcock. Why I tell you I won't.

Roff. Ha, ha, ha!

J. Woodcock. Huffey Huffey.

Roff. Ha, ha, ha!——Your servant, Sir, your servant.

J. Woodcock. Why, you impudent, audacious——

S.C E N E IX.

Justice Woodcock, Hawthorn.

Hawth. So, so, justice at odds with gravity ! his worship playing at romps ! —— Your servant, Sir.

J. Woodcock. Haw, friend Hawthorn !

Hawth. I hope I don't spoil sport, neighbour: I thought I had the glimpse of a petticoat as I came in here.

J. Woodcocl. Oh ! the maid. Ay, she has been gathering a sallad—But come hither, master Hawthorn, and I'll shew you some alterations I intend to make in my garden.

Hawth. No, no, I am no judge of it; besides, I want to talk to you a little more about this—Tell me, Sir Justice, were you helping your maid to gather a sallad here, or consulting her taste in your improvements, eh ? Ha, ha, ha ! Let me see, all among the roses; egad, I like your notion: but you look a little blank upon it: you are ashamed of the business, then, are you ?

A I R XXV.

Oons ! neighbour, ne'er blush for a trifle like this ;
What harm with a fair one to toy and to kiss ?

The greatest and gravest——a truce with grimace——
Would do the same thing, were they in the same place.

No age, no profession, no station is free ;
To sovereign beauty mankind bends the knee :
That power, resistless, no strength can oppose,
We all love a pretty girl——under the rose.

J. Woodcock. I profess, master Hawthorn, this is all Indian, all Cherokee language to me ; I don't under-stand a word of it.

Hawth. No, may be not : well, Sir, will you read this letter, and try whether you can understand that ; it is just brought by a servant, who stays for an answer.

J. Woodcock. A letter, and to me ! *(taking the letter.)* Yes it is to me ; and yet I am sure it comes from no correspondent, that I know of. Where are my spectacles ? not but I can *see* very well without them, master Haw-thorn ; but this seems to be a sort of a crabbed hand.

S I R,

I am ashamed of giving you this trouble ; but I am informed there is an unthinking boy, a son of mine, now disguised and in your service, in the capacity of a gardener : Tom *is a lit-tle wild, but an honest lad, and no fool either, tho' I am his father that say it.* Tom——oh, this is *Thomas,* our gar-dener ; I always thought that he was a better man's child than he appeared to be, though I never mentioned it.

Hawth. Well, well, Sir, pray let's hear the rest of the letter.

J. Woodcock. Stay, where is the place ? Oh, here: *I am come in quest of my runaway, and write this at an inn in your village, while I am swallowing a morsel of dinner : be-cause not having the pleasure of your acquaintance, I did not care to intrude, without giving you notice* (Whoever this person is, he understands good manners). *I beg leave to wait on you, Sir ; but desire you would keep my arrival a se-cret, particularly from the young man.*

WILLIAM MEADOWS.

I'll assure you, a very well worded, civil letter Do you know any thing of the person who writes it, neighbour?

Hawth. Let me consider—Meadows—by dad I believe it is Sir William Meadows of Northamptonshire; and, now I remember, I heard, some time ago, that the heir of that family had absconded, on account of a marriage that was disagreeable to him. It is a good many years since I have seen Sir William, but we were once well acquainted; and, if you please, Sir, I will go and conduct him to the house.

J. Woodcock. Do so, master Hawthorn, do so——But, pray what sort of a man is this Sir William Meadows? Is he a wise man?

Hawth. There is no occasion for a man that has five thousand pounds a year, to be a conjuror; but I suppose you ask that question because of this story about his son; taking it for granted, that wise parents make wise children.

J. Woodcock. No doubt of it, master Hawthorn, no doubt of it—I warrant we shall find now, that this young rascal has fallen in love with some mynx, against his father's consent—Why, Sir, if I had as many children as king Priam had, that we read of at school in the destruction of Troy, not one of them should serve me so.

Hawth. Well, well, neighbour, perhaps not; but we should remember when we were young ourselves; and I was as likely to play an old don such a trick in my day, as e'er a spark in the hundred; nay between you and me, I had done it once, had the wench been as willing as I!

A I R XXVI.

My Dolly was the fairest thing!
Her breath disclos'd the sweets of spring;
And if for summer you wou'd seek,
'Twas painted in her eye, her cheek;
Her swelling bosom, tempting ripe,
Of fruitful autumn was the type:
But, when my tender tale I told,
I found her heart was winter cold.

J. Woodcock. Ah, you were always a scape-grace rattle-cap.

Hawth.

Hawth. Odds heart, neighbour Woodcock, don't tell me, young fellows will be young fellows, though we preach till we'er hoarse again; and so there's an end on't.

SCENE X.

JUSTICE WOODCOCK'*s hall.*

HODGE, MARGERY.

Hodge. So, mistress, who let you in?

Marg. Why, I let myself in.

Hodge. Indeed! Marry come up! why, then pray let yourself out again. Times are come to a pretty pass; I think you might have had the manners to knock at the door first—What does the wench stand for?

Marg. I want to know if his worship's at home.

Hodge. Well, what's your business with his worship?

Marg. Perhaps you will hear that—Look ye, Hodge, it does not signify talking, I am come, once for all, to know what you intends to do; for I won't be made a fool of any longer.

Hodge. You won't.

Marg. No, that's what I won't, by the best man that ever wore a head; I am the make-game of the whole village upon your account; and I'll try whether your master gives you toleration in your doings.

Hodge. You will?

Marg. Yes that's what I will; his worship shall be acquainted with all your pranks, and see how you will like to be sent for a soldier.

Hodge. There's the door; take a friend's advice and go about your business.

Marg. My business is with his worship; and I won't go till I sees him.

Hodge. Look you, Madge, if you make any of your orations here, never stir if I don't set the dogs at you—Will you be gone?

Marg. I won't.

Hodge. Here Towzer, (*whistling*) whu, whu, whu.

AIR

A I R XXVII.

Was ever poor fellow so plagu'd with a vixen?
Zawns! Madge don't provoke me, but mind what I say;
You've chose a wrong parson for playing your tricks on,
So pack up your alls and be trudging away:
You'd better be quiet,
And not breed a riot;
S'blood must I stand prating with you here a'l day?
I've got other matters to mind;
May hap you may think me an ass;
But to the contrary you'll find:
A fine piece of work by the mass!

S C E N E XI.

ROSSETTA, HODGE, MARGERY.

Ross. Sure I heard the voice of discord here—as I live an admirer of mine, and, if I mistake not, a rival—I'll have some sport with them—how now fellow-servant, what's the matter?

Hodge. Nothing, Mrs. Rossetta, only this young woman wants to speak with his worship—Madge follow me.

Marg. No Hodge, this is your fine madam; but I am as good flesh and blood as she, and have as clear a skin too, tho'f I mayn't go so gay; and now she's here I'll tell her a piece of my mind.

Hodge. Hold your tongue, will you?

Marg. No, I'll speak if I die for it.

Ross. What's the matter, I say?

Hodge. Why nothing I tell you;—Madge—

Marg. Yes, but it is something, it's all along of she, and she may be ashamed of herself.

Ross. Bless me, child, do you direct your discourse to me?

Marg. Yes, I do, and to nobody else; there was not a kinder soul breathing than he was till of late; I had never a cross word from him till he kept you company; but all the girls about say, there is no such thing as keeping a sweetheart for you.

Ross. Do you hear this, friend Hodge?

Hodge.

Hodge. Why, you don't mind fhe I hope ; but if that
vexes her, I do like you, I do ; my mind runs upon
nothing elfe ; and if fo be as you was agreeable to it, I
would marry you to night, before to-morrow.

Marg. You're a nafly monkey, you are parjur'd, you
know you are, and you deferve to have your eyes tore
out.

Hodge. Let me come at her—I'll teach you to call
names, and abufe folk.

Marg. Do ftrike me ; you a man !

Roff. Hold, hold—we fhall have a battle here prefently, and I may chance to get my cap tore off—Never
exafperate a jealous woman, 'tis taking a mad bull by
the horns—Leave me to manage her.

Hodge. You manage her ! I'll kick her.

Roff. No, no, it will be more for my credit, to get the
better of her by fair means—I warrant I'll bring her to
reafon.

Hodge. Well, do fo then—But may I depend upon
you ? when fhall I fpeak to the parfon ?

Roff. We'll talk of that another time—Go.

Hodge. Madge, good bye.

Roff. The brutality of this fellow fhocks me !—Oh
man, man—you are all alike—A bumkin here, bred at
the barn-door ! had he been brought up in a court, could
he have been more fafhionably vicious ? fhew me the
lord, 'fquire, colonel, or captain of them all, can out-do
him.

<h3 style="text-align:center">A I R XXVIII.</h3>

Ceafe, gay feducers, pride to take,
  In triumphs o'er the fair ;
Since clowns as well can act the rake,
  As thofe in higher fphere.

Where then to fhun a fhameful fate
  Shall helplefs beauty go ;
In ev'ry rank, in ev'ry ftate,
  Poor woman finds a foe.

SCENE

SCENE XII.

ROSSETTA, MARGERY.

Marg. I am ready to burſt, I can't ſtay in the place any longer.

Roſſ. Hold child, come hither.

Marg. Don't ſpeak to me, don't you.

Roſſ. Well, but I have ſomething to ſay to you ot conſequence, and that will be for your good; I ſuppoſe this fellow promiſed you marriage.

Marg. Ay, or he ſhould never have prevail'd upon me.

Roſſ. Well, now you ſee the ill conſequence of truſting to ſuch promiſes: when once a man hath cheated a woman of her virtue, ſhe has no longer hold of him; he deſpiſes her for wanting that which he hath robb'd her of; and, like a lawleſs conqueror, triumphs in the ruin he hath occaſioned.

Marg.—Nan!

Roſſ. However, I hope the experience you have got, though ſomewhat dearly purchaſed, will be of uſe to you for the future; and as to any deſigns I have upon the heart of your lover, you may make yourſelf eaſy, for I aſſure you, I ſhall be no dangerous rival, ſo go your ways and be a good girl.

Marg. Yes—I don't very well underſtand her talk, but I ſuppoſe that's as much as to ſay ſhe'll keep him herſelf; well let her, who cares, I don't fear getting better nor he is any day of the year, for the matter of that; and I have a thought come into my head that may be will be more to my advantage.

A I R XXIX.

Since Hodge proves ungrateful, no further I'll ſeek,
But go up to the town in the waggon next week;
A ſervice in London is no ſuch diſgrace,
And Regiſter's office will get me a place:
Bet Bloſſom went there, and ſoon met with a friend;
Folks ſay in her ſilks ſhe's now ſtanding an end!
Then why ſhould not I the ſame maxim purſue,
And better my fortune as other girls do?

SCENE

SCENE XIII.

Enter ROSSETTA *and* LUCINDA.

Roff. Ha! ha! ha! Oh-admirable, moft delectably ridiculous. And fo your father is content he fhould be a mufic-mafter, and will have him fuch, in fpite of all your aunt can fay to the contrary?

Lucin. My father and he, child, are the beft companions you ever faw: and have been finging together the moft hideous duets! Bobbing Joan, and Old Sir Simon the King: Heaven knows where Euftace could pick them up; but he has gone through half the contents of Pills to purge Melancholy, with him.

Roff. And have you refolved to take wing to-night?

Lucin. This very night, my dear: my fwain will go from hence this evening, but no farther than the inn, where he has left his horfes; and at twelve precifely, he will be with a poft-chaife at the little gate that opens from the lawn into the road, where I have promifed to meet him.

Roff. Then depend upon it, I'll bear you company.

Lucin. We fhall flip out when the family are afleep, and I have prepared Hodge already. Well, I hope we fhall be happy.

Roff. Never doubt it.

A I R XXX.

In love fhould there meet a fond pair,
  Untutor'd by fafhion or art;
Whofe wifhes are warm and fincere,
  Whofe words are th' excefs of the heart:

If ought of fubftantial delight,
  On this fide the ftars can be found,
'Tis fure when that couple unite,
  And cupid by Hymen is crown'd.

SCENE XIV.

ROSSETTA, LUCINDA, HAWTHORN.

Hawth. Lucy, where are you ?

Lucin. Your pleasure, Sir ?

Ross. Mr. Hawthorn, your servant.

Hawth. What, my little water-wagtail! The very couple I wish'd to meet : come hither both of you.

Ross. Now, Sir, what would you say to both of us ?

Hawth. Why, let me look at you a little—have you got on your best gowns, and your best faces ? If not go and trick yourselves out directly, for I'll tell you a secret—there will be a young batchelor in the house, within these three hours, that may fall to the share of one of you, if you look sharp—but whether mistress or maid—

Ross. Ay, marry, this is something ; but how do you know whether either mistress or maid will think him worth acceptance ?

Hawth. Follow me, follow me ; I warrant you.

Lucin. I can assure you, Mr. Hawthorn, I am very difficult to please.

Ross. And so am I, Sir.

Hawth. Indeed !

A I R XXXI.

Well come, let us hear what the swain must possess
Who may hope at your feet to implore with success?

Ross.	*He must be, first of all,*
	Straight, comely, and tall:
Lucin.	*Neither aukward,*
Ross.	*Nor foolish,*
Lucin.	*Nor apish,*
Ross.	*Nor mulish ;*
Lucin. }	
Ross. }	*Nor yet should his fortune be small.*
Hawth.	*What think'st of a captain ?*
Lucin.	*All bluster and wounds !*
Hawth.	*What think'st of a 'squire ?*
Ross.	*To be left for his hounds.*

Lucin.

Lucin. *The youth that is form'd to my mind,*
Must be gentle, obliging and kind;
Of all things in nature love me.:

Roff. *Have sense both to speak and to see—*
Yet sometimes be silent and blind.

Hawth. *'Fore George a most rare matrimonial receipt!*

Roff. *Observe it, ye fair, in the choice of a mate;*

Lucin. *Remember, 'tis wedlock determines your fate.*

END OF THE SECOND ACT.

E 2

ACT

ACT III. SCENE I.

A parlour in JUSTICE WOODCOCK's *house.* *Enter Sir* WILLIAM MEADOWS, *followed by* HAWTHORN.

Sir Will. WELL this is excellent, this is mighty good, this is mighty merry, faith; ha! ha! ha! was ever the like heard of? that my boy, Tom, should run away from me, for fear of being forced to marry a girl he never saw? that she should scamper from her father; for fear of being forced to marry him; and that they should run into one another's arms this way in disguise, by mere accident; against their consents, and without knowing it, as a body may say! May I never do an ill turn, master Hawthorn, if it is not one of the oddest adventures partly—

Hawth. Why, Sir William, it is a romance; a novel; a pleasanter history by half, than the loves of Dorastus and Faunia: we shall have ballads made of it within these two months, setting forth, how a young 'squire became a serving man of low degree; and it will be stuck up with Margaret's Ghost and the Spanish Lady, against the walls of every cottage in the country.

Sir Will. But what pleases me best of all, master Hawthorn, is the ingenuity of the girl. May I never do an ill turn, when I was called out of the room, and the servant said she wanted to speak to me, if I knew what to make on't: but when the little gipsey took me siade, and told me her name, and how matters stood, I was quite astonished; as a body may say; and could not believe it partly; till her young friend, that she is with here, assured me of the truth on't: Indeed, at last, I began to recollect her face, though I have not set eyes on her before, since she was the height of a full-grown greyhound.

Hawth. Well, Sir William, your son as yet knows nothing of what has happened, nor of your being come hither!

hither; and, if you'll follow my counfel, we'll have fome fport with him.—He and his miftrefs were to meet in the garden this evening by appointment, fhe's gone to drefs herfelf in all her airs; will you let me direct your proceedings in this affair?

Sir Will. With all my heart, mafter Hawthorn, with all my heart, do what you will with me, fay what you pleafe for me; I am fo overjoyed, and fo happy—And may I never do an ill turn, but I am very glad to fee you too; ay, and partly as much pleafed at that as any thing elfe, for we have been merry together before now, when we were fome years younger: well, and how has the world gone with you, mafter Hawthorn, fince we faw one another laft?

Hawth. Why, pretty well, Sir William, I have no reafon to complain: every one has a mixture of four with his fweets: but, in the main, I believe, I have done in a degree as tolerably as my neighbours.

AIR XXXII.

The world is a well furnifh'd table,
Where guefts are promifc'oufly fet;
We all fare as well as we're able,
And fcramble for what we can get.
My fimile holds to a tittle,
Some gorge, while fome fcarce have a tafte;
But if I'm content with a little,
Enough is as good as a feaft.

SCENE II.

Sir WILL. MEADOWS, HAWTHORN, ROSSETTA.

Roff. Sir William, I beg pardon for detaining you, but I have had fo much difficulty in adjufting my borrowed plumes—

Sir Will. May I never do an ill turn but they fit you to a T. and you look very well, fo you do: Cockfbones how your father will chuckle when he comes to hear this!—Her father, mafter Hawthorn, is as worthy a man as lives by bread, and has been almoft out of his

fenfes

fenfes for the lofs of her—But tell me huffey, has not this been all a fcheme, a piece of conjuration between you and my fon? Faith I am half perfuaded it has, it looks fo like hocus pocus as a body may fay.

Rofs. Upon my honour, Sir William, what has happened has been the mere effect of chance; I came hither unknown to your fon, and he unknown to me: I never in the leaft fufpected that Thomas the gardner was other than his appearance fpoke him; and leaft of all, that he was a perfon with whom I had fo clofe a connection. Mr. Hawthorn can teftify the aftonifhment I was in when he firft informed me of it; but I thought it was my duty to come to an immediate explanation with you.

Sir Will. Is not fhe a neat wench, mafter Hawthorn? May I never do an ill turn but fhe is—But you little plaguy devil, how came this love affair between you?

Rofs. I have told you the whole truth very ingenuoufly, Sir: fince your fon and I have been fellow-fervants, as I may call it, in this houfe, I have had more than reafon to fufpect he had taken a liking to me; and I will own with equal franknefs, had I not looked upon him as a perfon fo much below me, I fhould have had no objection to receiving his courtfhip.

Hawth. Well faid, by the lord Harry, all above board, fair and open.

Rofs. Perhaps I may be cenfured by fome for this candid declaration; but I love to fpeak my fentiments; and I affure you, Sir William, in my opinion, I fhould prefer a gardner, with your fon's good qualities, to a knight of the fhire without them.

AIR XXXIII,

'Tis not wealth, it is not birth,
Can value to the foul convey;
Minds poffefs fuperior worth,
Which chance nor gives, nor takes away.
Like the fun true merit fheavs;
By nature warm, by nature bright;
With intred flames, he nobly glows,
Nor needs the aid of borrow'd light.

Hawth.

Hawth. Well, but, Sir, we lose time—is not this about the hour appointed to meet in the garden?

Ross. Pretty near it.

Hawth. Oons then what do we stay for? Come, my old friend, come along, and by the way we will consult how to manage your interview.

Sir Will. Ay, but I must speak a word or two to my man about the horses first.

SCENE III.

ROSSETTA, HODGE.

Ross. Well—What's the business?

Hodge. Madam—Mercy on us, I crave pardon!

Ross. Why Hodge, don't you know me?

Hodge. Mrs. Rossetta!

Ross. Ay.

Hodge. Know you, ecod I don't know whether I do or not: never stir, if I did not think it was some lady belonging to the strange gentlefolks: why you ben't dizen'd this way to go to the statute dance presently, be you?

Ross. Have patience and you'll see :—but is there any thing amiss that you came in so abruptly?

Hodge. Amiss! why there's ruination.

Ross. How, where!

Hodge. Why, with Miss Lucinda: her aunt has catch'd she and the gentleman above stairs, and over-heard all their love discourse.

Ross. You don't say so!

Hodge. Ecod, I had like to have pop'd in among them this instant; but, by good luck, I heard Mrs. Deborah's voice, and run down again, as fast as ever my legs could carry me.

Ross. Is your master in the house?

Hodge. What his worship! no, no, he is gone into the fields to talk with the reapers and people.

Ross. Poor Lucinda, I wish I could go up to her, but I am so engaged with my own affairs——

Hodge. Mistress Rossetta.

Ross. Well.

Hodge

Hodge. Odds bobs, I muſt have one ſmack of your ſweet lips.

Roſſ. Oh ſtand off, you know I never allow liberties.

Hodge. Nay, but why ſo coy, there's reaſon in roaſt-ing of eggs; I would not deny you ſuch a thing.

Roſſ. That's kind: ha, ha, ha—But what will become of Lucinda? Sir William waits for me, I muſt be gone. Friendſhip, a moment by your leave; yet as our ſuffer-ings have been mutual, ſo ſhall our joys; I already loſe the remembrance of all former pains and anxieties.

A I R XXXIV.

The traveller benighted,
*   And led thro' weary'd ways,*
The lamp of day new lighted,
*   With joy the dawn ſurveys.*

The riſing proſpects viewing,
*   Each look is forward caſt;*
He ſmiles, his courſe purſuing,
*   Nor thinks of what is paſt.*

S C E N E IV.

HODGE, *Mrs.* **DEBORAH WOODCOCK, LUCINDA.**

Hodge. Hiſt, ſtay! don't I hear a noiſe?

Lucin. *(within)* Well, but dear, dear aunt——

Mrs. Deb. *(within)* You need not ſpeak to me, for it does not ſignify.

Hodge. Adwawns they are coming here! ecod I'll get out of the way—Murrain take it, this door is bolted now —So, ſo.

Mrs. Deb. Get along, get along; *(driving in Lucinda before her)* you are a ſcandal to the name of Woodcock; but I was reſolved to find you out, for I have ſuſpected you a great while, though your father, ſilly man, will have you ſuch a poor innocent.

Lucin. What ſhall I do?

Mrs. Deb. I was determined to diſcover what you and your pretended muſic-maſter were about, and lay in wait

on purpofe : I believe he thought to efcape me, by flip
ing into the clofet when I knocked at the door; but I-
was even with him, for now I have him under lock and
key, and pleafe the fates there he fhall remain till your
father comes in : I will convince him of his error, whether he will or not.

Lucin. You won't be fo cruel, I am fure you won't : I
thought I had made you my friend by telling you the
truth.

Mrs. Deb. Telling me the truth, quotha! did I not
overhear your fcheme of running away to-night, thro' the
partition ? did not I find the very bundles pack'd up in
the room with you ready for going off? No, brazenface,
I found out the truth by my own fagacity, tho' your father
fays I am a fool, but now we'll be judged who is the
greateft.—And you, Mr. Rafcal, my brother fhall know
what an honeft fervant he has got.

Hodge. Madam !

Mrs. Deb. You were to have been aiding and affifting
them in their efcape, and have been the go-between, it
feems, the letter-carrier !

Hodge. Who, me, madam !

Mrs. Deb. Yes, you, firrah.

Hodge. Mifs Lucinda, did I ever carry a letter for
you ? I'll make my affidavy before his worfhip—

Mrs. Deb. Go, go, you are a villain, hold your
tongue.

Lucin. I own, aunt, I have been very faulty in this
affair ; I don't pretend to excufe myfelf ; but we are all
fubject to frailties ; confider that, and judge of me by
yourfelf ; you were once young, and inexperienced as I
am.

A I R XXXV.

If ever a fond inclination
   Rofe in your bofom to rob you of reft ;
Reflect with a little compaffion,
   On the foft pangs, which prevail'd in my breaft.
Oh where, where would you fly me ?
   Can you deny me thus torn and diftreft ?
Think, when my lover was by me,
   Wou'd I, how cou'd I, refufe his requeft ?

Kneeling

Kneeling before you, let me implore you ;
　Look on me sighing, crying, dying ;
Ah! is there no language can move ?
　If I have been too complying,
Hard was the conflict 'twixt duty and love.

Mrs. Deb. This is mighty pretty romantic stuff! but you learn it out of your play-books and novels. Girls in my time had other employments, we worked at our needles, and kept ourselves from idle thoughts: before I was your age, I had finished with my own fingers, a complete set of chairs, and a fire-screen in tent-stitch; four counterpanes in Marseilles quilting; and the creed and the ten commandments, in the hair of our family: it was fram'd and glaz'd, and hung over the parlour chimney-piece, and your poor dear grandfather was prouder of it than of e'er a picture in his house. I never looked into a book, but when I said my prayers, except it was the Complete Housewife, or the great family receipt-book: whereas you are always at your studies! Ah, I never knew a woman come to good, that was fond of reading.

Lucin. Well, pray, madam, let me prevail on you to give me the key to let Mr. Euſtace out, and I promise, I never will proceed a step farther in this business, without your advice and approbation.

Mrs. Deb. Have not I told you already my resolution ? —Where are my clogs and my bonnet ? I'll go out to my brother in the fields; I'm a fool, you know, child, now let's see what the wit's will think of themselves— Don't hold me—

Lucin. I'm not going ;—I have thought of a way to be even with you, so you may do as you please.

S C E N E V.

HODGE.

Well, I thought it would come to this, I'll be shot if I did'nt—So here's a fine job—But what can they do to me—They can't send me to jail for carrying a letter, seeing there was no treason in it; and how was I obligated

gated to know my mafter did not allow of their meet-
ings :—The worft they can do, is to turn me off, and I
am fure the place is no fuch great purchafe—indeed, I
fhould be forry to leave Mrs. Roffetta, feeing as how
matters are fo near being brought to an end betwixt
us ; but fhe and I may keep company all as one; and
I find Madge has been fpeaking with Gaffer Broad-
wheels, the waggoner, about her carriage up to London :
fo that I have got rid of fhe, and I am fure I have reafon to be main glad of it, for fhe led me a wearifome
life—But that's the way of them all.

A I R XXXVI.

A plague on thofe wenches, they make fuch a pother,
When once they have let'n a man have his will ;
They're always a whining for fomething or other,
And cry he's unkind in his carriage.
What tho'f he fpeaks them ne'er fo fairly,
Still they keep teazing, teazing on :
You cannot perfuade 'em,
'Till promife you've made 'em ;
And after they've got it,
They tell you———add rot it,
Their character's blafted, they're ruin'd undone :
And then to be fure, Sir,
There is but one cure, Sir,
And all their difcourfe is of marriage.

S C E N E VI.

A Greenhoufe.

Enter YOUNG MEADOWS.

Y. Meadows. I am glad I had the precaution to bring
this fuit of cloaths in my bundle, though I hardly know
myfelf in them again, they appear fo ftrange, and feel fo
unweildy. However, my gardener's jacket goes on no
more.—I wonder this girl does not come *(looking at his
watch)* : perhaps fhe won't come——Why then I'll go
into the village, take a poft-chaife and depart without
any farther ceremony.

A I R

A I R XXXVII.

How much superior beauty awes,
*   The coldest bosoms find;*
But with resistless force it draws,
*   To sense and sweetness join'd.*
The casket, where, to outward shew,
*   The workman's art is seen,*
Is doubly valu'd, when we know
*   It holds a gem within.*

Hark! she comes.

S C E N E VII.

Enter Sir WILLIAM MEADOWS *and* HAWTHORN.

Y. Meadows. Confusion! my father! What can this
mean?

Sir Will. Tom, are not you a sad boy, Tom, to bring
me a hundred and forty miles here—May I never do an
ill turn, but you deserve to have your head broke; and
I have a good mind, partly—What, sirrah, don't you
think it worth your while to speak to me?

Y. Meadows. Forgive me, Sir; I own I have been in
a fault.

Sir Will. In a fault? to run away from me because
I was going to do you good—May I never do an ill turn,
Mr. Hawthorn, if I did not pick out as fine girl for him,
partly, as any in England; and the rascal run away
from me, and came here and turn'd gardener. And pray
what did you propose to yourself, Tom? I know you
were always fond of Botany as they call it; did you intend to keep the trade going, and advertise fruit-trees
and flowering-shrubs, to be had at Meadow's nursery?

Hawth. No, Sir William, I apprehend the young
gentleman designed to lay by the profession; for he has
quitted the habit already.

Y. Meadows. I am so astonished to see you here, Sir,
that I don't know what to say; but I assure you, if you
had not come, I should have returned home to you directly. Pray, Sir, how did you find me out?

'Sir

Sir Will. No matter, Tom, no matter ; it was partly by accident, as a body may say ; but what does that signify—tell me, boy, how stands your stomach towards matrimony ; do you think you could digest a wife now ?

Y. Meadows. Pray, Sir, don't mention it : I shall always behave myself as a dutiful son ought ; I will never marry without your confent, and I hope you won't force me to do it against my own.

Sir Will. Is not this mighty provoking, master Hawthorn ? Why, sirrah, did you ever see the lady I defigned for you ?

Y. Meadows. Sir, I don't doubt the lady's merit ; but at prefent, I am not difpofed——

Hawth. Nay, but young gentleman, fair and foftly, you fhould pay fome refpect to your father in this matter.

Sir. Will. Refpect, master Hawthorn ! I tell you he fhall marry her, or I'll difinherit him ! there's once. Look you, Tom, not to make any more words of the matter, I have brought the lady here with me, and I'll fee you contracted before we part ; or you fhall delve and plant cucumbers as long as you live.

Y. Meadows. Have you brought the lady here, Sir ? I am forry for it.

Sir Will. Why forry ? what then you won't marry her ? we'll fee that ! Pray, master Hawthorn, conduct the fair one in.——Ay, Sir, you may fret, and dance about, trot at the rate of fifteen miles an hour, if you pleafe, but marry whip me, I'm refolv'd.

S C E N E VIII,

Sir WILLIAM MEADOWS, HAWTHORN, YOUNG MEADOWS, ROSSETTA.

Hawth. Here is the lady, Sir William.

Sir Will. Come in, madam, but turn your face from him—he would not marry you becaufe he had not feen you : but I'll let him know my choice fhall be his, and he fhall confent to marry you before he fees you, or not an acre of eftate—Pray, Sir, walk this way.

F

Y. Meadows.

Y. Meadows. Sir, I cannot help thinking your conduct a little extraordinary ; but, since you urge me so closely, I must tell you my affections are engaged.

Sir Will. How, Tom, how!

Y. Meadows. I was determined, Sir, to have got the better of my inclination, and never have done a thing which I knew would be disagreeable to you.

Sir Will. And pray, Sir, who are your affections engaged to ? Let me know that.

Y. Meadows. To a person, Sir, whose rank and fortune may be no recommendations to her : but whose charms and accomplishments entitle her to a monarch. I am sorry, Sir, it's impossible for me to comply with your commands, and I hope you will not be offended if I quit your presence.

Sir Will. Not I, not in the least ; go about your business.

Y. Meadows. Sir, I obey.

Hawth. Now, madam, is the time.

[*Rossetta advances, Young Meadows turns round and sees her.*]

A I R XXXVIII.

Ross. ' *When we see a lover languish,*
   ' *And his truth and honour prove,*
  ' *Ah! how sweet to heal his anguish,*
   ' *And repay him love for love.*'

Sir. Will. Well, Tom, will you go away from me now ?

Hawth. Perhaps, Sir William, your son does not like the lady ; and if so, pray don't put a force upon his inclination.

Y. Meadows. You need not have taken this method, Sir, to let me see you are acquainted with my folly, whatever my inclinations are.

Sir Will. Well, but Tom, suppose I give my consent to your marrying this young woman ?

Y. Meadows. Your consent, Sir !

' *Ross.* Come, Sir William, we have carried the jest ' far enough ; I see your son is in a kind of embarrass- ' ment, and I don't wonder at it ; but this letter, which ' I received from him a few days before I left my
father's,

‘ father's houfe, will, I apprehend, expound the riddle.
‘ He cannot be furprifed that I ran away from a gentle-
‘ man who expreffed fo much diflike to me; and what
‘ has happened fince chance has brought us together in
‘ mafquerade, there is no occafion for me to inform him
‘ of.

‘ *Y. Meadows.*’ What is all this? Pray don't make a
jeft of me.

Sir Will. May I never do an ill turn, Tom, if it is no
truth; this is my friend's daughter.

Y. Meadows. Sir!

Roff. Even fo; 'tis very true indeed. In fhort, you
have not been a more whimfical gentleman than I have a
gentlewoman; but you fee we are defigned for one another 'tis plain -

Y. Meadows. I know not, madam, what I either hear
or fee; a thoufand things are crowding on my imagination; while, like one juft awakened from a dream,
I doubt which is reality, which delufion.

Sir Will. Well then, Tom, come into the air a bit,
and recover yourfelf.

Y. Meadows. Nay, dear Sir, have a little patience;
do you give her to me?

Sir Will. Give her to you! ay, that I do, and my
bleffing into the bargain.

Y. Meadows. Then, Sir, I am the happieft man in the
world; I enquire no farther; here I fix the utmoft li-
mits of my hopes and happinefs.

A I R XXXIX.

Y. Mead.	*All I wifh in her obtaining,*
	Fortune can no more impart;
Roff.	*Let my eyes, my thoughts explaining,*
	Speak the feelings of my heart.
Y. Mead.	*Joy and pleafure never ceafing,*
Roff.	*Love with length of years increafing.*
Together.	*Thus my heart and hand furrender,*
	Here my faith and truth I plight;
	Conftant ftill, and kind, and tender,
	May our flames burn ever bright.

Haweth

Hawth. Give you joy, Sir; and you, fair lády——
And, under favour, I'll falute you too, if there's no fear
of jealoufy.

Y. Meadows. And may I believe this?—Pr'ythee tell
me, dear Roffetta.

Roff. Step into the houfe and I'll tell you every thing
—I muft intreat the good offices of Sir William, and Mr.
Hawthorn, immediately; for I am in the utmoft unea-
finefs about my poor friend Lucinda.

Hawth. Why, what's the matter?

Roff. I don't know, but I have reafon to fear I left
her juft now in very difagreeable circumftances; however, I hope, if there's any mifchief fallen out between
her father and her lover——

Hawth. The mufic mafter! I thought fo.

Sir Will. What, is there a lover in the cafe? May I
never do an ill turn, but I am glad, fo I am; for we'll
make a double wedding; and, by way of celebrating it,
take a trip to London, to fhew the brides fome of the
pleafures of the town. And, mafter Hawthorn, you fhall
be of the party—Come, children, go before us.

Hawth. Thank you, Sir William; I'll go into the
houfe with you, and to church to fee the young folks
married; but as to London, I beg to be excufed.

A I R XL.

If ever I'm catch'd in thofe regions of fmoke,
   That feat of confufion and noife,
May I ne'er know the fweets of a flumber unbroke,
   Nor the pleafure the country enjoys,
Nay more, let them take me, to punifh my fin,
   Where, gaping, the Cockneys they fleece,
Clap me up with their monfters, cry, mafters walk in,
   And fhew me for two-pence a piece.

SCENE

SCENE IX.

Justice WOODCOCK'*s Hall.*

Enter Justice WOODCOCK, *Mrs.* DEB. WOODCOCK, LU-
CINDA, EUSTACE, HODGE.

Mrs. Deb. Why, brother, do you think I can hear, or see, or make use of my senses? I tell you, I left that fellow locked up in her closet; and, while I have been with you, they have broke open the door, and got him out again.

J. Woodcock. Well, you hear what they say.

Mrs. Deb. I care not what they say; it's you encourage them in their impudence—Hark'e, huffey, will you face me down that I did not lock the fellow up?

Lucin. Really, aunt, I don't know what you mean; when you talk intelligibly, I'll answer you.

Eust. Seriously, madam, this is carrying the jest a little too far.

Mrs. Deb. What then, I did not catch you together in her chamber, nor over-hear your design of going off to-night, nor find the bundles packed up—

Eust. Ha, ha, ha.

Lucin. Why aunt you rave.

Mrs. Deb. Brother, as I am a Christian woman, she confessed the whole affair to me from first to last; and in this very place was down upon her marrow-bones for half an hour together, to beg I would conceal it from you.

Hodge. Oh Lord! Oh Lord!

Mrs. Deb. What, sirrah, would you brazen me too! Take that (*boxes him.*)

Hodge. I wish you would keep your hands to yourself; you strike me, because you have been telling his worship stories.

J. Woodcock. Why, sister, you are tipsey!

Mrs. Deb. I tipsey, brother!—I—that never touch a drop of any thing strong from year's end to year's end; but now and then a little aniseed water, when I have got the cholic.

Lucin.

Lucin. Well, aunt, you have been complaining of the stomach-ach all day ; and may have taken too powerful a dose of your cordial.

J. Woodcock. Come, come, I see well enough how it is ; this is a lye of her own invention, to make herself appear wise : but, you simpleton, did you not know I must find you out ?

SCENE X.

Enter Sir WILLIAM MEADOWS, HAWTHORN, ROS-SETTA, YOUNG MEADOWS.

Y. Meadows. Bless me, Sir ! look who is yonder.

Sir. Will. Cocksbones, Jack, honest Jack, are you there ?

Eust. Plague on't, this rencounter is unlucky——Sir William, your servant.

Sir Will. Your servant again, and again, heartily your servant ; may I never do an ill turn, but I am glad to meet you.

J. Woodcock. Pray, Sir William, are you acquainted with this person ?

Sir Will. What, with Jack Eustace ! why he's my kinsman : his mother and I was cousin-germans once removed, and Jack's a very worthy young fellow ; may I never do an ill turn if I tell a word of a lye.

J. Woodcock. Well, but Sir William, let me tell you, you know nothing of the matter ; this man is a music-master ; a thrummer of wire, and a scraper of cat-gut, and teaches my daughter to sing.

Sir Will. What Jack Eustace a music-master ! no, no, I know him better.

Eust. 'Sdeath, why should I attempt to carry on this absurd farce any longer ?——What that gentleman tells you is very true, Sir ; I am no music-master indeed.

J. Woodcock. You are not, you own it then ?

Eust. Nay, more, Sir, I am as this lady has represented me *(pointing to Mrs. Deborah)*, your daughter's lover ; whom, with her own consent, I did intend to have carried off this night ; but now that Sir William Meadows is here, to tell you who, and what I am ; I throw my-

self

felf upon your generofity, from which I expect greater advantages than I could reap from any impofition on your unfufpicious nature.

Mrs. Deb. Well, brother, what have you to fay for yourfelf now ? You have made a precious day's work of it ! Had my advice been taken : Oh. I am afhamed of you, but you are a weak man, and it can't be help'd ; however, you fhould let wifer heads direct you.

Lucin. Dear papa, pardon me.

Sir Will. Ay, do, Sir, forgive her; my coufin Jack will make her a good hufband, I'll anfwer for it.

Roff. Stand out of the way, and let me fpeak two or three words to his worfhip.——Come, my dear Sir, though you refufe all the world, I am fure you can deny me nothing : love is a venial fault—You know what I mean.——Be reconciled to your daughter, I conjure you, by the memory of our paft affections——What, not a word !

A'I R XLI.

Go, naughty man, I can't abide you ;
Are then your vows fo foon forgot ?
Ah ! now I fee if I had try'd you,
What would have been my hopeful lot.

But here I charge you—Make them happy ;
Blefs the fond pair, and crown their blifs :
Come be a dear good natur'd pappy,
And I'll reward you with a kifs.

Mrs. Deb. Come, turn out of the houfe, and be thankful my brother does not hang you, for he could do it, he's a juftice of peace ;—turn out of the houfe, I fay :——

J. Woodcock. Who gave you authority to turn him out of the houfe—he fhall flay where he is.

Mrs. Deb. He fhan't marry my neice.

J. Woodcock. Shan't he ? but I'll fhew you the difference now, I fay, he fhall marry her, and what will you do about it ?

Mrs. Deb. And you will give him your eftate too, will you ?

J. Woodcock.

J. Woodcock. Yes, I will.

Mrs. Del. Why I'm sure he's a vagabond.

J. Woodcock. I like him the better, I would have him a vagabond.

Mrs. Del. Brother, brother!

Hawth. Come, come, madam, all's very well, and I see my neighbour is what I always thought him, a man of sense and prudence.

Sir Will. May I never do an ill turn, but I say so too.

J. Woodcock. Here, young fellow, take my daughter, and bless you both together; but hark you, no money till I die; observe that.

Eust. Sir, in giving me your daughter, you bestow upon me more than the whole world would be without her.

Rof. Dear Lucinda, if words could convey the transports of my heart upon this occasion—

Lucin. Words are the tools of hypocrites, the pretenders to friendship; only let us resolve to preserve our esteem for each other.

Y. Meadows. Dear Jack, I little thought we should ever meet in such odd circumstances but here has been the strangest business between this lady and me——

Hodge. What then, Mrs. Rossetta, are you turned false-hearted after all; will you marry Thomas the gardener; and did I forsake Madge for this?

Rof. Oh lord! Hodge, I beg your pardon; I protest I forgot; but I must reconcile you and Madge, I think, and give you a wedding dinner to make you amends.

Hodge. N—ah.

Hawth. Adds me, Sir, here are some of your neighbours come to visit you, and I suppose to make up the company of your statute-ball; yonder's music too I see; shall we enjoy ourselves? If so give me your hand.

J. Woodcock. Why, here's my hand, and we will enjoy ourselves; Heaven bless you both, children, I say— Sister Deborah you are a fool.

Mr. Del. You are a fool, brother; and mark my words——But I'll give myself no more trouble about you.

Hawth. Fiddlers, strike up.

A I R

AIR XLII.

Hence with cares, complaints, and frowning,
  Welcome jollity and joy;
Ev'ry grief in pleasure drowning,
  Mirth this happy night employ:
Let's to friendship do our duty,
  Laugh and sing some good old strain;
Drink a health to love and beauty——
  May they long in triumph reign.

THE END

The Purchasers of BELL's EDITION of
The POETS of GREAT BRITAIN.

ARE respectfully informed by the Publisher, that the SEVENTY-SECOND Volume of that undertaking will be published on the 8th of MAY, 1781, being

HAMMOND's LOVE ELEGIES.

And his POETICAL WORKS compleat, including also several Originals which have not appeared in any other edition, embellished with a graceful PRINT, engraved by BARTALOZZI, from an interesting subject, designed by SIGNORA ANGELICA KAUFFMAN. The Life of the Author is also written by a GENTLEMAN OF EMINENCE, in a manner that will be highly acceptable to the Lovers of English Biography.

The following Poets are already published, in BELL's beautiful Edition.

	l.	s.	d.
Milton's Poetical Works compleat, 4 vols. neatly sewed in marble paper, price	0	6	0
Pope's Poetical Works compleat, 4 vols.	0	6	0
Dryden's Poetical Works compleat, 3 vols.	0	4	6
Butler's Poetical Works compleat, 3 vols.	0	4	6
Prior's Poetical Works, 3 vols.	0	4	6
Thomson's Poetical Works compleat, 2 vols.	0	3	0
Gay's Poetical Works compleat, 3 vols.	0	4	6
Young's Poetical Works compleat, 4 vols.	0	6	0
Waller's Poetical Works compleat, 2 vols.	0	3	0
Cowley's Poetical Works, 4 vols.	0	6	0
Spencer's Poetical Work, 8 vols.	0	12	0
Parnell's Poetical Works, 2 vols.	0	3	0
Congreve's Poetical Works, 1 vol.	0	1	6
Swift's Poetical Works, 4 vols.	0	6	0
Addison's Poetical Work, 1 vol.	0	1	6
Shenstone's Poetical Works, 2 vols.	0	3	0
Churchill's Poetical Works, 3 vols.	0	4	6
Pomfret's Poetical Works, 1 vol.	0	1	6
Donne's Poetical Works, 3 vols.	0	4	6
Hughe's Poetical Works, 2 vols.	0	3	0
Garth's Poetical Works, 1 vol.	0	1	6
Dyer's Poetical Works, 1 vol.	0	1	6
Denham's Poetical Works, 1 vol.	0	1	6
Fenton's Poetical Works, 1 vol.	0	1	6
Lansdown's Poetical Works, 1 vol.	0	1	6
Buckingham's Poetical Works, 1 vol.	0	1	6
Roscommon's Poetical Works, 1 vol.	0	1	6
Sommerville's Works, 2 vols.	0	3	0
Savage's Works, 2 vols.	0	3	0
Mallet's Poetical Works, 1 vol.	0	1	6

MISS CATLEY in the Character of RACHEL.

I mean, stark, errant, downright Beggars.

BELL'S EDITION.

THE
JOVIAL CREW.

A COMIC OPERA.

DISTINGUISHING ALSO THE

VARIATIONS OF THE THEATRE,

AS PERFORMED

IN THREE ACTS,

AT THE

Theatre-Royal in Covent-Garden.

Regulated from the Prompt-Book,

By *PERMISSION of the MANAGERS,*

By Mr. WILD, Prompter.

LONDON:

Printed for JOHN BELL, at the British Library, in the *Strand.*

MDCCLXXXI.

Dramatis Perſonæ.

M E N.

Oldrents,	Mr. *Sparks.*
Hearty,	Mr. *Beard.*
Springlove,	Mr. *Clark.*
Randal,	Mr. *Dunſtal.*
Oliver,	Mr. *Dyer.*
Vincent,	Mr. *Mattocks.*
Hilliard,	Mr. *Baker.*
Juſtice Clack,	Mr. *Shuter.*
Patrico,	Mr. *Marten.*
Martin,	Mr. *R. Smith.*
Sentwell,	Mr. *Gibbs.*
Firſt Beggar-man,	Mr. *Bennet.*
Second Beggar-man,	Mr. *Creſſwick.*
Third Beggar-man,	Mr. *Coſtollo.*
Fourth Beggar-man,	Mr. *Barrington.*
Fifth Beggar-man,	Mr. *Holtom.*
Sixth Beggar-man,	Mr. *Collins.*

W O M E N.

Rachel,	Miſs *Brent.*
Meriel,	Mrs. *Vincent.*
Amie,	Mrs. *Baker.*
Firſt Beggar-woman,	Mrs. *Stevens.*
Second Beggar-woman,	Miſs *Sledge.*
Third Beggar-woman,	Miſs *Mullart.*
Fourth Beggar-woman,	Miſs *Young.*

Dancers, Countrymen, Servants, and Beggars.

S C E N E Oldrents' *and Juſtice* Clack's *Houſe, and the Country adjacent.*

ACT I. SCENE I.

A Room in OLDRENTS’ *Houſe.*

Enter Oldrents *and* Hearty.

Old. IT has indeed, friend, much afflicted me.

Heart. And very juſtly, let me tell you, ſir, to give ear and faith too (by your leave) to fortune-tellers ! wizards, and gipſies.

Old. I have ſince been frighted with it in a thouſand dreams.

Heart. I wou’d go drunk a thouſand times to bed, rather than dream of any of their riddlemy riddleme-ries.

AIR I.

To-day let us never be ſlaves,
* Nor the fate of to-morrow enquire :*
Old wizards, and gipſies, are knaves,
* And the devil, we know, is a liar.*
Then drink off a bumper whilſt you may,
We’ll laugh, and we’ll ſing, tho’ our hairs are grey ;
* He’s a fool, and an aſs,*
* That will baulk a full glaſs,*
For fear of another day.

B   *Old.*

Old. Wou'd I had your merry heart!

Heart. I thank you, fir.

Old. I mean the like.

Heart. I wou'd you had! and I fuch an eftate as your's.——Four thoufand pounds a year, and fuch a heart as mine, would defy fortune, and all her babbling foothfayers.

Old. Come, I will ftrive to think no more on't.

Heart. Will you ride forth for the air then, and be merry?

Old. Your counfel, and example, may inftruct me.

Heart. Sack muft be had in fundry places too. For fongs I am provided.

<h3 style="text-align:center">AIR II.</h3>

In Nottinghamfhire,
 Let 'em boaft of their beer;
With a hay down, down, and a down!
 I'll fing in the praife of good fack:
 Old fack, and old fherry,
 Will make your heart merry,
Without e'er a rag to your back.

 Then caft away care,
 Bid adieu to defpair,
With a down, down, down, and a down!
 Like fools our own forrows we make:
 In fpite of dull thinking,
 While fack we are drinking,
Our hearts are too bufy to ache.

Enter Springlove, *with books and papers, and a bunch of keys. He lays them on the table.*

Old. Yet here comes one brings me a fecond fear, who has my care next unto my children.

Heart. Your fteward, fir, it feems, has bufinefs with you: I wifh you would have none with him.

Old. I'll foon difpatch it, and then be for our journey inftantly.

Heart. I'll wait your coming down, fir. [*Exit.*
              Old.

Old. But why, Springlove, is now this expedition?

Spr. Sir, 'tis duty.

Old. Not common among stewards, I confess, to urge in their accounts before the day their lords have limited.

Spr. Sir, your indulgence, I hope, shall ne'er corrupt me.—Here, sir, is the balance of the several accounts, which shews you what remains in cash; which added to your former bank, makes up in all————

Old. Twelve thousand and odd pounds.

Spr. Here are the keys of all: the chests are safe in your own closet.

Old. Why in my closet? Is not your's as safe?

Spr. Oh, sir, you know my suit.

Old. Your suit! what suit?

Spr. Touching the time of the year.

Old. 'Tis well nigh May. Why what of that Sringlove?   [*Birds sing.*

Spr. Oh, sir, you hear I am call'd!

Old. Are there delights in beggary? or if to take diversity of air be such a solace, travel the kingdom over; and if this yield not variety enough, try farther (provided your deportment be genteel) take horse, and man, and money, you have all, or I'll allow enough.

                    [*Nightingale, Cuckow, &c. sings.*

Spr. Oh, how am I confounded! dear sir, return me naked to the world, rather than lay those burdens on me; which will stifle me; I must abroad, or perish———— Have I your leave, sir?

Old. I leave you to dispute it with yourself: I have no voice to bid you go, or stay.

Spr. I am confounded in my obligations to this good man.

Enter Randal, *and three or four servants with baskets. The servants go off.*

Now, fellows, what news from whence you came?

Rand. The old wonted news, sir, from your guest-house, the old barn: they have all pray'd for you, and our master, as their manner is, from the teeth outward: Marry! from the teeth inward, 'tis enough to swallow

                    your

your alms, from whence, I think, their prayers feldom come.

Spr. Thou art old Randal ftill! ever grumbling! but ftill officious for 'em,

Rand. Yes, hang 'em, they know I love 'em well enough: I have had merry bouts with fome of 'em.

A I R III.

And he that will not merry, merry be,
  With a pretty lafs in a bed;
I wifh he were laid in our church-yard,
  With a tomb-ftone over his head.
He, if he could, to be merry, merry there,
  We to be merry, merry here;
For who does know, where we fhall go,
  To be merry another year,
Brave boys! to be merry another year.

Spr. Well, honeft Randal! thus it is———I am for a journey: I know not how long will be my abfence: but I will prefently take order with the cook and butler for my wonted allowance to the poor. And I will leave money with them to manage the affair till my return.

Rand. Then rife up Randal, bailey of the beggars.
[*Exeunt.*

S C E N E, *a Barn.*

The Beggars are difcovered in their Poftures: then they iffue forth, and at laft the Patrico.

Enter Springlove.

All the Beggars. Our mafter! our mafter! our fweet and comfortable mafter!

Spr. How chear, my hearts?

1 Beg. Moft crowfe! moft caperingly! fhall we dance? fhall we fing to welcome our king?

A I R

AIR IV.

1 *Beg. Wom. Tho' all are difcontented grown,*
    And fain would change condition;
    The courtier envies now the clown,
    The clown turns politician.

2 *Beg. Wom. Ambition ftill is void of wit,*
    And makes a woeful figure:
    For none of 'em all e'er envy'd yet,
    The life of a jovial beggar.

  Cho. Ambition ftill, &c.

3 *Beg. Wom. The man that hourly racks his brain,*
    To encreafe his ufelefs ftore,
    Still dreads a fall, and lives in pain,
    While we can fall no lower.

4 *Beg. Wom. The dame of rich attire that brags,*
    Wou'd willingly unrig her:
    Did fhe but know the joys of rags,
    And the life of a jovial beggar.

Chorus of all. The dame, &c.

Spr. What, is he there? that folemn old fellow?

2 *Beg. Man.* O, fir! the rareft of them all! he is a prophet; fee how he holds up his prognofticating nofe: he is divining now.

Spr. How! a prophet!

2 *Beg. Man.* Yes, fir, a cunning-man, and a fortune-teller; 'tis thought he was a great clerk before his decay; but he is very clofe, will not tell his beginning, nor the fortune he himfelf is fallen from. But he ferves us for a clergyman ftill, and marries us, if need be, after a new way of his own.

Spr. How long have you had his company?

2 *Beg. Man.* But lately come among us, but a very ancient ftroller all the land over; and has travell'd with gipfies, and is a Patrico.————Shall he read your fortune, fir?

Spr. If it pleafe him.

Pat. Lend me your hand, fir.
    By this palm I underftand
    Thou art born to wealth and land:

          And

And after many a bitter guft,
Shall build with thy great grandfire's duft.

Spr. Where fhall I find it ? but come, I'll not trouble my head with the fearch.

2 Beg Man. What fay you, fir, to our crew ? are we not well congregated ?

Spr. You are a jovial crew ! the only people whofe happinefs I admire.

3 Beg. Man. Will you make us happy in ferving you ? have you any enemies ? fhall we fight under ye ? will you be our captain ?

2 Beg. Man. Nay, our king !

3 Beg. Man. Command us fomething, fir !

Spr. Where's the next rendezvous ?

1 Beg. Man. Neither in village, nor in town,
                But three miles off, at Maple-down.

Spr. At evening, there I'll vifit you.

1 Beg. Man. And there you'll find us frolick.

AIR V.

1 Beg. Man. *We'll glad our hearts with the beft of our*
                cheer,
                Our fpirits we'll raife with his honour's
                ftrong beer ;
                All ftrangers to hope, and regardlefs of fear,
                We'll make this the merrieft night of the year.

Cho. *The year, we'll make this the merrieft night of the*
                year.

2 Beg. Man. *Nor forrow, nor pain, amongft us fhall be*
                found,
                To our mafter's good health fhall the cup be
                crown'd,
                That long he may live, and in blifs abound,
                Shall be every man's wifh, while the bowl
                goes round.

Cho. *Goes round, fhall be every man's wifh, &c.*

3 Beg. Man. *Our wants we can't help, nor our poverty*
      cure :
      To-morrow mayn't come, of to-night we'll
      make sure ;
      We'll laugh, and lie down, although we are
      poor,
      And our love shall remain, tho' the wolf's
      at the door.
Cho. *The door, and our love, &c.*

4 Beg. Man. *Then brisk, and smart, shall our mirth go*
      round,
      With antick measures we'll beat the ground,
      To pleasure our master, in duty bound,
      We'll dance till we're lame, and drink till
      we're found.
Cho. *We're found, we'll dance, &c.*

Spr. " So now away.   [*Exeunt beggars.*"
    They dream of happiness that live in state,
    But they enjoy it that obey their fate."   [*Exit.*

S C E N E, Oldrents' *House.*

Enter Vincent, Hilliard, Meriel, *and* Rachel.

Hill. I admire the felicity they take.

Vin. Beggars! they are the only people can boast the benefit of a free state, in the full enjoyment of liberty, mirth, and ease. Who would have lost this sight of their revels? how think you, ladies? Are they not the only happy in a nation?

Mer. Happier than we, I'm sure, that are pent up, and ty'd by the nose to the continual stream of hot hospitality here in our father's house, when they have the air at pleasure in all variety.

AIR

AIR VI.

In the charming month of May,
　When the pretty little birds begin to sing,
What a shame at home to stay,
　Nor enjoy the smiling spring ;
While the beggar that looks forlorn,
Tho' she's not so nobly born,
With her rags all patch'd and torn,
While she dances and sings with the merry men and maids,
　In her smiling eyes you may trace
　And her innocent chearful face,
　　Tho' she's poor, may be
　　More happy than she
That sighs in her rich brocades.

Rach. And tho' I know we have merrier spirits than they, yet to live thus confin'd, stifles me.

AIR VII.

See how the lambs are sporting !
　Hear how the warblers sing !
See how the doves are courting !
　All nature hails the spring.
Let us embrace the blessing,
　Beggars alone are free ;
Free from employment,
　Their life is enjoyment
　　Beyond expression ;
Happy they wander,
And happy sleep under
　The greenwood tree.

Hill. Why, ladies, you have liberty enough, or may take what you please.

Mer. Yes, in our father's rule and government, or by his allowance : what's that to absolute freedom ? Such as the very beggars have ; to feast and revel here to-day, and yonder to-morrow ; next day, where they please ; and so on still, the whole country or kingdom over. There's liberty ! the birds of the air can take no more.

Rach.

Rach. And then, at home here, or wherefoever he
comes, our father is fo penfive (what muddy fpirit fo-
e'er poffeffes him, wou'd I cou'd conjure it out) that he
makes us ever fick of his fadnefs, that were wont to do
any thing before him, and he would laugh at us.

Mer. Now he never looks upon us, but with a figh,
or tears in his eyes, tho' we fimper never fo demurely.
What tales have been told him of us, or what he fuf-
pects, I know not, but I am weary of his houfe.

Rach. Does he think us wanton tro, becaufe fometimes we talk as lightly as great ladies?

A I R   VIII.

How fweet is the evening air,
When the laffes all prepare,
  So trim and fo clean,
  To trip it o'er the green,
And meet with their fweet-hearts there?
  While the pale town lafs
  Difguifes her face,
To fqueak at a mafquerade;
  Where the proudeft prude
  May be fubdu'd,
  And when fhe cries, you're rude,
  You may conclude
She will not die a maid.

Rach. I can fwear fafely for the virginity of one of
us, fo far as word and deed goes ——Marry, thoughts
are free.

Mer. Which is that one of us, I pray? Yourfelf, or
me?

Rach. Good fifter Meriel, charity begins at home:
but I'll fwear, I think as charitable of thee, " and not
" only becaufe thou art a year younger, neither."

Mer. I am beholden to you.—— But dear Rachel, as
the faying is, a demure look is no fecurity for virtue.
But for my father, I would I knew his grief, and how
to cure him, or that we were where we cou'd not fee it.
It fpoils our mirth, and that has been better than his
meat to us.

Vinc.

Vinc. Will you hear our propofal, ladies?

Mer. Pſhah! you would marry us prefently out of his way, becaufe he has given you a foolifh kind of pro-mife: but we will fee him in a better humour firſt, and as apt to laugh, as we to lie down, I warrant him.

Hill. 'Tis like that courfe will cure him, would you embrace it.

Rach. We will have him cur'd firſt, I tell you, and you ſhall wait that feafon, and our leifure.

Mer. I will rather venture my being one of the ape-leaders, than to marry while he is fo melancholy.

Vinc. We are for any adventure with you, ladies.

Rach. And we will put you to't.——— Come afide, Meriel. I remember an old fong of my nurfe's, every word of which ſhe believed as much as her pfalter, that us'd to make me long, when I was a girl, to be abroad in a moon-light night.

AIR IX.

At night, by moon-light on the plain,
  With rapture, how I've feen,
Attended by her harmlefs train,
  The little fairy queen:
Her midnight revels fweetly keep,
While mortals are involv'd in fleep,
  They tript it o'er the green.
And where they danc'd their chearful round,
  The morning would difclofe,
For where their nimble feet do bound,
  Each flow'r unbidden grows:
The daify (fair as maids in May)
The cowflip, in his gold array,
  And blufhing violet 'rofe.

Mer. Come hither, Rachel.

Rach.
Mer. } Ha! ha, ha!

Vinc. What's the conceit, I wonder!

Rach.
Mer. } Ha! ha, ha!

Hill. Some merry one it feems, but I'll never pre-tend to guefs at a woman's mind.

A I R

AIR X.

The mind of a woman can never be known,
  You never can guess it aright :
I'll tell you the reason———she knows not her own,
  It changes so often e'er night.
    'Twou'd puzzle Apollo,
    Her whimfies to follow,
His oracle wou'd be a jeft ;
    She'll frown when she's kind,
    Then quickly you'll find,
    She'll change with the wind,
      And often abufes
      The man that she chufes,
    And what she refufes,
        Likes beft.

Rach. And then, Meriel,———hark again—ha, ha, ha!

Vinc. How they are taken with it?

Mer. Ha, ha, ha!—Hark again, Rachel,———I am of the girl's mind, who wou'd not take the man she lik'd beft, 'till she was fure he lov'd her well enough to live in a cottage with her.

Both. Ha, ha, ha!

Vinc. Now, ladies, is your project ripe? poffefs us with the knowledge of it. You know how, and what we have vow'd; to wait upon you any how, and any where.

Mer. And you will ftand to't?

Vinc. Ay, and go to't with you wherever it be.——— What fay you, are you for a trip to Bath?

Mer. No, no, not 'till the Doctor doesn't know what elfe to do with us.

Vinc. Well, would you be courted to go to London!

Rach. Few country ladies need be afk'd twice: but you're a bold man to propofe it.

AIR

A I R   XI.

How few like you, wou'd dare advise,
  To trust the town's deluding arts;
Where love, in daily ambush lies,
  And triumphs over heedless hearts:
How few, like us, wou'd thus deny
  T'indulge the tempting dear delight,
Where daily pleasures charm the eye,
  And joys superior crown the night.

Hill. In the name of wonder what would you do?

Mer. Pray tell it 'em, sister Rachel.

Rach. Why, gentlemen—ha, ha!—Then thus it is—you seem'd e'en now to admire the felicity of beggars.

Mer. And have engag'd yourselves to join with us in any course.

Rach. Will you now with us, and for our sakes, turn beggars?

Mer. It is our resolution, and our injunction on you.

Rach. But for a time, and a short progress.

Mer. And for a spring-trick of youth, now in the season.

Vinc. Beggars! what rogues, are these!

Hill. A simple trial of our loves and service!

Rach. Are you resolv'd upon't? If not farewel! We are resolv'd to take our course.

Mer. Let yours be to keep counsel.

Vinc. Stay, stay! beggars! Are we not so already?

A I R   XII.

Vinc. *We beg but in a higher strain,*
    Than sordid slaves, who beg for gain.

Hill. *No paltry gold, or gems, we want,*
    We beg what you alone can grant.

Vinc. *No lofty titles, no renown,*
    But something greater than a crown.

Hill. *We beg not wealth, or liberty,*

Both. *We beg your humble slaves to be.*

Vi

Vinc. *We beg your snowy hands to kiss,*
    Or lips, if you'd vouchsafe the bliss.
Hill. *And if our faithful vows can move,*
    (What gods might envy us) your love.
Vinc. *The boon we beg, if you deny,*
    Our fate's decreed, we pine and die.
Hill. *For life we beg, for life implore,*
Both. *The poorest wretch can beg no more.*

Rach. That will not serve—your time's not come for that yet. You shall beg victuals first.

Vinc. O! I conceive your begging progress is, to ramble out this summer among your father's tenants.

Mer. No, no, not so.

Vinc. Why so we may be a kind of civil beggars.

Rach. I mean, stark, errant, downright beggars. Ay, without equivocation, statute beggars.

Mer. Couchant and *passant, guardant,* and *rampant* beggars.

Vinc. Current and *vagrant.*

Hill. Stockant and *whippant* beggars.

Vinc. 'Fore heaven! I think they are in earnest; for they were always mad.

Hill. And we were madder than they, if we should lose 'em.

Vinc. 'Tis but a mad trick of youth, as they say, for the spring, or a short progress; and mirth may be made out of it, if we knew how to carry it.

Rach. Pray, gentlemen, be sudden. [*Cuckow without.*] Hark! you hear the cuckow?

A I R XIII.

Rach. *Abroad we must wander to hear the birds sing,*
    T' enjoy the fresh air, and the charms of the spring.
Mer. *We'll beg for our bread, then if the night's raw,*
    We'll keep ourselves warm on a bed of clean straw.
Rach. *How blest is the beggar, who takes the fresh air?*
Mer. *Tho' hard is his lodging, and coarse is his fare.*
Rach. *Confinement is hateful ————*
Mer. *———————————And pleasure destroys.*
Both. *'Tis freedom alone is the parent of joys.*

C

Enter

Enter Springlove.

Vinc. O! here comes Springlove! His great bene-factorship among the beggars, might prefer us with authority, into a ragged regiment, prefently. Shall I put it to him?

Rach. Take heed what you do! His greatnefs with my father will betray us.

Vinc. I will cut his throat, then————my noble Springlove! the great commander of the maunders, and king of canters: we faw the gratitude of your loyal fubjects, in the large tributary content they gave you in their revels.

Spr. Did you fo, fir?

Hill. We have feen all, with great delight and admiration.

Spr. I have feen you too, kind gentlemen and ladies, and over-heard you in your ftrange defign, to be partakers, and co-actors too, in thofe vile courfes, which you call delights, ta'en by thofe defpicable and abhorred creatures.

Vinc. Thou art a defpifer, nay a blafphemer, againft the maker of thofe happy creatures.

Rach. He grows zealous in the caufe: fure, he'll beg indeed.

Vinc. Art thou an hypocrite, then, all this while? only pretending charity, or ufing it to get a name and praife unto thyfelf; and not to cherifh and increafe thofe creatures in their moft happy way of living.

Mer. They are more zealous in the caufe, than we.

Spr. But are you, ladies, at defiance too with reputation, and the dignity due to your father's houfe, and you?

Rach. Hold thy peace, good Springlove; and tho' you feem to diflike this difcourfe, and reprove us for it, do not betray us in it. Your throat's in queftion; I tell you for good-will, good Springlove.

Spr. I have founded your faith, and am glad to find you all right. And for your father's fadnefs, I'll tell you the caufe on't; I over-heard it but this day, in private difcourfe with his merry mate, Hearty; he has been told by fome wizard, you both were born to be beggars!   *All.*

All. How! how!

Spr. For which he is fo tormented in mind, that he cannot fleep in peace, nor look upon you, but with heart's grief.

Vinc. This is moft ftrange!

Rath. Let him be griev'd then, 'till we are beggars, we have juft reafon to become fo now; and what we thought on but in jeft before, we'll do in earneft now.

Spr. I applaud this refolution in you; wou'd have perfuaded it; will be your fervant in't. For, look ye, ladies; the fentence of your fortune does not fay that you fhall beg for need, hunger, or cold neceffity. If therefore you expofe yourfelves on pleafure into it, you fhall abfolve your deftiny, neverthelefs, and cure your father's grief: I am overjoy'd to think on't;—I am prepar'd already for the adventure, and will with all conveniencies, furnifh, and fet you forth; give you rules, and directions, how I us'd to accoft paffengers, with a————good your good worfhip! the gift of one fmall penny to a poor cripple, and even to blefs, and reftore it to you in heaven.

All. A Springlove, a Springlove!

Spr. Follow me, gallants, then, as chearful as———
[*Birds whiftle without*] we are fummon'd forth.

All. We follow thee.

A I R XIV.

Mer. *To you, dear father and our home,*
    We bid a fhort adieu:
The tempting frolick has o'ercome,
    By force of being new.
But let not that your patience vex,
For, dear papa, you know our fex.
               With a fal, la, &c.

Rach. *Nor hope, good fir, to fpare your coft,*
    Nor think our fortune's paid;
No woman yet was ever loft,
    Tho' fometimes fhe's mif-laid:
For when the pleafure turns to pain,
Be fure we fhall come home again.
               With a fal, la, &c.

The End of the Firft Act.

ACT II.   SCENE I.

SCENE *continues*.

Enter Randal *with a bag of money in his hand.*

Rand. WELL, go thy ways! if ever any juſt and charitable ſteward was commended, ſure-ly thou ſhalt be at the laſt quarter-day. Here's five-and-twenty pounds for this quarter's beggars charge: and (if he return not by the end of this quarter) here's an order to a friend to ſupply for the next——If I now ſhould venture for the commendation of an unjuſt ſtew-ard, and turn this money to my own uſe? Ha! dear devil tempt me not! I'll do thee ſervice in a greater matter; but to rob the poor (a poor trick) every church-warden can do't.——Now ſomething whiſpers me, that my maſter, for his ſteward's love, will ſupply the poor, as I may handle the matter——then I rob the ſteward, if I reſtore him not the money at his return.——Away, temptation: leave me! I'm frail fleſh, yet I will fight with thee.—But ſay the ſteward never return—Oh! but he will return!———Perhaps he may not return. ———Turn from me, ſatan! ſtrive not to clog my conſcience.———I would not have this weight upon me for all thy kingdom.

Enter Hearty *ſinging, and* Oldrents.

AIR XV.

Let pleaſure go round,
Let us laugh and ſing, let us laugh and ſing, boys!
Let humour abound,
And joy fill the day.
If ſorrow intrude,
Drive it out again, drive it out again, boys!
If by griefs we're purſu'd,
Let us drink 'em away :
The pleaſure of wine
Makes a mortal divine.

For

For get but a bottle once into your noddle,
    No power, or art,
    Can such virtue impart,
For raising the spirits, and cheering the heart.

Remember, sir, your covenant to be merry.

Old. I strive, you see, to be so.————But do you see yon fellow?

Heart. I never noted him so sad before; he neither sings, nor whistles.

Old. Why, how now, Randal! where's Springlove?

Rand. Here's his money, sir; I pray that I be charg'd with it no longer. The devil and I have strain'd courtesy these two hours about it.————I would not be corrupted with the trust of more than is my own. Mr. Steward gave it me, sir, to order it for the beggars: he has made me steward of the barn, and them; while he is gone, he says, a journey, to survey and measure lands abroad about the countries; some purchase, I think, for your worship.

Old. I know his measuring of land! he's gone his old way, and let him go——Am not I merry, Hearty?

Heart. Yes, but not hearty merry.

Old. The poor's charge shall be mine: carry you the money to one of my daughters to keep for Springlove.

Rand. I thank your worship.   *[Exit.*

Old. He might have ta'en his leave, tho'.

Heart. I hope he's run away with some large trust: I never lik'd such demure, down-look'd fellows.

Old. You are deceiv'd in him.

Heart. If you be not, 'tis well.————But this is from the covenant.

Old. Well, sir, I will be merry: I'm resolv'd to force my spirit only unto mirth.————Should I hear now my daughters were misled, or run away, I would not send a sigh to fetch 'em back.

Heart. T'other old song for that.

There was an old fellow at Waltham-Cross
Who merrily sung when he liv'd by the loss.
He chear'd up his heart when his goods went to rack,
With a hem! boys, hem! and a cup of old sack.

Old. Is that the way on't? well, it shall be mine then.

Enter Randal.

Rand. My mistresses are both abroad, sir.

Old. How! since when?

Rand. On foot, sir, two hours since, with the two gentlemen their lovers. Here's a letter they left with the butler, and there's a muttering in the house.

Old. I will not read, nor open it, but conceive within myself the worst that can befall them; that they are lost, and no more mine. 'Grief shall lose her name, where I have being, and sadness from my farthest foot of land, while I have life, be banish'd.

Heart. What's the whim now!

Old. My tenants shall sit rent-free for this twelve-month, and all my servants have their wages doubled; and so shall be my charge in housekeeping: I hope my friends will find and put me to't.

Heart. For them I'll be your undertaker, sir. But this is over-done! I don't like it.

Old. And for thy news, the money that thou hast is now thy own: I'll make it good to Springlove. Be sad with it, and leave me; for I tell thee I'll purge my house of stupid melancholy.

Rand. I'll be as merry as the charge that's under me.

[*A confused noise of singing and laughing without.*]

The beggars, sir, d'ye hear them in the barn?

Old. I'll double their allowance too, that they may double their numbers, and increase their noise.

Rand.

Rand. Now you are fo nigh, fir, if you'll look in, I doubt not but you will find 'em at their high feaft already.

Heart. Pray let's fee 'em, fir.

Old. With all my heart.   [*Exeunt.*

SCENE *draws, and difcovers the Beggars.*

Re-enter Oldrents, Hearty, *and* Randal.

All Beg. Blefs his worfhip! his good worfhip! blefs his worfhip!

1 *Beg. Man.* Come, friends, let us give his worfhip a tafte of our mirth!———Hem! let us fing the part-fong that I made for you, that which contains all our characters, I mean thofe we had in better times : there is not fuch a collection of oddities, perhaps, in all Europe.———Hem! be filent there!

A I R XVII.

1 Beg. Man. *I once was a poet at London,*
   I keep my heart ftill full of glee ;
   There's no man can fay that I'm undone,
   For begging's no new trade to me.

      Tol derol, &c.

2 Beg. Man. *I was once an attorney at law,*
   And after a knight of the poft :
   Give me a brifk wench in clean ftraw,
   And I value not who rules the roaft,

      Tol derol, &c.

3 Beg. Man. *Make room for a foldier in buff,*
   Who valiantly ftrutted about ;
   'Till he fancy'd the peace breaking off,
   And then he moft wifely ——fold out.

      Tol derol, &c.

4 Beg.

4 *Beg. Man. Here comes a courtier polite, fir,*
Who flatter'd my lord to his face;
Now railing is all his delight, fir,
Because he mifs'd getting a place.

Tol derol, *&c.*

5 *Beg. Man. I ftill am a merry gut-fcraper,*
My heart never yet felt a qualm:
Tho' poor, I can frolick and vapour,
And fing any tune but a pfalm.

Tol derol, *&c.*

6 *Beg. Man. I was a fanatical preacher,*
I turn'd up my eyes when I pray'd;
But my hearers had half-ftarv'd their teacher,
For they believ'd not one word that I faid.

Tol derol, *&c.*

1 *Beg. Man. Whoe'er wou'd be merry and free,*
Let him lift, and from us he may learn;
In palaces who fhall you fee,
Half fo happy as we in a barn?

Tol derol, *&c.*

Crutch dance of Beggars.

Old. Good Heaven! how merry they are!

Heart. Be not you fad at that;

Old. Sad, Hearty! no; unlefs it be with envy at their full happinefs—What is an eftate of wealth and power, balanced with their freedom?

Heart. I have not fo much wealth to weigh me down, nor fo little, I thank chance, as to dance naked.

All Beg. Blefs his worfhip! his good worfhip, blefs his worfhip.　　　　　　　　　　　　*[Exeunt Beggars.*

Heart. How think you, fir? or what? or why d'ye think at all, unlefs on fack, or fupper-time! d'ye fall back? d'ye not know the danger of relapfes?

Old. Good Hearty! thou miftak'ft me; I was think-ing upon this Patrico, and that he has more foul than a born beggar in him.

Heart.

Heart. Rogue enough though, I warrant him.

Old. Pray forbear that language.

Heart. Will you then talk of fack that can drown fighing? Will you in to fupper, and take me there your gueft? or muft I creep into the barn among your welcome ones?

Old. You have rebuk'd me timely, and moft friendly. [*Exit.*

Heart. Would all were well with him!
[*Exit.* Patrico *fellows.*

Rand. It is with me.

A I R XVIII.

What, tho' thefe guineas bright, fir,
  Be heavy in my bag;
My heart is ftill the lighter,
  The more my pockets fwag:
    Let mufty fools
    Find out by rules
  That money forrow brings;
    Yet none can think
    How I love their chink;
Alas, poor things.

S C E N E, *the Fields.*

Enter Vincent *and* Hilliard *in their Rags.*

Hill. Is this the life we admired in others, with envy of their happinefs?

Vinc. Pray let us make a virtuous ufe of it, by fteering our courfe homewards ————Before I'll endure fuch another night!

Hill. What wou'dft thou do! I wifh thy miftrefs heard thee!

Vin. I hope fhe does not; for I know there's no altering our courfe before they make the firft motion; but 'tis ftrange we fhou'd be weary already, and before their fofter conftitution of flefh and blood.

Hill. They are the ftronger in will, it feems.

A I R

" A I R XIX.

" *Tho' women, 'tis true, are but tender,*
  " *Yet nature does strength supply:*
" *Their will is too strong to surrender,*
  " *They're obstinate still 'till they die.*
" *In vain you attack 'em with reason,*
  " *Your sorrows you only prolong;*
" *Disputing is always high-treason,*
  " *No woman was e'er in the wrong.*
" *Your only relief is to bear;*
  " *And when you appear content,*
" *Perhaps, in compassion, the fair*
  " *May persuade herself into consent.*"

Enter Springlove.

Spr. How now, comrades! repining already at your fulness of liberty! do you complain of ease?

Vin. Ease call'st thou it! didst thou sleep to-night?

Spr. Not so well this eighteen months, I swear, since my last walks.

Hill. Lightning and tempest is out of thy litany. Cou'd not the thunder wake thee?

Spr. Ha, ha, ha.

Vinc. Nor the noise of the crew in the quarter by us? Well! never did knights-errant in all adventures, merit more of their ladies, than we beggars-errant, or errant-beggars, do of ours.

Spr. The greater will be your reward, think upon that, and shew no manner of distaste to turn their hearts from you: you are undone then.

Vinc. Are they ready to appear out of their privy lodgings in the pig's palace of pleasure? Are they coming forth?

Spr. I left 'em almost ready, sitting on their pads of straw, helping to dress each other's head; the one's eye is t'other's looking-glass; with the prettiest coyle they keep to fit their fancies in the most graceful way of wearing their new dressing, that you wou'd admire.

Vin. I hope we are as gracefully set out, are we not?

Spr.

Spr. Indifferent well. But will you fall to practice.? let me hear how you can maund when you meet with paffengers.

Hill. We do not look like men, I hope, too good to learn.

Spr. Let me inftruct you, tho' [*Spring. inftructs them.*

Enter Rachel *and* Meriel *in Rags.*

Rach. Have a care, good Meriel; what hearts or· limbs foever we have, and tho' never fo feeble, let us fet our beft faces on't, and laugh our laft gafp out, before we difcover any diflike, or wearinefs to them. Let us bear it out till they complain firft, and beg to carry us home a-pick-a-pack.

Mer. I am forely tir'd with hoofing it already, and fo crampt with our hard lodging in the ftraw, " that——"

Rach. Think not on't. I am numb'd i'th' fhoulders too, a little; and have found the difference between a hard floor with a little ftraw, and a down bed with a quilt upon't. But no words, nor a four look, I pry'thee.

Hill. O! here they are! madam Few-cloaths, and my lady Bonny-rag.

Vin. Peace! they fee us.

Rach.
Mer. } Ha, ha, ha!

Vinc. We are glad the object pleafes you.

Rach. So does the fubject: now you appear the glories of the fpring, darling of Phœbus, and the fummer's heirs.

A I R XX.

Woe betide each tender fair,
  Who now beholds you, muft adore ye.
Such a fhape, and fuch an air,
  Muft make each beauty fall before ye.
Narciffus' fate and your s were one,
  Cou'd you but your own charms difcover,
You'd die, as many a fop has done,
  Only of himfelf a lover.

Hill.

Hill } Ha, ha, ha!
Vin. }

Rach. } Ha, ha, ha! we are glad you are so merry!
Mer. }

Vinc. Merry, and lusty too: This night will we lie together, as well as the proudest couple in the barn.

Spr. What! do we come for this? laugh and lie down when your bellies are full! Remember, ladies, you have not begg'd yet to quit your destiny, but have lived hitherto on my endeavours.——Who got your supper, pray, last night, but I? of dainty trencher-fees from a gentleman's house, such as the serving-men themselves sometimes would have been glad of: and this morning now, what comfortable chippings, and sweet butter-milk, had you to breakfast!

Rach. O! 'twas excellent! I feel it good still, here.

Mer. There was a brown crust amongst it that has made my neck so white, methinks! Is it not, Rachel?

Rach. Yes, yes, you gave me none on't; you ever covet to have all the beauty.

A I R XXI.

No woman her envy can smother,
Tho' never so vain of her charms;
If a beauty she spies in another,
The pride of her heart it alarms.
New conquests she still must be making,
Or fancies her power grown less:
Her poor little heart is still aching,
At sight of another's success.
But nature design'd,
In love to mankind,
That different beauties should move;
Still pleas'd to ordain,
None ever should reign,
Sole monarch in empire or love.
Then learn to be wise,
New triumphs despise,
And leave to your neighbours their due;
If one can't please,
You'll find by degrees,
You'll not be contented with two.

Vinc. They are pleas'd, and never like to be weary.

Hill. No more muft we, if we'll be theirs.

Spr. Peace! here comes paffengers; forget not your rules, quickly difperfe yourfelves, and fall to your calling. [*Exeunt.*

Enter Oliver.

Ol. Let me fee! here I am fent by my father, the worfhipful Juftice Clack, in great hafte to Mr. Oldrents', in fearch of my coufin Amie, who is run away with Martin, my father's clerk, and Hearty's nephew, juft when fhe fhould have been coupled to another: my bufinefs requires hafte; but my pleafure, and all the fearch I intend is, by hovering here, to take a 'review of a brace of the handfomeft beggar-wenches that ever grac'd ditch or hedge-fide: I paft by 'em in hafte, but fomething fo poffeffes me, that I muft—what the devil muft I?——— A beggar! why, beggars are flefh and blood, and rags are no difeafes; and there is wholfomer flefh under country dirt, than city painting.

Enter Rachel *and* Meriel.

'Oh! here they come! they are delicately fkinn'd and limb'd! now they fpy me.

Rach. Sir, I befeech you to look upon us with the favour of a gentleman. We are in a prefent diftrefs, and utterly unacquainted in thefe parts, and therefore forc'd by the calamity of our misfortunes, to implore the courtefy, or rather charity, of thofe to whom we are ftrangers.

Ol. Very fine, this!

Mer. Be therefore pleas'd, right noble fir, not only valuing us by our outward habits, " which cannot but appear loathfome or defpicable unto you," but as we are forlorn Chriftians, and in that eftimation, be compaffionately mov'd to caft a handful or two of your filver, or a few of your golden pieces unto us, to furnifh us with linen, and fome decent habiliments.

D *Ol.*

Ol. They beg in a high ſtrain ! ſure they are mad, or bewitch'd in a language they underſtand not.——The ſpirits of ſome decay'd gentry talk in them, ſure.

Rach. May we expect a gracious anſwer from you, ſir ?

Mer. And that as you can wiſh our virgin prayers to be propitious for you.

Rach.	*O ! may your miſtreſs ne'er deny,*
	The ſuit, which you ſhall humbly move !
Mer.	*And may the faireſt virgins vie,*
	And be ambitious of your love !
Rach.	*If honour lead,*
Mer.	*May you ſucceed,*
Rach.	*By love inſpir'd, with conqueſt crown'd.*
Mer.	*And when you wed,*
Rach.	*Your bridal bed*
Both.	*With wealth, and endleſs joys abound.*

Ol. This exceeds all that ever I heard, and ſtrikes me into wonder. Pray tell me how long you have been beggars ? or how chanced you to be ſo ?

Rach. By influence of our ſtars, ſir.

Mer. We are born to no better fortune.

Ol. How came you to talk, and ſing thus ? and ſo much above the beggars dialect ?

Rach. Our ſpeech came naturally to us ; and we ever lov'd to learn by rote as well as we cou'd.

Mer. And to be ambitious above the vulgar, to aſk more than common alms, whate'er men pleaſe to give us.

" *Ol.* Sure ſome well-diſpos'd gentleman, as myſelf,
" got theſe wenches. They are too well grown to be
" my own, and I cannot be inceſtuous with 'em.
" *Rach.* Pray, ſir, your noble bounty."

Ol. What a tempting lip that little rogue moves there ! and what an enticing eye the other !

A I R

AIR XXIII.

To Rach.   *Come hither pretty maid, with a black roll-*
            ing eye :
Aside.   *What a look was there ! does all my senses*
            charm.
To Mer.   *Come hither, pretty dear, for I swear, I*
            long to try
            A little, little love, which will do thee
            child no harm.
To Rach.   *That air, that grace,*
To Mer.   *That lovely milk-white skin.*
To both.   { *Oh ! which shall I embrace ?*
            {   *Oh ! where shall I begin !*
            { *For if I stay*
            {   *I both of them must wooe ;*
Aside.   { *I had better run away,*
            {   *Than deal at once with two.*

What's this ? a flea upon thy bosom ?
  Mer. Is it not a straw-coloured one, sir ?
  Ol. O what a provoking skin there ! that very touch
inflames me.

AIR XXIV.

Rach.   *Can nothing, sir, move you, our sorrows to mend ?*
         Have you nothing to give ! Have you nothing to
         lend ?
Mer.   *You see the sad fate we poor damsels endure ;*
         Can't charity move you to grant us a cure ?
Rach.   *My heart does so heave, I'm afraid it will break !*
         Of victuals we've scarce had a morsel this week.
Mer.   *How hard is your heart ! how unkind is your eye !*
         If nothing can move you, good sir, to comply.
Both.   *How hard is your heart, &c.*

  Rach. Are you mov'd in charity towards us yet ?
  Ol. Mov'd ! I am mov'd ; no flesh and blood more
mov'd.
  Mer. Then pray, sir, your benevolence.
              D 2   *Ol.*

Ol. Benevolence ! which shall I be benevolent to ? or which first ? I am puzzled in the choice. Wou'd some sworn brother of mine were here to draw a cut with me.

Rach. Sir, noble sir.

Ol. First let me tell you, damsels, I am bound by a strong vow to kifs all of your sex I meet this morning.

Mer. Beggars and all, sir !

Ol. All, all ; let not your coyness crofs a gentleman's vow, I befeech you.   [*Kiffes them both.*

Mer. You'll tell now.

Ol. Tell, quotha ! I could tell a thoufand on thofe lips, and as many upon thofe.————What life-restoring breaths they have ! milk from the cow fteems not fo fweetly.————" I must lay one of them aboard ; both, if my tackling hold."

   " *Rach.* } Sir ! fir !"
   " *Mer.* }

Ol. But how to bargain, now, will be the doubt : they that beg fo high, as by the handfuls, may expect for price above the rate of good men's wives.

Rach. Now, will you, fir, be pleas'd ?

Ol. With all my heart, fweet ! and I am glad thou know'ft my mind————Here's twelve-pence for you.

Rach. } We thank you, fir.
Mer. }

Ol. That's but an earneft ; I'll jeft away the reft with you.—Look here ! all this—Come, you know my meaning.

A I R XXV.

Rach.	*Wou'd you hurt a tender creature,*
	Whom your charity should fave ?
Mer.	*Is it in your gentle nature*
	Thus to triumph o'er a flave ?
Rach.	*Fye, for shame, fir !*
Mer.	*You're to blame, fir ;*
	Can your worship ftoop fo low ?
Rach.	*Tho' you're above me,*
Mer.	*'Twill behove me,*
	Still to anfwer, no, no, no.
Both.	*Still to anfwer, no, no, no.*

Ol.

Ol. Muſt you be drawn to't ? then I'll pull. Come away.

Rach.
Mer. } Ah ! ah !

Enter Springlove, Vincent, *and* Hilliard.

Vinc. Let's beat his brains out.

Ol. Come, leave your ſqueaking.

Spr. O ! do not hurt 'em, maſter.

Ol. Hurt 'em ! I mean 'em but too well ———— Shall I be ſo prevented ?

Spr. They be but young, and ſimple ; and if they have offended, let not your worſhip's own hands drag 'em to the law, or carry 'em to puniſhment : correct 'em not yourſelf, it is the beadle's office.

Ol. D'ye talk, ſhag-rag ?

Vinc.
Hill. } Shag-rag !

[*Offer to beat him with their crutches ; he runs off.*
Rach. Look you here, gentlemen, ſix-pence a piece !

Mer. Beſides fair offers, and large promiſes. What have you got to-day, gentlemen !

Vinc. More than (as we are gentlemen) we wou'd have taken.

Hill. Yet we put it up in your ſervice.

Rach.
Mer. } Ha, ha, ha ! ſwitches and kicks ! Ha, ha, ha !

Spr. Talk not here of your gettings, we muſt quit this quarter : the eager gentleman's repulſe may arm, and return him with revenge upon us ; we muſt therefore leap hedge and ditch, 'till we eſcape out of this liberty to our next rendezvous, where we ſhall meet the crew, and then, hey-tofs ! and laugh all night.

Mer. As we did laſt night.

Rach. Hold out, Meriel.

Mer. Lead on, brave general.

Vinc. What ſhall we do ? they are in heart ſtill : ſhall we go on !

Hill. There's no flinching back, you ſee.

Enter

Enter Martin *and* Amie, *in poor habits.*

Spr. Stay, here comes more paffengers ; fingle your-felves again, and fall to your calling difcreetly.

Hill. I'll fingle no more ; if you'll beg in full cry, I am for you.

Mer. Ay, that will be fine ! let's charm all together.

Spr. Stay firft, and liften a little.

Ma. Be of good cheer, fweetheart, we have efcaped hitherto, and I believe that all the fearch is now retired, and we may fafely pafs forward.

Am. I fhould be fafe with thee. But that's a moft lying proverb that fays, " where love is, there is no lack." I am faint, and cannot travel further without meat ; and if you lov'd me, you would get me fome.

Ma. We'll venture at the next village to call for fome ; the beft is, we want no money.

Am. We fhall be taken then, I fear ; I'll rather pine to death.

AIR XXVI.

The tuneful lark, who, from her neft,
  Ere yet well fledg'd, is ftol'n away,
With care attended, and carefs'd,
  She fometimes fings the live-long day.
Yet ftill her native fields fhe mourns,
Her goaler hates, his kindnefs fcorns ;
For freedom pants, for freedom burns.
That darling freedom once obtain'd,
  Unfkill'd, untaught to fearch for prey,
She mourns the liberty fhe gain'd,
  And hungry, pines her hours away.
Helplefs, the little wand'rer flies,
Then homeward turns her longing eyes,
And warbling out her grief, fhe dies.

Ma. I'm not fo fearful ; who can know us in thefe clownifh habits ?

Am. Our cloaths, indeed, are poor enough to beg with ; wou'd I cou'd beg, fo it were of ftrangers that

cou'd

cou'd not know me, rather than buy of thofe that wou'd betray us.

Ma. And yonder are fome that can teach us.

Spr. Thefe are the young couple of run-away lovers difguifed, that the country is fo laid for ; obferve, and follow now. Good loving meafter and meeftrefs, your bleffed charity to the poor, who have no houfe nor home, no health, no help, but your fweet charity.

Mer. No bands, or fhirts, to keep us from the cold.

Hill. No fmocks, or petticoats, " to hide our " fcratches."

Vinc. No fkin to our flefh, nor flefh to our bones, fhortly.

Rach. No fhoes to our legs, or hofe to our feet.

A I R XXVII.

Mer.　*Oh ! turn your eyes on me, and view my diftrefs !*
　　　Did you know my hard fate, you would pity my
　　　　cafe.
　　　Such a kind-hearted gentleman furely wou'd grant
　　　To a tender young virgin what'ere fhe did want.

A I R XXVIII.

Hill.　*Tho' old, my ftory, gentle lady, hear ;*
　　　　I am a wealthy farmer's fon,
　　　Who once cou'd gay and rich appear,
　　　　But now by fate I am undone.
　　　Reduc'd to want and wretchednefs,
　　　　And ftarv'd, alas ! I foon muft be,
　　　Unlefs you grant to my diftrefs
　　　　Some kind relief in charity.

A I R XXIX.

Vinc.　*I like a gentleman did live,*
　　　　I ne'er did beg before ;
　　　Some fmall relief you fure might give,
　　　　That wou'd not make you poor.

A I R

A I R　XXX.

Rach.　　*My daddy is gone to his grave ;*
　　　　　My mother lies under a ſtone ;
　　　　And never a penny I have,
　　　　　Alas ! I am quite undone :
　　　　My lodging is in the cold air,
　　　　　And hunger is ſharp, and bites :
　　　　A little ſir, good ſir, ſpare,
　　　　　To keep me warm o' nights.

Spr. Good worſhipful meaſter and meeſtreſs——

Ma. Good friend, forbear, here's no meaſter nor meeſtreſs, we are poor folks ; thou feeſt no worſhip upon our backs, I'm ſure ; and for within, we want as much as you, and would as willingly beg, if we knew how as well

Spr. Alack for pity ! you may have enough ; and what I have is your's, if you'll accept it. 'Tis wholeſome food from a good gentleman's gate———Alas ! good meeſtreſs——much good 'do' your heart ! how favourly ſhe feeds.

Ma. What, do you mean to poiſon yourſelf ?

Am. Do you ſhew love, in grudging me ?

Ma. Nay, if you think it hurts you not, fall to, I'll not beguile you. And here, mine hoſt, ſomething towards your reckoning.

" *Am.* This beggar is an angel, ſure !"

Spr. Nothing by way of bargain, gentle maſter ; 'tis againſt order, and will never thrive ; but pray, ſir, your reward in charity.

Ma. Here then, in charity.——This fellow would never make a good clerk.

Spr. What ! all this, maſter !

Am. What is it ? let me ſee it.

Spr. 'Tis a whole ſilver three-pence, miſtreſs.

Am. For ſhame ! ungrateful miſer.——Here, friend, a golden crown for thee.

Spr. Bountiful goodneſs ! gold ?

Am. I have robb'd thy partners of their ſhares too ; there's a crown more for them.

All.

All. Duly and truly pray for you.

Ma. What have you done ? lefs would have ferv'd ; and your bounty will betray us.

Am. Fy on your wretched policy !

Spr. No, no, good mafter; I knew you all this while, and my fweet miftrefs too. And now I'll tell you ; the fearch is every way, the country all laid for you, it's well you ftaid here. Your habits, were they but a little nearer our fashion, wou'd fecure you with us. But are you married, mafter and miftrefs ? are you joined in matrimony ? In heart, I know you are. And I will (if it pleafe you) for your great bounty, bring you to a curate that lacks no licence, nor has any living to lofe, that fhall put you together.

Ma. Thou art a heavenly beggar !

Spr. But he is fo fcrupulous, and feverely precife, that unlefs you, miftrefs, will affirm that you are with child by the gentleman, that you have at leaft flept together, he will not marry you. But if you have lain together, then 'tis a cafe of neceffity, and he holds himfelf bound to do it.

Ma. You may fay you have.

Am. I would not have it fo, nor make that lye againft myfelf, for all the world.

AIR XXXI.

Is there on earth a pleafure,
  Dearer than virtue's fame ?
In vain's the real treafure,
  When we have loft the name.
Then let each maid maintain it,
  'Twill afk the niceft care ;
Once loft fhe'll ne'er regain it,
  All, all is then defpair.

Spr. That I like well, and her exceedingly.

Ma. I'll do that for thee——thou fhalt never beg more.

Spr. That cannot be purchas'd fcarce, for the price of your miftrefs. Will you walk, mafter?——We ufe no compliments.

All. Duly and truly pray for you.   [*Exeunt.*

SCENE

SCENE, Oldrents' *House*.

Heart. Come, come, fir, this houfe is too melancholy for you, we muft e'en vary the fcene, and pay a
vifit to your merry neighbour Juftice *Clack*; his good
humour will ftrengthen mine, and help me to drive to
old care away.

Old. Good *Hearty*, you have kindly undertaken my
cure, and fhall find me a tractable patient.

Heart. T'other old fong for that, and then for the
Juftice.

AIR XXXII.

I made love to Kate, *long I figh'd for fhe,*
'Till I heard of late fhe'd a mind to me,
I met her on the green in her beft array,
So pretty fhe did feem, fhe ftole my heart away;
O then we kifs'd and prefs'd, were we much to blame,
Had you been in my place, you'd have done the fame.

As I fonder grew fhe began to prate,
Quoth fhe, I'll marry you, if you will marry Kate;
But then I laugh'd and fwore, I lov'd her more than fo,
For tied each to a rope's end 'tis tugging to and fro:
Again we kifs'd and preft, were we much to blame,
Had you been in my place, you'd have done the fame.

Then fhe figh'd and faid, fhe was wondrous fick,
Dicky Katy *led,* Katy *fhe led* Dick.
Long we toy'd and play'd under yonder oak,
Katy *loft the game, though fhe play'd in joke;*
For there we did alas ? what I dare not name,
Had you been in my place, you'd have done the fame.
Fal, lal, &c.

The End of the Second Act.

ACT III. SCENE I.

SCENE *a Wood.*

Enter Amie, Rachel, *and* Meriel.

Am. WELL, ladies, my confidence in you, that you are the same that you have protested yourselves to be, hath so far won upon me, that I confess myself well affected both to the mind and person of that Springlove; and if he be (as fairly as you pretend) a Gentleman, I shall easily dispense with Fortune.

Rach.
Mer. } He is a gentleman, upon my honour?

Am. How well that high engagement suits your habits!

Rach. Our minds and blood are still the same..

Am. I have past no affiance to the other, that stole me from my guardian, and the match he would have forced me to; from which I would have fled with any, or without a guide. Besides, to offer to marry me under a hedge, without a book or ring, by the Chaplain of the Beggars Regiment, your Patrico, only to save charges, was a piece of gallantry I shall not easily excuse.

Rach. I have not seen the wretch these three hours; whither is he gone?

Am. He told me to fetch horse and fit raiment for us, so to post me hence; but I think it was to leave me on your hands.

Mer. He has taken some great distaste sure, for he is very jealous.

Rach. Ay! didst thou mark what a wild look he cast, when Springlove tumbled her, and kiss'd her on the straw this morning?

A I R

AIR XXXIII.

" *Jealousy like a canker-worm.*
 " *Nips the tender flow'rs of love;*
" *Jealousy, raging like a storm,*
 " *Pray'rs can't molify, tears can't move.*
" *Love is the root of pleasures and joys;*
" *Jealousy all its fruit destroys:*
" *'Tis love, love, Jealousy, love,*
" *Our heav'n or hell still prove.*"

Enter Springlove, Vincent, *and* Hilliard.

But who comes here?

Spr. O ladies! you have left as much mirth as would
have filled up a week of holidays.

 [Springlove *takes* Amie *aside, and courts her in a
        genteel way.*

Vinc. I am come about again for the beggar's life,
now.

Rach. You are! I'm glad on't.

Hill. There is no life, but it.

Rach. I am glad you are so taken with your calling.

Mer. We are no less, I assure you; we find the sweetness of it now.

Rach. The mirth! the pleasure! the delights! No
ladies live such lives.

AIR XXXIV.

Tho' ladies look gay, when of beauty they boast,
 And misers are envy'd when wealth is increased;
The vapours oft kill all the joys of a toast;
 And the miser's a wretch, when he pays for the feast.
The pride of the great, of the rich, of the fair,
 May pity bespeak, but envy can't move;
 My thoughts are no farther aspiring,
 No more my fond heart is desiring,
 Than freedom, content, and the man that I love.

Vinc.

Vinc. They will never be weary.

Hill. Whether we feem to like, or to diflike, all's one to them.

Vinc. We muft do fomething to be taken by, and difcover'd, we fhall never be ourfelves, and get home again elfe. [Springlove *and* Amie *come to the reft.*

Spr. I am your's for ever. Well, ladies, you have mifs'd rare fport; thefe beggars lead fuch merry lives, as all the world might envy. But here they come; their mirth few partake of, tho' their vocation is in fome meafure practifed by all mankind.

Enter all the Beggars.

AIR XXXV.

Hill.   *That all men are beggars, you plainly may fee,*
For beggars there are of every degree,
Tho' none are fo bleft, or fo happy as we.
      Which nobody can deny.

Vinc.   *The tradefman, he begs that his wares you wou'd*
     buy;
Then begs you'd believe the price is not high;
And fwears 'tis his trade, when he tells you a lye.
      Which nobody can deny.

Hill.   *The lawyer he begs you would give him a fee,*
Tho' he reads not your brief, and regards not your
     plea;
Then advifes your foe how to get a decree.
      Which nobody can deny.

Mer.   *The courtier, he begs for a penfion, a place,*
A ribbon, a title, a fmile from his Grace,
'Tis due to his merit, is writ in his face.
      Which nobody fhou'd deny.

Rach.   *But if by mifhap he fhould chance to get none,*
He begs you'd believe that the nation's undone;
There's but one honeft man — and himfelf is that one.
      Which nobody dares deny.

E   Am,

Am.   *The fair one who labours whole mornings at home,*
         New charms to create, and much pains to consume,
         Yet begs you'd believe 'tis her natural bloom.
                   Which nobody thou'd deny.

Hill. *The lover he begs the dear nymph to comply,*
         She begs he'd be gone; but her languishing eye,
         Still begs he would stay——for a maid she can't die.
                   Which none but a fool wou'd deny.

Enter Patrico.

Pat. Alack and a welladay ! this is no time to sing, our quarter is beset, we are all in the net; leave off your merry glee.

Spr. Why, what's the matter ?

Within. Bing awaft, bing awaft; the quear cove, and the harman-beck.

Spr. We are beset indeed ! what shall we do ?

Vinc. I hope we shall be taken.

Hill. If the good hour be come, welcome be the grace of good fortune.

Enter Sentwell; Constable, Watch.   *The Crew slip away.*

Sent. Beset the quarter round ; be sure that none escape.

Spr. Blessed master, to a many distressed.—

Sent. A many counterfeit rogues ! so frolick and so lamentable all in a breath ? you were dancing and singing but now, incorrigible vagabonds ! If you expect any mercy, own the truth ; we are come to search for a young lady, an heirefs, among you ; where is she ? what have you done with her ?

Am. Who do you want, Mr. Sentwell ?

Sent. Precious ! how did my haste overfee her ! O, mistress Amie ! cou'd I, or your uncle justice Clack, a wifer man than I, ever ha' thought to have found you in such company ?

Am.

Am. Of me, fir, and my company, I have a ftory to delight you, which, on our march towards your houfe, I will relate to you.

Sent. And thither will I lead you as my gueft,
　　　But to the law furrender all the reft.
I'll make your peace.

Am. We muft fare all alike. [*Exeunt* Sent. *and* Amic.
Hill. Pray how are we to fare?
Rach. That's as you behave.　　　　　　[*Smiling.*

A I R   XXXVI.

Hill. 　*Sure, by that fmile, my pains are over!*
Rach. 　　　　*Don't be too fure.*
Hill. 　*Wou'd you then kill a faithful lover?*
Rach. 　　　　*Wait for your cure.*
Hill. 　*Women, regardlefs of our fate,*
　　　　Often prove kind, but kind too late.
Rach. *Women, alas! too foon furrender!*
Hill. 　　　　*That I deny*
Rach. *Men oft betray a heart too tender.*
Hill. 　　　　*Take me and try.*
Rach. *Love is a tyrant, under whofe fway,*
　　　　They fuffer leaft who beft obey.
Both. *Love is,* &c.　　　　　　　　　[*Exeunt.*

S C E N E, Juftice Clack's Houfe.

Enter Juftice Clack *and* Martin.

Cla. I have forgiven you, provided that my niece be fafely taken, and fo to be brought home fafely, I fay; that is to fay, unftain'd, unblemifh'd, undifhonour'd; that is to fay, with no more faults, criminal or accufitive, than thofe fhe carried with her.

Mar. Sir, I believe——

Cla. Nay, if we both fpeak together, how fhall we hear one another? You believe her virtue is armour of proof, without your counfel, or your guard, and therefore you left her in the hands of rogues and vagabonds, to make your own peace with me: you have it, provided, I fay (as I faid before) that fhe be fafe; that is

to fay, uncorrupted, undefiled ; that is to fay—as I faid
before.

Mar. Mine intent, fir, and mine only way—

Cla. Nay, if we both fpeak together, how fhall we
hear one another ?

Enter Sentwell.

O mafter Sentwell ! good news !

Sent. Of beggarly news, the beft you have heard.

Cla. That is to fay, you have found my niece among
the beggars ; that is to fay—

Sent. True, fir, I found her among them. And
they were contriving to act a play among themfelves,
juft as we furpriz'd 'em, and fpoil'd their fport.

Cla. A play ! are there players among them ! I'll
pay them above all the reft.

Enter Randal.

Rand. Sir, my mafter, Mr. Oldrents, and his friend,
Mr. Hearty, are come to wait upon you, and are impatient to behold the mirror of juftices ; and if you
come not at once, twice, thrice ! he's gone.

Cla. Good friend, I will fatisfy your mafter, without telling him—he has a faucy knave to his man.

[*Exit.* Clack.

Rand. Thank your worfhip.

Sent. Do you hear, friend, you ferve mafter Oldrents.

Rand. I cou'd ha' told you that.

Sent. Your name is Randal.

Rand. Are you fo wife ?

Sent. Ay ; and the two young ladies, your mafter's
daughters, with their lovers, are hard by, at my houfe
They directed me to find you, Randal, and bring you
to 'em.

Rand. Whaw, whaw, whaw, whaw !——Why do
we not go then ?

Sent. But fecretly, not a word to any body, for a
reafon I'll tell you.

Rand. Mum.——

A I R

AIR XXXVII.

The greatest skill in life,
For avoiding noise and strife,
Is to know when a man should be dumb, dumb, dumb.
When a knave, to gain his end,
Sifts you to betray your friend,
Let your answer be only, mum, mum, mum.
Wou'd you try to persuade
A pretty, pretty maid,
As ripe as a peach, or a plumb, plumb, plumb?
You've nothing more to do,
But to swear you will be true,
And then you may kiss! but———mum, mum, mum.

[Exeunt.

Enter Clack, Oldrents, Hearty, Oliver, *and* Martin.

Cla. A-hay! boy; y-hay! this is right; that is to say, as I wou'd have it; that is to say—a-hay! boys; a-hay! they are as merry without as we are within. A-hay! master Oldrents, and a-hay! master Hearty! and a-hay! son Oliver! and a-hay! clerk Martin! clerk Martin! the virtue of your company turns all to mirth and melody; with a-hay trollolly, lolly, lolly, is't not so, master Hearty?

AIR XXXVIII.

Heart.   *There was a maid, and she went to the mill,*
        Sing trolly, lolly, lolly, lolly, lo.
        The mill turn'd round, but the maid stood still.
Cla.   *Oh ho! did she so? did she so? did she so?*

Heart.   *The miller he kiss'd her, away she went;*
        Sing trolly, &c.
        The maid was well pleas'd, and the miller content;
Cla.   *O ho! was he so, &c.*

               Heart.

Heart. *He danc'd, and he sung, while the mill went*
                    clack ;
              Sing trolly, &c.
           And he cherish'd his heart with a cup of old sack.
Cla.   *Oh ho ! did he so, &c.*

Old. Why, thus it should be ! now I see you are a
good fellow.

Cla. Again, boys, again ; that is to say, a-hay,
boys ! a-hay !—

Old. But there is a play to be expected and acted by
beggars !

Cla. That is to say, by vagabonds ! that is to say,
by strolling players ; they are upon their purgation ; if
they can present any thing to please you, they may escape the law ; (that is, a-hay !) If not, to-morrow,
gentlemen, shall be acted, abuses stript and whipt among
'em ; with a-hay, master Hearty, you are not merry.

Enter Sentwell.

And a-hay ! master Sentwell, " where are your *dra-*
" *matis personæ ?* your prologues ? and your " *actus*
primus ? Ha' they given " you the slip, for fear of the
whip ? a-hay !" in.

Sent. A word aside, an't please you.

          [Sentwell *takes* Clack *aside, and gives him a paper.*
Cla. Send 'em in, master Sentwell. [*Exit.* Sent.] Sit,
gentlemen, the players are ready to enter ; and here's a
bill of their plays ; you may take your choice.

Old. Are they ready for them all in the same cloaths ?
read 'em, good Hearty.

Heart. First, here's *The two lost Daughters.*

Old. Put me not in mind of the two lost daughters, I
pr'y-thee.   What's the next ?

Heart. The Vagrant Steward.

Old. Nor of a vagrant steward ; sure some abuse is
meant me.

Heart. The Old Squire, and the Fortune Teller.

Old That comes nearer me ; away with it.

Heart. The Beggar's Prophecy.

                                        Old.

Old. All thefe titles may ferve to one play of a ftory that I know too well ; I'll fee none of them.

Heart. Then here's the *Jovial Crew.*

Old. Ay, that ; and let 'em begin. See, à moft folemn prologue !

Enter fix Beggars for the Prologue.

A I R XXXIX.

Beg.   *To knight, to fquire, and to the genteels here,*
    We wifh our play may with content appear ;
    We promife you no dainty wit of court,
    Nor city pageantry, nor country fport ;
    But a plain piece of action, very fhort and fweet,
    In ftory true, you'll know it when you fee't.   [Exit.

Old. True ftories, and true jefts, do feldom thrive on ftages.

Cla. They are beft to pleafe you with this tho', or, a-hay ! with a whip for them to-morrow.

Old. Nay, rather than they fhall fuffer, I will be pleas'd, let 'em play their worft.

Enter Patrico, *with* 1*ft Beggar, habited like* Oldrents.

See our Patrico among 'em.

Pat.   Your childrens fortunes I have told,
        Now hear the reafon why ;
    That they fhall beg, ere they be old,
        Is their juft deftiny.

    Your grandfather, by crafty wile,
        An heir of half his lands,
    By fhamelefs fraud did much beguile,
        Then left them to your hands.

1 *Beg.* That was no fault of mine, nor of my chil-dren.

Old. Doft note this, Hearty ?

Heart.

Heart. You faid you would be pleas'd, let 'em play their worft.

[1ft Beggar *walks fadly, beats his breaft,* &c.]

Enter 4th Beggar, dreffed like Hearty, *and feems to comfort him.*

Old. It begins my ftory, and by the fame fortune-teller that told me my daughters' fortunes, almoft in the fame words ; and he fpeaks in the play to one that perfonates me as near as they can fet him forth.

Cla. How like you it, fir ? you feem difpleas'd ; fhall they be whipp'd yet ? A-hay ! if you fay the word——

Old. O ! by no means, fir ; I am pleas'd.

4 Beg. Sad, for the words of a bafe fortune-teller ? Believe him ! hang him ; I'll truft none of 'em. They have all whims and double meanings in all they fay.

Old. Whom does he talk, or look like, now ?

Heart. It is no matter whom ; you are pleas'd, you fay.

4 Beg. Ha' you no fack i'th' houfe ? am not I here ? and never without a merry old fong.

<h2 style="text-align:center">A I R   XL.</h2>

Old fack, and old fongs, and a merry old crew,
Will fright away cares, when the ground looks blue.

And can you think on gypfy fortune-tellers ?

1 Beg. I'll think as little of 'em as I can.

4 Beg. Will you abroad then ? But here comes your fteward.

Enter Springlove, *as an actor.*

Old. Blefs me ! is not that Springlove ?

Heart. Is that you that talks to him, or that Coxcomb, I, do you think ? pray let them play their play ; the juftice will not hinder them, you fee ; he's afleep.

Spr.

Spr. Here are the keys of all my charge, fir; and my humble fuit is, that you will be pleas'd to let me walk upon my lawful occafions this fummer.

1 *Beg.* Fie! can'ft not yet leave off thofe vagrancies? but I will ftrive no more to alter nature. I will not hinder thee, nor bid thee go.

Old. My own words at his departure.

Heart. No matter; pray attend.

1 *Beg.* Come, friend, I'll take your counfel.
[*Excunt Beggars.*

Spr. I've ftriven with myfelf to alter nature in me
For my good mafter's fake, but all in vain;
For beggars (cuckow like) fly out again
In their own notes, and feafon.

Enter Rachel, Meriel, Vincent, *and* Hilliard.

Rach. Our father's fadnefs will not fuffer us
To live in's houfe.

Mer. And we muft have a progrefs.

Vinc. The affurance of your love hath engaged us.

Hill. We are determin'd to wait on you in any courfe.

Rach. Suppofe we'll go a begging!

Hill. We are for you.

Spr. And that muft be your courfe, and fuddenly,
To cure your father's fadnefs, who is told
It is your deftiny, which you may quit,
By making it a trick of youth, and wit,
I'll fet you in the way.

All. But how! but how?   [*All talk afide.*

Old. My daughters, and their lovers too! I fee the fcope of their defign, and the whole drift of all their action now, with joy and comfort.

Heart. But take no notice yet; fee a whim more of it. But the mad rogue that acted me, I muft make drunk, anon.

Spr. Now are you all refolv'd?

All. Agreed, agreed.

Spr. You beg to abfolve your fortune, not for need.
[*Excunt.*

Old.

Old. I muſt commend their act in that ; pr'ythee let's call 'em, and end the matter here.   The purpoſe of their play is but to work my friendſhip, or their peace with me, and they have it.

Heart. But ſee a little more, ſir.

Enter Randal.

Old. My man, Randal, too ! has he a part with 'em ?

Rand. They were well ſet to work when they made me a player ! What is it I muſt ſay ? and how muſt I act now ? Oh ! that I muſt be ſteward for the beggars in maſter ſteward's abſence, and tell my maſter he's gone to meaſure land for him to purchaſe.

Old. You, ſir, leave the work, you can do no better, and call the actors back again to me.

Ran. With all my heart, and glad my part is ſo ſoon done.   [*Exit.*

Enter Patrico.

Pat. Since you will then break off our play,
Something in earneſt I muſt ſay ;
But let affected rhiming go ;
I'll be no more a Patrico.

My name is Wrought-on————Grandſon to that unhappy Wrought-on, whom your grandfather craftily wrought out of his eſtate, by which all his poſterity were ſince expos'd to beggary.

                              [Patrico *takes* Oldrents *aſide.*
I had a ſiſter, who, among the race of beggars was the faireſt ; a gentleman, by her, in the heat of youth, did get a ſon, who now muſt call you father.

Old. Me ?

Pat. Yet attend me, ſir, your bounty then diſpos'd your purſe to her, in which, beſides
Much money (I conceive by your neglect)
Was thrown this jewel : do you know it ?

                                                                Old.

Old. The bracelet my mother gave me !
Does the young man live ?

Enter Springlove, Vincent, Hilliard, Rachel, *and*
Meriel.

Pat. Here, with the reſt of your fair children, ſir.
Old. My joy begins to be too great within me.
My bleſſing, and a welcome to you all ;
Be one another's, and you all are mine.
Vinc. } We are agreed on that.
Hill. }
Rach. Long ſince ; we only ſtay'd till you ſhook off
your ſadneſs.
Old. Now I can read the juſtice of my fate, and
yours.——
Cla. Ha ! juſtice ! are they handling of juſtice ?
Old. But more applaud great Providence in both.
Cla. Are they jeering of juſtices ? I watch'd for
that.
Heart. Ay, ſo methought ; no, ſir, the play is
done.

Enter Sentwell, Amie, *and* Oliver.

Sent. See, ſir, your niece preſented to you.
[Springlove *takes* Amie.
Cla. What, with a ſpeech by one of the players ?
Speak, ſir, and not be daunted ; I am favourable.
Spr. Then, by your favour, ſir, this maiden is my
wife.
Cla. Sure you are out o' your part ! that is to ſay,
you muſt begin again.
Spr. She's mine by ſolemn contract, ſir.

A I R

AIR XLI.

Amie.   *Alas ! fir, I have prov'd your clown,*
        Ey'd him,
        Try'd him,
    But muſt own,
So wretched a mortal ne'er was known ;
I had been with him undone.

If I muſt in bondage be,
To chuſe my chains, at leaſt I'm free.
    Since I am willing,
    To be billing,
Here's the man, the man for me.

Cla. You will not tell me that : are not you my niece ?

Am. I dare not, fir, deny't ; we are contracted.

Cla. Nay, if we both ſpeak together, how ſhall we hear one another.

Old. Hear me then for all. This gentleman that ſhall marry your niece, is my ſon, on whom I will ſettle a thouſand pounds a year, to make the match equal.—Do you hear me now ?

Cla. Now I do hear you, and muſt hear you ; that is to ſay, it is a match ; that is to ſay——as I ſaid before.

Spr. [*To* Oldrents.] Now, on my duty, fir, I'll beg no more, but your continual love, and daily bleſſing.

Rach. You, fir, [*To* Oliver.] are the gentleman that wou'd have made beggars ſport with us. Two at once.

Mer. Two for a ſhilling.

AIR

AIR XLII.

Rach.   *What haste you were in to be doing,*
When two at a time you were wooing ;
   You men are so keen,
   When once you begin,
You fancy you ne'er shall have done.

   What haste you were in to be billing,
With two at a time for a shilling ;
   Yet quickly you'd find,
   If any prove kind,
You'd work enough meet with one.

Oliv. There are some misunderstandings have happened : but, I hope, we are all friends.

Old. Ay, ay, we are all friends, and shall continue so ; and to shew we are friends, let us be merry : and to shew we are merry, let us have a song, " and after-" wards a dance."

AIR XLIII.

Hearty, To the men.

   Now then tell them fairly,
   You will love 'em dearly,
   May each of them be yearly
      Mother of a boy.

To the women.

   Ladies fair, adieu t'ye,
   Manage well your beauty,
   Keep your spouses true t'ye ;
      Be their only joy.

To

Come, my lads, be merry,
Bring us sack and sherry;
Call the pipe and tabor
Now, sir, cut a caper:
Here ends all our labour
   This happy wedding day.

Come, my lads, &c.

A Country Dance.

F I N I S.

A TABLE of SONGS.

ACT I.

ACT II.

XXVII.

Signora Baccelli in the Ballet (call'd) Les Amans Surpris

Mrs MAHON in the Character of FANNY.

How bountiful has Providence been, in allotting me such humane benefactors!

THE
ACCOMPLISH'D MAID.

A COMIC OPERA.

DISTINGUISHING ALSO THE

VARIATIONS OF THE THEATRE.

AS PERFORMED

IN THREE ACTS,

AT THE

𝕿𝖍𝖊𝖆𝖙𝖗𝖊-𝕽𝖔𝖞𝖆𝖑 𝖎𝖓 𝕮𝖔𝖛𝖊𝖓𝖙-𝕲𝖆𝖗𝖉𝖊𝖓.

Regulated from the Prompt-Book

By PERMISSION of the MANAGERS,

By Mr. WILD, Prompter.

THE MUSIC BY
SIG^r. NICCOLO PICCINI.

" Virtue never will be remov'd
" Tho' Lewdnefs court it in a Shape of Heav'n."

SHAKESPEARE.

LONDON:

Printed for JOHN BELL, at the Britifh Library, in the *Strand.*

MDCCLXXXI.

Dramatis Perſonæ.

M E N.

Lord Bellmour, in Love with Fanny. } Mr. *Mattocks.*

Sir John Lofty, contracted to Lady Lucy. } Mr. *Du-Bellamy.*

Kreigſman, a German Offi-cer. } Mr. *Shuter.*

Robin, a Gardener, in love with Fanny. } Mr. *Dibdin,*

Lady Lucy, Siſter to Lord Bellmour. } Mr. *Pinto.*

W O M E N.

Fanny, her Chambermaid, a Foundling. } Mrs. *Mattocks,*

Finet, Governeſs to Lady Lucy. } Mrs. *Thompſen.*

Suſan, a Dairy - Maid, in love with Robin. } Mrs. *Baker.*

An old Woman, Nurſe to Fanny.

Sportſmen, Servants, Ruffians, &c.

S C E N E

At, and near, Lord Bellmour's Country Seat.

A TABLE of SONGS.

ACT I.

ACT

ACT III.

N. B. The three fongs marked * were not originally in this opera; but are the compofition of the fame mafter.

PREFACE.

THIS drama is a tranflation from the celebrated Italian comic opera of Goldoni, LE BUONA FIGLIUOLA; which, as it owes its origin to an Englifh ftory, I hope it will not be thought prefumptuous to endeavour to reftore it to its native country, with all thofe additional embellifhments it has received by travel; I mean that of being formed into an opera, by fo celebrated a writer as Goldoni; and that greateft improvement, Italy was capable of beftowing on it, being fet to mufic, by that inimitable compofer, Signor Niccolo Piccini.

Goldoni, in his Preface, fays; " To render a per-
" formance worthy the regard and attention of the
" lovers of the theatre, he had chofen a ftory wherein
" the moft amiable character of innocence, was blend-
" ed with lighter comic ones; to raife thofe laudable
" fenfations in the mind, which create the mixture
" of *Utility* and *Delight*."

This

This tranflation is attempted, fo as to be fung to the original mufic, as performed in Italy ; wherefore, the verfification, it is hoped, will be confidered, as fubfervient to the mufical expreffion ; and of courfe cannot have that perfect harmony in poetry, which otherwife might have been given to it, had it been free from that reftriction. As the mufic of this opera has always been efteemed the moft capital work of that great compofer Piccini, the tranflator thought it more juft, to give up the claim to poetical harmony, rather than make the leaft infringement on the mufical accent. He likewife flatters himfelf, that it will not be lefs acceptable to an Englifh audience, by the dialogue's being without the incumbrance of recitative. All other alterations were made to adapt it to the Englifh ftage ; by giving to fome characters, fuch employmeats in life, as are more fuitable to rhe cuftoms of our own country.

Should this firft attempt of bringing an entire Italian mufical compofition on the Englifh ftage, by applying our language to the harmony of their moft eminent compofer, prove acceptable to the public, the tranflator's intention is fully anfwered, as it may be the means of exciting fome abler genius to tread the fame path.

N. B. This Opera is tranflated to the original mufic, performed at Rome in the year 1760.

ACCOMPLISH'D MAID.

ACT I.   SCENE I.

A Garden. FANNY difcovered at a Diftance gathering Flowers.

HOW delightful is the morning,
 Nature's richeft ftores adorning
  All the gay enamell'd ground;
Herbs and flow'rs each fenfe regaling,
Ev'ry breeze rich odours ftealing,
 Spreads the grateful fragrance round.

How bountiful has Providence been, in allotting me
fuch humane benefactors! who by kindnefs convert
misfortunes to a bleffing, and prevent every painful reflection which I muft feel, in not knowing the place of
my birth, or who my parents were.

Enter ROBIN.

Rob. Good morrow to you, Fanny.
Fan. Robin, good morning to you.
Rob. What are you about? I faw you bufy, and am
come to help you.

B

Fan.

Fan. I thank you; I was only gathering a few flowers for my lady's dreffing room, and I think thefe will be fufficient. How beautiful they look! how fweet they fmell! what pity they fhould fade fo foon.

Rob. They are indeed very pretty; but there's a flower that, when it is properly cultivated, is much more beautiful, and more lafting; but I'm affeard you don't know it.

Fan. Oh dear! tell me the name of it.

Rob. 'Tis called the flower of love.

Fan. I never heard of it; where does it grow? I long to carry fome to my lady.

Rob. It is indeed fcarce, but I'll tell you where it may be found, and how you may know it.

> *When you difcover*
> *A faithful lover,*
> *Who from his truth will ne'er depart,*
> *Then's in your power,*
> *Love's choiceft flower,*
> *If grafted in an honeft heart.*

Fan. If that's the flower, I believe it is fcarce enough; I remember now to have heard of it; but they told me, that, tho' it look'd fo very pretty, it was dangerous to gather; fo I never fought after it; and the defcription given, was quite the reverfe of yours.

> *When men purfuing,*
> *Girls to their ruin,*
> *Boaft that Love's flow'r in the heart fweetly blows;*
> *Tho' they proteft and fwear,*
> *Maids fhun the fubtle fnare,*
> *None e'er could tell where conftancy grows.*

Rob. There's a flower fomething like it, which is reckon'd a poifon; but the true one you will find in the heart of your faithful Robin: take it, my dear, Fanny, and——

Fan. Hufh, Robin; I can hear no more of this language; I have told you my fentiments before, and beg you will defift.

Rob.

Rob. What, have you no pity?

Fan. Yes, as much as you can defire.

Rob. And no love?

Fan. Yes, and love too, if you will be content with that which I fhould give to a brother, or a friend; the only love I can receive, and the only one I can give in return; let me defire, therefore, you will reft fatisfied, that I fo far take kindly your well-meant profeffions, that, if it ever be in my power to fhew my fenfe of them, you fhall fee I will not be ungrateful.

Rob. And may I then hope, my dear Fanny?

Fan. Miftake me not, good Robin! your love I can never requite, but with friendfhip; deceive not yourfelf by an expectation of what can never happen: that affection which is loft upon me, may make fome other happy: and one, perhaps, who, by being better qualified to make you fo, may better deferve that affection. Good morning to you.   [*Exit.*

Rob. Unkind girl, good day to you. Well, I don't defpair; tho' fhe now only promifes to love me as a brother, who knows but one day we may be nearer related.

I did not mean the love
Which friends and kindred prove;
If that is all fhe'll give,
I'll ftrive content to live.
Perhaps a brother's tender name,
In time may light a kinder flame;
And fifter change for life,
To dear and loving wife.   [*Exit.*

S C E N E   II.

Another Part of the Garden.

Enter FANNY, *and Lord* BELLMOUR, *meeting.*

L. Bell. Ah! Fanny here, fortunate opportunity. You are abroad early this morning, Fanny.

Fan. My lord, I have been gathering thefe flowers for my lady's dreffing-room, againft fhe rifes.

L. Bell. You are a good girl, and the diligent attention you conftantly pay to our fervice fhall not be unrewarded.

Fan. The leaft remiffnefs in duty, my lord, to benefactors, who have been fo liberal, would be wholly unpardonable: efpecially as duty is the only return I can make for your bounty. - ·

L. Bell. What has been already done, Fanny, is but little, compared to what I wifh ftill to do for you; and I hope you will be grateful. ·

Fan. I hope, my lord, I ever fhall be fo; has your lordfhip any commands?

L. Bell. Why in fuch hafte to be going?

Fan. To carry thefe flowers.————

L. Bell. Oh, you have time enough for that; my fifter is no early rifer, and I have fomething to fay——. Tell me, Fanny, have you ever been in love?

Fan. My lord!

L. Bell. Come, my fweet girl, let me hope the gratitude you fhew in your conftant endeavours to pleafe, is not without fome mixture of a more tender nature, and that————

Fan. My lord, I humbly beg leave to go.

L. Bell. You muft not, I cannot part with you—Oh, my hard fortune; that it fhould be difgraceful to my rank, to acknowledge a paffion fo well juftified by the charms of my fair one. My dear Fanny, tell me, fhould I love you with the utmoft ardour and fincerity— Why do you tremble?

Fan. Forgive me, my lord, I cannot ftay.——

L. Bell. You muft, you fhall, I will not lofe this opportunity.

Fan. Indeed, my lord, I ought not, therefore excufe me, I will not ftay.—— *(Runs off.)*

L. Bell. Foolifh girl! yet how graceful was her confufion? She muft, fhe fhall be mine. I may perhaps overtake her. [*Exit.*

Enter

Enter SUSAN, *with a Milk-pail.*

Oh! how cruel is my fate,
All my life to work like a slave;
Forc'd to labour early and late,
Neither pleasure nor comfort I have.
To a girl so young and tender,
Some help, Oh quickly lend her;
To carry so heavy a weight:
Oh! how cruel is my fate,
Forc'd to labour early and late.

Oh dear! 'twas not always so; time was, when Robin would have carried my pails, and have thanked me into the bargain; but he is turned false-hearted, and has left me for an upstart minx—Hey ho!

Enter Lord BELLMOUR.

L. Bell. How vexatious! she flew like lightning: Ha! this wench is Fanny's companion; her assistance may be useful—Suppose I forget my rank a-while—O tyrant love! to what condescensions and little artifices dost thou reduce us?—How do you do, Susan?

Su. Thank your honour, I am very well.

L. Bell. You look as fresh as a new blown rose this morning.

Su. Your honour is pleased to joke me.

L. Bell. Indeed I don't, set down your pail—I have something to say to you.

Su. La, your honour, the milk will be cold.

L. Bell. P'shaw! set it down—I stand in need of your assistance.

Su. Suppose he should be in love with me.   *(Aside)*

L. Bell. But before I trust you with this affair, tell me, and tell me sincerely, was you ever in love?

Su. Sir!—so, so ——

L. Bell. Do you know what it is to be in love?

Su. Why—why—

L. Bell. Come, come, tell me..

Su. Why—yes, Sir,

B 3

L. Bell.

L. Bell. And can you pity the pangs that lovers feel?

Su. Yes, Sir.

L. Bell. Then hear me—but I charge you be fecret.

Su. Yes, I will, Sir—'Tis plain enough, he is in love with me.   *(Afide.)*

L. Bell. I am deeply enamoured—and it is in your power————

Su. Your honour may command me freely.

L. Bell. Very well—I love————

Su. Yes; fo your honour faid before.

L. Bell. And doft thou know the beauteous objeƈt of my paffion?

Su. I believe, Sir, I can guefs.

L. Bell. As you hope for my future favours, I charge you be fecret.

Su. Oh, yes; I never tells tales.

L. Bell. I love Fanny to diftraƈtion.

Su. Fanny!—*(Looks difappointed and confufed.)*

L. Bell. You are intimate with her; among your-felves, you girls often talk of your admirers; do you privately mention my paffion to her, and perfuade her to make a proper return. I have attempted to tell her, but fhe ran from me, to avoid giving an anfwer—perhaps fhe will not be backward in fpeaking her mind to you.

Su. Pleafe your honour—I muft make bold to tell you—thou' I am but a poor, fimple girl—I don't care to do any fuch thing.

L. Bell. Pooh! filly; why won't you oblige me? it will make me your friend for ever, and I will reward you beyond your wifhes.

Su. Then, Sir, to be fure, I will do what your honour commands.

L. Bell. Tell her fhe has infpired me with a paffion, whofe violence I cannot refift—tell her, that her charming eyes have captivated my heart; tell her, I doat upon her, and cannot live without her.

Su. Yes, your honour; I'll be fure to fay fo—but if I am not even with them.   *(Afide.)*

(Curtfies and retires watching.)

L. Bell. How abfolute a tyrant is this paffion! I al-moft blufh to be thus fubdued, and yet am proud

of

of it—'Tis an infatuation bordering upon phrenzy—
reafon has no power, every word and thought is fondnefs and Fanny.

> *While her charms my thoughts employ,*
> *All is rapture, all is joy;*
> *When fhe fpeaks, how fweet to hear,*
> *Modeft, graceful, and fincere:*
>   *In her lovely fhape and face,*
>   *Center ev'ry charm and grace;*
> *Sure never nymph was half fo fair.*
>
>   *Not the idle, giddy, vain,*
>   *Nor the wanton flirting train,*
> *Did my cautious heart enfnare;*
>   *Net their artful, fubtle wiles,*
>   *Nor their foft deluding fmiles,*
> *Charming Fanny triumphs there.*   [Exit.

SUSAN, comes forward.

Su. Tell her, fpeak to her—yes, to be fure!——
thank you for nothing; I am not fuch a fool neither—
they fay Love is blind, fo it feems truly—for I think
I have as good pretenfions to a gentleman fweetheart,
as any girl in the parifh. The men are all bewitched,
I believe, both high and low—I'll be revenged of my
lord, I'll warrant him, for I'll go and tell my lady.

Enter Sir JOHN LOFTY.

Sir John. Good morrow, pretty lafs.
Su. Your fervant, fir.
Sir John. Do you belong to this houfe?
Su. Yes, Sir.
Sir John. Is your lady ftirring?
Su. I can't tell, fir; I have been out of the houfe a
long while.
Sir John. Will you enquire; and if fhe is, let her
know

know I am impatient to have the honour of feeing her ?

Su. Who muft I fay you are, fir?

Sir John. Say, Sir John Lofty is come to wait on her ?

Su. Oh la ! this is the gentleman fhe is going to be married to. This is fo lucky ! the charmingeft opportunity to fend it round to my lady.—Adod, I'll venture. *(Afide.)* I make bold to wifh you much joy, fir ; I will let my lady know directly; fhe is goodnefs itfelf; you will be vaftly happy with her : Heaven blefs you both together, I fay !—but I'm afraid—'tis a great pity to be fure—I am very forry for it—but 'tis not her fault, poor lady.

Sir John. Ha ! what does the wench mean ?

Su. Sir—I fcorn to fpeak ill of any body ; but—if you knew all, fir—'tis no bufinefs of mine—your fervant, fir.

Sir John. This muft mean fomething fure !—I'll humour it. *(Afide.)* Come hither, child, and tell me what is the matter ? here's fomething to buy you a top-knot.

Su. Thank you, fir——Why, fir, you muft know—but you won't tell ?

Sir John. No, no.

Su. My lord will never forgive me,—if he fhould know that I told any body.

Sir John. He fhall know nothing of the matter.

Su. For, to be fure, it does not become fervants to be tittle tattling of their mafters and miftreffes affairs, and telling the fecrets of a family to ftrangers, you know, fir.

Sir John. Well, well ; but you may tell it to me ; it feems to concern me.

Su. It does indeed, fir ; you are going to be one of the family, and fo there can be no harm in it.

Sir John. Not in the leaft, let me know what it is.

Su. And fo I think I may venture to tell you ; but I would not willingly do a wrong thing for the whole world.

Sir John. Come, come—keep me no longer in fufpence.

Su.

Su. You muſt know, ſir; that my lord is fallen deſperately in love.——

Sir John. Pooh!—is that all?

Su. All, ſir! yes, ſir.

Sir John. Well, and who is the lady?

Su. The lady, ſir!—Ay!—that's the caſe.——She is no lady, ſir, I aſſure you.

Sir John. What is ſhe?

Su. A ſtrange girl, that was brought up by charity, ſir; and nobody can tell who ſhe belongs to.

Sir John. Indeed!

Su. My lady took her into the houſe, to learn to be a ſervant; and my maſter is fallen ſo deſperately in love with her, that I verily believe he intends to marry her, ſir.

Sir John. How! to marry her! Is that poſſible?

Su. I aſſure you 'tis very true, ſir.—I think I ſhall be even with him now. ·　　　　　　　　*[Aſide.*

Sir John. But, child, how ſhould you know this?

Su. Sir, I heard him ſay ſo his ownſelf.

Sir John. Ay!—ſhould it prove ſo, I muſt conſider well before I take his ſiſter for a wife.

Su. I am ſo ſure, that I am ready to take my Bible oath of it.

Search thro' the world, ſir, you never will find
A girl more diſcreet, or to truth more inclin'd:
Envy and malice, I boldly defy
To prove that I ſlander, or flatter, or lie.
My ſimple maſter—but I'll ſay no more,
That wheedling creature—I've told you before.
　　　That's all I ſay,
　　　I wiſh you good day,
　　　For I cannot ſtay.　　　　　　　　　*[Exit.*

Sir John. Strange! that people ſhould debaſe their rank and birth!—It behoves me to uſe deliberation.—Though I ſincerely love lady Lucy, and am perfectly ſatisfied with the choice I have made; if this girl's tale be true, ſuch an alliance will bring diſgrace upon my family.——
　　　　　　　　　　　　　　　　　Perhaps

Perhaps 'tis not too late to prevent it; I will immediately try; and endeavour to act with a dignity becoming a descendant from illustrious ancestors.

> *Love and beauty mildly reigning,*
> *Gently sooth my captive heart ;*
> *　Rigid honour, both disdaining,*
> *Fiercely plays a tyrant's part.*
> *　Fondest love we may controul,*
> *Or by time, or absence cure ;*
> *　Sacred honour in the soul,*
> *Should unstain'd thro' life endure.*　　　　　[Exit.

S C E N E   III.

A Saloon, with a Prospect of the Garden.

Enter Lady LUCY.

L. Luc. How agreeable is this abode of peace and tranquility ! how infinitely preferable to the noise and bustle of the town. Here we breathe the purest air, and enjoy the beauties of nature in perfection. Yet cannot I be happy, while the object of my love is absent ; his presence would brighten every prospect, and compleat my joy.

> *Bring, ye tedious hours,*
> *The man my heart adores,*
> *　My love-sick soul to cheer ;*
> *Retir'd from pomp and noise,*
> *We'll taste the tranquil joys.*
> *　Untainted, flowing here.*

Enter FINET.

Fin. My lady, Sir John Lofty is come to wait on your ladyship.

L. Lu. Run, fly ; tell him I am impatient to see him.

Fin.

Fin. Ay, to be fure! my lady is in a great hurry.
[*Afide and Exit.*

L. Lu. How fweet is the affurance of a reciprocal affection! I may, truly, think my lover's heart doth perfectly fympathize with mine, he comes fo opportunely
to my wifh.

Enter Sir JOHN *and* FINET.

Fin. Pray walk in, fir,—Blefs me! how can a man
move fo flow towards his bride?

L. Luc. Good morning to you, fir John.

Sir John. Lady Lucy, your fervant.

L. Luc. Blefs me! are you not well? your countenance has loit its ufual chearfulnefs.

Fin. Indeed, I think fo too; he looks quite ftupi-
fied.

L. Luc. Pray inform me, what is it affects you?

Sir John. I am to afk your ladyfhip's pardon;—
fomething indeed hangs heavy on my mind. My temper ought to be known to you. When ftrong fufpicion
makes my heart uneafy, I cannot, I would not wifh to
conceal it; but let my countenance always declare my
real fentiments.

Fin. Have I liv'd to fee one fincere man! To be fure
he is a prodigy.   [*Afide.*

L. Lu. What can this mean? Sufpicions! of whom?
pray explain yourfelf.

Sir John. I am informed your brother is in love with
a low bred girl.

L. Lu. My brother!

Sir John. Nay, more; that he is fo extravagantly
infatuated, 'tis to be fear'd he will difgrace his noble
family, by marrying her.

L. Lu. Is it poffible? who is fhe?

Sir John. One in the houfe, whofe parents are unknown. Is there not fuch a perfon?

L. Lu. There is; yet I know not how to fufpect her
of an indifcretion—Are you well informed?

Sir John. I think I am.

L. Lu. I hope it will not prove fo: the girl has a
prudence uncommon at her years; and I think I know
my

my brother's principles too well. Yet, suppofing he fhould imprudently yield to the force of an unruly paffion, and demean himfelf by fo unequal a match, would his actions deprive me of your affections?

Sir John. I know not——the queftion is too nice—I cannot at prefent determine—allow me fome time to confider. I love you with the tendereft, the fincereft paffion; I doat on you to diftraction; and the thought of lofing you is infupportable. Yet I ought not to bring difgrace on my family. Endeavour, before it is too late, to prevent this misfortune; and think how ftrong that motive muft be, which can tear me from you.   *[Exit.*

L. Lu. Amazement deprives me of the power of fpeech.

Fin. Why, my lady, this agrees exactly with a thing that Sufan told me happened in the garden, this morning. My lord wanted to bribe her to affift him.

L. Lu. Indeed!

Fin. Notwithftanding Fanny's demure looks, in your ladyfhip's prefence, I believe fhe has more mifchief in her heart than we are aware of, and more art to difguife it.

L. Lu. Can fuch be the return for all my care! have I nurfed a ferpent in my bofom, to fting me in the tendereft part! muft I, for her, lofe the man I love!

Fin. There is feldom any good comes of educating girls above their ftation in life.

L. Lu. Where is fhe?

Fin. I will fend her to you, and I hope your ladyfhip will feverely reprimand the forward creature.

> *I hate a proud, a faucy flirt,*
>   *Who flaunts about fo gay and vain :*
> *Shall paltry girls, who fprung from dirt,*
>   *A noble lord prefume to gain?*
>   *No longer now among girls we fee,*
>   *Proportion kept in due degree,*
>   *All ape the airs of quality.*
> *The lifp of the tongue, the tottering tread;*
> *The flirt of the fan, the tofs of the head;*
> *They giggle, and ftare at, whoever they meet,*
> *And look fo affected, it fhocks one to fee't.*   *[Exit.*

L. Lu. I'll fend the girl from hence immediately; fhe fhall be reduced to her original ftate of penury and want, to mortify her pride and ambition. To avoid a rupture with my brother, I muft ftifle my anger awhile. Some excufe muft be thought of. Here fhe comes.—How innocent fhe looks! The artful hypocrite! But paffion would demean me; for the fake both of my pride and love, prudence muft direct at prefent.

Enter FANNY.

Fan. In obedience to your ladyfhip's commands.—

L. Lu. Come hither, Fanny! I hope I fhall always find you as good a girl, as you have hitherto proved, and ready to oblige me.

Fan. Your ladyfhip makes me blufh to hear you fpeak fo; my ftudy and delight is to receive, and obey your commands.

L. Lu. Very well. In return for your good behaviour, I would not willingly omit any opportunity that offers for your advancement; I have none in my own family; but my fifter Laura has taken a great liking to you, and defired me to fend you to wait upon her; I have promifed fo to do.

Fan. Alas!   *[Afide.*

L. Lu. Why don't you fpeak?

Fan. If your ladyfhip does not chufe to keep me any longer—I am forry my earneft endeavours to pleafe are not acceptable—fince your ladyfhip does not approve my fervices————

L. Lu. That is not the point. I only part with you to my neareft relation, for your own immediate advantage.

Fan. You are always increafing my gratitude; but, if your ladyfhip pleafes, I would much rather continue under your protection, than reap the largeft benefits elfewhere.

L. Lu. Do you fay this from affection?

Fan. Indeed I do, I folemnly avow it.

L. Lu. If your affection for me does not confift in profeffions only, fhew the fincerity of it, by a ready obedience.

C

Fan.

Fan. I humbly beg your ladyſhip's pardon—does my lord know ?

L. Lu. 'Tis no concern of his ; go, and get ready immediately.

Fan. I will obey your ladyſhip—but ſhould his lord-ſhip ———

L. Lu. Am not I your miſtreſs ? Do as I command.

Fan. You are, indeed, my honoured miſtreſs and benefactreſs ; yet would it not be uncivil to go—

L. Lu. What a civil laſs you are grown ! but no more words : at your peril get ready this inſtant.

Fan. I am moſt unhappy to have diſobliged your la-dyſhip.   *(Weeps and is going.)*

Enter Lord BELLMOUR.

L. Bell. Fanny here ! in tears ! what can it mean ? Where are you going ? You look diſturbed, ſiſter ! what has happened ?

Fan. My lord—her ladyſhip is diſpleaſed with me ; why, I know not—I am not conſcious of any offence.

L. Lu. Dare you appeal from my commands !——Be gone this inſtant.

Fan. I obey.

See a poor, a friendleſs creature,
   Never knew a parent's care ;
'Tis too cruel thus to treat her,
   Oh ! 'tis more than I can bear.
Yes, my lady, I will go,
Since you pleaſe to have it ſo.
   Tho' deſerted, helpleſs, poor,
   Tho' I beg from door to door,
Gracious Heav'n will not deſert
An innocent, an honeſt heart.   [Exit.

L. Bell. For Heaven's ſake, what is the meaning of all this ?

L. Lu. Nothing, but that my ſiſter has deſired me to ſend her Fanny ; and I cannot with politeneſs refuſe the requeſt ; it will be greatly to the girl's advantage ;
                                        and,

and, as I fhall foon leave.this place, there is no proper employment for her here.

L. Bell. But, my dear fifter, there is a difficulty, you perhaps are not aware of—Suppofe I don't chufe to part with her ?

L. Lu. No! what can be the reafon for fo abfurd——

L. Bell. No matter—here fhe fhall ftay.

L. Lu. Have you confidered what the world will fay ?

B. Bell. The world is at liberty to fay whatever it pleafes; I defpife its cenfures or applaufe.

L. Lu. Indeed—very extraordinary, this !—you chufe a very uncommon method of fhewing a regard for your fifter.

L. Bell. I have ever fhewn you the tendereft regard, and finceteft affection ; as my fifter, I highly efteem you ; but, remember, I am, and will be, mafter of my own actions.   [*Exit.*

L. Lu. So peremptory !—Sir John's intelligence was true then ! My brother's defigns are too evident, either to ruin the girl, or marry her. But it fhall be my aim, by every means, to prevent his fuccefs in either : this obftacle to my wifhes fhall inftantly be removed—Muft my views of happinefs give place to her's !—No— feverely fhall fhe feel the vengeance of a difappointed woman.

> *Come, dire revenge, infpire me,*
>   *Thy dreadful force employ ;*
> *Pride and refentment fire me,*
>   *To blaft their blooming joy.*
>
> *Come fury, rage, difdain,*
>   *With all your fatal train ;*
> *Ruin, deftruction, let them prove,*
> *Ere I lofe the man I love.*   [Exit.

                    SCENE

S C E N E IV.

A Thicket, with a View of the Country.

Enter FINET *and* SUSAN.

Fin. You are sure you cannot tell where Fanny is gone?

Su. Indeed I can't; she went out crying, but I don't know which way; however, I am heartily glad her tricks are found out at last.

Fin. I never knew these upstart favourites come to any good; her mock-modesty had so far gain'd upon my lady, that no other servant was regarded; and nothing was right, forsooth, but what she said and did.

Su. I wish she was an hundred miles off, with all my heart; she is continually followed by all the young fellows hereabout.

Fin. I can't endure such forward sluts!

Su. There's Robin the gardener, who used to be very fond of me, has quite forsaken me, and is always dangling after her. I wonder what they can see in her, for my part.

Fin, Men have no taste, now a-days!—to admire such a little paltry chit! that nobody knows.

Su. I have heard she was found quite an infant, by the road side?

Fin. She was so; and I wish my good old lady had sent her to the parish work-house; she would not then have been the cause of so much mischief, and set the family in an uproar.

Su. To be sure her parents must be thieves, to leave her in that manner.

Fin. I believe she is some gipsy's brat.—

Su. Hush!—As I am alive, here she comes—let us watch her.

Enter

Enter FANNY.

QUINTETTO.

Fan.	*Forlorn I wander, scorn'd, rejected,*
	By ev'ry former friend neglected;
	Where e'er I go, a lead I bear
	Of helpless life, and dark despair.
Su. }	*Pray, good madam, what are you doing?*
Fin. }	*Pray, dear madam, where are you going?*
Fan.	*Dearest friends, I cannot tell.*
	Adieu—farewell—
	I go to find, a fate more kind—
	A happier destiny,
	Heaven has, I hope, in store for me. [Going.
Su. }	*See the fruits of your intrigues,*
Fin. }	*Get you gone a thousand leagues.*

Enter ROBIN.

Rob.	*Stay, my dear—Ah! Fanny, why*
	Will you from your true love fly?
Fin. }	*Yes, 'tis certain she must go,*
Su. }	*'nd her train of lovers too.*
Fan.	*Can you so inhuman be,*
	To insult my misery:
	Have you lost all charity?
Su. }	*We are sorry,——* (Sneering.)
Fin. }	*Pray excuse the liberty.*
Rob.	*Come, my dear, and let me prove,*
	('Tis all I ask) a sister's love.
Fan.	*Come then, Robin, and be my friend;*
	A poor, a helpless girl defend.
Su. }	*Robin, pray take her, and lead her away,*
Fin. }	*His lordship, no doubt, her protector will pay—*
	Go on foolish cully—for what do you stay?
	Booby, booby, take her away.
Rob.	*Is she my lord's?*
Su. }	*Yes, 'tis true—*
Fin. }	*The dainty bit is not for you.*

C 3

Rob.

Rob. *Stay there, stay there, stay where you are,*
   Of other men's girls I'll take no care.
Fan. *In my ruin, all things join,*
   All the world 'gainst me combine.

Enter Lord BELLMOUR.

L. Bell. *Will you leave me, cruel fair !*
   Thus abandon'd to despair !
   Where dost thou go ? Ah ! tell me where ?
Su.   }
Fin. } *With the gard'ner, sir, we guess ;*
   He's the happy, happy swain ;
   He alone her heart could gain.
L. Bell. *With Robin !*
Su.   }
Fin. } *Yes, sir, yes.*
L. Bell. *Hence, ungrateful wretch, be gone !*
   All my tender thoughts are flown ;
   Now you'll find, when 'tis too late,
   Gentle love will turn to hate.
Fan. *What will, alas ! become of me,*
   Expos'd to want and misery ?
L. Bell. *Go to thy happy swain.*
Rob. *Go to my lord again.*
Su.   }
Fin. } *Charming, charming ; how they snub her !*
   I wish, with all my heart, they'd drub her.
Fan. *Hear, my lord—*
L. Bell. *No ; get ye gone.*
Fan. *Hear me, you—*
Rob, *No ; I have done.*
Fan. *Hear me, friends, for charity.*
Su.   }
Fin. } *We're very sorry.*   [*Sneering.*
   Pardon our temerity.
Fan. *Do you then no pity know ?*
L. Bell.] *Go——*
Su. | *None to you will pity shew.*
Fin.   { *With one lover not content,*
Rob.   ] *Now your jilting you'll repent.*
All.   }
Four. } *None to you will pity shew.*
Fan. *Gracious heaven, some pity shew.*

END OF THE FIRST ACT.

A C T II.

S C E N E I. *A Wood.*

Enter Lord BELLMOUR.

L. Bell. WHERE can she be! Oh! curfed foolifh jealoufy! My impetuous temper too haftily took fire; like a mad man, I fpurned her from me, and now find her innocent. I feel I cannot live without her; nor will I reft, till I have difcovered her.

> *Where is my deareft Fanny gone!*
> *Where is the lovely wand'rer flown?*
>   *How could my ftubborn heart,*
>   *Act fuch a rigid part?*
>   *Barbarous fate! fortune fevere!*
> *Where is my love? Ah, tell me where.*   [*Exit.*

S C E N E II. *Another Part of the Wood.*

Enter Sir John LOFTY *and* FANNY, *guarded by fome armed Men.*

Sir John Conduct this creature carefully to town: and deliver her fafe to the perfon to whom this letter is directed.

Fan. Hear me, Sir, in pity.

Sir John. Away with her this inftant, and your reward fhall equal your diligence.   [*Exit.*

Fan. Alas, alas, what will become of me? [*Exeunt.*

Enter

Enter ROBIN.

Rob. O! poor dear Fanny, what are they going to do with her?—What a fool was I to believe such a story! I must be jealous truly! and so have lost her—— Ay, I deserve it. I will follow and see what becomes of her, tho' I die for it.

—Here are some gentlemen shooting; I will ask them to help me to take her away from them. [*Enter some sportsmen.*] Let me beseech you, good gentlemen, to have compassion upon an innocent girl, and save her from villains; they have carried away my poor sister; and I am afraid they will murder her.

1st Sports. Which way are they gone?

Rob. By that tree.

2d Sports. How long since?

Rob. This moment, they are hardly out of sight; you will soon overtake them; I'll shew you! [*Exeunt.*

Fanny and her guard are seen at the farther end of the stage. [Enter the sportsmen.] *and they attack them. Fanny runs to the front of the stage; the guards are beaten off, and one of them drops his sword.*

Fan. Robin has procured my liberty; but my unkind lord has cruelly abandoned me to distress and persecution.

Rob. My dear Fanny!

Fan. You have preserv'd my life.

Rob. May I now hope you will love me?

Fan Give me time to recover myself——I am greatly terrified.

Rob. Come home with me, and rest yourself.—— Gentlemen, I return you a thousand thanks.

1st Sports. Take care of your sister for the future.

2d Sports. Where do you live?

Rob. At Bellmour-Hall.

1st Sports. Oh!—Here's my lord.

Enter Lord BELLMOUR.

2d Sports. Your lordship's most obedient.

L. Bell. Gentlemen, your most humble servant—— Ha! Fanny here! [*Aside.*

1st Sports.

1ſt Sportſ. Does this pretty laſs belong to your lordſhip?

L. Bell. Yes, ſir—How came ſhe here?

2d Sportſ. Some men were forcing her away, and we
have prevented them.

L. Bell. I am much obliged to you.

1ſt Sportſ. We are glad to have done any ſervice that
is acceptable to your lordſhip, and wiſh you a good
day.

L. Bell. I return you my thanks—I wiſh you good
ſport.

2d Sportſ. You ſeem to promiſe yourſelf ſome, or I
am much miſtaken.————   [*Aſide.*
                                 [*Exeunt ſportſmen.*

L. Bell. My dear girl, how happy am I to have
found you; come with me, I will defend you againſt
all future attempts.   [*Exit with Fanny.*

Rob. Oh la! oh la! Muſt I bear all this? He has
ſnatch'd the precious morſel out of my mouth, when
I thought I was quite ſure of it. I ſaved her from
being run away with; and when I had fairly courſed
her down, comes another, and ſnaps her up.—What
plaguy ill luck!—I ſhall go mad for vexation—I am
quite deſperate—I'll go hang myſelf, or drown myſelf
—or—no—I'll kill myſelf with this ſword I am determined, for what is life without Fanny?

> *Oh! my Fanny, thy true ſwain,*
> *Will for thee this life reſign————*
> *But, my trembling heart ſays no————*
> *Pray forbear, ah! don't do ſo————*
> *Riſe my courage, fear defy————*
> *Now I am reſolv'd to die.*
>
>   [Going to ſtab himſelf.

Enter KREIGSMAN.

Kreigſ. Hault!————[*Stops him.*] Der divel! Vat
is dis?

Rob. Pray, ſir, let me alone; I am a deſperate man.

Kreigſ. You be ein coward, ein boldroon, to run
dyſelf drew for teſhbair.—If thou vilt tie as cin clever
oneſt mans, come to dee vars, and tie as ein ſoldier.
                                                Rob.

Rob. Yes—captain,—I will go along with you, and turn foldier, 'tis the only way to forget Fanny.

Kriegf. Aw! Vat is dat Fanny?

Rob. 'Tis a very pretty young girl, that I am in love with—and I have loft her.

Kriegf. Vat! Vil dee Englifh mans pee in tefhbair for de oomans! De Germans care nichts apout 'em: dey vil tie in de vars vid onnor, put never for ficht dryfels. Come, come mit me—dere pe oomans enough every vere.

Rob. Pray, fir, who are you?

Kreigf. I pe ein goot foldier, dat ferve mein fheneral, I have peen in England pefore, and now pecome again to fearch for ein yoong ferr.

Rob. I don't underftand you; but be what you will, I'll go along with you; I can't bear to ftay here—it was too cruel to fnatch her away, juft when——

Kriegf. Friend, friend; tinck nicht more of dee oomans, come mit me to de vars, and dou fhalt pe happy; in de camb, dere pe all kind of teverfions.

Dere pe de drumbets, horns, and trums,
Dere pe guittars, and dere pe fifes.
And dey altogether blay;
  Dere the nimpel laffes comes,
Singing, tancing, night and tay.

  Ven de enemy pe var,
Trinka vine mit fholly poys;
  If de enemy come near,
Den pe hufh, and make no noife

Come to de camb, trive love away;
I'll go to fight, put you may ftay:
Trink, and fing, and tance, and blay;
And pe merry night and tay.   [*Exeunt.*

SCENE

SCENE III. *A Parlour.*

Enter Lady LUCY *and Sir* JOHN LOFTY.

L. Lu. And fo, you have conveyed the troublefome girl away?

Sir John. I have fent her guarded to town, where fhe will be clofely confined; and my lord fhall never fee her more.

L. Lu. May I believe you are now fatisfied?

Sir John. Yes, my deareft life, I am quite eafy and happy.

L. Lu. I wifh you always fo, but for me———

Sir John. What means your ladyfhip?

L. Lu. I fear the ficklenefs of your temper; I muft confefs you had reafon to be offended, but not with me. A fincere and encouraged lover, fhould not have made any action of my brother's, a pretence to forfake me.

Sir John. Forfake you! I never had the leaft intention———

L. Lu. You furely feem'd to threaten it, as if———

Sir John. Forgive me. Paffion too often makes us propofe things in hafte, which in our cooler moments we find impoffible to execute. This nice trial of my heart, has only convinced me, that I adore you with fincerity and vehemence, which will triumph over every other confideration.

> *Tho' in my breaft contending*
> *Tumultuous paffions roll;*
> *The conflict here is ending;*
> *Love has poffefs'd my foul.*   [*Exit.*

L. Lu. What he fays is reafonable; but I muft be fully fatisfied, that his love and regard for me is free from all referve.

Enter FINET *and* SUSAN, *talking foftly to each other.*

Su. Well, I vow, I could never have thought of fuch a ftrange thing happening.

Fin.

Fin. I don't know how to tell it to my lady, it will be very difagreeable to her.

Su. We may tell it between us.

L. Lu. What is the meaning of that whifpering?

Fin. Madam, does your ladyfhip know that Fanny——

L. Lu. Yes, yes; I know fhe is gone from hence.

Fin. But fince that—do you tell the reft.　[*To hufan.*

L. Lu. Has any thing particular happened?

Su. Yes, and pleafe your ladyfhip; foon after fhe was fent away—I have begun, now 'tis your turn.　[*To Fin.*

L. Lu. Why do you hefitate? Speak out.

Fin Your ladyfhip muft know————

L. Lu. What muft I know?

Fin That fhe is come back again.

L. Lu. How! Come back again?

Su. Yes, my lady.

L. Lu. Come back again!——Why?——Thro' what means?—— Where is fhe?

Su. My lord has lock'd her up.

L. Lu. Is it poffible, Sir John would deceive me? Or has my head-ftrong brother ufed fome violence?

Fin. I wifh they don't both deceive you.

L. Lu. Run you, and find out Sir John; tell him I wifh to fpeak with him this inftant.　　　[*To Fin.*

Fin. Yes, my lady,

L. Lu. Go you to my brother, and tell him, I defire the favour of feeing him directly.　　　[*To Sufan.*

Su. I'll go this minute.

L. Lu. Yet ftay—come back again—I have not yet determined what I fhall fay, I muft confider—firft let me know what Fanny is doing; from thence I may form fome judgment how to proceed.

Fin. We are gone, madam——Come along.

[Exeunt both.

L. Lu. Be quick, and bring me word here; that done, it will be time enough to go to Sir John, and my brother. What can I determine? How fhall I act? That it fhould be in the power of fuch a creature, to give vexation to a heart like mine!

Re-enter

Re-enter FINET.

D U E T T O.

Fin.
Thro' the key hole I was peeping,
There I saw the girl a weeping;
First she rav'd, and then look'd sad,
I believe she's gone stark mad.　　　　[Exit.

Re-enter SUSAN.

Su.
Round the room, I saw her walking,
Wringing thus her hands and talking;
Then she'd stop, and wildly stare,
Like a creature in despair.　　　　[Exit.

Re-enter FINET.

Fin.
Look, I see his lordship come,
He is hast'ning to the room;
Some glad tydings sure he bears,
That will dry his fav'rite's tears.

Re-enter SUSAN.

Su.
Tho' I met my lord just now,
Yet I could not speak, I vow;
Nor have I the message told,———
He might think I was too bold.

Fin.
See Fanny's coming out !———
Where can she be roving ?

Su.
His lordship follows quick,———
They seem very loving.

Both.
'Tis an intricate affair,
We had had better to declare,　　　　[Aside.
We'll have nothing more to do.
Madam, we are forc'd to own,
There is nothing can be done,
Please to give us leave to go.　　　　[Exeunt.

D

L. Lu.

L. Lu. Perplexing beyond meafure! I wifh to avoid difobliging my brother—fome expedient muft be devifed—I will fee Sir John, and afk his counfel; he will not furely forfake me, after the folemn vows and proteftations he has fo repeatedly made.

> *I know his foul difdains*
> *All falfhood, fraud and art ;*
> *Strick honour nobly reigns,*
> *Triumphant in his heart.*   [Exit.

SCENE IV.   *A Chamber.*

Lord BELLMOUR, *and* FANNY, *difcovered.*

Fan. My lord, I humbly beg permiffion to go.

L. Bell. Where ?

Fan. To throw myfelf at my lady's feet, and implore her forgivenefs for the confufion and uneafinefs which I have innocently occafioned.

L. Bell. You fhall not do it,——her prefent warmth of temper, may influence her to treat you in fuch a manner, as her cooler reafon would, I am confident, difdain.

Fan. Yet furely, my lord, I ought to try: if fhe infifts upon my going, I cannot ftay: as her fervant, 'tis my duty to obey.

L. Bell. My dear Fanny, you are very good.

Fan. Pardon me, my lord, I fear I do not merit your praife, or I fhould have gone, without hefitation, to Lady Laura; and (altho' her fevere temper terrifies me) fhould not have caufed fuch difturbance in a family, where I lay under the higheft obligations.

L. Bell. 'Tis but a momentary ftorm, raifed by an exceptious and a hafty lover's breath.

Fan. That alone is a fufficient reafon for my going; ought I to interrupt the happinefs of my benefactrefs ? I own myfelf wrong, I have acted in a very unbecoming manner; but will inftantly make all the reparation in my power.

L. Bell. Come, come, no more of this; my fifter is out of the queftion; fhe is very foon going; you fhall ftay and command here.

Fan. My lord !————

L. Bell. Say you will love me; I will place you above the reach of malice or reproach : my whole fortune shall be at your disposal.

Fan. For goodness sake, my lord, no more.

L. Bell. Come, my charmer, say you will consent, and seal it with a kiss.

Fan. Pray, my lord, forbear, left I forget the respect due to you.

L. Bell. Equipage and splendor shall attend you.

Fan. I disdain them. Tho' poor and friendless, I will not purchase grandeur with infamy.

L. Bell. 'Tis in vain to deny me——you must—— you must——

Fan. If you persist, I will fly from you, and shun you as my greatest enemy.

L. Bell. I'll follow you thro' the world.

Fan. For pity's sake, let me alone——good Heaven protect me !.

> *Off, my lord, pray forbear, let me go,*
> *These are freedoms no maid must allow.*
> *Too severe, too severe is the smart,*
> *And the anguish that rends my poor heart.*
>   *Unhappy me, by ills inclos'd;*
>   *To ev'ry insult thus expos'd.*
> *No, my lord, to virtue true,*
>   *All due respect I'll show.*
> *What honour dictates still pursue,*
>   *Away—unhand me—let me go.*   [*Exit.*

L. Bell. How cowardly is vice ! This girl's superior virtue appears with a dignity, that makes me despicable to myself. How charming was her honest indignation ! Had I found her easy and complying, she might have gratified my passion, but could not have raised my admiration ! Tyrant custom ! That denies her virtue the reward I would joyfully bestow ! Yet, to marry a woman, whom the world would treat with contempt—— No, no,—it must not be—-I cannot bear the thought— she shall go to my sister, and I will go to town ; in the variety of amusements, I hope I shall soon forget her ;

D 2

she

fhe will be properly fituated—and I fhall—I'll think no
more; but give orders for my journey—and make my
fifter and her lover eafy, by this conqueft over' my
inclinations.   [*Exit.*

SCENE V. *A Court-yard before Lord Bellmour's*
Houfe.

Enter KREIGSMAN.

Kreigf. Aw! dis is de blace.   [*Knocks at the gate.*

Enter a Servant.

Whofe houfe is dis!
Serv. Sir!
Kreigf. Who is de maifter of dis houfe?
Serv. Lord Bellmour, Sir.
Kreigf. Aw! Tas is right; I vou'd fpeak mit him.
Serv. I will let him know—my lord is coming this
way.   [*Exit.*

Enter Lord BELLMOUR.

Kreigf. Are you de maifhter of dis houfe, mein herr?
L. Bell. Sir, the houfe is mine.
Kreigf. I vou'd fbake mit you.
L. Bell. I am at your fervice.
Kreigf. How long have you peen the maifhter of it?
L. Bell. I inherited it of my father; it has been in
my family many ages.
Kreigf. Aw! Tas is good, I have peen in dis con-
dry before, and den der vas loofe——
L. Bell. Stay; fir, before you proceed, I muft defire
to know, why you afk thefe queftions, and by whom
commiffioned?
Kreigf. Py mein badron.
L. Bell. Who is your patron?
Kreigf. Ein, who ift not afraid or afhamed to pe
known to all de lords in the vorld—He is general of de
cavalry, and ein paron.
L. Bell. Very well—now proceed.

                                            Kreigf.

Kreigf. Mein herr—der vas—fday—how long? Aw! de many years baft—der vas—aw der devil—dis great blague to de Germans to fhbake your Englifh; dake defe babers mein herr, dey will dalk blainer I pelieve dan me. *(Lord Bellmour infpeƈts them.)* Aw! I pring mein fheneral fome good news, he will brefer me in de army, and I might come to pe ein fheneral.

L. Bell. What do I fee?—and yet it cannot be—my fond hopes but miflead me—the time feems to cor-refpond; but then the name——'Tis worth enquiry, however: if you will follow me, monfieur——

Kreigf. Der divel! Me monfieur! I pe ein German —I pe nicht monfieur—you muft call me herr—never you ein German monfieur.

L. Bell. Well then, herr! Go with me into the houfe; I will fend for a perfon, who can better fatisfy your enquiries than myfelf.

Kreigf. Aw! Fat berfon?

L. Bell. One that remembers every tranfaƈtion in this family, for more than double the time your letters mention; an elderly woman.

Kreigf. Ein old oomans?

L. Bell. Ouy, monfieur.

Kreigf. Der devil! Ich nicht monfieur.

L. Bell. I beg your pardon—but this woman——

Kreigf De old oomans nicht do mein badron's bufi-nefs—I vant de young ferr.

L. Bell. There is a young one too who may perhaps. —Fond bufy hopes prefs not too far!

Kreigf. De young one—aw! Dat vill be goot——

L. Bell. Come, follow me.

Kreigf. Hark you friend——have you good rhine fine in the houfe?

L. Bell. Yes, plenty.

Kreigf. Aw! Tas is right, to trinka de rhine fine pe ferry goot for de healt.

L. Bell. You fhall have as much as you pleafe.

Kreigf Hark you, friend, is de young ferr hanfum?

L. Bell. Handfome!

Come

> *Come and see the lovely creature,*
> *My delight, and pride of nature!*
> *Sparkling eyes, to blifs inviting,*
> *Ev'ry glance the heart delighting.*
> *None with her we can compare,*
> *She is the faireft of the fair.*
> *Ah! come in, come in monfieur——*
> *No, mein herr—excufe the word,*
> *Let's be friends, put up your fword;*
> *Trinka vine, be blyth and gay,*
> *Sing, and drive old care away.*   [*Exeunt.*

S C E N E VI.   *A Grove.*

Enter FANNY.

To whom can I fly? Or who will now affift me? From birth I have been the fport of fortune: O! When will it defift from perfecuting me?—Among all its cruelties, the bafe defigns of my lord, wound me the fevereft. *(Sighs.)* Ungenerous man! to feek the ruin of a defencelefs orphan!—I am weary and can go no farther. I will reft a-while under the fhadow of thefe trees—Did but I know my parents, I might fly to their protection; they would correct my unexperienced youth, if it has erred—But, ah! that happinefs is denied, and I am quite deftitute. My eyes grow heavy; I will indulge the call of friendly fleep, to eafe my agitated mind; and may the guardian powers of innocence protect me.

> *Come, balmy fleep, relieve my woes,*
> *In thy foft bands, my eye-lids clofe;*
> *To my breaft bring foft repofe.*   [*Sleeps.*

Enter KREIGSMAN, *and Lord* BELLMOUR'S *Servant.*

Serv. This was the way, my lord was informed, fhe went—if we could but find her.

Kreigf. Aw! And if fhe broves to pe de oomans I fant, I fill have de bleafure to kill mein badron mit fhoy.

Serv. Let us look farther on——

Kreigf.

Kreigſ. Aw! Who is dis?   [*Seeing Fanny.*

Serv. 'Tis her, and aſleep—the very perſon we were looking for—Will you pleaſe, ſir, to ſtay here, and watch her, while I go and acquaint my lord?   [*Exit.*

Kreigſ. Yaw, yaw, Aw! *Mein ſchatz.*

Fan. (*Dreaming*) Save me, ſave me, dear papa!

Kreigſ. Ich believe ſhe call me—no—ſhe is ſhleeben. Aw! ſhleeben on, *mein ſchatz.*

Fan. (*Dreaming*) Come, and embrace your child.

Kreigſ. Aw! I fill emprace mit dee.

Enter FINET *and* SUSAN : *they ſtand obſerving* KREIGS-
MAN.

Kreigſ. She is fery hanſum!

Fan. (*Dreaming*) Save your helpleſs child.

Kreigſ. I pe ein happy German!—I feel—I nicht tell fat is de matter mit me.

Fan. (*Dreaming*) Dear papa, in pity come—

Kreigſ. Dee boor little *young ferr ſlaupen,* and call for her baba!—

Fin. So, ſo, fine doings, truly!

Su. Well done, ſoldier.

Fin. How came you here?

Kreigſ Oomans, fat do you fant here?

Su. He's a man of taſte.

Kreigſ. Oomans, pekawn—

Fan. (*Waking*) Where am I?—what man is that?

QUINTETTO.

Fin.	⎫	*Madam, we have ſeen it all,*	
Su.	⎬	*As upon the bank you lay,*	
	⎭	*With a ſoldier ſtout and tall,*	
		You divert the hours away.	
Fan.		*Do I dream! How came I here?*	
		What's the matter? What d'ye ſay?	
		Ah! will fate be ſtill ſevere!	
Kreigſ.		*Dis young ferr pelong to me,*	[To Fin.
		Get you gone, afvay, afvay;	[and Su.
		I mit her alone fil ſhtay—	
		From mein badron I pe come,	[To Fan.
		For to pring you ſhafely home.	

Fan.

Fan.	*Pray who are you, fir ?*
Kreigſ.	*I'm a foldier —*
Fin. } Su.	*Your dear lover.*
Kreigſ.	*I pe fent to——*
Fin. } Su.	*Yes, we faw you.*
Kreigſ.	*Let me fhbake—mein fheneral—*
Fin. } Su.	*We can't believe you.*
Kreigſ.	*He did ſend me——*
Fin. } Su.	*It is not true.*
Kreigſ.	*Here to find—*
Fin. } Su.	*He don't know what to fay.*
Kreigſ,	*Blague confound you, get you fvay.*
Fan.	*I don't know.*
Fin. } Su.	*But we know it well.*
Fan.	*I was fleeping—*
Fin. } Su.	*And can you deny?*
Fan.	*I know nothing —*
Fin. } Su	*Come, don't tell a lie.*
Kreigſ.	*Blague confound you, get you afay.*
Fin.	*Saucy fellow, fcurvy knave !* [To him.
Su.	*My lord fhall know how you behave.* [To her.
Fan. }	*Arm'd in confcious innocence,* *I defpife your infolence.*
Kreigſ. }	*Oomans, oomans, get ye hence ;* *Curfe your rude inbertincnce.*

Enter Lord BELLMOUR.

L. Bell.	*Ah ! my charmer, come with me,* *Come, and tafte felicity ;* *Ev'ry fear and doubt fhall ceafe,* *Ev'ry hour bring joy and peace.*
Fan.	*O ! my lord——*

Fin.

Fin. Su. }	*That confident huffy—*
Kreigf.	*Ich fas here—*
Fin. Su. }	*Careffing his doxy.*
Fan.	*I know nothing—*
Fin. Su. }	*She's fallen in love, fir.*
Kreigf.	*Aw! boor greature.*
Fin. Su. }	*They were embracing —*
Fan. Kreigf. }	*'Tis not true, 'tis not true—*
Fin. }	*Sir 'tis true—'twas juft fo—*
Su. }	*That's her fav'rite lover now.*
L. Bell.	*Embracing !*
Su.	*Thus, my lord.*
L. Bell.	*He her lover ?*
Fin.	*'Pon my word.*
Su.	*Punifh her, fir—*
Fin.	*And fend her away.*
Fan. Fin. Su. Kreigf }	*Now he's mufing !—what will he fay ?* [*Afide.*
L. Bell.	*Lovely creature, no more languifh ;* [*To Fan.* *(Foolifh girls, I fent him here :* *Go, and no more interfere.)* *I am come to heal your anguifh ;* [*To Fan.* *Stop ! ah ! ftop that ftarting tear,*
Fin. Su. }	*Sure he's crazy !*
Kreigf.	*Dat is fel.*
Fan.	*Send this foldier, fir, away.*
L. Bell.	*He hath fome good news to tell.* *No, my charmer, he muft ftay.*
Fan. }	*Much good may't do you, noble fir :* [*To L. B⸗*
Su. }	*Much good may't do you, blufterer.* [*To Kr.*
L. Bell. Kreigf. }	*Infolent wenches, hence, and leave us.*
Fin. Su. }	*Is he fo filly as not to believe us !* [*Afide.*

L. Bell.

L. Bell.   *Give him your hand—*   [To Fanny.
Fan.   *No, no, away.*
L. Bell.   *'Tis my command, you muſt obey*
Fin.
Su.   } *Part them, ſir, ſee what they do.*   [To L. B.
L. Bell. |
Kreigſ. | *Saucy wenches, hence, begone;*
           Learn a due reſpect to ſhew.
Fin.
Su.   } *Let us leave them, come along.*
Fin.   *'Tis provoking, can it be ?*
Su.   *Well, he'll heartily repent.*
         Muſt I know more miſery !
Fan.   *Will ſtern fortune ne'er relent ?*
L. Bell.   *Come my deareſt, you ſhall ſee*
Kreigſ.   *Pleaſure, joy, and true content.*

END OF THE SECOND ACT.

ACT   III.

SCENE. I.   *A. Parlour.*

Enter Lady LUCY, *Sir.* JOHN *and* FINET.

L. Lu. IS this poſſible ?

Fin.   Indeed, my lady, it was juſt as I tell you. It would make one die with laughing, to think that my lord ſhould pretend to be ſo much in love with Fanny, and then leave her with a foreign ſoldier.

Sir John. Surely his love cannot be ſo violent, as we imagined.

Fin. A girl in low circumſtances, with a pretty face, is ſure to be mark'd out by intriguing men as a victim to ruin.

                                                    Sir

Sir John. Who can this foldier be?

Fin. I don't know. My lord and he feem to under-ftand one another very well.

L. Lu. I fuppofe my brother has properly confidered the affair, and provided a hufband for her.

Sir John. The more I think of it, the more extra-ordinary it appears in every circumftance.

Fin. I take it to be fo common a cafe, that I am not in the leaft furprized at it.

" *Some men with artful pràife,*
    To girls will figh and whine;
And vain ideas raife,
    To ferve a bafe defign.

    The flatter'd lafs,
    Confults her glafs,
And on the object dwells:
Sees all her beauties blooming,
    Fantaftic airs affuming!
And growing more prefuming,
    Cries, Yes, 'tis truth he tells.

Seduc'd by wheedling and fighing,
If fhe prove kind and complying,
    How foon the delufion appears!
    The fubtle deceiver,
    In triumph will leave her,
Nor heed her reproaches and tears.

Young maids in time take warning,
Such fly deluders fcorning;
    From flatterers turn your ear,
    Difdain their tales to hear,
They never, never prove fincere." [*Exit.*

L. Lu. I believe my governefs judges very right; what is your opinion, Sir John?

Sir John. Tho' it may in general be too true, yet I could name a very ftrong proof of the contrary.

L. Lu. No doubt—you are fincerity and conftancy itfelf.

Enter

Enter a SERVANT, *with a letter.*

Serv. For your ladyship.   [*Exit.*

L. Lu. 'Tis my brother's hand; will you give me leave, Sir John?—I fee your name in the firft line, fo beg you will read it.

Sir John. (Reads.) " Let my fifter's, and Sir John's
" happinefs be no longer delayed by fcrupulous fears
" for my honour and conduct. Fanny is no longer a
" fervant in this houfe, but is otherwife provided for.
" My affections are plac'd on a baronefs, the daughter of
" an eminent general ; a woman of honour and fortune.
" I fhall foon introduce her ; and intend to compleat
" the ceremony this day: if my friend's happinefs
" may be confirmed at the fame time, it will double
" that of

" Your affectionate Brother,

" BELLMOUR."

Sir John. Bleft fortune ! May we rely on this ?

L. Lu. You may—I know my brother's honour ; he will not falfify his word.

Sir John. Then every obftacle is remov'd, and I am truly happy. Let us, my deareft love, prepare for the folemn union ; and put it out of the power of chance to difturb our felicity.

> *Doubts and fears are gone,*
>   *But fweet content remains ;*
> *Sorrow away is flown,*
>   *And love triumphant reigns.*
> *In thy foft fmiles, my fair,*
>   *In thofe confenting eyes,*
> *I fee the end of care,*
>   *And pledge of future joys.*   [*Exit.*

L. Lu. 'Tis a happinefs, beyond expectation, to have thefe alarming fears fo foon vanifh: I could not have imagined, my brother would thus eafily have
                    conquer'd

conquer'd his attachment. But who can this baroneſs be ?

Enter SUSAN.

Su. Madam, has your ladyſhip heard the news?

L. Lu. What news ?

Su. That my lord is going to be married to Fanny !

L. Lu. Pſhaw ! Fooliſh ! Why do you think ſo ?

Su. Becauſe I was juſt now told, he has ordered the ſteward to get every thing ready for a wedding, as faſt as poſſible

L. Lu. I know it—It is for mine.

Su. Indeed, I was told for certain, that he ordered it for his own.

L. Lu. That may be too ; for he is to be married to a lady of quality.

Su. La, madam ! How can that be, when——

L. Lu. Pr'ythee never trouble thy inquiſitive brain how it comes about ; be ſatisfied that it is ſo.

Su. And Fanny——

L. Lu. Is otherwiſe diſpoſed of—begone—I deſire to be entertained no further, at preſent, either with her or you.

Su. But, madam——

L. Lu. No more, I ſay, but vaniſh—I will not ſuffer the ſmalleſt doubt, to cloud the ſerene proſpect of my preſent happineſs.

Soothing hopes excite me,
Happy hours invite me,
To baniſh ev'ry fear :
See love and joy attending,
Our conſtant hearts befriending,
A ſweet reward prepare.

[Exit.

Su. So, Miſs Fanny ! Your high airs will be pull'd down at laſt ; my lord has no farther occaſion for you. I am glad of it—I thought how matters were going, when I ſaw my lord ſo intimate with the ſtrange ſoldier. I would fain ſee her once again methinks ; I ſuppoſe I ſhall find her hankering about my lord's dreſſing-room— It would be rude, not to bid the lady good bye—Yes— This is generally the end of all ſuch conceited things,

E

as have a better opinion of themfelves, than any body elfe has !—A faucy minx, to pretend to fet herfelf up above me, and fteal every girl's fweetheart in the parifh ! Oh ! here's Robin ; fhe inveigled him too: now fhe's fent packing, his dainty chops may come fimpering to me again—and if he does—but hold—I'll make no rafh refolutions, for fear of the worft.

Enter ROBIN.

Rob. Sufan, is this true that I have heard ? .

Su. And pray what is it you may have heard ?

Rob. Why, that my lord is going to be married to a great lady.

Su. Yes, it is very true. And is this all you have heard ?

Rob. Yes.

Su. Then I can tell you more news ; you may take leave of your fine mifs Fanny.

Rob. Dear me, why fo ?

Su. Becaufe fhe is going to be married, and fent away the lord knows where.

Rob. Married !

Su. Yes—to an outlandifh foldier—fhe muft now learn to wafh her own linnen ; tuck up her coats and follow the army into foreign parts, thro' all weathers: it is much more befitting for her, than fetting herfelf up for a fine lady.

Rob. How can you talk fo cruelly ?——And where is fhe going ?

Su. Among the Mallots and Blackamoors, for aught I know.

Rob. I am fure I am very forry for it.

Su. O ! poor fellow ! have you loft your deary ? Ha ! Ha ! Ha ! I am glad of it—I fuppofe, I fhall foon have you come cringing to me again ; with a forrowful face, and a whining tale——

Rob. And would you not take pity of me ?

Su. I can't promife that—I don't know—remember what a falfe hearted wretch you have been—but who knows what may happen ? A kind word may do fome-thing—yet I don't promife—No, no ; nor I don't de-ny—I am very good natur'd.

My

My heart is soft, relenting,
  And easy to regain ;
Your broken vows repenting,
  A pardon may obtain.
Ah! poor forsaken fellow !
And must you wear the willow ?
  Come, never pine and grieve,
  Don't despair, I may forgive.   [*Exit*

Rob. 'Tis very hard upon me, that I must lose my dear Fanny : but since she is gone, I am resolved, I will never break my heart after any woman again as long as I live.—If Susan won't have me, I will look out for another ; there is variety enough.

I saw the black, the brown, and fair,
Each had charms a heart t'ensnare :
Prove they true, we bliss obtain ;
If deceitful, grief and pain :
He that takes a wife on chance relies,
In the dark his fortune tries ;
And lucky is he, that has a prize. }   [*Exit*

S C E N E II. *A Parlour.*

Enter Lord BELLMOUR, KREIGSMAN, *and a* SERVANT,
with a Bottle and Glass.

L. Bell. Set down the wine, and leave us.
                              [*Exit Servant.*
Kreigs. Dis is all goot luck—Der Divel ! Fie you nicht trinka ?
L. Bell. Pray excuse me ; I cannot in the morning.
Kreigs. De good rhine Fine nefer hurt any pody.
                              [*Drinks.*

L. Bell. The dear girl, as yet, is ignorant of her good fortune
Kreigs. Fere is she ?
L. Bell. She flew from us, and shut herself up.
Kreigs. I wou'd see her, I wou'd shbake mit her.
L. Bell. She denied me admittance ; but I have sent a woman to her, with whom she is very intimate ; the very person who found her, eighteen years ago.
Kreigs. Aw ! Tas is right, *Mein Herr.*
                    E 2   *L. Bell.*

L. Bell. Her account agrees exactly with that in the letters you have produc'd; and she has inform'd me of some particular circumstances I did not know before.

Kreigs. Fat pe dey?

L. Bell. When she was found an infant by the road side, my mother ordered her to be taken care of, and call'd her Fanny. At her death, she recommended her to mine, and my sister's care; I was too young to take any particular notice of the object, and the story was familiar to me: but when I return'd from my travels, I found her the most accomplish'd creature I ever saw.

Kreigs. She is her moder's bicdure. Mein Badron, hafe shent many letters, put could nefer hear of her; put fen his son fas tie, he tid send me to find her.

L. Bell. (*Looking on the Papers.*) The mark on her neck!

Kreigs. I fish you shoy of dat.   [*Drinks.*

L. Bell. The things found with her!

Kreigs. Choy of dat.   [*Drinks.*

L. Bell. The time, the place, all correspond, and fully prove, my dear Fanny, my lovely girl, a baroness.

Kreigs. Aw! prave English mans! *Mein Leeber Her!* I fish you shoy of all togeder.   [*Drinks.*

L. Bell. I am the happiest of mankind! The dearest wish of my heart is accomplish'd; I can marry her, without disgusting my family, or drawing on me the reproaches of the world—I fly to tell her—follow me—

Kreigs. We vilth shake mit her, and ten I will go tirectly to de sheneral mein Badron, and fight de Durks—I nicht liff put fen I pe shopping off de heads of de enemy.

> *Aw! fat a bleasure, shoy, and telight,*
> *Dis to be marshing out to de fight;*
> *Drenshes pe oben, foes pe in fight:*
> *Fen all de colours flying pefore,*
> *And de loud dundering cannons do roar.*

> *Quick to de preash we mount shord in hant,*
> *Cutting and flashing all dat fidshtant;*
> *Ich pe most happys fen I go fight,*
> *War is my bleasure, shoy, and telight.*   [*Exit.*

SCENE

SCENE III. *A Chamber.*

Enter FANNY.

Fan. How am I agitated by a variety of paffions! Fortune feems to fport with my anxieties.—Why am I here?—Yet my nurfe fpoke fo urgent, fo perfuafive—'tis ftrange! Would I could fee an end to—but I am the child of Chance, and, bound by birth-right to endure her chaftifements.

Enter SUSAN.

Su. Your ladyfhip's moft obedient. Is there any fervices I can do for your ladyfhip, before your ladyfhip goes away?

Fan. Sufan! I don't underftand you—

Su No! Sure your ladyfhip has a very pretty found with it—and my lord has a very pretty look—and your ladyfhip has a pretty look—and I dare fay, you would have made a very pretty couple.

Fan. I don't know how I have deferv'd this treatment, I never injur'd you.

Su. It did not happen to be in your ladyfhip's power —and yet 'tis a pity—for you would have made a fweet miftrefs of a family—I hope tho' you won't fettle a great way off—we fhall fee you fometimes!—Oh!— yonder is my lord---your lord I mean; I beg your ladyfhip's pardon---you may have fome private bufinefs together, before you go away for ever; I am forry I am obliged to make my vifit fo fhort. Your ladyfhip's moft obedient humble fervant. [*Exit.*

Fan. How fhall I behave---where fhall I turn!

Enter Lord BELLMOUR.

L. Bell. You are not going, Fanny?

Fan. I don't know, my lord, how---I am quite at a lofs---yet I have been affur'd, on your lordfhip's honour, I might venture to come *here*, without apprehenſion of danger.

L. Bell. You may, indeed.

Fan. I wait your commands.

L. Bell. Why do you tremble? I want you to get a noſegay.

Fan. Yes, my lord.   [*Going.*

L. Bell. You don't enquire who it is for?

Fan. 'Tis my duty to obey, without aſking queſtions.

L. Bell. Stay---you have more right to know it, than any perſon; the noſegay is for my bride.

Fan. Alas!---   [*Sighs.*

L. Bell How! Is my approaching happineſs diſagreeable to you?

Fan. No, my lord; 'tis my ſincereſt, my moſt earneſt wiſh, and conſtant prayer; may you enjoy unbounded felicity.   [*Going.*

L. Bell. Stay, Fanny; ſhould not you like to know who is to be my bride?

Fan. I know ſhe will be the happieſt of women; it does not become me to enquire further.

L. Bell. You are more concern'd in it, than you at preſent imagine; ſhe is a German baroneſs.

Fan. Permit me to depart.

L. Bell. Her name Louiſa; ſhe is remarkably handſome; but the beauties of her mind, far exceed thoſe of her perſon.

Fan. For pity's ſake, let me go——

L. Bell. I love her with extreme fondneſs; and ſhall, as long as I live.

Fan. How cruel to detain me.

L. Bell. (Kneels.) You are my charming Louiſa; the idol of my heart.

Fan. Are my misfortunes become the mark of public ſport; can your noble heart deſcend to mock me?

L. Bell. By the bright flame that glows within my boſom, 'tis truth I tell---Oh! ſtop thoſe tears.

Fan. Let them plead for me; let them excite your compaſſion for a helpleſs orphan, expos'd to all the inſults of cruel fortune, and perſecuted by every means, that malice and envy can invent. Let me conjure you, my lord, in the name of your honoured mother---think

of

of the noble precepts she taught; think of her dying request; and cease, Oh! cease, to torment me.

L. Bell. By the dear memory of her, you have invoked, I do not attempt to deceive you; you were born a lady.

Fan. It cannot be; 'tis beyond probability!——

L. Bell. Your name Louisa; your father a baron, a great general; he sent the officer you saw, to search for you; come with me, he is ready to clear every doubt, by the most convincing proofs.

Fan. Do not, my honoured lord, delude, or betray me——My heart throbs——What can I think?—— What can I say?——

L. Bell. Be chearful, my dearest love; think it the reward of Heaven for your steady virtue; say, you will consent to be mine, and make me the happiest of mortals.

Fan. Am I not Fanny? Am I not your servant?

L. Bell. You are my Louisa, the beloved of my heart.

Fan. May I believe? May I give way to hope?

L. Bell. Depend upon my honour, my sincerity, my love.

Fan. Yet I fear——

L. Bell. Banish your fears; the proofs are waiting to convince you, your consent is all that is wanting to compleat our felicity.

Fan. I fear you have read too plainly the sentiments of my unexperienced heart—I will no longer hesitate, but rely upon your honour.

L. Bell. Thus let me seize your hand, as the dear, dear pledge of every joy.

D U E T T O.

L. Bell. " *The merchant fraught with treasure*
    By restless billows tost,
    At length beholds with pleasure,
    His wished-for destin'd coast:
    On dangers past he thinks no more,
    But fondly eyes the welcome shore.

Fan,

Fan.	*From noxious dews descending,*
	  The lilly clos'd all night;
	Itself from blasts defending,
	  Preserves its native white:
	At morn unfolds its snow white leaves,
	And vital heat and strength receives."

L. Bell.	*In thee each wish obtaining.*
Fan.	*No more of fate complaining,*
Both.	*What language can impart* *The transports of my heart!*
L. Bell.	*A thousand raptures fill my breast,* *They glow intense in ev'ry vein;*
Fan.	*Shall my tortur'd mind have rest?* *Shall I know an end of pain?*
L. Bell.	*Sorrow now no more shall wound thee,* *Love and peace shall hover round thee.*
Both.	*Joys unknown now fill my breast,* *Joys too great to be express'd;* *Am I with a parent blest!* *O what transports fill my breast;* *Joys too great to be express'd:* *Of my utmost wish possest.*

      Fortune relenting,
      Fond hearts consenting;
      Prove ev'ry blessing
        Mortals can know.
      Thus to behold thee,
      Thus to enfold thee;
      Joys past expressing
        Ever shall flow.   [*Exeunt.*

SCENE IV. *A Grand Hall.*

Enter Lady LUCY. *and Sir* JOHN, FINET, SUSAN,
and ROBIN.

  L. Lu. It is not possible—I cannot believe it—my
brother would not attempt so gross an imposition.

  Sir John. I am unwilling to think he would, after
the assurances he has given.

                         Fin.

Fin. My lord and Fanny have been in his dressing-room some time.

Su. They are just gone very lovingly together into the parlour, where the soldier is.

Fin. I will engage it will prove so.

Su. I am sure of it.

Rob. Now 'tis my thoughts, my lord is too much of a gentleman to play tricks.

Enter Lord BELLMOUR.

L. Bell. Every thing is prepared; let us conclude the ceremony without more delay,

L. Lu. Where is your bride?

L. Bell. She is at hand.

Sir John. My lord, I cannot help looking on this affair in a very serious light.

L. Bell. A few moments shall convince you, I agree to your opinion; and am going to produce the proof of it.   [*Exit.*

Sir John. I cannot help observing, that there is something very mysterious in all this.

L. Lu. After his public declaration, I have not a doubt remaining.

" *Thus the sun at morn appearing,*
  Darts around a splendid ray;
All the face of nature cheering,
  Drives the gloomy shades away,
In promise of a glorious day."

A Door opens in the Back SCENE.

Enter FANNY, *handed by Lord* BELLMOUR, *and*
  KREIGSMAN. *An old Woman following them.*

Fin. There, my lady!

Su. There, Sir! just as I said.

L. Lu. Imposing, deceitful man!   [*To L. B.*

Sir John. Is this, my lord, the behaviour of a man of honour? 'Tis an insult that demands——

                                        ' *L. Bell.*

L. Bell. If you find it fuch, you fhall have ample fatisfaction. This is the German baronefs; thefe tefti-
monials will prove it beyond a doubt. *(Gives the letters
to L. Lucy and Sir John.)* This woman has the things
which were found with her, they anfwer in the minuteft
article: examine them attentively, and act as reafon
fhall direct.

[*L. Lucy, Sir John, and the old Woman retire.*
Kreigf. I remember (Fat do you call dat ting dere)
it fas lofe mit de fhild fen wee marfh of a fudden in the
tark night; and if any pody tout de drut of it, Der
divel! I fil broof it, as becomes ein goot foldier.

[*Takes hold of his fword.*
Fin. O! I believe it, fir!
Su. And fo do I!
Rob. For my part—I always thought fhe was a lady,
and too good for me. Well, Sufan, fhall we make up
our quarrel, and do as our betters?
Su. I think I may as well take you now you are in
the mind, or may hap you may flip through my fingers
again.
L. Lu. Thefe proofs are inconteftible.
Sir John. My lord, I am fully fatisfied, and afk your
pardon.
Kreigf. Der divel! I pe an honeft German, and wear
ein fhword——
L. Lu. I need not repeat what my objections were,
and am fincerely glad they are removed; I always lov'd
her, and will moft cordially continue it. May you be
happy in each other.
Sir John. Accept, my lord, my hearty congratula-
tions; let us be folemnly united, and forget the anxieties of the few paft hours.
L. Bell. I join in every wifh for our general happinefs; nor can I doubt its proving truly fo. Love,
when founded on virtue, enfures felicity in marriage.
Come, my love, my bride; foregoing pains give a
double relifh to fucceeding pleafures.
Fan. I would willingly do my duty by all; but my
heart is ftill wavering between fear and joy, and I cannot exprefs as I ought, my acknowledgments of your
favours; my future behaviour muft convince you, I
am not undeferving of your good opinions.

FINALE.

L. Bell.	*My charmer's hand thus preffing,* *I'm ev'ry blifs poffeffing,* *In thee, my deareft love.*
Fan.	*My heart with joy overflowing,* *With gratitude now glowing,* *Shall ever humble prove.*
L. Lu.	*A fifter's love fincere,* *I hope you won't refufe.*
Sir John	*Not knowing who you were,* *Mademoifelle, pray excufe* ———
Kreigf.	*(She nicht Mamzell* *She is ein German—)*
Fan.	*I'll conftantly endeavour,* *To deferve your love and favour,* *Your affection and regard.*
Fin. Su.	*Forgive us, good my lady.*
Fan.	*Your pardon's feal'd already.*
Rob.	*Oh! pray forgive me too,* *For daring to love you;* *Forgive for charity.*
Fan.	*I thank, and will reward,* *Your care and honefty.*

CHORUS.

Love, when conftant hearts unite,
Rewards their pangs with true delight;
To make the gen'rous paffion laft,
Let truth, and virtue, bind it faft.

END OF THE OPERA.

[illegible]

Roberts del.   Publish'd for Bells British Theatre July 10 1781.   Thornthwait Sc

Mrs BADDELEY in the Character of CLARISSA.

"Can you forsake me?

LIONEL and CLARISSA:

OR, A

SCHOOL FOR FATHERS.

A COMIC OPERA.

AS IT IS PERFORMED AT THE

Theatre-Royal in Drury-Lane.

DISTINGUISHING ALSO THE

VARIATIONS OF THE THEATRE.

Regulated from the Prompt-Book,

By PERMISSION of the MANAGERS,

By Mr. HOPKINS, Prompter.

LONDON:

Printed for JOHN BELL, at the BRITISH LIBRARY in the *Strand.*

M DCC LXXXI.

ADVERTISEMENT.

HAVING, for some years, met with very great
success in my productions of the musical kind;
when I wrote the following opera, it was with unusual
care and attention; and it was the general opinion of all
my friends, some of whom rank among the best judges,
that of all my trifles, Lionel and Clarissa was the most
pardonable: a decision in its favour which I was the
prouder of, because, to the best of my knowledge,
through the whole, I had not borrowed an expression, a
sentiment, or a character, from any dramatic writer
extant.

When Mr. GARRICK thought of performing this piece
at Drury-lane theatre, he had a new singer to bring out,
and every thing possible for her advantage was to be
done; this necessarily occasioned some new songs and
airs to be introduced; and other singers, with voices of
a different compass from those who originally acted the
parts, occasioned still more; by which means the greatest
part of the music unavoidably became new. This is the
chief, and indeed the only alteration made in the opera;
and even to that, I should, in many places, have been
forced, much against my will, had it not given a fresh
opportunity to Mr. Dibdin to display his admirable
talents as a musical composer. And I will be bold to
say, that his airs, serious and comic, in this opera, will
appear to no disadvantage by being heard with those of
some of the greatest masters.

The SCHOOL FOR FATHERS is added to the
title, because the plot is evidently double; and that of
Lionel and Clarissa alluded to but one part of it, as the
readers and spectators will easily perceive.

J. B.

DRAMATIS PERSONÆ.

SIR JOHN FLOWERDALE,	MR. AICKIN.
COLONEL OLDBOY,	MR. PARSONS.
CLARISSA,	MRS. BADDELEY.
LIONEL,	MR. VERNON.
MR. JESSAMY,	MR. DODD.
LADY MARY OLDBOY,	MRS. HOPKINS,
DIANA,	MRS. WRIGHTEN,
HARMAN,	MR. FAWCET.
JENNY,	
JENKINS,	MR. BANNISTER.

SCENE, the COUNTRY.

LIONEL and CLARISSA.

ACT I. SCENE I.

A Chamber in Colonel OLDBOY's House: Colonel OLDBOY is discovered at breakfast reading a news-paper; at a little distance from the tea-table sits JENKINS; and on the opposite side DIANA, who appears playing upon a harpsicord. A Girl attending.

A. 2.

> *AH how delightful the morning,*
>   *How sweet are the prospects it yields;*
> *Summer luxuriant adorning*
>   *The gardens, the groves, and the fields.*
>
>   *Be grateful to the season,*
>   *It's pleasures let's employ;*
> *Kind Nature gives, and Reason*
>   *Permits us to enjoy.*

Col. Well said Dy, thank you Dy. This, master Jenkins, is the way I make my daughter entertain me every morning at breakfast. Come here and kiss me you slut, come here and kiss me you baggage.

Dian. Lord, papa, you call one such names——

Col. A fine girl, master Jenkins, a develish fine girl! she has got my eye to a twinkle. There's fire for you—spirit!—I design to marry her to a Duke: how much money do you think a Duke would expect with such a wench?

Jen.

Jen. Why, Colonel, with submission, I think there is no occasion to go out of our own country here; we have never a Duke in it I believe, but we have many an honest gentleman, who, in my opinion, might deserve the young lady.

Col. So, you would have me marry Dy to a country 'squire, eh! How say you to this Dy! would not you rather be married to a Duke?

Dian. So my husband's a rake, papa, I don't care what he is.

Col. A rake! you damned confounded little baggage; why you wou'd not wish to marry a rake, wou'd you? So her husband is a rake, she does not care what he is! Ha, ha, ha, ha!

Dian. Well, but listen to me, papa—When you go out with your gun, do you take any pleasure in shooting the poor tame ducks, and chickens in your yard? No, the partridge, the pheasant, the woodcock are the game; there is some sport in bringing them down because they are wild; and it is just the same with an husband or a lover. I would not waste powder and shot, to wound one of your sober pretty behaved gentlemen; but to hit a libertine, extravagant, madcap fellow, to take him upon the wing—

Col. Do you hear her, master Jenkins? Ha, ha, ha!

Jen. Well, but, good Colonel, what do you say to my worthy and honourable patron here, Sir John Flowerdale? He has an estate of eight thousand pounds a year as well paid rents as any in the kingdom, and but one only daughter to enjoy it; and yet he is willing, you see, to give this daughter to your son.

Dian. Pray, Mr. Jenkins, how does Miss Clarissa and our university friend Mr. Lionel? That is the only grave young man I ever liked, and the only handsome one I ever was acquainted with, that did not make love to me.

Col. Ay, master Jenkins, who is this Lionel? They say he is a damn'd witty knowing fellow; and egad I think him well enough for one brought up in a college.

Jen. His father was a general officer, a particular friend of Sir John's, who, like many more brave men, that live and die in defending their country, left little else than honour behind him. Sir John sent this young man, at

his

his own expence, to Oxford; where, while his son lived, they were upon the same footing: and since our young gentleman's death, which you know unfortunately happened about two years ago, he has continued him there. During the vacation he is come to pay us a visit, and Sir John intends that he shall shortly take orders for a very confiderable benefice in the gift of the family, the present incumbent of which is an aged man.

Dian. The last time I was at your house, he was teaching Miss Clarissa mathematics and philosophy. Lord, what a strange brain I have! If I was to sit down to distract myself with such studies—

Col. Go, hussey, let some of your brother's rascals inform their master that he has been long enough at his toilet; here is a message from Sir John Flowardale—— You a brain for mathematics indeed! We shall have women wanting to head our regiments to-morrow or next day.

Dian. Well, papa, and suppose we did. I believe, in a battle of the sexes, you men would hardly get the better of us.

To rob them of strength, when wise Nature thought fit
   By women to still do her duty,
Instead of a sword she indu'd them with wit,
  And gave them a shield in their beauty.

Sound, sound then the trumpet, both sexes to arms!
   Our tyrants at once and protectors!
We quickly shall see, whether courage or charms,
  Decide for the Helens or Hectors.

SCENE II.

Colonel OLDBOY, JENKINS.

Col. Well, master Jenkins! don't you think now that a Nobleman, a Duke, an Earl, or a Marquis, might be content to share his title—I say, you understand me—— with a sweetener of thirty or forty thousand pounds, to pay off mortgages? Besides, there's a prospect of my whole eftate ; for I dare fwear, her brother will never have any children.

Jen. I fhould be concerned at that, Colonel, when there are two fuch fortunes to defcend to his heirs, as yours and Sir John Flowerdale's

Col. Why look you, mafter Jenkins, Sir John Flowerdale is an honeft gentleman ; our families are nearly related ; we have been neighbours time out of mind ; and if he and I have an odd difpute now and then, it is not for want of a cordial efteem at bottom. He is going to marry his daughter to my fon ; fhe is a beautiful girl, an elegant girl, a fenfible girl, a worthy girl, and—a word in your ear—damn me if I ant very forry for her.

Jen. Sorry ! Colonel ?

Col. Ay——between ourfelves, mafter Jenkins, my fon won't do.

Jen. How do you mean ?

Col. I tell you, mafter Jenkins, he won't do—he is not the thing, a prig——At fixteen years old, or thereabouts, he was a bold, fprightly boy, as you fhould fee in a thoufand ; could drink his pint of port, or his bottle of claret——now he mixes all his wine with water.

Jen. Oh ! if that be his only fault, Colonel, he will ne'er make the worfe hufband, I'll anfwer for it.

Col. You know my wife is a woman of quality—— I was prevailed upon to fend him to be brought up by her brother Lord Jeffamy, who had no children of his own, and promifed to leave him an eftate——he has got the eftate indeed, but, the fellow has taken his Lordfhip's name for it. Now, mafter Jenkins, I would be glad to know, how the name of Jeffamy is better than that of Oldboy.

Jen. Well ! but, Colonel, it is allowed on all hands that his Lordfhip has given your fon an excellent education.

Col. Pfha ! he fent him to the univerfity, and to travel forfooth ; but what of that ; I was abroad, and at the univerfity myfelf, and never a rufh the better for either. I quarelled with his Lordfhip about fix years before his death, and fo had not an opportunity of feeing how the youth went on ; if I had, mafter Jenkins, I would no more have fuffered him to be made fuch a monkey of——

He

He has been in my houfe but three days, and it is all turned topfy turvey by him and his rafcally fervants——then his chamber is like a perfumer's fhop, with wafh-balls, paftes, and pomatum——and do you know he had the impudence to tell me yefterday at my own table, that I did not know how to behave myfelf?

Jen. Pray, Colonel, how does my Lady Mary?

Col. What my wife? In the old way, mafter Jenkins; always complaining; ever fomething the matter with her head, or her back, or her legs——but we have had the devil to pay lately—fhe and I did not fpeak to one another for three weeks.

Jen. How fo, Sir?

Col. A little affair of jealoufy—you muft know my game-keeper's daughter has had a child, and the plaguy baggage takes it into her head to lay it to me—Upon my foul it is a fine fat chubby infant as ever I fet my eyes on; I have fent it to nurfe; and between you and me, I believe I fhall leave it a fortune.

Jen. Ah, Colonel, you will never give over.

Col. You know my Lady has a pretty vein of poetry; fhe writ me an heroic epiftle upon it, where fhe calls me her dear falfe Damon; fo I let her cry a little, promifed to do fo no more, and now we are as good friends as ever.

Jen. Well, Colonel, I muft take my leave; I have delivered my meffage, and Sir John may expect the plea-fure of your company to dinner.

Col. Ay, ay, we'll come—pox o' ceremony among friends. But won't you ftay to fee my fon; I have fent to him, and fuppofe he will be here as foon as his valet-de-chambre will give him leave.

Jen. There is no occafion, good Sir: prefent my hum-ble refpects, that's all.

Col. Well, but, zounds, Jenkins, you muft not go till you drink fomething—let you and I have a bottle of hock—

Jen. Not for the world, Colonel; I never touch any thing ftrong in the morning.

Col. Never touch any thing ftrong! Why one bottle won't hurt you man, this is old and as mild as milk.

Jen. Well, but, Colonel, pray excufe me.

To

To tell you the truth,
In the days of my youth,
   As mirth and nature bid,
I lik'd a glass,
And I lov'd a lass,
   And I did as younkers did.

But now I am old,
With grief be it told, .
   I must those freaks forbear ;
At sixty-three,
'Twixt you and me,
   A man grows worse for wear.

S C E N E III.

Mr. JESSAMY, *Lady* MARY OLDBOY, *and then Colonel*
OLDBOY.

Lady M. Shut the door, why don't you shut the door
there ? Have you a mind I should catch my death ?
This house is absolutely the cave of Æolus ; one had as
good live on the eddy stone, or in a wind-mill.

Mr. Jeſſ. I thought they told your Ladyship that there
was a messenger here from Sir John Flowerdale.

Col. Well, Sir, and so there was ; but he had not patience to wait upon your curling-irons. Mr. Jenkins was
here, Sir John Flowerdale's steward, who has lived in
the family these forty years.

Mr. Jeſſ. And pray, Sir, might not Sir John Flowerdale have come himself : if he had been acquainted with
the rules of good breeding, he would have known that I
ought have been visited.

Lady M. Upon my word, Colonel, this is a solecism.

Col. 'Sblood, my Lady, it's none. Sir John Flowerdale came but last night from his sister's seat in the west,
and is a little out of order. But I suppose he thinks he
ought to appear before him with his daughter in one
hand, and his rent roll in the other, and cry, Sir, pray
do me the favour to accept them.

Lady M. Nay, but, Mr. Oldboy, permit me to say—

Col.

Col. He need not give himfelf fo many affected airs ; I think it's very well if he gets fuch a girl for going for ; fhe's one of the handfomeft and richeft in this country, and more than he deferves.

Mr. Jeff. That's an exceeding fine china jar your Ladyfhip has got in the next room ; I faw the fellow of it the other day at Williams's, and will fend to my agent to purchafe it : it is the true matchlefs old blue and white. Lady Betty Barebones has a couple that fhe gave an hundred guineas for, on board an Indiaman ; but fhe reckons them at a hundred and twenty-five, on account of half a dozen plates, four Nankeen beakers, and a couple of fhaking Mandarins, that the cuftom-houfe officers took from under her petticoats.

Col. Did you ever hear the like of this ! He's chattering about old china, while I am talking to him of a fine girl. I tell you what, Mr. Jeffamy, fince that's the name you choofe to be called by, I have a good mind to knock you down.

Mr. Jeff. Knock me down ! Colonel ? What do you mean ? I muft tell you, Sir, this is a language to which I have not been accuftomed ; and, if you think proper to continue to repeat it, I fhall be under a neceffity of quitting your houfe ?

Col. Quitting my houfe ?

Mr. Jeff. Yes, Sir, incontinently.

Col. Why, Sir, am not I your father, Sir, and have I not a right to talk to you as I like ? I will, firrah. But, perhaps, I mayn't be your father, and I hope not.

Lady M. Heavens and earth, Mr. Oldboy !

Col. What's the matter, Madam ! I mean, Madam, that he might have been changed at nurfe, Madam ; and I believe he was.

Mr. Jeff. Huh ! huh ! huh !

Col. Do you laugh at me, you faucy jackanapes !

Lady M. Who's there, fomebody bring me a chair. Really, Mr. Oldboy, you throw my weakly frame into fuch repeated convulfions—but I fee your aim ; you want to lay me in my grave, and you will very foon have that fatisfaction.

Col. I can't bear the fight of him.

Lady M. Open that window, give me air, or I fhall faint.

Mr.

Mr. Jeff. Hold, hold, let me tie a handkerchief about my neck firſt. This curſed ſharp north wind—Antoine, bring down my muff.

Col. Ay, do, and his great-coat.

Lady M. Marg'ret ſome harts-horn. My dear Mr. Oldboy why will you fly out in this way, when you know how it ſhocks my tender nerves?

Col. 'Sblood, Madam, its enough to make a man mad.

Lady. M. Hartſhorn! Hartſhorn!

Mr. Jeff. Colonel!

Col. Do you hear the puppy?

Mr. Jeff. Will you give me leave to aſk you one queſ-tion?

Col. I don't know whether I will or not.

Mr. Jeff. I ſhould be glad to know, that's all, what ſingle circumſtance in my conduct, carriage, or figure you can poſſibly find fault with—Perhaps I may be brought to reform—Pr'ythee let me hear from your own mouth, then, ſeriouſly what it is you do like, and what it is you do not like.

Col. Hum!

Mr. Jeff. Be ingenuous, ſpeak and ſpare not.

Col. You would know?

Zounds Sir! then I'll tell you without any jeſt,
The thing of all things, which I hate and deteſt;
　　A coxcomb, a fop,
　　A dainty milk-ſop;
Who, eſſenc'd and dizen'd from bottom to top,
Looks juſt like a doll for a milliner's ſhop.
　　A thing full of prate,
　　And pride and conceit;
　　All faſhion, no weight;
　　Who ſhrugs and takes ſnuff,
　　And carries a muff;
　　　A minikin,
　　　Finiking,
　　French powder-puff:
And now Sir, I fancy, I've told you enough.

SCENE

SCENE IV.

Lady MARY OLDBOY, *Mr.* JESSAMY.

Mr. Jeff. What's the matter with the Colonel, Madam; does your ladyfhip know?

Lady M. Heigho! don't be furprifed, my dear; it was the fame thing with my late dear brother, Lord Jeffamy; they never could agree: that good natured friendly foul, knowing the delicacy of my conftitution, has often faid, fifter, Mary, I pity you. Not but your father has good qualities, and I affure you I remember him a very fine gentleman himfelf. In the year of the hard froft, one thoufand feven hundred and thirty-nine, when he firft paid his addreffes to me, he was called agreeable Jack Oldboy, though I married him without the confent of your noble grandfather.

Mr. Jeff. I think he ought to be proud of me: I believe there's many a Duke, nay Prince, who would efteem themfelves happy in having fuch a fon——

Lady M. Yes, my dear; but your fifter was always your father's favourite: he intends to give her a prodigious fortune, and fets his heart upon feeing her a woman of quality.

Mr. Jeff. He fhould wifh to fee her look a little like a gentlewoman firft. When fhe was in London laft winter, I am told fhe was taken notice of by a few men; But fhe wants air, manner——

Lady M. And has not a bit of the genius of our family, and I never knew a woman of it but herfelf without. I have tried her: about three years ago I fet her to tranflate a little French fong: I found fhe had not even an idea of verfification; and fhe put down love and joy for rhyme—fo I gave her over.

Mr. Jeff. Why, indeed, fhe appears to have more of the Thaleftris than the Sapho about her.

Lady M. Well, my dear, I muft go and drefs myfelf, though I proteft I am fitter for my bed than my coach. And condefcend to the Colonel a little—Do my dear, if it be only to oblige your mamma.

SCENE V.

Mr. Jessamy.

Let me confider: I am going to vifit a country Baronet here: who would fain prevail upon me to marry his daughter: the old gentleman has heard of my parts and underftanding, Mifs of my figure and addrefs. But, fuppofe I fhould not like her when I fee her? Why, pofitively, then I will not have her; the treaty's at an end, and, fans compliment, we break up the congrefs. But, won't that be cruel, after having fuffered her to flatter herfelf with hopes, and fhewing myfelf to her. She's a ftrange dowdy I dare believe: however, fhe brings provifion with her for a feparate maintenance.

Antoine, appretez la toilet. I am going to fpend a curfed day, that I perceive already; I wifh it was over, I dread it as much as a general election.

When a man of fafhion condefcends,
To herd among his country friends,
 They watch his looks, his motions:
One booby gapes, another ftares,
And all he fays, does, eats, drinks, wears,
 Muft fuit their ruftic notions.

But as for this bruitifh old clown here;
S'death, why did I ever come down here!
 The favage will now never quit me:
  Then a confort to take,
  For my family's fake,
I'm in a fine jeopardy, fplit me!

SCENE VI.

Changes to a Study in Sir John Flowerdale's *Houfe; two Chairs and a Table, with Globes and Mathematical Inftruments.* Clarissa *enters, followed by* Jenny.

Clar.   *Immortal pow'rs protect me,*
   Affift, fupport, direct me;

Relieve

Relieve a heart oppreſt:
Ah! why this palpitation!
Ceaſe buſy perturbation,
And let me, let me reſt.

Jen. My dear lady, what ails you?

Clar. Nothing Jenny, nothing.

Jen. Pardon me, Madam, there is ſomething ails you indeed. Lord! what ſignifies all the grandeur and riches in this world, if they can't procure one content. I am ſure it vexes me to the heart, ſo it does, to ſee ſuch a dear, ſweet, worthy young Lady, as you are, pining yourſelf to death.

Clar. Jenny, you are a good girl, and I am very much obliged to you for feeling ſo much on my account; but in a little time, I hope I ſhall be eaſier.

Jen. Why, now, here to day, Madam, for ſartain you ought to be merry to day, when there's a fine gentleman coming to court you; but, if you like any one elſe better, I am ſure, I wiſh you had him, with all my ſoul.

Clar. Suppoſe, Jenny, I was ſo unfortunate, as to like a man without my father's approbation; would you wiſh me married to him?

Jen. I wiſh you married to any one, Madam, that could make you happy.

Clar. Heigho!

Jen. Madam! Madam! yonder's Sir John and Mr. Lionel on the terras: I believe they are coming up here. Poor, dear Mr. Lionel, he does not ſeem to be in over great ſpirits either. To be ſure, Madam, it's no buſineſs of mine; but, I believe, if the truth was known, there are thoſe in the houſe, who wou'd give more than ever I ſhall be worth, or any the likes of me, to prevent the marriage of a ſartain perſon that ſhall be nameleſs.

Clar. What do you mean? I don't underſtand you.

Jen. I hope you are not angry, Madam?

Clar. Ah! Jenny ——

Jen. Lauk! Madam, do you think, when Mr. Lionel's a clergyman, he'll be obliged to cut off his hair? I'm ſure it will be a thouſand pities, for it is the ſweeteſt colour, and looks the niceſt put up in a cue—and your

great

great pudding-sleeves! Lord! they'll quite spoil his shape, and the fall of his shoulders. Well! Madam, if I was a lady of large fortune, I'll be hanged if Mr. Lionel should be a parson, if I could help it.

Clar. I'm going into my dressing-room—It seems then Mr. Lionel is a great favourite of yours; but, pray Jenny, have a care how you talk in this manner to any one else.

Jan. Me talk! Madam, I thought you knew me better; and, my dear Lady, keep up your spirits. I'm sure I have dressed you to day as nice as hands and pins can make you.

I'm but a poor servant 'tis true, Ma'am;
But was I a lady like you, Ma'am;
In grief would I sit! The dickens a bit;
No faith, I would search the world thro' Ma'am,
To find what my liking could hit.

Set in case a young man,
In my fancy there ran;
It might anger my friends and relations:
But, if I had regard,
It should go very hard,
Or I'd follow my own inclinations.

SCENE VII.

Sir JOHN FLOWERDALE, LIONEL.

Sir John. Indeed, Lionel, I will not hear of it. What! to run from us all of a sudden, this way; and at such a time too; the eve of my daughter's wedding, as I may call it; when your company must be doubly agreeable, as well as necessary to us? I am sure you have no studies at present, that require your attendance at Oxford: I must, therefore, insist on your putting such thoughts out of your head.

Lion. Upon my word, Sir, I have been so long from the university, that it is time for me to think of returning. It is true, I have no absolute studies; but, really,

Sir,

Sir, I fhall be obliged to you, if you will give me leave to go.

Sir John. Come, come, my dear Lionel, I have for fome time obferved a more than ordinary gravity growing upon you, and I am not to learn the reafon of it: I know, to minds ferious, and well inclined, like yours, the facred functions you are about to embrace——

Lion. Dear Sir, your goodnefs to me, of every kind, is fo great, fo unremitted! Your condefcenfion, your friendly attentions—in fhort, Sir, I want words to exprefs my fenfe of obligations——

Sir John. Fie, fie, no more of them. By my laft letters, I find that my old friend, the rector, ftill continues in good health, confidering his advanced years. You may imagine I am far from defiring the death of fo worthy and pious a man; yet, I muft, own, at this time, I could wifh you were in orders, as you might then perform the ceremony of my daughter's marriage; which would give me a fecret fatisfaction.

Lion. No doubt, Sir, any office in my power, that could be inftrumental to the happinefs of any in your family, I fhould perform with pleafure.

Sir John. Why, really, Lionel, from the character of her intended hufband, I have no room to doubt, but this match will make Clariffa perfectly happy: to be fure, the alliance is the moft eligible, for both families.

Lion. If the gentleman is fenfible of his happinefs in the alliance, Sir.

Sir John. The fondnefs of a father is always fufpected of partiality; yet, I believe, I may venture to fay, that few young women will be found more unexceptionable than my daughter: her perfon is agreeable, her temper fweet, her underftanding good; and, with the obligations fhe has to your inftruction——

Lion. You do my endeavours too much honour, Sir; I have been able to add nothing to Mifs Flowerdale's accomplifhments, but a little knowledge in matters of fmall importance to a mind already fo well improved.

Sir John. I don't think fo; a little knowledge, even in thofe matters, is neceffary for a woman, in whom, I am far from confidering ignorance as a defireable characteriftic: when intelligence is not attended with impertinent

 affectation,

affectation, it teaches them to judge with precifion, and gives them a degree of folidity neceffary for the companion of a fenfible man.

Lion. Yonder's Mr. Jenkins: I fancy he's looking for you, Sir.

Sir John. I fee him; he's come back from Colonel Oldboy's; I have a few words to fay to him; and will return to you again in a minute.

S C E N E VIII.

LIONEL : *afterwards* CLARISSA, *and then* JENNY, *who enters abruptly and runs out again.*

Lion. To be a burthen to one's felf, to wage continual war with one's own paffions, forced to combat, unable to overcome! But fee, fhe appears, whofe prefence turns all my fufferings into tranfport, and makes even mifery itfelf delightful.

Perhaps, Madam, you are not at leifure now; otherwife, if you thought proper, we would refume the fubject we were upon yefterday.

Clar. I am fure, Sir, I give you a great deal of trouble.

Lion. Madam you give me no trouble; I fhould think every hour of my life happily employed in your fervice; and as this is probably the laft time I fhall have the fatisfaction of attending you upon the fame occafion——

Clar. Upon my word, Mr. Lionel, I think myfelf extremely obliged to you; and fhall ever confider the enjoyment of your friendfhip——

Lion. My friendfhip, Madam, can be of little moment to you; but if the moft perfect adoration, if the warmeft wifhes for your felicity, though I fhould never be witnefs of it: if thefe, Madam, can have any merit to continue in your remembrance, a man once honoured with a fhare of your efteem——

Clar. Hold Sir—I think I hear fomebody.

Lion. If you pleafe, Madam, we will turn over this celeftial globe once more—Have you looked at the book I left you yefterday?

Clar.

Clar. Really, Sir, I have been so much disturbed in my thoughts for these two or three days past, that I have not been able to look at any thing.

Lion. I am sorry to hear that Madam; I hope there was nothing particular to disturb you. The care Sir John takes to dispose of your hand in a manner suitable to your birth and fortune.

Clar. I don't know, Sir;—I own I am disturbed; I own I am uneasy; there is something weighs upon my heart, which I would fain disclose.

Lion. Upon your heart, Madam! did you say your heart?

Clar. I did, Sir,—I——

Jen. Madam! Madam! Here's a coach and six driving up the avenue: It's Colonel Oldboy's family; and, I believe the gentleman is in it, that's coming to court you.—Lord, I must run and have a peep at him out of the window.

Lion. Madam, I'll take my leave.

Clar. Why so Sir?—Bless me, Mr. Lionel, what's the matter!—You turn pale.

Lion. Madam!

Clar. Pray speak to me, Sir.—You tremble:—Tell me the cause of this sudden change.—How are you.—. Where's your disorder?

Lion. Oh fortune! fortune!

> *You ask me in vain,*
> *Of what ills I complain,*
> *Where harbours the torment I find;*
> *In my head, in my heart,*
> *It invades ev'ry part,*
> *And subdues both my body and mind.*
>
> *Each effort I try,*
> *Ev'ry med'cine apply,*
> *The pangs of my soul to appease;*
> *But doom'd to endure,*
> *What I mean for a cure,*
> *Turns prison and feeds the disease.*

 SCENE

SCENE IX.

CLARISSA, DIANA.

Dian. My dear Clariſſa—I'm glad I have found you alone.—For Heaven's ſake, don't let any one break in upon us ;—and give me leave to ſit down with you a little :—I am in ſuch a tremour, ſuch a panic.—

Clar. Mercy on us, what has happened ?

Dian. You may remember I told you, that when I was laſt winter in London, I was followed by an odious fellow, one Harman ; I can't ſay but the wretch pleaſed me, though he is but a younger brother, and not worth ſix pence : And—in ſhort, when I was leaving town, I promiſed to correſpond with him.

Clar. Do you think that was prudent ?

Dian. Madneſs ! But this is not the worſt ; for what do you think, the creature had the aſſurance to write to me about three weeks ago, deſiring permiſſion to come down and ſpend the ſummer at my father's.

Clar. At your father's !

Dian. Ay, who never ſaw him, knows nothing of him, and would as ſoon conſent to my marrying a horſe jockey. He told me a long ſtory of ſome tale he intended to invent to make my father receive him as an indifferent perſon ; and ſome gentlemen in London, he ſaid, would procure him a letter that ſhould give it a face ; and he longed to ſee me ſo, he ſaid, he could not live without it ; and if he could be permitted but to ſpend a week with me ——

Clar. Well, and what anſwer did you make ?

Dian. Oh ! abuſed him, and refuſed to liſten to any ſuch thing—But—I vow I tremble while I tell it you— Juſt before we left our houſe, the impudent monſter arrived there, attended by a couple of ſervants, and is now actually coming here with my father.

Clar. Upon my word, this is a dreadful thing.

Dian Dreadful, my dear !—I happened to be at the window as he came into the court, and I declare I had like to have fainted away.

Car. Isn't my Lady below ?

Dian.

Dian. Yes, and I muſt run down to her. You'll have my brother here preſently too, he would fain have come in the coach with my mother and me, but my father inſiſted on his walking with him over the fields.

Clar. Well, Diana, with regard to your affair—I think you muſt find ſome method of immediately informing this gentleman that you conſider the outrage he has committed againſt you in the moſt heinous light, and inſiſt upon his going away directly.

Dian. Why, I believe that will be the beſt way—— but then he'll be begging my pardon and aſking to ſtay.

Clar. Why then you muſt tell him poſitively you won't conſent to it; and if he perſiſts in ſo extravagant a deſign, tell him you'll never ſee him again as long as you live.

Dian. Muſt I tell him ſo ?

Ah ! pr'ythee ſpare me, deareſt creature !
How can you prompt me to ſo much ill-nature ?
Kneeling before me,
Shou'd I hear him implore me ;
Cou'd I accuſe him,
Cou'd I refuſe him
The boon he ſhou'd aſk ?
Set not a lover the cruel taſk.

No, believe me, my dear,
Was he now ſtanding here,
In ſpite of my frights, and alarms
I might rate him, might ſcold him——
But ſhou'd ſtill ſtrive to hold him——
And ſink at laſt into his arms.

SCENE X.

CLARISSA.

How eaſy to direct the conduct of others, how hard to regulate our own ! I can give my friend advice, while I am conſcious of the ſame indiſcretions in myſelf. Yet is it criminal to know the moſt worthy, moſt amiable man in the world, and not to be infenfible to his merit? But my father, the kindeft, beft of fathers, will he approve the choice I have made? Nay, has he not made another choice for me? And, after all, how can I be fure that the man I love, loves me again? He never told me fo; but his looks, his actions, his prefent anxiety fufficiently declare what his delicacy, his generofity, will not fuffer him to utter.——

Ye gloomy thoughts, ye fears perverfe,
Like fullen vapours all difperfe,
And fcatter in the wind;

Delufive phantoms, brood of night,
No more my fickly fancy fright,
No more my reafon blind:

'Tis done; I feel my foul releas'd;
The vifions fly, the mifts are chas'd,
Nor leave a cloud behind.

SCENE XI.

Changes to a Side View of Sir JOHN FLOWERDALE's *Houfe, with Gates, and a Profpect of the Garden.*

HARMAN *enters with Colonel* OLDBOY.

Col. Well, and how does my old friend Dick Rantum do? I have not feen him thefe twelve years: he was an honeft worthy fellow as ever breathed; I remember he kept a girl in London, and was curfedly plagued by his wife's relations.

Har. Sir Richard was always a man of fpirit, Colonel.

Col. But as to this bufinefs of yours, which he tells me of in his letter—I don't fee much in it—An affair with a citizen's daughter—pinked her brother in a duel— Is the fellow likely to die?

Har. Why, Sir, we hope not; but as the matter is dubious, and will probably make fome noife, I thought it was better to be for a little time out of the way; when

hearing

hearing my cafe Sir Richard Rantum mentioned you; he faid, he was fure you would permit me to remain at your houfe for a few days, and offered me a recommendation.

Col. And there's likely to be a brat in the cafe—And the girl's friends are in bufinefs—I'll tell you what will be the confequence then—They will be for going to law with you for a maintenance—but no matter, I'll take the affair in hand for you—make me your folicitor; and, if you are obliged to pay for a fingle fpoonful of pap, I'll be content to father all the children in the Foundling Hofpital.

Har. You are very kind, Sir.

Col. But hold—hark you—you fay there's money to be had—fuppofe you were to marry the wench?

Har. Do you think, Sir, that would be fo right after what has happened? Befides, there's a ftronger objection—To tell you the truth, I am honourably in love in another place.

Col. Oh! you are.

Har. Yes, Sir, but there are obftacles—A father—In fhort, Sir, the miftrefs of my heart lives in this very county, which makes even my prefent fituation a little irkfome.

Col. In this county! Zounds! Then I am fure I am acquainted with her, and the firft letter of her name is——

Har. Excufe me, Sir, I have fome particular reafons——

Col. But look who comes yonder—Ha! ha! ha! My fon picking his fteps like a dancing-mafter. Pr'ythee, Harman, go into the houfe, and let my wife and daughter know we are come, while I go and have fome fport with him: they will introduce you to Sir John Flowerdale.

Har. Then, Sir, I'll take the liberty——

Col. But d'ye hear, I muft have a little more difcourfe with you about this girl; perhaps fhe's a neighbour of mine, and I may be of fervice to you.

Har. Well, remember Colonel I fhall try your friendfhip.

Indulgent

Indulgent pow'rs, if ever
You mark'd a tender vow,
O bend in kind compaſſion,
And hear a lover now :

For titles, wealth, and honours,
While others crowd your ſhrine ;
I aſk this only bleſſing,
Let her I love be mine.

SCENE XII.

Colonel OLDBOY, *Mr.* JESSAMY, *and ſeveral Servants.*

Col. Why, Zounds ! one would think you had never
put your feet to the ground before ; you make as much
work about walking a quarter of a mile, as if you had
gone a pilgrimage to Jeruſalem.

Mr. Jeſſ. Colonel, you have uſed me extremely ill, to
drag me through the dirty roads in this manner; you
told me the way was all over a bowling-green ; only ſee
what a condition I am in !

Col. Why, how did I know the roads were dirty ? is
that my fault ? Beſides, we miſtook the way. Zounds,
man, your legs will be never the worſe when they are
bruſhed a little.

Mr. Jeſſ. Antoine ! have you ſent La Roque for the
ſhoes and ſtockings ? Give me the glaſs out of your pocket—not a duſt of powder left in my hair, and the friſ-
ſure as flat as the fore-top of an attorney's clerk—get
your comb and pomatum ; you muſt borrow ſome powder ; I ſuppoſe there's ſuch a thing as a dreſſing-room in
the houſe ?

Col. Ay, and a cellar too, I hope, for I want a glaſs
of wine curſedly—but hold ! hold ! Frank, where are
you going ? Stay, and pay your devoirs here, if you
pleaſe ; I ſee there's ſomebody coming out to welcome us.

SCENE

SCENE XIII.

Colonel OLDBOY, *Mr.* JESSAMY, LIONEL, DIANA,
CLARISSA.

Lion. Colonel your moſt obedient ; Sir John is walking with my Lady in the garden, and has commiſſioned
me to receive you.

Col. Mr. Lionel, I am heartily glad to ſee you—come
here, Frank—this is my ſon, Sir.

Lion. Sir, I am exceeding proud to——

Mr. Jeſſ. Can't you get the powder then ?

Col. Miſs Clary, my little Miſs Clary—give me a kiſs
my dear—as handſome as an angel by heavens—Frank,
why don't you come here ? this is Miſs Flowerdale.

Dian. Oh Heavens Clariſſa! Juſt as I ſaid, that impudent devil is come here with my father.

Mr. Jeſſ. Had'nt we better go into the houſe ?

	To be made in ſuch a pickle !
	Will you pleaſe to lead the way, Sir ?
Col.——	*No, but if you pleaſe, you may Sir,.*
	For precedence none will ſticle.
Dian.——	*Brother, no politeneſs ? Bleſs me !*
	Will you not your hand beſtow ?
	Lead the Lady.
Clar.——	——————*Don't diſtreſs me;*
	Dear Diana let him go.
Mr. Jeſſ.	*Ma'am permit me.*
Col.——	—————————*Smoke the beau.*
A. 2.	*Cruel muſt I, can I bear ;*
	Oh adverſe ſtars!
	Oh fate ſevere !
	Eaſet, tormented,
	Each hope prevented :
Col.	*Non but the brave deſerve the fair,*
	Come Ma'am let me lead you :
	Now, Sir, I precede you.
A. 5.	*Lovers muſt ill uſage bear.*
	Oh adverſe ſtars! oh fate ſevere !
	None but the brave deſerve the fair.

A C T

ACT II. SCENE I.

A Hall, in Sir John FLOWERDALE'S *House, with the View of a grand Stair-case, through an Arch. On either Side of the Stair-case below, two Doors, leading from different Apartments.*

LIONEL *enters followed by* JENNY.

Jen. Well, but Mr. Lionel, confider, pray confider now; how can you be fo prodigious undifcreet as you are, walking about the hall here, while the gentlefolks are within in the parlour! Don't you think they'll wonder at your getting up fo foon after dinner, and before any of the reft of the company?

Lion. For Heaven's fake, Jenny, don't fpeak to me: I neither know where I am, nor what I am doing; I am the moft wretched and miferable of mankind.

Jen. Poor dear foul I pity you. Yes, yes, I believe you are miferable enough indeed; and I affure you I have pitied you a great while, and fpoke many a word in your favour, when you little thought you had fuch a friend in a corner.

Lion. But, good Jenny, fince, by fome accident or other, you have been able to difcover what I would willingly hide from all the world; I conjure you, as you regard my intereft, as you value your Lady's peace and honour, never let the moft diftant hint of it efcape you; for it is a fecret of that importance—

Jen. And, perhaps, you think I can't keep a fecret. Ah! Mr. Lionel, it muft be hear, fee, and fay nothing in this world, or one has no bufinefs to live in it; befides who would not be in love with my Lady? There's never a man this day alive but might be proud of it; for fhe is

the

the handfomeft, fweeteft temperdeft! And I am fure one of the beft miftreffes, ever poor girl had.

Lion. Oh Jenny! She's an angel.

Jen. And fo fhe is indeed—Do you know that fhe gave me her blue and filver fack to day, and it is every crum as good as new; and, go things as they will, don't you be fretting and vexing yourfelf, for I am mortally fartain fhe would liverer fee a toad than this Jeffamy. Though I muft fay, to my thinking, he's a very likely man; and a finer pair of eye-brows, and a more delicate nofe I never faw on a face.

Lion. By Heavens I fhall run mad.

Jen. And why fo? It is not beauty that always takes the fancy: moreover, to let you know, if it was, I don't think him any more to compare to you, than a thiftle is to a carnation: and fo's a fign; for, mark my words, my Lady loves you, as much as fhe hates him.

Lion. What you tell me, Jenny, is a thing I neither merit nor expect: No, I am unhappy, and let me continue fo; my moft prefumptuous thoughts fhall never carry me to a wifh that may affect her quiet, or give her caufe to repent.

Jen. That's very honourable of you I muft needs fay! but for all that, liking's liking, and one can't help it; and if it fhould be my Lady's cafe it is no fault of yours. I am fure, when fhe called me into her dreffing-room, before fhe went down to dinner, there fhe ftood with her eyes brim full of tears; and fo I fell a crying for company—and then fhe faid fhe could not abide the chap in the parlour; and at the fame time, fhe bid me take an opportunity to fpeak to you, and defire you to meet her in the garden this evening after tea; for fhe has fomething to fay to you.

Lion. Jenny, I fee you are my friend; for which I thank you, though I know it is impoffible to do me any fervice; take this ring and wear it for my fake.

Jen. I am very much obliged to your honour; I am your friend indeed—but, I fay, you won't forget to be in the garden now; and in the mean time keep as little in the houfe as you can, for walls have eyes and ears; and I can tell you the fervants take notice of your uneafinefs, tho' I am always defiring them to mind their own bufinefs.

Lion.

Lion. Pray have a care Jenny, have a care my dear girl, a word may breed fufpicion.

Jen. Pſha ! have a care yourfelf; it is you that breeds fufpicion, fighing and pining about ; you look for all the world like a ghoſt ; and if you don't pluck up your fpirits you will be a ghoſt foon ; letting things get the better of you.   Though to be fure when I thinks with myfelf, being crofs'd in love is a terrible thing—There was a young man in the town where I was born made away with himſelf upon the account of it.

Lion. Things ſhan't get the better of me Jenny.

Jen. No more they don't ought.   And once again I fay, fortune is thrown in your diſh and you are not to fling it out ; my Lady's eſtate will be better than three biſhopricks if Sir John could give them to you.   Think of that Mr. Lionel, think of that.

Lion. Think of what ?

Oh talk not to me of the wealth ſhe poſſeſſes,
My hopes and my views to herſelf I confine ;
The ſplendour of riches but ſlightly impreſſes
A heart that is fraught with a paſſion like mine.

By love, only love, ſhould our ſouls be cemented ;
No int'reſt, no motive, but that wou'd I own ;
With her in a cottage be bleſſ and contented,
And wretched without her, tho' placed on a throne.

SCENE II.

JENNY, *Colonel* OLDBOY.

Col. Very well, my Lady, I'll come again to you prefently, I am only going into the garden for a mouthful of air.   Aha ! my little Abigal ! Here Molly, Jenny, Betty ! What's your name ? Why don't you anfwer me, huſſey, when I call you ?

Jen. If you want any thing, Sir, e'll call one of the footmen.

Col. The footmen ! the footmen ! Damn me, I never knew one of them, in my life, that would'nt prefer a

raſcal

rafcal to a gentleman—Come here, you flut, put your hands about my neck and kifs me.

Jen. Who, I, Sir!

Col. Ay, here's money for you; what the devil are you afraid of? I'll take you into keeping; you fhall go and live at one of my tenant's houfes.

Jen. I wonder you are'nt afhamed, Sir, to make an honeft girl any fuch propofial; you that have a worthy gentlewoman, nay, a Lady of your own—To be fure fhe's a little ftricken in years; but why fhculdn't fhe grow elderly as well as yourfelf?

Col. Burn a lady, I love a pretty girl—

Jen. Well, then you may go look for one, Sir, I have no pretenfions to the title.

Col. Why, you pert baggage, you don't know me.

Jen. What do you pinch my fingers for? Yes, yes, I know you well enough, and your charekter's well known all over the country, running after poor young creatures as you do, to ruinate them.

Col. What, then people fay——

Jen. Indeed, they talk very bad of you; and whatever you may think, Sir, tho' I'm in a menial ftarion, I'm come of people that won'd'nt fee me put upon; there are thofe that wou'd take my part againft the proudeft he in the land, that fhould offer any thing un-civil.

Col. Well, come, let me know now, how does your young Lady like my fon?

Jen. You want to pump me do you? I fuppofe you would know whether I can keep my tongue within my teeth.

Col. She does'nt like him then?

Jen. I don't fay fo, Sir—Isn't this a fhame now—I fuppofe to-morrow or next day it will be reported that Jenny has been talking, Jenny faid that, and t'other— But here, Sir, I ax you, Did I tell you any fuch thing?

Col. Why yes, you did.

Jen. I!—Lord blefs me, how can you——

Col. Ad I'll mouzle you.

Jen. Ah! ah!

Col. What do you bawl for?

Jen. Ah! ah! ah!

D

Indeed,

Indeed, forfooth, a pretty youth,
'To play the am'rous fool;
At fuch an age, methinks your rage
Might be a little cool.

Fie, let me go, Sir.
Kifs me!—No, no, Sir.

You pull me and fhake me,
For what do you take me,
This figure to make me ?
I'd have you to know
I'm not for your game, Sir ;
Nor will I be tame, Sir.
Lord, have you no fhame, Sir,
To tumble one fo ?

SCENE III.

Colonel OLDBOY, *Lady* MARY, DIANA, HARMAN.

Lady M. Mr. Oldboy, won't you give me your hand to lead me up ftairs, my dear ?—Sir, I am prodigioufly obliged to you ; I proteft I have not been fo well, I don't know when : I have had no return of my bilious complaint after dinner to day ; and eat fo voracioufly ! Did you obferve Mifs ? Doctor Arfnic will be quite aftonifhed when he hears it ; furely his new invented medicine has done me a prodigious deal of fervice.

Col. Ah ! you'll always be taking one flop or other till you poifon yourfelf.

Lady M. It brought Sir Barnaby Drugg from death's door, after having tried the Spaw and Briftol waters without effect : it is good for feveral things, in many fovereign, as in colds and confumptions, and lownefs of fpirits ; it corrects the humours, rectifies the juices, regulates the nervous fyftem ; creates an appetite, prevents flufhings and ficknefs after meals ; as alfo vain fears and head-achs ; it is the fineft thing in the world for an

afthma ;

aſthma ; and no body that takes it, is ever troubled with hyſterics.

Col. Give me a pinch of your Lordſhip's ſnuff.

Lady. M. This is a mighty pretty ſort of man, Colonel, who is he !

. *Col.* A young fellow, my Lady; recommended to me.

Lady M. I proteſt he has the ſweeteſt taſte for poetry ! —He has repeated to me two or three of his own things ; and I have been telling him of the poem my late brother Lord Jeſſary made on the mouſe that was drowned.

Col. Ay, a fine ſubject for a poem ; a mouſe that was drowned in a——

Lady M. Huſh, my dear Colonel, don't mention it ; to be ſure the circumſtance was vaſtly indelicate ; but for the number of lines, the poem was as charming a morſel —I heard the Earl of Punley ſay, who underſtood Latin, that it was equal to any thing in Catullus.

Col. Well, how did you like your ſon's behaviour at dinner, Madam ? I thought the girl looked a little aſkew at him—Why, he found fault with every thing, and contradicted every body !

Lady M. Softly—Miſs Flowerdale I underſtand has deſired a private conference with him..

Col. What, Harman, have you got entertaining my daughter there ? Come hither, Dy.; has he been giving you a hiſtory of the accident that brought him down here ?

Dian. No, Papa, the gentleman has been telling he—

Lady M. No matter what Miſs—'tis not polite to repeat what has been ſaid.

Col. Well, well, my Lady, you know the compact we made ; the boy is yours, the girl mine——Give me your hand Dy.

Lady M. Colonel I have done—Pray, Sir, was there any news when you left London ; any thing about the Eaſt-Indies, the miniſtry, or politics of any kind ? I am ſtrangely fond of politics : but I hear nothing ſince my Lord Jeſſamy's death ; he uſed to write to me all the affairs of the nation, for he was a very great politician himſelf. I have a manuſcript ſpeech of his in my cabinet—He never ſpoke it, but it is as fine a thing as ever came from man ?

D 2

Col.

Col. What is that crawling on your Ladyſhip's petticoat ?

Lady M. Where! Where!

Col. Zounds ! a ſpider with legs as long as my arm.

Lady M. Oh Heavens! Ah don't let me look at it;
I ſhall faint, I ſhall faint ? A ſpider ! a ſpider ! a ſpider !

SCENE IV.

Colonel OLDBOY, DIANA, HARMAN.

Col. Hold; zounds let her go; I knew the ſpider
would ſet her a galloping, with her damned fuſs about
her brother my Lord Jeſſamy.—Harman come here.—
How do you like my daughter ? Is the girl you are in
love with as handſome as this ?

Har. In my opinion, Sir.

Col. What, as handſome as Dy !—I'll lay you twenty
pounds ſhe has not ſuch a pair of eyes.——He tells me
he's in love, Dy ; raging mad for love, and, by his talk,
I begin to believe him.

Dia. Now, for my part, Papa, I doubt it very much;
though, by what I heard the gentleman ſay juſt now
within, I find he imagines the lady has a violent partiality for him ; and yet he may be miſtaken there too.

Col. For ſhame, Dy, what the miſchief do you mean ?
How can you talk ſo tartly to a poor young fellow under misfortunes ? Give him your hand, and aſk his pardon.—Don't mind her, Harman.——For all this, ſhe is
as good-naturn'd a little devil, as ever was born.

Har. You may remember, Sir, I told you before dinner, that I had for ſome time carried on a private correſpondence with my lovely girl ; and that her father,
whoſe conſent we deſpair of obtaining, is the great ob-
ſtacle to our happineſs.

Col. Why don't you carry her off in ſpight of him,
then ?—I ran away with my wife—aſk my Lady Mary,
ſhe'll tell you the thing herſelf.—Her old conceited Lord
of a father thought I was not good enough ; but I
mounted a garden-wall, notwithſtanding their cheveux-
de-frize of broken glaſs bottles, took her out of a three

pair

pair of ſtairs window, and brought her down a ladder in my arms ——By the way, ſhe would have ſqueezed through a cat-hole to get at me.—And I would have taken her out of the Tower of London, damme, if it had been ſurrounded with the three regiments of guards.

Dia. But ſurely, Papa, you would not perſuade the gentleman to ſuch a proceeding as this is ; conſider the noiſe it will make in the country ; and if you are known to be the adviſer and abettor — -

Col. Why, what do I care ? I ſay, if he takes my advice he'll run away with her, and I'll give him all the aſſiſtance I can.

Har. I am ſure, Sir, you are very kind ; and, to tell you the truth, I have more than once had the very ſcheme in my head, if I thought it was feaſible, and knew how to go about it.

Col. Feaſible, and knew how to go about it ! The thing's feaſible enough, if the girl's willing to go off with you, and you have ſpirit ſufficient to undertake it.

Har. O, as for that, Sir, I can anſwer.

Dia. What, Sir, that the lady will be willing to go off with you ?

Har. No, Ma'am, that I have ſpirit enough to take her, if ſhe is willing to go ; and thus far I dare venture to promiſe, that between this and to-morrow morning I will find out whether ſhe is or not.

Col. So he may ; ſhe lives but in this county ; and tell her, Harman, you have met with a friend, who is inclined to ſerve you. You ſhall have my poſt-chaiſe at a minute's warning ; and if a hundred pieces will be of any uſe to you, you may command 'em.

Har. And you are really ſerious, Sir ?

Col. Serious ; damme if I an't. I have put twenty young fellows in the way of getting girls that they never would have thought of : and bring her to my houſe ; whenever you come you ſhall have a ſupper and a bed ; but you muſt marry her firſt, becauſe my Lady will be ſqueamiſh.

Dia. Well, but, my dear Papa, upon my word you have a great deal to anſwer for : ſuppoſe it was your own caſe to have a daughter in ſuch circumſtances, would you be obliged to any one—

D 3

Col.

Col. Hold your tongue, huffy, who bid you put in your oar ? However, Harman, I don't want to fet you upon any thing ; 'tis no affair of mine to be fure ; I only give you advice, and tell you how I would act if I was in your place.

Har. I affure you, Sir, I am quite charm'd with the advice ; and fince you are ready to ftand my friend, I am determined to follow it.

Col. You are———

Har. Pofitively———

Col. Say no more then ; here's my hand :—You un‑ derftand me—No occafion to talk any further of it at pre‑ fent—When we are alone—Dy, take Mr. Harman into the drawing-room, and give him fome tea.—I fay, Har‑ man, Mum.—

Har. O, Sir.

Col. What do you mean by your grave looks, mi‑ ftrefs ?

How curfedly vext the old fellow will be,
  When he finds you have fnapt up his daughter ;
But fhift as he will, leave the matter to me,
  And I warrant you foon fhall have caught her.

What, a plague and a pox,
Shall an ill-natur'd fox,
Prevent youth and beauty
From doing their duty ?
He ought to be fet in the flocks.
  He merits the law ;
And if we can't bite him,
By gad we'll indite him.
  Ha, ha, ha, ha, ha, ha, ha.

S C E N E V.

Diana, Harman.

Dian. Sir, I defire to know what grofs acts of impru‑ dence you have ever difcovered in me, to authorize you in this licence, or make you imagine I fhould not fhew

fuch

fuch marks of my refentment as your monftrous treatment of me deferves.

Har. Nay, my dear Diana, I confefs I have been ra-ther too bold ;—but confider, I languifh'd to fee you ; and when an opportunity offer'd to give me that pleafure without running any rifque, either of your quiet or re-putation, how hard was it to be refifted ? 'Tis true, I little thought my vifit would be attended with fuch happy confequences as it now feems to promife.

Dian. What do you mean ?

Har. Why, don't you fee your father has an inclina-tion I fhould run away with you, and is contriving the means himfelf ?

Dian. And do you think me capable of concurring ? Do you think I have no more duty ?

Har. I don't know that, Madam ; I am fure your re-fufing to feize fuch an opportunity to make he happy, gives evident proofs that you have very little love.

Dian. If there is no way to convince you of my love but by my indifcretion, you are welcome to confider it in what light you pleafe.

Har. Was ever fo unfortunate a dog ?

Dian. Very pretty this upon my word ; but is it pof-fible you can be in earneft ?

Har. It is a matter of too much confequence to jeft about.

Dian. And you ferioufly think I ought—

Har. You are fenfible there are no hopes of your fa-ther's cooly and wittingly confenting to our marriage ; chance has thrown in our way a whimfical method of fur-prizing him into a compliance, and why fhould not we avail ourfelves of it ?

Dian. And fo you would have me—

Har. I fhall fay no more, Ma'am.

Dian. Nay, but, for Heaven's fake——

Har. No, Madam no ; I have done.

Dian. And are you pofitively in this violent fufs about the matter, or only giving yourfelf airs ?

Har. You may fuppofe what you think proper, Ma-dam.

Dian. Well, come ;—let us go into the drawing-room and dring tea, and afterwards we'll talk of matters.

Har.

Har. I won't drink any tea.

Dian. Why so?

Har. Becaufe I don't like it.

Dian. Not like it! Ridiculous.

Har. I wifh you would let me alone.

Dian. Nay, pr'ythee——

Har. I won't.

Dian. Well, will you if I confent to act as you pleafe?

Har. I don't know whether I will or not.

Dian. Ha, ha, ha, poor Harman.

 Come then, pining, peevifh lover,
  Tell me what to do and fay;
 From your doleful dumps recover,
  Smile, and it fhall have its way.

 With their humours, thus to teaze us,
  Men are fure the ftrangeft elves!
 Silly creatures, would you pleafe us,
  You fhould ftill feem pleas'd yourfelves.

SCENE VI.

HARMAN.

Say'ft thou fo, my girl! Then Love renounce me, if I drive not old Truepenny's humour to the uttermoft.—Let me confider;—what ill confequence can poffibly attend it?—The defign is his own, as in part will be the execution.—He may perhaps be angry when he finds out the deceit.—Well;—he deceives himfelf; and faults we commit ourfelves we feldom find much difficulty in pardoning.

 Hence with caution, hence with fear,
  Beauty prompts, and naught fhall ftay me;
 Boldly for that prize I fteer;
  Rocks, nor winds, nor waves difmay me.

Yet

Yet, rash lover, look behind,
Think what evils may betide you ;
Love and fortune both are blind,
And you have none else to guide you.

SCENE VII.

Changes to a handsome Dressing-room, supposed to be CLA-
RISSA's. *On one Side, between the Wings, is a Table*
with a Glass, Boxes, and two Chairs. DIANA *enters*
before JESSAMY.

Dian. Come, brother, I undertake to be miſtreſs of
the ceremony upon this occaſion, and introduce you to
your firſt audience.——Miſs Flowerdale is not here, I
perceive ; but no matter.——

Mr. Jeſſ. Upon my word, a pretty elegant dreſſing-
room this ; but confound our builders, or architects, as
they call themſelves, they are all errant ſtone-maſons ;
not one of them know the ſituation of doors, windows,
or chimnies ; which are as eſſential to a room as eyes,
noſe and mouth to a countenance. Now, if the eyes are
where the mouth ſhould be, and the noſe out of proportion
and its place, *quel horrible phiſiognomie.*

Dian. My dear brother, you are not come here as a
virtuoſo to admire the temple ; but as a votary to ad-
dreſs the deity to whom it belongs. Shew, I beſeech
you, a little more devotion, and tell me, how do you
like Miſs Flowerdale ? don't you think her very handſome ?

Mr. Jeſſ. Pale ;——but that I am determined ſhe ſhall
remedy ; for, as ſoon as we are married, I will make
her put on rouge :—Let me ſee ;—has ſhe got any in her
boxes here ; *Veritable toilet a la Angloiſe.* Nothing but a
bottle of Hungary-water, two or three rows of pins, a
paper of patches, and a little bole-armoniac by way of
tooth-powder.

Dian. Brother, I would fain give you ſome advice upon
this occaſion, which may be of ſervice to you : You are
now going to entertain a young Lady——Let me prevail

upon

upon you to lay aside thofe airs, on account of which some people are impertinent enough to call you a coxcomb; for, I am afraid, fhe may be apt to think you a coxcomb too, as I affure you fhe is very capable of diftinguifhing.

Mr. Jeff. So much the worfe for me.—If fhe is capable of diftinguifhing, I fhall meet with a terrible repulfe. I don't believe fhe'll have me.

Dian. I don't believe fhe will, indeed.

Mr. Jeff. Go on, fifter,—ha, ha, ha.

Dian. I proteft I am ferious—Though, I perceive, you have more faith in the counfellor before you there, the looking-glafs. But give me leave to tell you, it is not a powder'd head, a lac'd coat, a grimace, a fhrug, a bow, or a few pert phrafes, learnt by rote, that conftitute the power of pleafing all woman.

Mr. Jeff. You had better return to the gentleman and give him his tea, my dear.

Dian. Thefe qualifications we find in our parrots and monkies. I would endertake to teach Poll, in three weeks, the fafhionable jargon of half the fine men about town; and I am fure it muft be allowed, that pug, in a fcarlet coat, is a gentleman as degage and alluring as moft of them.

Ladies, pray admire a figure,
Fait felon le derniere goût.
Firft, his hat, in fize no bigger
Than a Chinefe woman's fhoe;
Six yards of ribbon bind
His hair en baton behind;
While his fore-top's fo high,
That in crown he may vie
With the tufted cockatoo.

Then his waift fo long and taper,
'Tis an abfolute thread-paper:
Maids refift him, you that can;
Odd's life, if this is all th' affair,
I'll clap a hat on, club my hair,
And call myfelf a Man.

SCENE

SCENE VIII.

CLARISSA, *Mr.* JESSAMY.

Clar. Sir, I took the liberty to defire a few moments private converfation with you—I hope you will excufe it—I am, really, greatly embarrafs'd. But, in an affair of fuch immediate confequence to us both—

Mr. Jeff. My dear creature, don't be embarras'd before me; I fhould be extremely forry to ftrike you with any awe; but, this is a fpecies of mauvaife honte, which the company I fhall introduce you to, will foon cure you of.

Clar. Upon my word, Sir, I don't underftand you.

Mr. Jeff. Perhaps you may be under fome uneafinefs left I fhould not be quite fo warm in the profecution of this affair, as you could wifh: it is true, with regard to quality, I might do better; and, with regard to fortune, full as well—But, you pleafe me—Upon my foul, I have not met with any thing more agreeable to me a great while.

Clar. Pray, Sir, keep your feat.

Mr. Jeff. Mauvaife honte again. My dear, there is nothing in thefe little familiarities between you and me— When we are married, I fhall do every thing to render your life happy.

Clar. Ah! Sir, pardon me. The happinefs of my life depends upon a circumftance——

Mr. Jeff. Oh! I underftand you—You have been told, I fuppofe, of the Italian opera girl—Rat peoples tongues —However, 'tis true, I had an affair with her at Naples, and fhe is now here. But, be fatisfied: I'll give her a thoufand pounds, and fend her about her bufinefs.

Clar. Me Sir! I proteft nobody told me—Lord! I never heard any fuch thing, or enquired about it.

Mr. Jeff. Nor, have they not been chattering to you of my affair at Pifa, with the Principeffa del——

Clar. No, indeed, Sir.

Mr. Jeff. Well, I was afraid they might, becaufe, in this rude country—But, why filent on a fudden?—don't be afraid to fpeak.

Clar.

Clar. No, Sir, I will come to the fubject, on which I took the liberty to trouble you—Indeed, I have great reliance on your generofity.

Mr. Jeff. You'll find me generous as a prince, depend on't.

Clar. I am blefs'd, Sir, with one of the beft of fathers: I never yet difobeyed him; in which I have had little merit; for his commands hitherto have only been to fe-cure my own felicity.

Mr. Jeff. Apres ma chere.

Clar. But now, Sir, I am under the fhocking necef-fity of d'fobeying him, or being wretched for ever.

Mr. Jeff. Hem!

Clar. Our union is impoffible—my prefent fithation—the gloomy profpect before me—the inquietude of my mind——

> *Poor panting heart, ah! wilt thou ever*
> *Throb within my troubl'd breaft;*
> *Shall I fee the moment never*
> *That is doom'd to give thee reft?*

> *Cruel ftars! that thus torment me,*
> *Still I feek for eafe in vain,*
> *All my efforts but prefent me*
> *With variety of pain.*

SCENE IX.

JESSAMY, JENKINS.

Mr. Jeff. Who's there?

Jen. Do you call, Sir?

Mr. Jeff. Hark you, old gentleman; who are you?

Jen. Sir, my name is Jenkins.

Mr. Jeff. Oh! you are Sir John Flowerdale's fteward; a fervant he puts confidence in.

Jen. Sir, I have ferved Sir John Flowerdale many years: he is the beft of mafters; and, I believe, he has fome dependance on my attachment and fidelity.

Mr.

Mr. Jeff. Then, Mr. Jenkins, I shall condescend to speak to you. Does your master know who I am? Does he know, Sir, that I am likely to be a Peer of Great Britain? That I have ten thousand pounds a year; that I have passed through all Europe with distinguished éclat; that I refused the daughter of Mynheer Van Slokenfolk, the great Dutch burgomaster; and, that, if I had not had the misfortune of being bred a protestant, I might have married the niece of his present holiness the Pope, with a fortune of two hundred thousand piasters?

Jen. I am sure, Sir, my master has all the respect imaginable——

Mr. Jeff. Then, Sir, how comes he, after my shewing an inclination to be allied to his family; how comes he, I say, to bring me to his house to be affronted? I have let his daughter go; but, I think, I was in the wrong; for a woman that insults me, is no more safe than a man. I have brought a Lady to reason before now, for giving me saucy language; and left her male friends to revenge it.

Jen. Pray, good Sir, what's the matter?

Mr. Jeff. Why, Sir, this is the matter, Sir—your master's daughter, Sir, has behaved to me with damn'd insolence, and impertinence; and you may tell Sir John Flowerdale, first, with regard to her, that, I think she is a silly, ignorant, awkward, ill-bred country puss.

Jen. Oh! Sir, for Heaven's sake——

Mr. Jeff. And, that, with regard to himself, he is, in my opinion, an old, doating, ridiculous, country 'squire, without the knowledge of either men or things; and, that he is below my notice, if it were not to despise him.

Jen. Good Lord! Good Lord!

Mr. Jeff. And, advise him and his daughter to keep out of my way; for, by gad, I will affront them, in the first place I meet them——And, if your master is for carrying things further; tell him, I fence better than any man in Europe.

In Italy, Germany, France have I been;
Where princes I've liv'd with, where monarchs I've seen;
 The great have caress'd me,
 The fair have addres'd me,
Nay, smiles I have had from a queen.

And,

And, now, shall a pert,
Insignificant flirt,
With insolence use me,
Presume to refuse me!
She fancies my pride will be hurt.

But tout au contraire,
I'm pleas'd I declare,
Quite happy, to think, I escape from the snare:
Serviteur Mam'selle; my claim I withdraw.
Hey! where are my people?   Fal, lal, lal lal, la.

S C E N E X.

JENKINS.

I must go and inform Sir John of what has happened;
but, I will not tell him of the outrageous behaviour of
this young spark; for he is a man of spirit, and would
resent it.   Egad, my own fingers itched to be at him,
once or twice; and, as stout as he is, I fancy these old
fists would give him a bellyful.   He complains of Miss
Clarissa; but she is incapable of treating him in the manner he says.   Perhaps, she may have behaved with some
coldness towards him; and yet, that is a mystery to me
too.

We all say the man was exceedingly knowing,
And knowing most surely was he,
Who found out the cause of the ebbing and flowing,
The flux and reflux of the sea.

Nor was he in knowledge far from it,
Who first mark'd the course of a comet;
To what it was owing,
Its coming and going,
Its wanderings hither and thither;
But the man that divines
A Lady's designs,
Their cause, or effect,
In any respect,
Is wiser than both put together.

SCENE

SCENE XI.

Changes to Sir JOHN FLOWERDALE's *Garden; with a View of a Canal, by Moon-light: the Side Scenes reprefent Box-hedges, intermixed with Statues and Flowering Shrubs.* LIONEL *enters, leading* CLARISSA.

Lion. Hift—methought I heard a noife—fhould we be furprized together, at a juncture fo critical ; what might be the confequence—I know not how it is ; but, at this the happieft moment of my life, I feel a damp, a tremor, at my heart——

Clar. Then, what fhould I do ? If you tremble, I ought to be terrified indeed, who have difcovered fenti-ments, which, perhaps, I fhould have hid, with a frank-nefs, that, by a man lefs generous, lefs noble minded than yourfelf, might be conftrued to my difadvantage.

Lion. Oh ! wound me not with fo cruel an expreffion—You love me, and have condefcended to confefs it—You have feen my torments, and been kind enough to pity them—The world, indeed, may blame you——

Clar. And, yet, was it proclaimed to the world, what could the moft malicious fuggeft ? They could but fay, that, truth and fincerity got the better of forms ; that the tongue dar'd to fpeak, the honeft fenfations of the mind ; that, while you aimed at improving my underftanding, you engaged, and conquered my heart.

Lion. And, is it ! is it poffible !

Clar. Be calm, and liften to me : what I have done has not been lightly imagined, nor rafhly undertaken : it is the work of reflection, of conviction ; my love is not a facrifice to my own fancy, but a tribute to your worth ; did I think there was a more deferving man in the world——

Lion. If, to doat on you more than life, be to deferve you, fo far I have merit ; if, to have no wifh, no hope, no thought, but you, can entitle me to the envied dif-tinction of a moment's regard, fo far I dare pretend.

Clar. That, I have this day refufed a man, with whom I could not be happy, I make no merit : born for quiet and fimplicity, the crouds of the world, the noife attend-

ing

ing pomp and diftinction, have no charms for me: I wifh to pafs my life in rational tranquility, with a friend, whofe virtues I can refpect, whofe talents I can admire; who will make my efteem the bafis of my affection.

Lion. O charming creature! yes, let me indulge the flattering idea; form'd with the fame fentiments, the fame feelings, the fame tender paffion for each other; Nature defign'd us to compofe that facred union, which nothing but death can annul.

Clar. One only thing remember. Secure in each others affections, here we muft reft; I would not give my father a moment's pain, to purchafe the empire of the world.

Lion. Command, difpofe of me as you pleafe; angels take cognizance of the vows of innocence and virtue; and, I will believe that ours are already, regifter'd in Heaven.

Clar. I will believe fo too.

> *Go, and, on my truth relying,*
> *Comfort to your cares applying,*
> *Bid each doubt and forrow flying,*
> *Leave to peace, and love your breaft.*
>
> *Go, and may the Pow'rs that hear us,*
> *Still, as kind protectors near us,*
> *Through our troubles fafely fteer us,*
> *To a port of joy and reft.*

S C E N E XII.

LIONEL, *Sir* **JOHN FLOWERDALE.**

Sir John. Who's there? Lionel!

Lion. Heav'ns! 'tis Sir John Flowerdale.

Sir John. Who's there?

Lion. 'Tis I, Sir; I am here, Lionel.

Sir John. My dear lad, I have been fearching for you this half hour, and was at laft told you had come into the garden: I have a piece of news, which I dare fwear will fhock and furprize you; my daughter has refufed

Colonel

Colonel Oldboy's son, who is this minute departed the houfe in violent refentment of her ill treatment.

Lion. Is he gone, Sir?

Sir John. Yes, and the family are preparing to follow him. Oh! Lionel, Clariffa has deceived me: in this affair fhe has fuffered me to deceive myfelf. The meafures which I have been fo long preparing are broken in a moment—my hopes fruftrated; and both parties, in the eye of the world, rendered light and ridiculous.

Lion. I am forry to fee you fo much moved; pray, Sir, recover yourfelf.

Sir John. I am forry, Lionel, fhe has profited no better by your leffons of philofophy, than to impofe upon and diftrefs fo kind a father.

Lion. Have jufter thoughts of her, Sir: fhe has not impofed on you, fhe is incapable—have but a little patience and things may yet be brought about.

Sir John. No, Lionel, no; the matter is paft, and there's an end to it; yet I would conjecture to what fuch an unexpected turn in her conduct can be owing; I would fain be fatisfied of the motive that could urge her to fo extraordinary a proceeding, without the leaft intimation, the leaft warning to me, or any of her friends.

Lion. Perhaps, Sir, the gentleman may have been too impetuous and offended Mifs Flowerdale's delicacy—certainly nothing elfe could occafion——

Sir John. Heaven only knows——I think, indeed, there can be no fettled averfion, and furely her affections are not engaged elfewhere.

Lion. Engag'd Sir——No, Sir.

Sir John. I think not, Lionel.

Lion. You may be pofitive, Sir,—I'm fure——

Sir John. O worthy young man, whofe integrity, opennefs, and every good quality have rendered dear to me as my own child; I fee this affair troubles you as much as it does me.

Lion. It troubles me indeed, Sir.

Sir John. However, my particular difappointment ought not to be detrimental to you, nor fhall it: I well know how irkfome it is to a generous mind to live in a ftate of dependance, and have long had it in my thoughts to make you eafy for life.

E 3

Lion.

Lion. Sir John, the situation of my mind at present is a little disturb'd—spare me—I beseech you, spare me; why will you persist in a goodness that makes me asham'd of myself?

Sir John. There is an estate in this county which I purchased some years ago ; by me it will never be missed,. and who ever marries my daughter will have little reason to complain of my disposing of such a trifle for my own gratification. On the present marriage I intended to per-- fect a deed of gift in your favour, which has been for some time prepared ; my lawyer has this day completed: it, and it is yours, my dear Lionel, with every good wish that the warmest friend can bestow.

Lion. Sir, If you presented a pistol with design to shoot me, I would submit to it; but you must excuse me, I cannot lay myself under more obligations.

Sir John. Your delicacy carries you too far ; in this, I confer a favour on myself : however, we'll talk no more on the subject at present, let us walk towards the house,. our friends will depart else without my bidding them adieu.

SCENE XIII.

DIANA, CLARISSA, *and afterwards* LIONEL.

Dian. So then, my dear Clarissa, you really give credit to the ravings of that French wretch, with regard to a. plurality of worlds ?

Clar. I don't make it an absolute article of belief, but I think it an ingenious conjecture with great probability on its side.

Dian. And we are a moon to the moon ! Nay, child,. I know something of astronomy, but that—that little shining thing there, which seems not much larger than a silver plate, should, perhaps, contain great cities like London ; and who can tell but they may have kings there and parliaments, and plays and operas, and peo- ple of fashion ! Lord the people of fashion in the moon must be strange creatures.

Clar.

Clar. Methinks Venus shines very bright in, yonder corner.

Dian. Venus! O pray let me look at Venus; I suppofe, if there are any inhabitants there, they muft be all, lovers.

Lion. Was even fuch a wretch—I can't ftay a moment in a place; where, is my repofe?—fled with my virtue. Was I then born for falfhood and diffimulation? I was, I was, and I live to be confcious of it; to impofe upon my friend; to betray my benefactor and lie to hide my ingratitude—a monfter in a moment—No, I may be the moft unfortunate of men, but I will not be the moft odious; while my heart is yet capable of dictating what is honeft, I will obey its voice.

SCENE XV.

DIANA, CLARISSA, LIONEL, *Colonel* OLDBOY, HARMAN.

Col. Dy, where are you? What the mifchief, is this a time to be walking in the garden? The coach has been ready this half hour, and your Mama is waiting for you.

Dian. I am learning aftronomy, Sir; do you know Papa, that the moon is inhabited?

Col. Huffy, you are half a lunatic yourfelf; I come here, things have gone juft as I imagin'd they wou'd, the girl has refus'd your brother, I knew he muft difguft her.

Dian. Women will want tafte now and then, Sir.

Col. But I muft talk to the young Lady a little.

Har. Well, I have had a long conference with your father about the elopement, and he continues firm in his opinion that I ought to attempt it: in fhort, all the neceffary operations are fettled between us, and I am to leave his houfe to-morrow morning, if I can but perfuade the young Lady——

Dian. Ay, but I hope the young Lady will have more fenfe—Lord, how can you teaze me with your nonfenfe. Come, Sir, is'nt it time for us to go in? Her Ladyfhip will be impatient.

Col.

Col. Friend Lionel, good night to you ; Mifs Clariffa, my dear, tho' I am father to the puppy who has difpleafed you, give me a kifs ; you ferv'd him right, and I thank you for it.

Col. *O what a night is here for love !*
   Cynthia brightly fhining above ;
   Among the trees,
   To the fighing breeze,
   Fountains tinkling ;
   Stars a twinkling :
Dian. *O what a night is here for love !*
   So may the morn propitious prove ;
Har. *And fo it will if right I guefs ;*
   For fometimes light,
   As well as night,
   A lover's hopes may blefs.

A 2. *Farewell my friend,*
   May gentle reft
   Calm each tumult in your breaft,
   Every pain and fear remove.

Lion. *What have I done ?*
   Where fhall I run,
   With grief and fhame at once opprefs ;
   How my own upbraiding fhun,
   Or meet my friend diftrefs ?

A. 3. *Hark to Philomel, how fweet,*
   From yonder elm.
Col.   *Tweet, tweet, tweet, tweet.*
A. 5. *O what a night is here for love !*
   But vainly nature ftrives to move.
   Nor nightingale among the trees,
   Nor twinkling ftars, nor fighing breeze,
   Nor murm'ring ftreams,
   Nor Phæbe's beams,
   Can charm unlefs the heart's at eafe.

ACT III. SCENE I.

A Room in Colonel OLDBOY*'s House.* HARMAN *enters, with his Hat, Boots, and Whip, followed by* DIANA.

Dian. Pry'thee, hear me.

Har. My dear, what would you say?

Dian. I am afraid of the step we are going to take; indeed, I am: 'tis true, my father is the contriver of it; but, really, on consideration, I think, I should appear less culpable if he was not so; I am at once criminal myself and rendering him ridiculous.

Har. Do you love me?

Dian. Suppose I do, you give me a very ill proof of your love for me, when you would take advantage of my tenderness, to blind my reason: how can you have so little regard for my honour as to sacrifice it to a vain triumph? For it is in that light I see the rash action you are forcing me to commit; nay, methinks my consenting to it should injure me in your own esteem. When a woman forgets what she owes herself, a lover should set little value upon any thing she gives to him.

Har. Can you suppose then, can you imagine, that my passion will ever make me forget the veneration—— And, an elopement is nothing, when it is on the road to matrimony.

Dian. At best, I shall incur the censure of disobedience, and indiscretion; and, is it nothing to a young woman, what the world says of her? Ah! my good friend, be assured, such a disregard of the world is the first step towards deserving its reproaches.

Har. But, the necessity we are under—Mankind has too much good sense, too much good nature—.

Dian.

Dian. Every one has good fenfe enough to fee other people's faults, and good nature enough to overlook their own. Befides, the moft facred things may be made an ill ufe of, and even marriage itfelf, if indecently and improperly—

Har. Come, get yourfelf ready: where is your band-box, hat, and cloak? Slip into the garden; be there at the iron-gate, which you fhewed me juft now; and, as the poft-chaife comes round, I will ftep and take you in.

Dian. Dear Harman, let me beg of you to defift.

Har. Dear Diana, let me beg of you to go on.

Dian. I fhall never have refolution to carry me thro' it.

Har. We fhall have four horfes, my dear, and they will affift us.

Dian. In fhort—I——cannot go with you.

Har. But before me—Into the garden—Wont you?

Dian.   *How can you, inhuman! perfift to diftrefs me?*
     My danger, my fears, 'tis in vain to difguife:
     You know them, yet ftill to deftruction you prefs me,
     And force that from paffion which prudence denies.

     I fain would oppofe a perverfe inclination;
     The vifions of fancy, from reafon divide;
     With fortitude baffle the wiles of temptation,
     And let love no longer make folly its guide.

SCENE II.

Colonel OLDBOY, HARMAN.

Col. Hey-dey! what's the meaning of this? Who is it went out of the room there? Have you and my daughter been in conference, Mr. Harman?

Har. Yes, faith, Sir, fhe has been taking me to tafk here very feverely, with regard to this affair; and fhe has faid fo much againft it, and put it into fuch a ftrange light——

Col. A bufy, impertinent baggage; egad I wifh I had catched her meddling, and after I ordered her not: but

you

you have fent to the girl, and you fay fhe is ready to go with you ; you muft not difappoint her now.

Har. No, no, Colone ; I always have politenefs enough to hear a lady's reafons ; but conftancy enough to keep a will of my own.

Col. Very well—now let me afk you,—don't you think it would be proper, upon this occafion, to have a letter ready writ for the father, to let him know who has got his daughter, and fo forth ?

Har. Certainly, Sir ; and I'll write it directly.

Col. You write it! you be damn'd ! I won't truft you with it ; I tell you, Harman, you'll commit fome curfed blunder, if you don't leave the management of this whole affair to me : I have writ the letter for you myfelf.

Har. Have you, Sir ?

Col. Ay—here, read it ; I think it's the thing : how-ever, you are welcome to make any alteration.

Har. " Sir, I have loved your daughter a great while, fecretly ; fhe affures me there is no hopes of your con-fenting to our marriage ; I therefore take her without it. I am a gentleman who will ufe her well : and, when you confider the matter, I dare fwear you will be wil-ling to give her a fortune. If not you fhall find I dare behave myfelf like a man—A word to the wife—You muft expect to hear from me in another ftile."

Col. Now, Sir, I will tell you what you muft do with this letter : as foon as you have got off with the girl, Sir, fend your fervant back to leave it at the houfe, with orders to have it deliver'd to the old gentleman.

Har. Upon my honour, I will, Colonel.

Col. But, upon my honour, I don't believe you'll get the girl : come, Harman, I'll bet you a buck, and fix doz-en of Burgundy, that you won't have fpirit enough to bring this affair to a crifis.

Har. And, I fay done firft, Colonel.

Col. Then look into the court there, Sir ; a chaife with four of the prettieft bay geldings in England, with two boys in fcarlet and filver jackets, that will whifk you along.

Har. Boys ! Colonel ? Little cupids, to tranfport me to the fummit of my defires.

Col.

Col. Ay, but for all that, it mayn't be amifs for me to talk to them a little out of the window for you. Dick, come hither; you are to go with this gentleman, and do whatever he bids you; and take into the chaife whoever he pleafes; and, drive like devils, do you hear; but, be kind to the dumb beafts.

Har. Leave that to me, Sir——And fo, my dear Colonel,

> *To fear a ftranger,*
>   *Behold the foldier arm;*
> *He knows no danger,*
>   *When honour founds the alarm;*
> *But dauntlefs goes,*
> *Among his foes.*
>
> *In Cupid's militia,*
> *So fearlefs I iffue;*
>   *And, as you fee,*
>   *Arm'd cap-a-pie,*
> *Refolve on death or victory.*

SCENE III.

Colonel OLDBOY, *Lady* MARY, *and then* JENNY.

Lady M. Mr. Oldboy, here is a note from Sir John Flowderdale it is addrefs'd to me, intreating my fon to come over there again this morning. A maid brought it: fhe is in the anti-chamber—We had better fpeak to her—Child, child, why don't you come in?

Jen. I chufe to ftay where I am, if your Ladyfhip pleafes.

Lady M. Stay where you are! why fo?

Jen. I am afraid of the old gentleman there.

Col. Afraid of me, huffy.

Lady M. Pray, Colonel, have patience—Afraid—Here is fomething at the bottom of this—What did you mean by that expreffion, child?

Jen. Why the Colonel knows very well, Madam, he wanted to be rude with me yefterday.

Lady

Lady M. Oh Mr. Oldboy !

Col. Lady Mary don't provoke me, but let me talk to the girl about her bufinefs. How came you to bring this note here ?

Jenny. Why, Sir John gave it to me, to deliver to my uncle Jenkins, and I took it down to his houfe ; but while we were talking together, he remembered that he had fome bufinefs with Sir John, fo he defired me to bring it, becaufe he faid it was not proper to be fent by any of the common fervants.

Lady M. Colonel, look in my face, and help blufhing if you can.

Col. What the plague's the matter, my Lady ! I have not been wronging you now, as you call it.

Jenny. Indeed, Madam, he offer'd to make me his kept Madam : I am fure his ufage of me put me into fuch a twitter, that I did not know what I was doing all the day after.

Lady M. I don't doubt it, tho' I fo lately forgave him ; but as the poet fays, his fex is all deceit. Read Pamela, child, and refift temptation.

Jenny. Yes, Madam, I will.

Col. Why I tell you, my Lady, it was all a joke.

Jenny. No, Sir, it was no joke, you made me a proffer of money, fo you did, whereby I told you, you had a lady of your own, and that though fhe was old you had no right to difpife her.

Lady M. And how dare you miftrefs, make ufe of my name ? Is it for fuch trollops as you to talk of perfons of diftinction behind their backs ?

Jenny. Why, Madam, I only faid you was in years.

Lady M. Sir John Flowerdale fhall be inforin'd of your impertinence, and you fhall be turn'd out of the family ; I fee you are a confident creature, and I believe you are no better than you fhould be.

Jenny. I fcorn your words, Madam.

Lady M. Get out of the room ; how dare you ftay in this room to talk impudently to me ?

Jenny. Very well, Madam, I fhall let my Lady know how you have us'd me ; but I fhan't be turn'd out of my place, Madam, nor at a lofs, if I am ; and if you are an-

gry

gry with every one that won't fay you are young, I believe there is very few you will keep friends with.

> *I wonder, I'm fure, why this fufs fhould be made;*
> *For my part I'm neither afham'd nor afraid*
> *Of what I have done, nor of what I have faid.*
> *A fervant, I hope is no flave;*
>   *And tho', to their fhames,*
>   *Some ladies call names,*
> *I know better how to behave.*
>   *Times are not fo bad,*
>   *If occafion I had,*
> *Nor my character fuch I need ftarve on't.*
>   *And for going away,*
>   *I don't want to flay,*
> *And fo I'm your Ladyfhip's fervant.*

SCENE IV.

Colonel OLDBOY, *Lady* MARY, *Mr.* JESSAMY,

Mr. Jeff. What is the matter here?

Lady M. I will have a feparate maintenance, I will indeed. Only a new inftance of your father's infidelity, my dear. Then with fuch low wretches, farmers daughters, and fervant wenches: but any thing with a cap on, 'tis all the fame to him.

Mr. Jeff. Upon my word, Sir, I am forry to tell you, that thofe practices very ill fuit the character which you ought to endeavour to fupport in the world.

Lady M. Is this a recompence for my love and regard; I, who have been tender and faithful as a turtle dove?

Mr. Jeff. A man of your birth and diftinction fhould, methinks, have views of a higher nature, than fuch low, fuch vulgar libertinifm.

Lady M. Confider my birth and family too, Lady Mary Jeffamy might have had the beft matches in England.

Mr. Jeff. Then, Sir, your grey hairs.

Lady M. I, that have brought you fo many lovely fweet babes.

Mr. Jeff.

Mr. Jeff. Nay, Sir, it is a reflection on me.

Lady M. The heinous sin too——

Mr. Jeff. Indeed, Sir, I blush for you.

Col. S'death and fire, you little effeminate puppy, do you know who you talk to?—And you, Madam, do you know who I am!—Get up to your chamber, or zounds I'll make such a——

Lady M. Ah! my dear come away from him.

SCENE V.

Colonel OLDBOY, Mr. JESSAMY, a SERVANT.

Col. Am I to be tutor'd and call'd to an account! How now, you scoundrel, what do you want?

Serv. A letter, Sir.

Col. A letter, from whom, sirrah?

Serv. The gentleman's servant, an't please your honour, that left this just now in the post-chaise—the gentleman my young lady went away with.

Col. Your young lady, sirrah—Your young lady went away with no gentleman, you dog—What gentleman! What young lady, sirrah!

Mr. Jeff. There is some mystery in this—With your leave, Sir, I'll open the letter: I believe it contains no secrets.

Col. What are you going to do, you jackanapes? you shan't open a letter of mine—Dy—Diana—Somebody call my daughter to me there—" To John Oldboy, Efq.—" Sir, I have lov'd your daughter a great while secretly—" Confenting to our marriage——"

Mr. Jeff. So fo.

Col. You villain—you dog, what is it you have brought me here?

Serv. Pleafe your honour, if you'll have patience, I'll tell your honour—As I told your honour before, the gentleman's servant that went off just now in the post-chaise, came to the gate, and left it after his master was gone. I faw my young lady go into the chaife with the gentleman.

F 2

Mr. Jeff.

Mr. Jeff. A very fine joke indeed ; pray, Colonel, do you generally write letters to yourself ? Why this is your own hand.

Col. Call all the servants in the house, let horses be saddled directly—every one take a different road.

Serv. Why, your honour, Dick said it was by your own orders.

Col. My orders ! you rascal ? I thought he was going to run away with another gentleman's daughter—Dy— Diana Oldboy.

Mr. Jeff. Don't waste your lungs to no purpose, Sir ; your daughter is half a dozen miles off by this time.

Col. Sirrah, you have been brib'd to further the scheme of a pick-pocket here.

Mr. Jeff. Besides, the matter is intirely of your own contriving, as well as the letter and spirit of this elegant epistle.

Col. You are a coxcomb, and I'll disinherit you ; the letter is none of my writing, it was writ by the devil, and the devil contrived it. Diana, Margaret, my Lady Mary, William, John——

Mr. Jeff. I am very glad of this, prodigiously glad of it, upon my honour—he ! he ! he !—it will be a jest this hundred years. (*bells ring violently, on both sides.*) What's the matter now ? O ! her Ladyship has heard of it, and is at her bell ; and the Colonel answers her. A pretty duet ; but a little too much upon the forte methinks : it would be a diverting thing now, to stand unseen at the old gentleman's elbow.

> *Hist, soft ; let's hear how matters go ;*
> *I'll creep and listen ;—so, so, so,*
> *They're all together by the ears ;——*
> *Oh, horrid ! how the savage swears.*
> *There too again ; ay, you may ring ;*
> *Sound out th'alarm-bell—ding, ding, ding—*
> *Dispatch your scouts, 'tis all in vain,*
> *Stray maids are seldom found again.*
>
> *But hark, the uproar hither sounds ;*
> *The Colonel comes with all his hounds ;*
> *I'll wisely leave them open way,*
> *To hunt with what success they may.*

SCENE

SCENE VI.

Colonel OLDBOY *re-enters, with one Boot, a Great-Coat on his Arm, &c. followed by several Servants..*

She's gone, by the Lord ; fairly ſtole away, with that poaching, coney-catching raſcal ! However, I won't follow her ; no, damme ; take my whip, and my cap, and my coat, and order the groom to unſaddle the horſes ; I won't follow her the length of a ſpur-leather. Come here, you Sir, and pull off my boot ; (*whiſtles*) ſhe has made a fool of me once, ſhe ſhan't do it a ſecond time ; not but I'll be reveng'd too, for I'll never give her ſix-pence ; the diſappointment will put the ſcoundrel out of temper, and he'll thraſh her a dozen times a day ; the thought pleaſes me, I hope he'll do it.

What do you ſtand gaping and ſtaring at, you impu-dent dogs ? are you laughing at me ? I'll teach you to be merry at my expence.——

A raſcal, a buſſey ; zounds ! ſhe that I counted
In temper ſo mild, ſo unpractis'd in evil:
I ſet her a horſe-back, and no ſooner mounted,
Than, crack, whip and ſpur, ſhe rides poſt to the devil.
But there let her run,
Be ruin'd, undone ;
If I go to catch her,
Or back again fetch her,
I'm worſe than the ſon of a gun.

A miſchief poſſeſs'd me to marry ;
And further my folly to carry,
To be ſtill more a ſot,
Sons and daughters I got,
And pretty ones, by the Lord Harry.

SCENE VII.

Changes to CLARISSA's *Dressing-room;* CLARISSA *enters melancholy, with a Book in her Hand, followed by* JENNY.

Clar. Where have you been Jenny? I was enquiring for you—why will you go out without letting me know?

Jen. Dear Ma'am, never any thing happen'd so unlucky; I am sorry you wanted me—But I was sent to Colonel Oldboy's with a letter; where I have been so used—Lord have mercy upon me—quality indeed—I say quality—pray, Madam, do you think that I looks any ways like an immodest parson—to be sure I have a gay air, and I can't help it, and I loves to appear a little genteel-ish, that's what I do.

Clar. Jenny, take away this book.

Jen. Heaven preserve me, Madam, you are crying.

Clar. O my dear Jenny!

Jen. My dear mistress, what's the matter?

Clar. I am undone.

Jen. No, Madam; no, Lord forbid!

Clar. I am indeed—I have been rash enough to discover my weakness for a man, who treats me with contempt.

Jen. Is Mr. Lionel ungrateful, then?

Clar. I have lost his esteem for ever, Jenny. Since last night, that I fatally confess'd what I should have kept a secret from all the world, he has scarce condescended to cast a look at me, nor given me an answer when I spoke to him, but with coldness and reserve.

Jen. Then he is a nasty, barbarous, unhuman brute.

Clar. Hold, Jenny, hold; it is all my fault.

Jen. Your fault madam! I wish I was to hear such a word come out of his mouth! if he was a minister to-morrow, and to say such a thing from his pulpit, and I by, I'd tell him it was false upon the spot.

Clar. Somebody's at the door; see who it is.

Jen. You in fault indeed—that I know to be the most virtuousest, nicest, most delicatest——

Clar. How now?

Jen.

Jen. Madam, its a meſſage from Mr. Lionel. If you are alone, and at leiſure, he would be glad to wait upon you: I'll tell him, Madam, that you are buſy.

Clar. Where is he, Jenny?

Jen. In the ſtudy the man ſays.

Clar. Then go to him, and tell him I ſhould be glad to ſee him: but do not bring him up immediately, becauſe I will ſtand in the balcony a few minutes for a little air.

Jen. Do ſo, dear madam, for your eyes are as red as ferrets, you are ready to faint too; mercy on us, for what do you grieve and vex yourſelf—if I was as you—

Clar. Oh!

Why with ſighs my heart is ſwelling,
Why with tears my eyes o'erflow;
Aſk me not, 'tis paſt the telling,
Mute involuntary woe.

Who to winds and waves a ſtranger,
Ventrous tempts the inconſtant ſeas,
In each billow fancies danger,
Shrinks at every riſing breeze.

SCENE VIII.

Sir JOHN FLOWERDALE, JENKINS.

Sir John. So then, the myſtery is diſcovered :—but is it poſſible that my daughter's refuſal of Colonel Oldboy's ſon ſhould proceed from a clandeſtine engagement, and that engagement with Lionel?

Jenk. My niece, Sir, is in her young Lady's ſecrets, and Lord knows ſhe had little deſign to betray them; but having remarked ſome odd expreſſions of hers yeſterday, when ſhe came down to me this morning with the letter, I queſtioned her; and, in ſhort, drew the whole affair out; upon which I feigned a recollection of ſome buſineſs with you, and deſired her to carry the letter to Colonel Oldboy's herſelf, while I came up hither.

Sir

Sir John. And they are mutually promifed to each other, and that promife was exchanged yefterday?

Jenk. Yes, Sir, and it is my duty to tell you; elfe I would rather die than be the means of wounding the heart of my dear young lady; for if there is one upon earth of truly noble and delicate fentiments——

Sir John. I thought fo once, Jenkins.

Jen. And think fo ftill: O good, Sir John, now is the time for you to exert that character of worth and gentlenefs which the world fo defervedly has given you. You have indeed caufe to be offended; but confider, Sir, your daughter is young, beautiful, and amiable; the poor youth unexperienced, fenfible, and at a time of life when fuch temptations are hard to be refifted: their opportunities were many, their caft of thinking the fame.——

Sir John. Jenkins, I can allow for all thefe things; but the young hypocrites, there's the thing, Jenkins; their hypocrify, their hypocrify wounds me.

Jen. Call it by a gentler name, Sir, modefty on her part, apprehenfion on his.

Sir John. Then what opportunity have they had? They never were together but when my fifter or myfelf made one of the company; befides, I had fo firm a reliance on Lionel's honour and gratitude.——

Jenk. Sir, I can never think that nature ftamp'd that gracious countenance of his, to mafk a corrupt heart.

Sir John. How! at the very time that he was confcious of being himfelf the caufe of it, did he not fhew more concern at this affair than I did? Nay, don't I tell you that laft night, of his own accord, he offered to be a mediator in the affair, and defired my leave to fpeak to my daughter? I thought myfelf obliged to him, confented; and, in confequence of his affurance of fuccefs, wrote that letter to Colonel Oldboy, to defire the family would come here again to-day.

Jenk. Sir, as we were ftanding in the next room, I heard a meffage delivered from Mr. Lionel, defiring leave to wait upon your daughter; I dare fwear they will be here prefently; fuppofe we were to ftep into that clofet, and overhear their converfation?

Sir John. What, Jenkins, after having lived so many years in confidence with my child, shall I become an eves-dropper to detect her?

Jenk. It is necessary at present.—Come in, my dear master, let us only consider that we were once young like them; subject to the same passions, the same indiscretions; and it is the duty of every man to pardon errors incident to his kind.

> *When love gets into a youthful brain,*
> *Instruction is fruitless, and caution vain:*
> *Prudence may cry do so;*
> *But, if Love says No;*
> *Poor Prudence may go,*
> *With her preaching,*
> *And teaching,*
> *To Jericho.*
> *Dear Sir, in old age,*
> *'Tis not hard to be sage,*
> *And 'tis easy to point the way;*
> *But do or say,*
> *What we may,*
> *Love and youth will have their day.*

S C E N E IX.

CLARISSA, LIONEL.

Clar. Sir, you desired to speak to me; I need not tell you the present situation of my heart; it is full. Whatever you have to say, I beg you will explain yourself; and, if possible, rid me of the anxiety under which I have laboured for some hours.

Lion. Madam, your anxiety cannot be greater than mine; I come, indeed, to speak to you; and yet, I know not how, I come to advise you, shall I say as a friend? yes, as a friend to your glory, your felicity; dearer to me than my life.

Clar. Go on, Sir.

Lion. Sir John Flowerdale, Madam, is such a father as few are blessed with; his care, his prudence has pro-

vided

vided for you a match—Your refufal renders him in-
confolable. Liften to no fuggeftions that would pervert
you from your duty, but make the worthieft of men
happy by fubmitting to his will.

Clar. How, Sir, after what paffed between us yefterday evening, can you advife me to marry Mr. Jeffamy?

Lion. I would advife you to marry any one, Madam,
rather than a villain.

Clar. A villain, Sir.

Lion. I fhould be the worft of villains, Madam, was I
to talk to you in any other ftrain: Nay, am I not a villain, at once treacherous and ungrateful? Received into
this houfe as an afylum: what have I done! Betrayed
the confidence of the friend that trufted me; endeavoured
to facrifice his peace, and the honour of his family, to
my own unwarrantable defires.

Clar. Say no more, Sir; fay no more; I fee my error too late; I have parted from the rules prefcribed to
my fex; I have miftaken indecorum for a laudable fincerity; and it is juft I fhould meet with the treatment
my imprudence deferves.

Lion. 'Tis I, and only I, am to blame; while I took
advantage of the father's fecurity, I practifed upon the
tendernefs and ingenuity of the daughter; my own imagination gone aftray, I artfully laboured to lead yours
after it: but here, Madam, I give you back thofe vows
which I infidioufly extorted from you; keep them for
fome happier man, who may receive them without
wounding his honour, or his peace.

Clar. For Heaven's fake!

Lion. Why do you weep?

Clar. Don't fpeak to me.

Lion. Oh! my Clariffa, my heart is broke; I am
hateful to myfelf for loving you;—yet, before I leave
you for ever, I will once more touch that lovely hand—
indulge my fondnefs with a laft look——pray for your
health and profperity.

Clar. Can you forfake me?—Have I then given my
affections to a man who rejects and difregards them?—
Let me throw myfelf at my father's feet; he is generous
and compaffionate:—He knows your worth——

Lion.

Lion. Mention it not ; were you ſtript of fortune, reduced to the meaneſt ſtation, and I monarch of the
globe, I ſhould glory in raiſing you to univerſal empire ;
but as it is ————

Clar. Yet hear me——

Lion. Farewel, farewel !

> *O dry theſe tears ! like melted ore,*
> *Faſt dropping on my heart they fall :*
> *Think, think no more of me ; no more*
> *The mem'ry of paſt ſcenes recall.*

> *On a wild ſea of paſſion toſs'd,*
> *I ſplit upon the fatal ſhelf ;*
> *Friendſhip and love at once are loſt,*
> *And now I wiſh to loſe myſelf.*

SCENE X.

CLARISSA, JENNY, *then Sir* JOHN FLOWERDALE *and*
JENKINS, *and afterwards* LIONEL.

Jenny. O Madam ! I have betray'd you. . I have gone
and ſaid ſomething I ſhould not have ſaid to my uncle
Jenkins ; and, as ſure as day, he has gone and told it all
to Sir John.

Clar. My father !

Sir John. Go, Jenkins ; and deſire that young gentleman to come back—ſtay where you are—But what have
I done to you my child ? How have I deſerv'd that you
ſhould treat me like an enemy ? Has there been any un-
deſigned rigour in my conduct, or terror in my looks ?

Clar. Oh Sir !

Jenk. Here is Mr. Lionel.

Sir John. Come in—When I tell you that I am in-
ſtructed in all your proceedings, and that I have been
ear-witneſs to your converſation in this place ; you will,
perhaps, imagine what my thoughts are of you, and the
meaſures which juſtice preſcribes me to follow.

Lion. Sir, I have nothing to ſay in my own defence ;
I ſtand before you, ſelf-convicted, ſelf-condemn'd, and
ſhall

ſhall ſubmit without murmuring to the ſentence of my judge.

Sir John. As for you, Clariſſa, ſince your earlieſt infancy, you have known no parent but me ; I have been to you, at once, both father and mother ; and, that I might the better fulfill thoſe united duties, tho' left a widower in the prime of my days, I would never enter into a ſecond marriage—I loved you for your likeneſs to your dear mother ; but that mother never deceiv'd me— and there the likeneſs fails—you have repaid my affection with diſſimulation—Clariſſa you ſhould have truſted me.

Jenny. O my dear, ſweet Lady.

Sir John. As for you, Mr. Lionel, what terms can I find ſtrong enough to paint the exceſs of my friendſhip ! —I loved, I eſteemed, I honoured your father : he was a brave, a generous, and a ſincere man ; I thought you inherited his good qualities—you were left an orphan, I adopted you, put you upon the footing of my own ſon ; educated you like a gentleman ; and deſigned you for a profeſſion, to which, I thought, your virtues would have been an ornament.

Jen. Dear me, dear me.

Jenk. Hold your tongue.

Sir John. What return you have made me, you ſeem to be acquainted with yourſelf ; and, therefore, I ſhall not repeat it—Yet, remember, as an aggravation of your guilt, that the laſt mark of my bounty was conferr'd upon you in the very inſtant, when you were undermining my deſigns. Now, Sir, I have but one thing more to ſay to you—Take my daughter : was ſhe worth a million, ſhe is at your ſervice.

Lion. To me Sir !—your daughter—do you give her to me ?—Without fortune—without friends !—without—

Sir John. You have them all in your heart ; him whom virtue raiſes, fortune cannot abaſe.

Clar. O, Sir, let me on my knees kiſs that dear hand —acknowledge my error, and intreat forgiveneſs and bleſſing.

Sir John. You have not erred, my dear daughter ; you have diſtinguiſh'd. It is I ſhould aſk pardon, for this little trial of you ; for I am happier in the ſon-in-law you have given me, than if you had married a prince——

Lion.

Lion. My patron—my friend—my father—I would fain fay fomething ; but, as your goodnefs exceeds all bounds——

Sir John. I think I hear a coach drive into the court ; it is Colonel Oldboy's family ; I will go and receive them. Don't make yourfelf uneafy at this ; we muft endeavour to pacify them as well as we can. My dear Lionel, if I have made you happy, you have made me fo; Heaven blefs you, my children, and make you deferving of one another.

SCENE XI.

CLARISSA, LIONEL, JENNY.

Jen. O dear, Madam, upon my knees, I humbly beg your forgivenefs—Dear Mr. Lionel, forgive me—I did not defign to difcover it, indeed——and you won't turn me off, Madam, will you?—I'll ferve you for nothing.

Clar. Get up, my good Jenny ; I freely forgive you if there is any thing to be forgiven. I know you love me ; and, I am fure here is one who will join with me in rewarding your fervices.

Jen. Well, if I did not know, as fure as could be, that fome good would happen, by my left eye itching this morning.

Lion. *O blifs unexpefted ! my joys overpow'r me !*
 My love, my Clariffa, what words fhall I find?
 Remorfe, defperation, no longer devour me——
 He blefs'd us, and peace is reftor'd to my mind.

Clar. *He blefs'd us ! O rapture ! Like one I recover*
 Whom death had appul'd without hope, without aid ;
 A moment depriv'd me of father and lover ;
 A moment reftores, and my pangs are repaid.

G

Lion.

Lion. Forsaken, abandoned,

Clar. ——————————What folly! what blindness!

Lion. We fortune accus'd;

Clar. ——————————— and the fates that decreed:

A. 2. But pain was inflicted by Heaven, out of kindness,
    To heighten the joys that were doom'd to succeed.
    Our day was o'ercast:
       But brighter the scene is,
       The sky more serene is,
    And softer the calm for the hurricane past.

S C E N E XII.

Lady MARY OLDBOY *leaning on a Servant, Mr.* JESSAMY
leading her; JENNY; *and afterwards Sir* JOHN FLOWER-
DALE *with Colonel* OLDBOY.

Lady M. 'Tis all in vain, my dear;—set me down any
where; I can't go a step further———I knew, when Mr.
Oldboy infisted upon my coming, that I should be seized
with a meagrim by the way; and it's well I did not die
in the coach.

Mr. Jeff. But, pr'ythee, why will you let yourself be
affected with such trifles—Nothing more common than
for young women of fashion to go off with low fellows.

Lady M. Only feel, my dear, how I tremble! Not a
nerve but what is in agitation; and my blood runs cold,
cold!

Mr. Jeff. Well, but, Lady Mary, don't let us expose
ourselves to those people; I fee there is not one of the
rafcals about us, that has not a grin upon his countenance.

Lady M. Expose ourselves! my dear? Your father
will be as ridiculous as Hudibras, or Don Quixote.

Mr. Jeff. Yes, he will be very ridiculous indeed.

Sir John. I give you my word, my good friend, and
neighbour, the joy I feel upon this occasion, is greatly
allayed by the difappointment of an alliance with your family; but I have explained to you how things have happened———You fee my fituation; and, as you are kind
enough to confider it yourfelf, I hope you will excufe it
to your fon.

Lady

Lady M. Sir John Flowderdale, how do you do ? You fee we have obey'd your fummons ; and I have the pleafure to affure you, that my fon yielded to my intreaties with very little difagreement : in fhort, if I may fpeak metaphorically, he is content to ftand candidate again, notwithftanding his late repulfe, when he hopes for an unanimous election.

Col. Well, but, my Lady, you may fave your rhetoric.; for the borough is difpofed of to a worthier member.

Mr. Jeff. What do you fay, Sir ?

S C E N E XIII.

Sir John Flowerdale, *Lady* Mary Oldboy, *Mr.* Jessamy, *Colonel* Oldboy, Lionel, Clarissa, Jenny.

Sir John. Here are my fon and daughter.

Lady M. Is this pretty, Sir John ?

Sir John. Believe me, Madam, it is not for want of a juft fenfe of Mr. Jeffamy's merit, that this affair has gone off on any fide :. but the heart is a delicate thing ; and after it has once felt, if the object is meritorious, the impreffion is not eafily effac'd ; it would therefore have been an injury to him, to have given him in appearance what another in reality poffeffed.

Mr. Jeff. Upon my honour, upon my foul, Sir John, I am not in the leaft offended at this *contre temps*—Pray Lady Mary, fay no more about it.

Col. Tol, lol, lol, lol.

Sir John. But, my dear Colonel, I am afraid, after all, this affair is taken amifs by you ; yes, I fee you are angry on your fon's account ; but let me repeat it, I have a very high opinion of his merit.

Col. Ay ! that's more than I have. Taken amifs ! I don't take any thing amifs ; I never was in better fpirits, or more pleafed in my life.

Sir John. Come, you are uneafy at fomething, Colonel.

Col. Me ! Gad I am not uneafy—Are you a juftice of peace ? Then you could give me a warrant, cou'dn't you ? You muft know, Sir John, a little accident has

hap-

happen'd in my family fince I faw you laft, you and I may fhake hands—Daughters, Sir, daughters! Your's has fnapt at a young fellow without your approbation ; and how do you think mine has ferv'd me this morning? —only run away with the fcoundrel I brought to dinner here yefterday.

Sir John. I am exceffively concerned.

Col. Now I'm not a bit concern'd—No, damn me, I am glad it has happened ; yet, thus far, I'll confefs, I fhould be forry that either of them would come in my way, becaufe a man's temper may fometimes get the better of him, and I believe I fhould be tempted to break her neck, and blow his brains out.

Clar. But pray, Sir, explain this affair.

Col. I can explain it no farther—Dy, my daughter Dy, has run away from us.

S C E N E XIV.

Sir JOHN FLOWERDALE, *Colonel* OLDBOY, *Lady* MARY OLDBOY, *Mr.* JESSAMY, CLARISSA, LIONEL, JENNY, DIANA, HARMAN, JENKINS.

Dian. No, my dear papa, I am not run away; and, upon my knees, I intreat your pardon for the folly I have committed ; but, let let it be fome alleviation, that duty, and affection, were too ftrong to fuffer me to carry it to extremity : and, if you knew the agony I have been in, fince I faw you laft——

Lady M. How's this ?

Har. Sir, I reftore your daughter to you ; whofe fault, as far as it goes, I muft alfo take upon myfelf ; we have been known to each other for fome time ; as Lady Richly, your fifter, in London, can acquaint you——

Col. Dy, come here——Now, you rafcal where's your fword ; if you are a gentleman you fhall fight me; if you are a fcrub, I'll horfe-whip you—Draw, Sirrah— Shut the door there, don't let him efcape.

Har. Sir, don't imagine I want to efcape; I am extremely forry for what has happened, but am ready to give you any fatisfaction you think proper.

Col.

Col. Follow me into the garden then—Zounds! I have no fword about me—Sir John Flowerdale—lend us a cafe of piftols, or a couple of guns; and, come and fee fair play.

Clar. My dear papa!

Dian. Sir John Flowerdale—O my indifcretion—we came here, Sir, to beg your mediation in our favour.

Lady M. Mr. Oldboy, if you attempt to fight I fhall expire.

Sir John. Pray, Colonel, let me fpeak a word to you in private.

Col. Slugs and a faw-pit——

Mr. Jeff. Why, Mifs Dy, you are a perfect heroine for a romance—And, pray who is this courteous knight?

Lady M. O Sir, you that I thought fuch a pretty behav'd gentleman!

Mr. Jeff. What bufinefs are you of friend?

Har. My chief trade, Sir, is plain dealing; and, as that is a commodity you have no reafon to be very fond of, I would not advife you to purchafe any of it by impertinence;

Col. And is this what you would advife me to?

Sir John. It is, indeed, my dehr old friend; as things are fituated, there is in my opinion, no other prudent method of proceeding; and it is the method I would adopt myfelf, was I in your cafe.

Col. Why, I believe you are in the right of it—fay what you will for me then.

Sir John. Well! young people, I have been able to ufe a few arguments, which have foftned my neighbour here; and in fome meafure pacified his refentment. I find, Sir, you are a gentleman by your connections?

Har. Sir, till it is found that my character and family will bear the ftricteft ferutiny, I defire no favour—And for fortune—

Col. Oh! Rot your fortune, I don't mind that—I know you are a gentleman, or Dick Rantum would not have recommended you. And fo, Dy, kifs and friends.

Mr. Jeff. What, Sir, have you no more to fay to the man who has ufed you fo ill?

Col. Us'd me ill!—That's as I take it—he has done a mettled thing; and, perhaps, I like him the better for it;

it's

it's long before you would have fpirit enough to run away
with a wench—Harman give me your hand; let's hear no
more of this now——Sir John Flowerdale, what fay you?
fhall we fpend the day together, and dedicate it to love
and harmony?

Sir John. With all my heart.

Col. Then take off my great coat.

Lion. *Come then, all ye focial pow'rs,*
      Shed your influence o'er us,
    Crown with blifs the prefent hours,
      And lighten thofe before us.
    May the juft, the gen'rous kind,
      Still fee that you regard 'em;
    And Lionels for ever find,
      Clariffas to reward 'em.

Clar. *Love, thy godhead I adore,*
      Scurce of facred paffion;
    But will never bow before
      Thofe idols, wealth, or fafhion.
    May, like me, each maiden wife,
      From the fop defend her;
    Learning, fenfe, and virtue prize,
      And fcorn the vain pretender.

Har. *Why the plague fhould men be fad,*
      While in time we moulder?
    Grave, or gay, or vex'd, or glad,
      We ev'ry day grow older.
    Bring the flafk, the mufic bring,
      Joy will quickly find us;
    Drink, and laugh, and dance, and fing,
      And caft our cares behind us.

Dian. *How fhall I efcape—fo naught,*
      On filial laws to trample;
    I'll e'en curtfey, own my fault,
      And plead papa's example.
    Parents 'tis a hint to you,
      Children oft are fhamelefs;
    Oft tranfgrefs—the things too true—
      But are you always blamelefs?

One

One word more before we go;
  Girls and boys have patience;
You to friends must something owe,
  As well as to relations.
These kind gentlemen address—
  What tho' we forgave 'em
Still they must be lost, unless
  You lend a hand to save 'em.

END OF THE OPERA.

www.ingramcontent.com/pod-product-compliance
Lightning Source LLC
Chambersburg PA
CBHW031137120726
47905CB00006B/1723